Also by Luana DaRosa

Pregnancy Surprise with the Greek Surgeon
Falling for Her Miami Rival
Faking It with the Doctor Prince

Valentine Flings collection

Hot Nights with the Arctic Doc

Also by Sue MacKay

Healing the Single Dad Surgeon
Brooding Vet for the Wallflower
Wedding Date with the ER Doctor
Parisian Surgeon's Secret Child

Discover more at millsandboon.co.uk.

FALLING FOR THE GP NEXT DOOR

LUANA DaROSA

A FLING WITH THE ER DOC

SUE MacKAY

MILLS & BOON

First published in Great Britain 2025
by Mills & Boon, an imprint of HarperCollins*Publishers* Ltd,
1 London Bridge Street, London, SE1 9GF

www.harpercollins.co.uk

HarperCollins*Publishers* Macken House, 39/40 Mayor Street Upper,
Dublin 1, D01 C9W8, Ireland

Falling for the GP Next Door © 2025 Luana DaRosa

A Fling with the ER Doc © 2025 Sue MacKay

ISBN: 978-0-263-32525-6

11/25

MIX
Paper | Supporting responsible forestry
FSC™ C007454
www.fsc.org

This book contains FSC™ certified paper
and other controlled sources to ensure responsible forest management.

For more information visit www.harpercollins.co.uk/green.

Printed and Bound in the UK using 100% Renewable Electricity
at CPI Group (UK) Ltd, Croydon, CR0 4YY

FALLING FOR THE GP NEXT DOOR

LUANA DaROSA

MILLS & BOON

CHAPTER ONE

HOW COULD DRIVING down one street feel *this* familiar? Tess hadn't set foot in Invercaillie in three years, yet the moment she turned into the little road, the utter familiarity of the place struck her. She slowed down the car as she spotted the house with its yellow-painted walls at the end of the street.

The entire neighbourhood was quiet, not a single light shining through the windows, which only heightened the nervous energy bubbling up within Tess. Even though she drove slowly, the sound of her car echoed back from the walls, and she couldn't help it—she felt like an intruder.

No, she *was* an intruder, if she paid mind to Zara Ellis and her opinion. They'd had one tense phone conversation before shifting all their communication to email. Which, in hindsight, had been a mistake because, without hearing the words, Tess wasn't sure if they'd come to an agreeable cohabitation plan. If she'd interpreted the other woman's words correctly, the answer was no.

Not that Tess was thrilled to be here in Invercaillie, either. But after the complete implosion of her life had left her homeless, wife-less and with a job she resented, she needed to leave London and come back to Scotland.

Now she could take her time to put herself together, figure out what she wanted in life.

And confront the two people that had been living in Tess's ancestral home ever since the passing of her sister Sabrina: Sabrina's daughter, Helly, and her legal guardian, Zara.

The light on the porch flickered to life as she pulled up to the old house. Her eyes darted over the façade, searching for a disturbance of the curtains or a glimpse of the person now living there. A house where Tess and her sister used to live right until Tess had left for medical school. One their parents had left to her and Sabrina in their will. It had stood empty until Sabrina had packed up her entire life—including her best friend, Zara—four years ago to move up here for a fresh start.

The day the two women left had been the last time Tess had seen her sister. And the last time she'd seen Zara had been at Sabrina's funeral three years ago, clutching a crying Helly to her chest while her own tears fell.

Fresh start. In an echo of what had brought her sister back to Invercaillie, Tess now found herself in the same position.

She took a few deep breaths as she wrestled with the anxiety wrapping around her chest. She was here because of Helly. With how absent she'd been from her sister's life, she knew she had a lot to make up. Lost time to reclaim. But she suspected Zara wouldn't make any of this easy on her—not with the history they shared.

They'd never spoken about it. Not properly. And maybe it hadn't meant as much to Zara. Maybe it *should* mean nothing now. Why was Tess even thinking about moments two decades in the past? They'd been teenagers and those feelings were designed to be fleeting.

Get out of the car and walk up to the house. She knows you're here. The hesitation was ridiculous. What was she scared of?

They'd had a tension-filled dynamic from the start. Zara had been fifteen, newly folded into the Sinclair household as Sabrina's best friend; Tess had been seventeen and immediately off balance by what her sister's new friend had brought to the house. There'd been something about her—too bright, too charming, too hard not to notice.

Despite the code of conduct among siblings marking Zara as forbidden, they'd circled each other for months. Lots of eye contact, words shot at each other that had been designed to tease as much as to cut. Then one night, it had escalated. A tentative kiss. An exploring one had followed after that. Tess didn't let herself remember it in too much detail, but it had been real. Messy and charged. And something they'd both immediately pretended never happened.

So, instead, Tess had channelled those confusing feelings into derision, building up a rivalry that Zara had leaned into with enthusiasm. Not a day had gone by back then when they hadn't had a verbal sparring match.

Tess let out a sigh, pressing her head against the steering wheel as a bone-deep tiredness swept through her. The drive up here had taken twelve hours. She'd distracted herself most of the trip by listening to an audiobook about a man and an alien becoming best friends, but the closer she'd got to her destination, the more anxious she'd grown, leaving her unable to listen to the words.

Maybe she could sneak around the back of the house and get into the cottage without facing Zara. It would be easier to talk to her in the morning, after a shower and a coffee. Thankfully she wouldn't have to live *with* Zara in the same house. That they had to share a property was already contentious enough.

A property and their place of work. Tess was here on a locum assignment at the GP surgery attached to the one local hospital within a few miles' radius. Not a choice she'd *wanted* to make, but with her life falling apart around her, she'd needed to get out. Needed to—

A sharp knock ripped her out of her thoughts and her heart stuttered in her chest when she looked up and found two brown eyes staring at her through narrowed slits.

'Are you going to come in or do you plan on sleeping in your car?' Zara said, her voice muffled through the glass.

'You would like that, wouldn't you?' Tess mumbled, then grabbed the key from the ignition and slung the backpack sitting on the passenger seat over her shoulder as she pushed the car door open.

Zara needed to relax. Grasping the keys in a death grip, she unlocked the door of the small cottage at the back of the property with stiff fingers.

The moment she'd seen Tess's car crawl down the street, something in her had gone rigid. Not just nerves, but something older. Heavier.

She stepped into the warmth and left the door open

behind her. Tess followed, silent and close enough for Zara to feel her presence linger in the air, even without a word said between them.

It had been years. But hearing that voice again—first on the phone, then just now when she'd approached the other woman's car—had tugged something loose. Some coil of a memory and wariness and…something else Zara had no interest in naming.

'I've turned on the electric heater earlier today so it's not freezing cold in here. But putting on a fire is better for the electricity bill. There's some chopped wood next to the fireplace that you can use.' Zara flicked the lights on, bathing them both in the pale-yellow light of the last-century light bulb still in the fixture.

The door clicked closed as Tess drew it shut, and Zara turned around even though a part of her brain was telling her not to. That something would happen to that incessant buzzing inside her if she was confronted with the full force of Tess Sinclair's presence. With the darkness outside it had been hard to make out more than shapes, but now—

'Thanks,' Tess said, her backpack coming down on the floor with a *thunk* and, yup—Zara shouldn't have turned around.

Her heart leapt into her throat at the flash of teeth in Tess's tired smile. The purple shadows under her eyes said more than the twelve-hour drive ever could, and a part of Zara itched to know why she was here—after years of radio silence. Years of not showing up for her sister. For Helly.

But the part of her that knew better didn't care. Or

wouldn't let itself care. Tess was just another person who'd walked out on her.

Zara had been left before. Her dad hadn't stuck around long enough to be anything more than a ghost, and her mum—when sober enough to care—had always chosen the pub over parenting. That was how she'd ended up in the Sinclair household. A family so warm and kind, they felt fictional. Whether Sabrina's parents ever saw how bad things were at home, Zara would never know. But they'd treated her like one of their own.

And then they were gone, snatched away by an accident.

Tess had come for the funeral but left before people had even said their condolences, leaving her little sister to wade through grief and paperwork alone. That was when the crack between Tess and Sabrina split wide open. The sisters had started to drift, and Zara had always wondered if she was the cause.

Sabrina had said no, years later. That they'd just never had much in common without their parents holding them together. It hadn't made the abandonment easier. Tess had walked away—from Sabrina, from Helly, from Zara.

And now she was back.

Looking at her now, Zara could feel the old pull kicking to life in her chest as though it had never left. It had no right to still feel this electric. But it did.

Tess stood in the entryway as if she belonged here. Hair a little shorter, shoulders broader, eyes just as sharp. Her jumper stretched across her chest in a way that caught Zara off guard. She looked tired—maybe a flicker of uncertainty—but still infuriatingly magnetic.

'There's some stuff in the fridge, in case you're hungry,' Zara said—mostly to distract herself from her thoughts straying. The absolute last thing she should focus on was Tess and how well she remembered the feel of those hands on her body.

It had been twenty years. How was there even a memory to recall?

Tess looked down at her shoes, the braid of light brown hair flopping over her shoulder in a gesture that looked oddly tired for hair. Then she let out a sigh, her shoulders slumped. 'Look… I've had a long drive, and I was hoping to just get into the shower, wash this day off, and get some sleep before we get into all of *this*.'

Zara blinked, taken aback by Tess's tone. As if she were the one being unreasonable. 'Don't worry, we don't have to get into anything *at all*,' she snapped, forgetting about the memories that had made her tense up a second ago. 'I should've realised you're only here because you need a place to stay.'

She turned, heart thudding when she heard Tess mutter behind her, quiet but loaded: 'That is exactly what I wanted to avoid.'

Zara stopped short. 'Excuse me?'

Tess let out a sigh as she slumped against the door. She raked both hands through her dishevelled hair, loosening the already disintegrating braid. 'Sorry, this is not—I'm not trying to be complicated. I'm just—' Tess interrupted herself with a shake of her head, and something about the gesture struck Zara. They were both tired and on edge.

'It's been a long day, Tess. How about I let you get some rest, and we can talk when we've both had some sleep?' It was the smallest of olive branches Zara could muster and even that felt like more than Tess deserved. But they were adults now and, at the very least, they needed to find a way to be civil. For Helly.

Not that Zara had any plans to rush Helly into the arms of her aunt. Outside Zara herself, Tess might be the only family Helly had left. But as Zara was her guardian, it was her responsibility to prevent any further harm when the little girl still struggled with the loss of her mother. She didn't want her to get attached to Tess only for her to bail on her the way she had on other people in her life.

Blood didn't guarantee consistency. And if Tess was only here to play at being aunt for a few weeks, Zara wasn't going to make it easy. Tess had yet to make her intentions clear.

'I'll get out of your hair. We can chat tomorrow before work, okay?' She took a step towards the exit. Tess shuffled away from the door, dragging her backpack with her, and their shoulders grazed as they passed each other in the narrow space of the little cottage. Zara flinched from that slight touch, the tiny bump of skin against skin enough to send lightning racing down her spine.

Another reason to get out of here as soon as possible.

Zara's hand closed around the door handle when Tess said, 'Can I see her?'

Zara sighed. Something inside her had anticipated the question and had wanted to get out before Tess could voice it. Now, with it out in the open, Zara had to address it. Shooting Tess a look over her shoulder, she shook her head and bit down the need to comfort the other woman when she saw something infinitely fragile flutter over her expression. 'Not right now. Helly is sleeping and I don't want to risk waking her.' She paused, finding another piece of the olive branch. 'Do you want to see some pictures?'

Tess's entire face lit up, every line on her face disappearing momentarily, and Zara's breath stuttered out of her. This was not good. The last thing she needed in her life was old feelings turning into something fresh.

Tess shouldn't be this aware of the space between her and Zara. Yet she was. Just as she was aware of the scent drifting around her being so specifically Zara's. Because why would she remember that about the other woman? It had been three years since she'd last seen her and even longer since Tess had breathed in this blend of floral and spices, yet the recognition was instant.

'This was Helly's first day at the day care of the hospital. She was so agitated,' Zara said as she angled her phone towards Tess, showing her a red-faced Helly with tears staining her cheeks. 'Before everything, Sabrina and I used to alternate our shifts, so that Helly was always at home. The new environment was a lot of stress for her.'

Tess looked at the picture of her niece and, as with all the other pictures Zara had been kind enough to show her, she felt the pressure in her chest tightening. As if the years she'd spent avoiding this place were all piling up on top of her, crushing her with the weight of her decisions.

She'd wanted to come back earlier. She'd meant to. There had been a moment—just after Helly was born— when Sabrina had reached out, and Tess had written back. But seeing Sabrina and Zara so fully entwined in that new life, co-parenting like a unit, had scraped against something inside her. Tess knew it had been irrational. They were best friends and had been since their youth. Their faith in each other made Tess's marriage seem even more hollow but, instead of seeing that, she'd told herself it was better to stay away. To focus on fixing her marriage and salvage what she'd built.

Tess couldn't undo any of it now. But she could be different. She could be here—for Helly. She would do anything to fix this. Which meant finding a way to co-exist with Zara. 'Is she better now?' she asked with a nod towards the picture.

Zara nodded. 'So much better. She loves it now. Helly is best friends with everyone there and she's always the first one to play with any newcomers.'

'That's good to know,' Tess said, taking a breath as awkwardness settled in between them. She tried to recall how she and Zara used to get along. After realising the tension between them was rooted in attraction, both had quickly course-corrected into sniping at each other. The jabs and barbs had been easy, almost affectionate at times, even if neither of them had wanted to admit that.

'Thank you for letting me stay here. I know that's inconvenient for you and probably not something you want to deal with, so I appreciate it,' Tess said, looking around the cottage. It had been the only thing available at short notice as she started her locum position, but she hoped to use it to her advantage with Helly.

'Well, half of this house does technically belong to you,' Zara said, stuffing her phone back in her pocket before shifting in her seat. 'I don't think I could legally prevent you from coming here.'

Tess stiffened at those words. She had known from the get-go that she would be an intruder, but some tiny part of her had hoped to receive a warm welcome anyway. A warm-ish welcome? A welcome that fell on the cosier side of frosty maybe? Whatever her hope had been, hearing that she was tolerated here because legally Zara had to tolerate her was not what she had wanted to hear.

'I will find somewhere else to stay sooner if necessary. If me being here is an imposition, I'd rather not—'

Zara raised her hands. 'No, it's totally fine for you to stay here. The cottage has everything you need. It's just been sitting there, empty.' She hesitated. 'I was just trying to wind you up. You know—banter? Like we used to talk to each other.' Her shoulders crept up. 'Too soon?'

Tess blinked several times, absorbing the other woman's words. The way they used to be? No, that was a dangerous place. One that so many years later shouldn't even exist, yet the faint tugging at the bottom of her stomach was there as she sat next to Zara, keenly aware of the narrow space between them.

'Oh…' That was all her tired and confused brain could muster. Then, to change the topic to something slightly less uncomfortable, she asked, 'What is Helly like?'

'She's really great.' The lines around Zara's eyes softened and the genuine love lighting up her face stole the breath from Tess's lungs. 'She communicates really well and now that she's figured out a few phrases, she never shuts up. The staff at the day care love her because she's so soft and kind to everyone she meets. And she...'

Her words trailed off, eyes darting down to where her long fingers played with the hem of her shirt. Tess took a steadying breath, prompting her with a quiet 'what?' when she didn't continue.

'She's excited to meet her aunt. Helly knows the concept from her friends at the day care, and when I told her you'd be living with us for a bit, she got excited.' This pause was less foreboding, but it still hit Tess with the might of a slap.

Of course she'd imagined her niece's reaction to her. But all the scenarios that had spawned in her head had been negative. That Helly would be scared of her. Or resent her presence. Or even reject her.

Too little, too late.

'Thank you for telling me,' Tess managed to say through a throat thick with emotions.

Zara's hand came up, as if to touch her. Or was that what Tess *wanted* to happen? But instead of reaching across the space, it hovered in the air for a second. Then it came down in the space between them. Far away still—but also closer.

Another peace offering?

'I should get back. She still wakes up sometimes at night looking for—' This time Zara's words didn't trail off. No, this interruption was intentional, clamping her mouth shut before she could mention the one person neither of them had brought up yet.

Why was this conversation even necessary? It wasn't as if she were here for Zara's sake. She'd come back to Invercaillie for Helly and to finally be part of her niece's life. Zara was only involved because of her role as Helly's legal guardian.

But outside that, did they really have to establish a relationship that went beyond cordial? Maybe it would be better if they *didn't*. Considering the tension that had snapped into place the second they'd entered each other's orbit.

'Right. I should get some rest. It was a—'

'—long drive, yeah,' Zara finished her sentence. Then she got to her feet and left without a backwards glance at Tess, leaving her in the tiny cottage stuffed full of memories from her youth.

And the soft scent of roses Tess was far too familiar with.

CHAPTER TWO

THE FIRST MEETING between Helly and her aunt hadn't gone as predicted, which had left Tess in a sour mood. Or at least Zara thought this was what a bad mood looked like on Tess Sinclair. The woman had perfected the resting-bitch face, so Zara wasn't sure if her feelings were hurt or if that was just her face.

Her impassive, stupidly pretty face with skin still as flawless as Zara remembered from her youth. Weren't people supposed to get wrinkles? Zara had.

'Helly got overwhelmed with excitement and that can go one of many ways,' she said, trying to get through to the other woman again.

When Tess had joined them for breakfast and Zara had introduced her as her aunt, Helly had stared at Tess with wide eyes. But the moment her aunt had taken a step closer, the little girl had burst into tears as she'd scrambled out of her seat to hide behind Zara's back. No amount of coaxing and prodding had helped with the situation, leaving Zara with no other choice than to tell Tess to go ahead and they'd catch up at the surgery.

Zara tried not to read too much into it, but failed at keeping her own scepticism in check. Did Helly sense her aunt's impermanence too and was she trying to tell her something? Would Tess take Helly's reaction as a reason to distance herself even though she'd just arrived?

'I told you it's fine,' Tess replied, but the tone of her voice conveyed it might not be fine.

'We can try again in the evening after I pick her up from day care. After a day of playing with her friends, she might be tired and less excitable.'

They walked down the corridors of the small hospital until they arrived at a door on the ground floor. Pushing through, Zara looked behind her to check on Tess, whose scowl had lessened only a fraction. Maybe it wasn't just Helly? Maybe she resented being here altogether? But then why had she come?

Zara pushed that tiny bubble of anxiety away with a shake of her head. It wasn't any of her business to theorise about Tess's motivations. Trying to do that was like reading tea leaves. She'd tried—failed—to do that in the past. But now Zara was a different person. Older and less susceptible to the mystery of an unapproachable woman.

With Helly's guardianship and a full-time job to boot, Zara had no time for women, mysterious or otherwise. Tess was here because of her own messy circumstances and once she had those sorted out, Zara had no guarantee that she would stick around. So what she needed to concentrate on was Helly, and Tess's relationship with her. Make sure she'd protect Helly's emotional well-being from a woman she knew to be unreliable.

'And this is the GP surgery attached to the hospital,' Zara said, forcing herself to focus on the present. She had more to navigate than just introducing Helly to Tess. She also needed to figure out how to work with

Tess daily since she would be here for the next three months at least.

'And it'll be just the two of us?' Tess asked, reading her mind. The sharp edges of her tone weren't lost on Zara. The other woman thought their working relationship would be contentious as well? Though she bristled at the thought of Tess feeling the same way. What right did she have to be annoyed or upset? Tess had been the one to make all the choices that had led her away from Sabrina—and from Zara by extension.

'Pretty much. On slow days in the hospital, I sometimes get one of the A & E doctors to help. But usually Tracey and I could handle the patient load between us.' Tracey Frazier was the woman who'd started working at the GP surgery some weeks after Sabrina's passing. And Tess was here because Tracey had gone on parental leave. A part of Zara panicked at the thought her colleague might not want to return.

Sabrina almost hadn't after giving birth. But if Tracey didn't, the locum position Tess occupied would become a permanent one.

Zara shoved the thought aside. It wasn't her decision. It wasn't even a conversation. And yet, her stomach knotted all the same.

'You mentioned shifts yesterday,' Tess said while looking at her, one delicate eyebrow pulled upwards.

'Oh, that's nothing to worry about right now. We did quite a few house calls and do the odd weekend shift when A & E is short-staffed. It's a give and take. They help us, we help them.' Zara kept her tone neutral. 'Your schedule should stay fairly regular over the next few months.'

Tess's scowl deepened. 'This isn't my first job right out of medical school. If you need me to take shifts or do house calls, I'll do it.'

The edge in her voice made something rise in Zara's throat—an old, defensive instinct. Now Tess wanted to prove herself? After walking out on the only family she had? Zara didn't know much about the circumstances of Tess's life back in the south, but she suspected Tess was only back because of convenience. Something had gone wrong and she was here to lick her wounds.

Zara wouldn't entrust her with the more specialised care of her community if she wasn't certain she could trust Tess.

'I'm not saying you can't handle it,' she said, voice sharper than she meant. 'I'm saying it's different here. You worked in private, right? This is a rural GP surgery. People need more than prescriptions. They need someone who knows them, their name, their history, their circumstances. Someone permanent in their lives.' She could see the words land. Could see Tess bristle, but Zara didn't budge. She wasn't just guarding herself. She was guarding her people, who had stood by her through so much of her turbulent early years. Tess had left like so many others for greener pastures, only returning to her home town because of necessity rather than wanting to be a part of the community again.

'I don't see how working with private patients is any different from this. They all need the same care.' Tess folded her arms in front of her and damn Zara's traitorous eyes as they flicked downward for a brief second— checking the other woman out.

Wait, what on earth was she doing? Judging by the

slight widening of Tess's eyes, she'd noticed Zara's straying gaze as well. Great. That wouldn't send the wrong
message at all. Nor would it interfere with their forced
cohabitation.

Ugh. She needed to get away from her.

'This will be your office. All the passwords and access you need to the system are printed out and on your
desk. You should have a light schedule today to get
used to our routine. But if you have any questions, I'll
be right next door.' Before Tess could drag her into another argument, Zara turned on her heel and walked
through her own office door, closing it behind her. Only
once she heard Tess do the same did she relax, slump-
ing against the door and taking a deep breath to calm
her racing heart.

Why was she even trying to be friendly with Tess?
She had accepted her olive branch, but the moment
Zara had slipped back into their old communication
style, she'd pulled back. Which should be a clear sign
for her. Tess was only interested in Helly. Zara didn't
need to waste her time and effort fixing their inter-
personal relationship. Fine. She wouldn't. In fact, she
hadn't even thought about doing that. Why would she?
That woman meant nothing to her. The pitter patter of
her heart against her sternum was because Zara hated
confrontation. No other reason.

So she would simply stay away from Tess. Easy, right?

Tess frowned at the patient's chart in front of her, reading over the notes that Dr Frazier had left on this man's
past check-up.

Patient reports unexplained weight loss, irregular bowel habits, and occasional blood in stool. No fever, no recent travel history, no obvious dietary triggers. Mild lower abdominal tenderness on exam. No palpable masses.

Provisional diagnosis: IBS. Recommended trial of low-FODMAP diet. Advised patient to follow up in six weeks if symptoms persist. If no improvement, consider inflammatory markers and referral for further testing.

IBS? But that didn't explain all his symptoms. Not with the bit about the bleeding. She put a smile on her face as she turned towards Robert. 'So you don't feel like your change in diet has improved your condition?' she asked, taking mental notes when he nodded.

'Dr Frazier said to give it a few weeks. But the pain some evenings is too much for me to handle, and it disrupts my working day as well,' he replied. Tess's eyes darted to the chart, and she frowned again when she noticed the occupation field of his chart was empty.

Sloppy paperwork.

'I see Dr Frazier's notes here, but I want to make sure we're not missing anything,' Tess said, then walked Robert through a few follow-up questions—his energy levels, weight trends, dietary changes, and the pattern of the pain.

The physical exam was unremarkable: mild tenderness in the lower abdomen, but no masses, no alarming sounds. Enough to raise concern but it didn't help her reach any conclusions on the diagnosis.

'You can get dressed now,' she said, stepping back. As Robert pulled his shirt down, Tess reviewed her notes.

The symptoms didn't sit right with IBS—especially not the bleeding. Though it was too early to jump to any conclusions, she had a suspicion that warranted further investigation.

When Robert sat back down, she turned towards him. 'It's still too early to say what's going on,' she said. 'But since the change in diet hasn't helped, I'd like to run some blood work and stool tests. That will give us a clearer picture of whether we're looking at something like inflammatory bowel disease or something else entirely.'

Robert's shoulders tensed. 'You think it's something serious?'

'I think it's something worth looking into further. Let's take it one step at a time. If anything flags on the tests, we can move forward with a referral for a colonoscopy. But right now, the focus is on narrowing things down.'

'Okay...' Robert sighed out the word after a beat of silence. 'I just need this to stop.'

Tess smiled, knowing it wouldn't set her patient at ease, but still hoping it would do something until they could get the diagnosis nailed down. 'We will get this sorted out. Once the results are in, I'll be in touch to talk again.'

She pushed to her feet and so did Robert, giving her a weak smile as he walked towards the door with her at his heel. 'Thanks, Dr Sinclair,' he said, then paused as if a thought had just occurred to him. 'You know, a previous doctor at this clinic had the same name. What are the chances?'

Tess could feel his scrutiny as his eyes travelled over her face, looking for the similarities between his previous doctor and her. One she knew was there but had hoped would remain undetected for, well, the duration of her stay. She knew that had been unlikely to happen, but she hadn't even lasted three patients before someone had noticed.

'Yes, we are related. *Were* related. She was my sister,' she said through a throat much thicker than it should be. She couldn't get emotional at work under any circumstances.

'Oh, right. She was—'

'The front desk will set you up with everything necessary for the testing. Once that's done, we'll be in touch to set up another appointment.' Tess knew she shouldn't interrupt her patient, but he'd been about to bring up Sabrina—clearly not remembering her passing. Which was fair. Why would he? But she didn't think she could listen to someone talk about her right now, as she was standing in the office where her sister used to work.

Not when the mere mention of her sister caused the tight ball of emotion living in the pit of her stomach to coil up even further. Whatever Tess liked to tell herself, she was not in control of the situation and so she did what she'd done for the last two-plus years: she shoved it away.

Avoided it. Nobody could make her face the ever-mounting guilt and regret coiling within her.

Except now that she was working in the office that used to be Sabrina's, living in the house that used to be hers and trying her best to form a relationship with Sabrina's child, her avoidance tactics became less and less workable.

Tess needed to do something about that. She had no idea what.

Once her last patient left, Tess tucked herself behind the computer and started typing up all of her notes. With this assignment's temporary nature, she needed to leave Dr Frazier as much context as possible on what decisions she'd made for her patients in her absence. Tess also took this opportunity to familiarise herself with tomorrow's schedule and what she could learn about her patients.

With all those tasks done, she was about to head out when a knock sounded at her door. One that wasn't soft enough to be the front desk or any of the nurses. Before she could say something, the door flew open and Zara stormed in, furrows already crinkling her brow.

'You're referring Robert Fern for a colonoscopy?' the woman said, skipping any of the pleasantries Tess might have expected from another colleague. Of course, Zara wasn't any other colleague and apparently she was also hell-bent on bringing their past conflict to work with them. Otherwise, why else would she be standing there now, questioning the diagnostic plan of her fellow GP?

And just to rub it in, Tess said, 'Hello to you, too.'

She got exactly the response she wanted when Zara bristled at her words. The thrill racing down Tess's spine at the reaction was unreasonable. Far more childish than she should behave. But it also temporarily emptied her mind of anything else whenever she focused on Zara. The tight ball of chaos in the pit of her stomach, the shadows lurking in the quiet of her mind, and the incessant nagging to be doing something so idleness couldn't catch up with her—these things all disappeared the second Zara was near her.

Or at least that was what had happened yesterday. And what was happening right now. Might be worth exploring some more. If only that didn't mean putting herself in the way of a woman that clearly loathed her.

'Why are we doing such an invasive procedure for IBS?' Zara said, as if her last question had not readily conveyed that meaning.

'I'm not referring him. If you had read the notes properly, you'd realise we're running tests before going to a colonoscopy. And I noted that because Robert doesn't have IBS. Which you would know if he was your patient. But he's mine. Which brings me to the question—' Tess leaned forward, weaving her fingers together and dropping her chin on top of her hands as she looked up at Zara '—why are you looking at my patient charts and referrals unprompted?'

GPs looking at each other's files wasn't anything out of the ordinary. But they did that for specific reasons. Either they were covering for someone, or their colleague had asked for advice. But sniffing around in someone's notes just to inform themselves was poor conduct—and looking at the blush creeping up Zara's face, Tess knew that she knew it and yet still hadn't been able to stop herself from barging in here.

Zara crossed her arms in front of her. She'd rolled the sleeves of her lab coat up, exposing the pale skin underneath, and Tess watched with far too much awareness as the muscles in the other woman's forearms pulsed as her hands dug into her biceps. She radiated tension, but there was something else underneath it. All of Tess's instincts told her not to focus on that something and to keep her attention above Zara's neckline.

'You're telling me you wouldn't check up on a new doctor after their first day?'

Tess fought the smirk tugging at her lips because why was she even amused? That—and the pinprick of heat appearing at the base of her spine when she looked at Zara—needed to stop. Too much had gone awry between them to still feel this way whenever she saw Zara.

'You know I would. But instead of snooping through their patient files and referrals, I would rather, you know, ask them how their day was. Which was good, by the way.'

Zara's eyes flared, letting Tess know she had hit a mark she hadn't even aimed at. But the satisfaction that washed through her was as good as if she'd done it on purpose. She knew she shouldn't enjoy the verbal sparring matches with Zara the way she used to as a teenager. She hadn't found pleasure in it last night. But then again, she'd been on the road for twelve hours, leaving behind a life she'd thought would never have failed her—except it had.

Now she found herself in a new clinic, stuck with the one person who had been continuously haunting her dreams with ethereal *what ifs*, even when she hadn't seen the other woman in several years.

After Robert had identified her as Sabrina's sister, Tess had been off in her head, barely able to focus on the rest of her patients. A part of her was dreading the end of the day and how Helly might react to her. If this morning had been any indicator, then building a relationship with her niece would be harder than she'd anticipated.

But something about this moment right now, as Zara's eyes narrowed on her and her chin jutted out in a defiant stance, emptied Tess's brain of all those thoughts and insecurities. Gone was the breakdown of her marriage that had seen her flee up here to Invercaillie. So were the words she burned to say to Sabrina and never could. And the regrets she had on missing so much of Helly's life so far.

Because all she could focus on in the presence of this woman was *her*.

Tess knew she shouldn't lean in, but the freedom— the reprieve from the thoughts dwelling within—was as seductive as Zara herself. The years gone by had turned her into a stunning woman. And because of that emptiness in her mind, Tess leaned in.

'Or are you just so obsessed with me you have to look at my files? You can't talk to me because I might make you blush more?' Tess braced her arms on her desk as she said that, leaning forward enough to make the flirty intentions of her words clear.

The reaction was everything she'd hoped for. Zara's eyes widened, the colour on her cheeks deepening to where Tess could almost feel the heat radiating from her. Zara's lips opened in a silent gasp, and for a few seconds, the only noise filling the room was her breath. 'I'm not—how can you even suggest—?' Zara shook her head and Tess traced every small movement with her eyes, drinking in the tiny shiver she could see clawing down her body even if she didn't say anything.

Zara didn't need to. Even after all these years, the connection neither of them had ever wanted—and only acted upon once—remained alive and that thread binding them meant Tess still knew how to read her. How to interpret her various moves.

'A colonoscopy is a highly invasive procedure for someone in their mid-thirties,' Zara said, and Tess couldn't help the smirk from unfurling on her lips this time at the other woman's avoidance.

'And I won't order one if he doesn't need it. But he *might* because he doesn't have IBS. Dr Frazier took a well enough guess, but the follow-up today showed it's the wrong one.' Tess didn't mention that Dr Frazier's notes hadn't even hinted at an alternative diagnosis. That wasn't her problem to solve as a locum doctor.

Zara straightened at those words. 'What do you suspect it is, then?'

'Some other inflammatory bowel disease. With the symptoms he presented today, it could be Crohn's. I've ordered some samples from him and bloodwork to run tests before the colonoscopy,' she said, though a part of her didn't want to. After this, there was nothing else to discuss, and Zara had no reason to stick around.

Tess had no reason to *ask* her to stay. No reason other than when they were arguing, she could forget about all the other worries pressing against her. That Zara had somehow become her messed-up antidote. She searched for something to say, but when she reached inside herself, the wrong thing came out.

'Robert was one of Sabrina's patients, wasn't he? He asked me about her as he was leaving,' Tess said, and regretted it the moment the words formed.

The warm colour drained from Zara's cheeks. 'What did he ask?'

'If we were related. Given we have the same surname.'

Zara's retreat—both mentally and physically—was obvious the moment Tess said her sister's name. The woman took a step back, blinked several times and when her back bumped against the door, Tess saw her hand grip the door handle so tight, her knuckles turned white. Of course Sabrina remained a difficult—*impossible*—topic to discuss, but it still struck her how fast they'd gone from needling each other to Zara retreating as fast as she could.

'Zara—' Tess started, but the other woman shook her head, dark curls bouncing around her head. Then the door opened with a small squeak and Zara stepped out.

'I'll see you at home,' she said, closing the door before Tess could even get another word in to ask her to stay. Only why? They'd discussed what they needed to, with Zara giving her far more time than she required.

That Zara was still processing the loss of Sabrina was obvious, and Tess had expected nothing else. Yet her hurried departure tasted like rejection. Maybe the problem was that Tess hadn't come here with *any* expectation of how to navigate the one thing they both still struggled with: Sabrina's death.

A part of Tess wanted to move on—choose to be healthy and happy and find the lightness in her life again. But could she do that without the one person who had been closest to her sister until the end of her life? The one person who also managed to quiet her mind whenever she was near?

It had been not even a day, yet the struggle was becoming more than apparent.

Shaking her head, Tess shut off the computer and pushed herself to her feet. There was someone else to focus on and that should be her *only* focus: Helly. The meeting this morning hadn't gone well, but that shouldn't deter her. How hard could it be to befriend a three-year-old child?

CHAPTER THREE

ONE WEEK. THAT WAS how long it took for Helly to warm up to Tess enough that they could spend some time alone without Zara's supervision. She wasn't sure if Helly was picking up on how anxious Tess was to get along with her niece, or if the family resemblance between her aunt and her late mother was too much for her to process.

Zara had briefly talked to Matt, her neighbour and a child psychologist who had worked with Helly when she'd become old enough to articulate her thoughts, about how to handle this evolving situation. And he'd assured her that as long as Zara didn't shy away from discussing Sabrina's death with Helly in a manner appropriate for her age, she wouldn't get confused.

Zara always spoke about Sabrina whenever Helly brought up her mum—but *only* with Helly. Anyone else bringing her up made something inside Zara clamp shut. As if the already fragile memories of Sabrina would float away on the wind if she let them out. But if she kept them in, they'd stay there. Preserved.

The moment from last week replayed in her mind as she opened her car door to squeeze behind the wheel. Tess had flirted with her. Not in an obvious way and anyone looking on would have thought they were having a contentious conversation. Only the two women knew the truth of how they spoke to each other—of the things that slumbered underneath their barbed words for each other.

She'd enjoyed their verbal sparring matches way too much, to the point where she was actively avoiding Tess in the clinic because Tess's presence distracted her. The way Tess moved through her spaces—both at home in the cottage and at the clinic—pulled at Zara's attention far more than it should. Zara had caught herself watching her in the hallway, or through the kitchen window when Tess walked across the back garden to the cottage, shirt sleeves rolled up, a mug of coffee in her hand. It was irritating. The way her chest tightened. The way her eyes lingered. The way her body reacted as though it hadn't forgotten what it once wanted.

Or maybe she was avoiding her because Zara knew Tess wanted to talk about Sabrina. Though what was the point? Tess had made her choice years ago to immerse herself in her new life down in the south. Zara knew Sabrina had wanted to see her sister more. They'd grown distant when Tess had left for medical school, and a part of Zara still wondered to this day if it had been *her* fault. That because of how joined at the hip she'd been with Sabrina, Tess had also needed to distance herself from her sister to get rid of the feelings for Zara.

It would explain Tess's reaction after the one night when things had gone too far…

Zara squeezed her eyes shut, shaking her head to dispel the thoughts. Nothing good could come from dwelling on this—another thing Matt had told her when she'd opened up about her thoughts of Tess returning to Invercaillie. Both Tess and Sabrina had made their decisions as adults, regardless of what feelings Zara might or might not have inspired.

She knew it was true, but, in the current circumstances, this was harder to remember than she liked. Tess's constant presence in her life wouldn't go away any time soon, so she needed to find a better way of dealing with it.

Maybe they should talk about Sabrina, no matter how little Zara wanted to do that. Her breath began to shake on its way out of her body as she contemplated the idea of that conversation, and the hints of panic gnawed at the edges of her vision.

Zara stuck the key into the ignition and began the drive home before her brain could catch up with her.

The lights in both the house and the little cottage in the back were off when Zara pulled up. She'd received a call a few hours ago for an out-of-hours visit to an elderly patient suffering from a heart condition. The carer couldn't move them safely enough to bring them to the hospital, so Zara had offered to come by and assess the situation before deciding if an ambulance was necessary.

Thankfully it hadn't been and with some additional medication and follow-up appointments, she'd been satisfied enough to leave things be for the evening.

When such situations arose, Zara would usually ask Matt to take care of Helly for a couple of hours. Being next door and working regular office hours, unlike Zara, he'd become her default childminder when she needed to work late and couldn't keep Helly at the hospital's day care.

When she'd received the call, she'd been halfway to Matt's house when a movement had caught her attention: Tess moving around in her cottage.

Zara had hesitated, her step faltering. She'd been ready to dismiss the idea out of hand—but it snagged on something jagged inside her, still raw from Sabrina's loss. Tess might have returned to Invercaillie because she had nowhere else to go.

And yet…there had been moments. Little things that made Zara wonder if Tess's desire to be involved with her niece might be genuine. But wanting wasn't the same as staying. And wanting wasn't enough.

As Helly's guardian, Zara had a responsibility to protect her from hope that came too easily. Especially when it came from someone with a history of walking away.

But she owed her a chance, no? What if Tess proved her wrong?

So she'd swallowed her apprehension, had changed course and asked Tess if she could watch Helly for the evening as she needed to head out and see a patient. To Tess's credit, she hadn't even hesitated before agreeing.

Snow crunched under her boots as Zara walked to the front door. It opened with a small squeal that made her wince. Helly should be asleep at this time, but if she woke up, it could take a while for her to settle back down.

The house was quiet, all the lights off, and when Zara had peeled herself out of all the layers and padded down the corridor to the living room, she found evidence of them playing together—pillows dragged from the sofa onto the floor, picture books stacked haphazardly, a half-drunk glass of milk left on the side table.

When she poked her head into Helly's room, Zara's chest eased. The girl was tucked into bed, bunny clutched to her chest, one foot already free of the blanket. Her breathing was deep and even. No disturbances there.

It was only when Zara stepped back into the living room that she spotted Tess, curled on the floor by the sofa, clearly asleep. She was using one of Helly's oversized plushies as a pillow, her arms folded beneath her cheek, the bare skin prickled with goosebumps.

Zara hovered. She should leave her. Shouldn't care. But that didn't stop her from stepping over to the armchair, grabbing the crochet blanket and kneeling to drape it over Tess's shoulders with careful hands.

She meant to get back up immediately.

But her hand hesitated, just briefly, brushing a loose strand of hair away from Tess's forehead.

And that was when Tess stirred.

Zara pulled back instantly, as if Tess's skin had been too hot to touch, and curled her fingers into a fist by her side. A beat of quiet stretched between them.

'Hey.' It was the first thing to pop into her head. Greeting her, as any person would another one. *You haven't forgotten how to be a human, have you?*

Apparently, whenever she was near Tess, she had to remind herself of the fundamental basics.

Tess blinked blearily, shifting upright with a groan and rolling her neck. 'What time is it?' she mumbled, rubbing at her eyes.

'Late,' Zara said, voice low. 'But Helly's in bed. You don't need to stay down here.'

Tess pushed herself to her feet slowly, stretching her arms overhead. 'Yeah. No idea how I fell asleep on the floor. My spine's going to file a complaint.'

By the time Zara had made it to the kitchen to put the kettle on, Tess had followed—barefoot, yawning, her hair a sleep-mussed mess that Zara refused to find endearing.

Her thoughts stalled when she looked around the kitchen, spotting a dirty pan in the sink. Then the smell hit her nose and her stomach gave a loud squeak that echoed through the quiet of her cosy kitchen.

Zara whirled around when Tess snorted. The sound was so foreign to the woman she knew, whose amusement she'd only ever seen in the context of derision. But this sounded nothing like that. 'What?' That one word had a serrated edge to it, the immediate response to anything Tess related, but if the woman caught it, she didn't let on.

Instead, she stood up from her chair and walked over to the microwave and turned it on. It came alive with a familiar whirring sound, and moments later the air filled with the scent of food. Zara followed Tess with her eyes as the other woman opened the drawers in the kitchen with an efficient familiarity. By the time she'd arranged cutlery and a placemat on the kitchen island, the microwave pinged.

'I made some extra food after feeding Helly and myself. I reckon you haven't eaten?' Tess asked, but Zara was too stunned by the food appearing in front of her to answer straight away.

Too surprised by the level of care it implied. 'Thank you,' she said when she'd gathered herself enough to form words. 'I scoffed down a protein bar I found at the bottom of my bag. Good for an emergency, but nothing this nutritious.'

'Been there,' Tess said, lingering next to her for a few heartbeats and only retreating back to her chair across the kitchen island when Zara picked up the fork and speared some of the buttered and steamed vegetables onto it.

The taste was exquisite, and Zara couldn't help herself. Her eyelids fluttered shut and a near pornographic moan escaped her lips at the explosion of flavour.

When had been the last time someone had cooked for her? Zara made sure that Helly had access to fresh food but, with how picky the three-year-old could be, it was often easier to just make food for the child and then live off protein bars and instant porridge between patients.

'You've had your fair share of handbag bars?' Zara said around a mouthful of chicken breast.

'I think we all have. You've been a trainee doctor. There's not much time to cook in those days. You're either working or studying.' Tess shrugged. 'I enjoy cooking a lot more now because of that struggle. There's something nice about switching off for thirty minutes while busying your hands.'

Zara looked down at the plate and then back up at Tess. 'I didn't know you could cook.'

Tess was quiet for a moment, her green eyes sparkling in the darkness with something Zara failed to name. But it raked through her in a shiver that was both hot and cold. 'There are a lot of things you don't know about me,' she said after another beat of silence, and the *something* got so intense, Zara had to break the connection by staring down at the plate.

'Did Helly eat all of this?' she asked, needing to change the topic. There *were* a lot of things she didn't know about Tess, and that should remain as such. Their proximity to each other was a result of Tess needing to come back here—not *wanting* to. With Tess's motives as murky as they were, Zara couldn't risk getting attached to her presence.

'She was sceptical, and I have to admit it hurt my ego a bit to see her pull a face at my food. But she got around to it eventually. And seeing you enjoy it is almost enough to prop me back up.'

Her tone was soft, her words dancing on the edge of playfulness. Just as they had last week when Zara had confronted her about a patient's diagnostic plan. A dumb thing to do, she could now admit, and Zara still wasn't sure what had possessed her. With any other colleague, she would never have overstepped like that, but something about Tess made her act before she could think things through.

Not good.

'Thank you for feeding her. And looking after her. I appreciate it,' she said, again attempting to steer the conversation into a direction where that spark in Tess's eyes would fade. She couldn't have her looking at her like that, or she would—

Would what?

Tess shook her head. 'Thanks for letting me hang out with her. I'd be more than happy to do this more often without there being any medical emergencies. If you want to have some time to yourself, we can…share the responsibility.'

But for how long? That was the question echoing in

Zara's mind as Tess said that. When they'd spoken about her coming back here and needing a place to stay because of her divorce, neither had really talked about how long-term this solution would be. Her placement at the clinic would only be for three months, after which Dr Frazier would come back from her parental leave. Then what? Would Tess fade out of her life again, the same way she had after her and Sabrina's parents' death? She couldn't possibly plan on staying in Invercaillie when she'd been so keen to leave the moment she'd turned eighteen.

Zara didn't trust her, but she had to give her some grace. For Helly. Even if her gut was telling her this wouldn't end well.

'Sure, if something comes up, I'll let you know. You can also hang out here with her any time you want. You know…' She paused as the words formed in her head, but then she said them anyway. 'As long as you cook for me.'

It sounded far too flirty the moment she said it, but the slow smile unfurling on Tess's lips wiped her doubts away and replaced them with something even more reckless that Zara was too afraid to name. The swooping sensation in her stomach was a familiar one even so many years later, and it spelled nothing but trouble.

'You have a deal, Ellis.'

CHAPTER FOUR

COOKING DINNER FOR Zara had turned into a peace offering in a way Tess hadn't expected. Sure, while she'd
told her she'd simply made too much food that evening,
the truth looked different. Even before her divorce, she
and her ex-wife, Giulia, had rarely eaten together, to
the point where Tess had become proficient enough in
cooking food for one person.

Turned out while she'd been having dinners alone at
their home, Giulia had been spending her time at the
other side of the city entertaining her girlfriend. Not a
fond memory by any mile.

Unlike the one that kept creeping back into her mind
whenever she let herself go idle. Zara standing at the
kitchen island, eating the food she'd made for her, and
the surprised little sounds each bite had wrung from her.
The pleasure Tess derived from that should embarrass
her. It didn't, though. Instead, she clung to it, remembered that moment—and any subsequent one she could
steal whenever Zara came home and beelined straight
for the food after settling Helly down.

They'd settled into a routine like that. Tess cooking
dinner at night, leaving enough leftovers for Zara to feed
herself the next day. Most of the time they were quiet,

the only real conversation when either of them spoke to Helly. Though each evening Tess found herself lingering just a bit longer, soaking up Zara's presence even if they weren't talking.

Some nights they'd even quietly watched a show together, each woman occupying a side of the couch. She caught Zara stealing glances at her now and then—but only because she was doing the same thing, trying to watch her when she wasn't aware of it.

Was she lonely? That was the only explanation she had for how much she tried to be around a woman who clearly only tolerated her in her life for the sake of Helly.

Maybe they needed to clear the air, and then all of this would go away. Talk about whatever was still sore between them. Was it the rift between her and Sabrina? Or was the tension about their past attraction and just how much of the idea still lingered in the air between them?

That was the thought Tess clung to, so she didn't have to consider what other sources the draw towards Zara had. Because even though they'd found a state of truce that let Tess get to know Helly better and look after her on her own, when it came to Zara, they still didn't exchange more than the odd word. In fact, most of their conversations were about the logistics within the GP surgery and patient care.

Like right now.

Zara stuck her head through the door after knocking. 'Hey, did you see the alert come in?' she asked, and Tess shook her head. She'd been sightlessly staring at her monitor for the last few minutes as she tried to figure out if this form of relationship she had with Zara would be enough to tide them over until Helly was old enough to be more independent.

'No, what's going on?' She clicked to her emails, opening the top one with the foreboding subject line Red Weather Warning. Do not leave shelter. Tess looked up at Zara, one eyebrow raised. 'I imagine that people still go outside far too often and all hell is about to break loose at A & E?'

Zara's smirk was like a tonic to Tess's frayed nerves, and she pushed the pleasure away as quickly as it surfaced. Maybe this was the real problem in all of this. She had a cordial relationship with Zara and yet her body reacted to different signals from the other woman as if they were teenagers again, dancing around feelings they thought had been forbidden.

'I just checked with them and they have it all covered. But we have a few patients who need their prescription medicine and if the storm lasts as long as the Met Office seems to suggest, we need to make the rounds now and distribute them before we're stuck.' Tess nodded, bringing up the schedule, and her eyes widened when she found it empty. 'I already cancelled all the appointments and have a list of people we have to see in the next three hours before we need to shelter, too.'

Shutting off the PC, Tess got to her feet. 'Okay, tell me who to visit and what to bring.'

An expression passed over Zara's face, too fleeting for Tess to pin down but showing just enough that she could jump to all sorts of conclusions. Apprehension? Hesitation? Did she not trust her to do her job and do it well? After the incident with Robert—who had just received his diagnosis of Crohn's disease the other day—

she'd thought they were on a better path both at home and here at the clinic.

Zara put a stop to her spiral when she cleared her throat. Looking down at the notebook she held open, she said, 'It's the trust's policy that we don't do home visits by ourselves during severe weather. Someone once got stuck having to move a patient by themselves and it didn't end well for either of them.'

'So, what is the—? Oh.' The words tapered off into a surprised sound when the meaning of Zara's words clicked into place. 'You're saying we have to do this together.'

Zara's nod was tight. 'I know that's not how either of us prefers it, but it's safer this way. The snow can be unpredictable.'

How wrong Zara was about her assumption. The only reason Tess felt apprehensive about this entire idea was because of how clearly she could see Zara's feelings about the situation. She'd rather be doing it with anyone else.

How had they got themselves in this situation? Sure, they had never been friends, but even in their relentless teasing and needling they'd been closer than the icy rift that now lived between them.

'Understood. Are we setting off right away?'

Zara nodded again and turned to leave when Tess quickly packed up her stuff.

Spending the next few hours with Zara in close proximity set something off in Tess. It was a moment existing outside their careful bubble where they had Helly as a buffer. Even if the girl was sleeping in her bed and

Tess lingered in the main house, she had her niece as a cover for why she was there.

Especially considering the things that had sneaked in between them in those quiet moments. Lately, there'd been too many of those—silent glances exchanged across the kitchen; Zara's hand brushing hers when they reached for the same mug—the time they spent together stretching too long at night when Helly was asleep. Nothing had happened. And yet something kept pulsing beneath the surface, taut and electric. Tess tried to ignore it, to file it under nostalgia or loneliness, but it was getting harder to pretend it wasn't real.

Pushing those thoughts away, Tess found Zara waiting at the entrance and hurried after her. They had a job to do, and that was the only thing that mattered right now.

Tess had never been in a snowstorm like this. Or at least she couldn't remember it though she'd grown up in Invercaillie and was used to the fickle temperament of the Scottish Highlands.

'One more person and we're good to go home,' Zara said as she squeezed herself behind the steering wheel of her car. Flurries of snow tried to squeeze their way into the car as she closed to the door. It shut when the wind pushed against it and the windows rattled from the impact.

'Are we going to make it?' The thought had bubbled up in Tess two patients ago and had only grown in severity as she watched the storm gather force. The only thing keeping her calm was Zara and how unfazed she still was.

Except the thin lines around her eyes were now

deeper, leaving Tess with the impression that she might be thinking the same thing. So it wasn't much of a relief when she shook her head only reluctantly. 'I've seen worse. And they all need their medication to survive. So there really isn't another choice. When Sabrina and I—'

Zara's mouth clamped shut just as Tess caught the name of her sister, turning around to look at the other woman. But she refused to meet her eye. She stuck the key into the ignition, the car coming to life with a roar of its engine and then they were creeping down the street as the snow kept piling up. Luckily, their last patient was located on the same street.

At this point, Tess had received the message loud and clear several times over. Sabrina was a topic of conversation that Zara didn't want to discuss. But her late sister—what her life had been like up until the aneurysm had wiped it out—was the one thing she wanted to know about. No, that wasn't entirely true. There was one other thing that kept Tess's attention, and that was the woman driving the car right now.

Nothing good could come of digging up her old feelings for Zara. Who knew if they would even translate well into adulthood? For all she knew, these were just stray thoughts and would fall apart the moment she looked at them too closely. Who could honestly say that their teenage infatuation had survived?

'Why do you not want to talk about her?' Tess asked, knowing well enough she shouldn't.

'About—'

'Sabrina,' she clarified before Zara could feign ignorance. 'You let me back into your life so I could have a relationship with Helly. But you refuse to say anything

relating to Sabrina—going as far as interrupting yourself when you accidentally share a memory of her.'

Zara's knuckles turned white as she gripped the steering wheel tighter, her eyes trained on the now barely
visible road in front of them. With a flick of her finger,
she turned the high beams on, though they did little to
illuminate their way through the growing dark.

'What's the point of talking about her? She's gone and
reminiscing isn't going to bring her back,' Zara said after
a few beats of silence, her voice bare of any inflection
that could help Tess interpret her words.

'You're the only one left who knows about her, and
I—I would like to hear about her life. About what happened. Find some way to—'

'*You're* looking for closure?' A sharpness edged her
voice, and, though Tess recoiled, she preferred it to the
recent robotic tone. At least this offered some leverage,
however painful the outcome.

Before she could say anything, Zara continued. 'You
had the choice to actually be in her life instead of now
hearing things from me posthumously. But you decided
you didn't want to be there for her—not even after she
told you she was pregnant. And now that she's lost to
us for ever, that's when you want to reconnect with her?
When it's too late?'

The words poured out of Zara; an avalanche of emotion crashing right into Tess and stunning her to silence. The words shouldn't be unexpected. Tess knew
she'd made some choices—some she regretted more
than others. They'd made plans to meet up, for Tess to
come back and meet Helly. For them to talk, but then...

'I thought we had more time,' she said, the snowstorm clawing at the windows of the car almost swallowing her words whole. But by the way Zara's spine stiffened, she knew she'd heard her. 'Our relationship—though casual—was working well enough, while other parts of my life *weren't* working, so I focused on those parts. I thought—of course I thought I could come back here eventually and pick things up where we left off. We had plans together.'

Sabrina had died of an undiagnosed aneurysm. Tess had seen the medical file the coroner had been kind enough to share with her after the funeral. There hadn't been anything anyone could have done to prevent her death. It had been a freak accident. Somehow that made it so much worse. As if they were all here on borrowed time.

Zara pulled into a driveway that was already over-flowing with freshly fallen snow. The lights in the car's cabin came on when she twisted the key out of the ignition. But instead of getting out of the car, Zara sat there, staring ahead and taking a few deep breaths. When she finally turned her head towards Tess, Tess saw the spark of determination in the other woman's eyes that made her stomach plummet.

'Okay, let's talk about this after we're home,' Zara said, and Tess almost couldn't believe her ears. From Zara's outburst, it was clear that she had some opinions on the choices Tess had made regarding Sabrina, and she knew that she would have to weather them all if she wanted to put things with Sabrina to a rest.

And once she'd done that, hopefully she would finally

be able to move on with her life and decide what to do next. Because Tess knew she couldn't remain in this holding pattern indefinitely while avoiding the sharp edges inside her.

Agreeing to talk about Sabrina would no doubt come back to haunt her. But Zara couldn't worry about that right now. Not even a second after they knocked on the door, it flew open and a panicked man urged them to step in with a frantic wave of his arms.

'Silvano, what's the matter?' Zara asked, looking over her shoulder to make sure Tess had made it in as well. They hadn't parked more than a few steps away from the house, but these snowstorms could be treacherous even at such a short distance.

'It's Noel. Something's wrong with him. I called the ambulance, but they s-said they couldn't get through and he's—' Silvano broke off, his words turning into a choking sound as he hurried them down the corridor and into the bedroom.

Noel, Silvano's brother, lay in bed with his eyes closed, sweat beading his face. His fingers stretched and contracted in an irregular rhythm as if he was trying to grab onto something but couldn't. Zara put down her bag and hurried over to the bed, tearing off her gloves as she knelt down. Brushing her hand over Noel's neck to find his pulse point, she counted for a few seconds. His skin was cold and clammy, his pulse only faint against her fingertips.

'Noel, can you hear me? It's Zara.' The man stirred when he heard her voice, his lips moving without making a sound. Zara's frown deepened. Silvano was the one they came to see for his medication, as he needed insulin for his diabetes. She couldn't even remember the last time Noel had come into the clinic for a check-up.

'When did all of this start?' Tess asked behind her, going down the same route of thought as Zara. First thing they needed to establish was when this had started.

Silvano, hovering at the other side of the bed, squeezed his eyes shut. 'He was a bit more lethargic this week, but we both thought it was maybe just a cold or some pressure from the oncoming storm.'

Zara bit on her lip to swallow her reply. The weather had nothing to do with Noel's worsening condition, but now was not the time to educate Silvano on what kinds of symptoms he needed to keep an eye on.

'What about eating and drinking?' Tess asked. 'Was he eating normally? Drinking enough water?'

Zara nodded. 'If he was feeling unwell, this might be dehydration.'

Silvano shrugged, shoulders tense as he pulled them up, and Zara could see how hard he was trying to keep the panic at bay. 'He didn't eat anything today because he barely got out of bed. His appetite wasn't strong yesterday, either, I think? But I don't know. We haven't been…' The man trailed off, and out of the corner of her eye Zara saw Tess step closer and put a reassuring hand on his shoulder.

'It's okay. Take a few deep breaths and try to remember.'

They listened to Silvano recite all the times he'd seen his brother in recent days, how he'd seemed sluggish but not really to an extent that had worried him. 'We were fighting about something dumb, and so I was ignoring him the last few days,' Silvano croaked out at the end, and Zara's eyes dropped down to where Tess was still holding onto the man. Watched as her grip tightened with sympathy.

'Let's get some fluids in him and then we'll see how it progresses,' Zara said, swallowing the lump appearing in her throat. Two siblings fighting and now one of their lives hung in the balance? Even looking at it from the outside, the story mirrored the one of the Sinclair sisters. Would Tess be okay?

She searched the other woman's face for a sign that this was too much for her, but she could see nothing but the professional mask she saw on her day in, day out at the surgery. Tess merely nodded, then moved to the large bag they'd dragged to every single patient visit for situations exactly like that. Better to be over-prepared than lack something in a storm like this one.

Unzipping the top of the bag, Tess brought over a bag of saline solution and a sterile kit with which to get the intravenous access going. 'Are you good, or do you want me to do it?'

Zara looked at Tess and Noel. 'You do it. I'll get the portable monitor set up. We need to check his oxygen levels.'

She couldn't see any signs of cyanosis—his lips were more white than pink but not turning blue. Neither were his fingertips. So even though his breath was laboured, oxygen was reaching his brain.

Not wanting to let Noel out of sight of either of them, Zara waited until Tess had sat herself across the bed and when the other woman pulled the gloves on, she moved to the same bag and brought out a vital signs monitor. Plugging it into an empty wall socket, she powered it on and clipped the pulse oximeter onto Noel's trembling finger. The numbers blinked across the screen as the machine calibrated.

SpO_2: 93%
Heart Rate: 114 bpm
BP: 88/60 mmHg

Zara's stomach tightened. Too low. All of it. His blood pressure was dropping fast, his heart racing to compensate.

'He's hypotensive,' she muttered under her breath, adjusting the oximeter to make sure it wasn't a faulty reading. But the numbers didn't improve.

Across the bed, Tess had a tourniquet secured around Noel's arm, palpating for a vein. 'He's severely dehydrated—his veins are practically collapsing.'

Silvano let out a strangled breath. 'Is he—?'

'He's still with us,' Tess assured him, reaching for the IV cannula, hands steady despite the tension humming in the room. 'But we need to get these fluids in now.'

Zara finished setting up the infusion set, spiking the saline bag and holding it aloft as Tess angled the needle into the antecubital vein on Noel's forearm. She advanced the catheter, blood flashing into the chamber before she secured it in place.

'Line's in,' Tess said, taping the IV down and attaching the fluids. 'Starting at a slow bolus—let's see how he responds before we push too much.'

Tess adjusted the drip rate, eyes darting to the BP monitor. The systolic number flickered up slightly—92/62. Still too low, but an improvement.

'Good,' Zara said. 'But his heart rate's still too high.'

Tess didn't look up. 'Give it a minute. His body's been running on fumes. The fluids should help stabilise him.'

Zara exhaled, the weight in her chest only slightly easing. Noel still wasn't over the hill, but the improving vitals were a good sign. To think they'd come here to drop off some medication for Silvano, only to find his brother in a state like this.

She glanced outside the window when it rattled in its frame, the storm picking up pace. Each moment they spent here would make it harder to get home, but they couldn't rush this situation. Thankfully Helly was safely tucked away with Matt.

Zara turned back to Silvano. 'Silvano, does he take any medications he might have got from another doctor? Blood pressure meds, anything for his heart?' She hadn't seen him in the surgery for a while, but maybe he'd gone somewhere else? A private GP maybe?

Silvano shook his head. 'No, he's—' His voice cracked. 'He doesn't really go to the doctor.'

'His lungs are still clear,' Tess noted, pressing the stethoscope to his chest. 'No crackles, no wheezing.'

Zara nodded, thankful for the small reprieve. 'Which means this isn't heart failure yet. But if we don't get his pressure up, we'll be dealing with something worse.'

Then the monitor gave a beep.

Tess flicked her gaze to it, then to Zara. Their eyes met. Zara knew that look, had given it to other doctors throughout her career. But it had never sent a jolt through her the way it did with Tess.

Something wasn't right.

'Noel?' Tess squeezed his shoulder, trying to rouse him. He had responded before, but now—

His breathing hitched. His eyelids fluttered. A violent hacking cough tore through him. Noel's entire body jolted as a choking, wet sound rattled in his chest. Reaching out to steady him, Zara's hands froze mid-motion. The sound sent every warning bell blaring in her head.

Tess reacted first. 'Turn him on his side—now!'

Zara grabbed Noel's shoulder, rolling him just as he coughed again, and pink-tinged froth bubbled up from his mouth. Zara's mind sprinted through the possibilities. Pulmonary oedema. Fluid backing into his lungs. Heart failure hitting them in real time.

She snatched the stethoscope from around her neck, pressing it against Noel's chest. Hadn't Tess just confirmed his lungs were clear? Zara glanced at her wristwatch, swallowing a curse. That had been less than five minutes ago. With a case like this, every second could come with a new surprise.

'He's going into acute heart failure,' Tess said before Zara could. 'We need to push a diuretic.'

Zara was already reaching into their bag, fingers closing around a vial of furosemide and saying a silent prayer for their storm protocol dictating they bring almost their entire portable clinic with them. With the snow raging outside, she wasn't sure an air ambulance could get here on time, never mind a car.

She barely had the syringe prepped before Noel seized, his body convulsing.

'Damn!' Tess was already checking his airway, rolling him onto his back. 'He's crashing.'

Zara's stomach plummeted, and she forced herself to stay calm. 'He's hypoxic.'

Noel's face was losing colour, his lips paling even further. The monitor gave an alert when it couldn't detect a pulse. Everything slowed, then snapped into focus.

Tess's eyes met Zara's, and they both nodded.

Adrenaline.

Zara grabbed the emergency syringe while Tess tilted Noel's head back, securing his airway. Zara injected the adrenaline into his thigh, pressing the plunger down with force. And then she held her breath.

Five seconds.

Ten.

Nothing.

Tess slammed her hands over his chest. 'Starting compressions. One, two—'

Zara grabbed the bag-valve mask, sealing it over Noel's mouth. 'Breathe, Noel.'

Fifteen seconds.

Twenty.

Zara had never been so glad to hear a weak, gasping breath. Noel's body jerked. His chest rose and fell in an uneven rhythm that was music to their ears. Tess slowed her compressions, and Zara's fingers flew back to his carotid pulse. Weak but there.

Zara let out a shaky breath. 'He's back.'

Tess didn't reply. Just sat back, hands braced on her

knees, breathing hard. Meanwhile, Silvano collapsed onto the bed, pressing a shaking hand over Noel's shoulder.

Zara let the weight of the moment settle for just a second—then pushed past it. They weren't done yet.

She turned to Tess. 'We'll need to let the ambulance service know that we need a pick-up.' She glanced towards the window, unable to see anything but darkness interspersed with flurries of snow. 'Given the situation, I think we have to stay and monitor him. Either until they get here or the storm dies down.'

Tess nodded, still catching her breath. They'd probably both already mentally prepared for this when they'd seen the state Noel had been in. They wouldn't be able to leave until the storm cleared, and that wasn't projected to happen for another few hours. Shaking off the shock that had set in right after Noel had come back to them, Zara approached the distressed Silvano, putting a gentle hand on his shoulder to grab his attention.

'He's stable now, Silvano. Dr Sinclair and I will stay with you until he gets picked up by an ambulance, okay?' Silvano sat up but kept one hand threaded around that of his brother, who was slowly regaining his colour.

'Is he going to be okay?' he asked, his voice a whisper—as if he didn't want to put those words into the universe in case the answer wasn't favourable.

'It's unclear right now,' Tess said from behind her, having taken a step closer. 'We don't know what caused his sudden heart failure and pulmonary oedema. He'll have to be admitted to hospital until the doctors there can figure out how this happened.'

Zara nodded to reinforce Tess's point. As far as she

could tell from the patient history she remembered, nothing pointed towards this. There were cases where hearts had just given out, but it was more likely that Noel had been carrying some underlying condition around for a while.

'I'll contact the ambulance service and, depending on how long it'll take them to get here, I'll take the first watch.' She looked at Tess, who nodded.

CHAPTER FIVE

'How is he doing?' Zara's voice ripped Tess out of her silent contemplation. She blinked as she gathered herself, then looked at the other woman.

'Good. Vital signs holding strong and he's been mostly sleeping. Woke up an hour ago to ask about what had happened but quickly ran out of energy,' she said, gesturing at Noel from where she sat in the armchair.

Since Noel was stable and no longer under direct life threat, the ambulance service had triaged him as a less severe case and he'd only be picked up once they'd sorted out all the more severe cases. That meant a few more hours of waiting until they would be able to leave. Though one glance out of the window told her they weren't going anywhere any time soon.

'I finally got Silvano to lie down as well. Poor man has been pacing up and down the kitchen to burn off the worry. He needs some rest.'

Tess raised an eyebrow. 'Shouldn't you be sleeping as well?' Silvano had given them all they needed to make themselves comfortable in his living room.

'I should, but I thought I'd check in first. My adrenaline is still pumping high, even though it's been a couple of hours.' Zara rolled her shoulders as she said that and

Tess let out a low laugh. She knew, yes. They'd been coming down from the adrenaline spike that had let them act as fast as they had to save Noel's life. Working at a GP surgery almost her entire career, she hadn't needed to handle acute emergencies like this one for many years. And even though she was glad emergency medicine wasn't her career, it was good to know that she still knew what to do from instinct alone.

Or rather, that *they* could do it. Tess wasn't certain how things would have turned out if she'd been all by herself with Noel.

The moment it had become clear that they were dealing with an urgent medical emergency here, something had clicked into place between them. It had had nothing to do with their past feelings for each other. Or maybe it had, and it was something underneath that blanket of feelings that they'd tapped into.

Whatever it had been, they'd worked together as if they had done that for their entire careers, one person reading the other's mind as they'd worked in unison. It was such a stark difference from the woman that had questioned her diagnostic capabilities just a few weeks ago.

'This was nice,' Tess said, lacking grander words to express herself. Something Zara made her aware of when she quirked an eyebrow. Tess let out a scoff that blended into a laugh. 'You know what I mean.'

Zara's expression softened and then she pushed herself off the doorframe, plopping down on the other armchair next to hers. 'Yeah, I know what you mean. I'm glad I wasn't dealing with it by myself.'

Tess nodded. Then the quiet set in between them, the

way it always did. They'd spent a lot more time together since Tess had arrived back in Invercaillie some weeks past now, but it had always been either at work or when Helly was around—neither scenario was a good one to discuss the things Tess wanted to talk about. No, *wanted* was too strong a word.

Maybe compelled fitted better? There was something floating between them, unresolved. And Tess wasn't sure if it was about how things between Tess and Sabrina had deteriorated after Tess had left for medical school and never really looked back to her home here in Scotland. Or if this was about the pesky attraction that seemed to have survived many years of no contact between her and Zara.

'I think we can admit that we can trust each other's capabilities as medical professionals,' Tess said, grabbing at the familiarity of slightly barbed words. Before they'd stepped into this house, they'd agreed they would talk about things. Hell, Tess had been the one to push for it since she could no longer keep it all bottled up. But now that they had some space to sit and not worry about anything else, she didn't know if she could be this vulnerable. Admitting as much as she had in the car had already taken something out of her, and she didn't expect Zara to be gentle or to understand her.

So when Zara rolled her eyes at her, Tess clung to the spark of excitement that cascaded through her. 'Please, that was one time, and you've humbled me three times over at this point. Robert got his right diagnosis and I'll have to deal with Tracey once she's back. Not that she has a leg to stand on when her patients are getting the right care.'

Now it was Tess's turn to laugh. 'Don't sound so disappointed.'

'I'm not.' Zara shot her a sideways glance that trickled a warm shiver through her, and Tess fought a visible reaction, but from the way the other woman's eyes narrowed on her, she knew anyway.

The past few weeks had turned into a rhythm she couldn't break. Every conversation walked a tightrope—Zara teasing one second, then putting distance between them. Tess never knew what version of her she'd get. But her body remembered them all. The flicker of awareness when Zara brushed past her in the hallway. The way her chest tightened when Zara laughed at something Helly said and then immediately looked away, as if joy were dangerous. Nothing between them was steady, but all of it felt alive.

She braced herself for another retort, something that would sting and remind her that even though this attraction between them had a mind of its own, they were still the same people they'd been many years ago. That exchanging verbal volleys was all they knew and would ever know of each other.

But instead of saying something, Zara sighed. Her gaze travelled from the sleeping Noel to the monitor showing his vital signs and then to the window, where a wall of darkness was occasionally interrupted by a flurry of snow beating against the glass.

'Sabrina and I got stuck in a storm once. The pharmacy asked us to deliver some medication to our patients, and we got to the last stop just like here. The storm was raging by the time we'd arrived and I'd said we could still make it even though things were deteriorating fast.' She paused, her gaze dropping down to her hands that were curling into fists in her lap. 'That's when she told me she was pregnant and too scared to risk driving home.'

Tess let out a shaky breath, only realising now that she'd been holding it for the time Zara had been speaking. The glimpse into her sister's life was both exciting and heartbreaking, twisting deep into her chest.

'She called me a few days after this happened, or at least that's what I gather now,' Tess said, remembering the day she'd learned about her sister's pregnancy. 'Months would go by without us talking to each other, and even then, it would mostly be some polite messages sent on birthdays or Christmas to fulfil some familial duties. With our parents gone, we—or, I should say, *I*—at least felt an obligation to maintain rudimentary contact. But when she got in contact with the news, she sounded different. She said—'

A lump appeared in Tess's throat, stopping her from going on. She closed her eyes, pushing down on the pressure building behind her eyelids, and forced down a few breaths.

She opened her eyes when a warm hand wrapped around her clenched fist. One by one, Zara prised her fingers open, laying them flat against her own palm in a move to comfort—to anchor her. And then she waited, letting the silence settle between them until Tess continued.

'She said she really wanted me to be a part of her child's life. That her child should know their family, and asked if, for their sake, we could just sit down and talk.'

Zara remained quiet, but her eyes were glassy as their

gazes locked. A tremble went through her hand when the other woman squeezed tighter. Her recollection was having an effect on both of them and, even though each word felt like a knife slicing through her, relief chased right after the pain. Not erasing it, but soothing along the jagged edges.

'I thought to myself: I have time. Babies take time to grow. Once it's here, I'll go visit. We'll sit down and talk about the things we've ignored.' Tess took a deep breath. 'Then Helly was born what felt like almost the next day. Sabrina reached out. And my life…it was chaos. Giulia and I had just started couples therapy to figure out if we could work things out between us. She had—there was someone else, and she'd planned on leaving me. Had it all sorted out. But for some reason, I—' Tess interrupted herself with a shake of her head.

What had happened between her and Giulia wasn't relevant. Zara didn't need—and probably also didn't want—to know about how desperate Tess had been to save her marriage, even though she'd got cheated on. That *she'd* been the one to ask Giulia to stay. Not because the marriage was precious to her, but because if this relationship didn't work out, then she would have spent years burying herself in it at the expense of other relationships in her life.

Zara turned her head to look at the monitor, blinking several times as she took the same steadying breaths Tess needed. Neither of them had expected this moment to get as emotionally charged as it just had. But it was good, right? Tess didn't feel all that better, but she had to believe it would come with time.

Maybe now things between her and Zara would get

easier. She could let go of the underlying tension and focus on being the steadfast aunt she wanted to be for Helly.

'I, uhm… I can't speak for Sabrina, and I don't know if it's right for me to tell you about her thoughts. I don't know if she would have wanted…' Zara's voice trailed off, the struggle within her clear to see through the ripple of emotions on her face.

Oh damn, Tess had overshared way too much, hadn't she? It was the couples therapist that had pointed out how much time Tess spent intellectualising her feelings until they fitted into a neat category where she could file them away—without dealing with the impact. But instead of having a measured discussion about it, she'd blurted them all out just because Zara had shared one memory about Sabrina. Zara had reached out a hand and, desperate as she was to reconnect with her sister even after her death, Tess had grabbed her entire arm.

Except Zara's hand was still on hers, their palms pressed against each other. Tess stared at where they were connected, keeping her fingers stretched out even though the need to curl them and grasp Zara tight rippled through her. But she was afraid she would push too hard and let old feelings take root where they shouldn't.

Then—as if she'd somehow shared those thoughts with Zara through their connecting hands—Zara did exactly what she'd thought of doing. Her fingers curled around Tess's hand, giving it a squeeze that landed on the wrong side—the *right* side?—of closeness. The connection they'd always shared flared alive between them at that small touch.

Sure, they'd touched before—passing plates, brush-

ing shoulders in narrow doorways, the occasional ac-
cidental graze that lingered a second too long. But this
wasn't ambient proximity. This was intentional, unmis-
takable. Skin to skin, and not just tolerated—wanted.

The room grew quiet outside the regular beeping of
the monitor, the occasional gust of wind pressing against
the window and their breaths coming in and out of their
bodies in an unsteady rhythm. Zara swallowed, and Tess
gazed down to where her throat bobbed; enjoying the
smooth expanse of dark skin way too much.

She shouldn't be looking at her like that. Not when
Zara was a part of all those complicated feelings, too.
A part they hadn't discussed and one Tess wasn't sure
they ever would.

'I thought it was my fault you weren't talking to each
other,' Zara said just as the wind died down, making her
words echo loud in Tess's ears.

'What?' Her gaze darted up, shock rippling through
her as the meaning of Zara's words unravelled within
her.

'I'm the common denominator between you two,
right? Before I arrived and basically started living at
your house, you guys were fine. But then I befriended
Sabrina and, because of that, *we* spent more time together, too. Then that night, when we...'

'We were kids,' Tess said, too quickly. Heat crawled
up her neck. 'I don't think you could've expected us to
handle it any better than we did.'

They'd never talked about it—not really. Pretended
nothing had shifted. But after that night, the sharpness
between them had dulled into something quieter, more

avoidant. The words they exchanged had got fewer. And less charged.

She didn't want to speak on it now. If they did, she wasn't sure she'd be able to put it all back into its box.

Zara exhaled, eyes fixed on the monitor's steady pulse. 'Sure. But even though we may have been young…did we ever grow out of it? You left. And things never got better. Not between you and her. Adulthood didn't fix it. And sometimes—' She paused, voice brittle. 'Sometimes I wonder if I made her choose. And she chose me.'

Tess shook her head before the words even settled. 'Don't do that,' she said, quieter now. 'Don't carry that. You didn't break our relationship. For better or for worse, I made my choices.'

Zara didn't answer right away. A beat passed. Then: 'You can't know that.'

Tess hesitated. Her throat felt thick. 'No. But I know it wasn't only about you.'

It wasn't a full confession—not yet. She could've said more. Could've told Zara about the space she'd thought she needed. How she'd convinced herself there was always time to fix things. But she couldn't bring herself to say it.

'I promised her I'd come back,' she murmured. 'And then I didn't.'

'She wanted you in her life.' Zara's voice was soft, almost too soft. But the impact landed hard, like something closing over her chest.

Silence stretched between them again, filled only by the monitor's steady beep. Tess's voice, when it came again, was barely above a whisper. 'I know.'

Now, three years and some later, she also knew that she'd wanted to be in Sabrina's life. But that was a decision she couldn't take back, couldn't fix. So why dwell on it? It would only push her down a path she didn't want to go down.

'I'll get some rest. Let me know if the ambulance service calls,' Zara said, then got up and left before Tess could say anything else.

Not that she had any words left. Her decision had hurt Zara, too, and now she knew the other woman had her own feelings wrapped up in all of it. She'd gone on believing that Tess had distanced herself from her sister because of their attraction to one another. But that wasn't it. It was the convenient excuse Tess had latched onto. But what had happened between them went way beyond that. Had far more to do with how her parents had always had such high expectations of Tess, while Sabrina could do whatever she wanted. How the eldest daughter had been expected to always be proper, to study hard, to *excel*.

And the first time she'd managed to shake the mantle of the eldest daughter had been away at medical school. *Everything* had been easier then, so she had never looked back. Even though she should have.

CHAPTER SIX

THE AMBULANCE ARRIVED just after dawn. Luckily, Noel held steady, had even woken up a couple of times to talk to his brother, which had helped to set him at ease. Tess had checked in with Zara throughout her shift when they'd swapped over again and, though they hadn't picked up the conversation from where they'd left it, something had shifted. And in the space created, they had at least been able to talk about Sabrina. About some of their fonder memories of her. Though when Zara had approached the question of how long Tess planned on staying, the conversation had ended. Leaving her to float around in limbo.

When they handed Noel over to the other crew, Zara and Tess made quick work of disassembling the equipment and loading it all up into the car before driving home in a tense silence.

Zara didn't pause for a second when they pulled up to the house. She threw the door of the car open, took out her bags and equipment and piled them in the corridor. Then, without looking back at the car, she walked to the neighbouring house and let herself in.

Warmth seeped through all the layers of her clothes in an instant, and Zara let out a sigh as she leaned against the door. Her eyes fluttered shut as some of the tension drained out of her body. But then the pattering of tiny feet waddling down the corridor became louder.

'Mummy's back!' Helly's voice kicked an avalanche of emotions loose inside her. Relief that her little girl had stayed safe and sound and cared for during the storm. And something tighter, sharper—because even though Zara knew she was Helly's mum just as much as Sabrina, she'd still corrected Helly once or twice in the early days. Out of habit. Or maybe fear. How would people react hearing it?

She spoke about Sabrina often—told Helly stories, showed her photos—made sure her daughter knew where she came from. That she had been deeply wanted and loved. But still, some small part of her worried: did it look as though she was taking something that wasn't hers?

Matt appeared from around the corner, a soft smile on his rugged face. 'Welcome back. We were just about to have some breakfast. Why don't you join us?'

Zara bent down and scooped Helly into her arms, giving her a tight squeeze and a kiss before setting her back on the floor. 'I missed you, munchkin.' Helly beamed up at her, and Zara's heart squeezed tight. After the night she'd had, she'd really needed to see her cute little face. 'Go sit back down with your uncle while I get undressed.'

She watched Helly pad away, then peeled herself out of her various layers. When she hung up her coat, she looked out of the window and stared across the expanse of white snow towards her own house—and the small cottage beyond. The lights were on in the cottage, and her chest tightened at the sight, though Zara wasn't entirely sure why.

Something had stirred back alive within her with Tess's arrival. Something she'd buried a long time ago. Not grief. Not exactly. Just…all the things they'd never addressed. All the glances, the tension, the unspoken *thing* that had once crackled between them and never really gone away. Zara had told herself she'd moved past it. That what had happened back then hadn't meant anything.

But the way her stomach dipped when she saw that light? It said otherwise.

'Porridge is getting cold,' Matt's voice sounded from the kitchen, shaking Zara out of her reverie. Letting go of the thoughts with a sigh, she followed the voice down the corridor and plopped down on a chair opposite Matt, who eyed her with a raised eyebrow.

'Rough night?' he asked, and she barked out a laugh.

'You could say that. I got stuck at Noel Packham's place overnight. We were there to deliver his brother's insulin when Noel crashed. Had to stay up monitoring him until an ambulance freed up to transport him.' For a fraction of a second Zara entertained the futile thought Matt might leave it at that. That maybe he wouldn't remember who exactly was with her because she had stupidly texted him her and Tess were doing the medication runs together.

'So you were stuck overnight with Tess Sinclair?' His eyebrows rose even higher, which didn't help with Zara's anxiety about the events of last night. How much they'd spoken. It almost felt as if they'd found some common ground. Of course, all of that had crumbled the moment Tess had reminded her she was still the person who chose to leave.

'Yes, given the rule that we can't be out in storms on our own, Tess and I paired up,' she said, every word measured as she looked over to Helly, who sat at her own little table with her bowl of porridge and a court of stuffed animals surrounding her. However Zara might currently feel about Tess, she didn't ever want to influence Helly's mind.

'And how was it?' he asked, voice far too innocent for her comfort. Of course he would ask—he knew the history. Zara had told him everything in the weeks after Sabrina died, when the weight of it all had left her overwhelmed and alone.

Back then, she and Sabrina had decided—half joke, half pact—that they'd raise a child together. Two perpetually single women tired of waiting for the mythical Right Person to appear. Sabrina had tried, once. A serious relationship that ended badly enough to push her towards IVF. Zara, meanwhile, had never made it that far. Living where she did, eligible lesbians were rare to begin with—and none of her brief encounters had ever sparked anything worth staying for. Not since that night with Tess in her youth…

Now she was raising Helly on her own. Every day a new challenge.

'Fine. We didn't kill each other,' she said, still fighting to tell him everything, even though she knew he was eventually going to pull it out of her. Time for plan B: changing the subject. 'How were things with Helly?'

They both looked to the side, watching Helly try to feed a spoonful of porridge to her stuffed unicorn. 'She was fine. Didn't even notice the storm. The power went out late at night, but they've already restored it.'

'You had a power outage down here? Must have been localised. We didn't have to deal with that.' A power failure would have added just another layer of complication to their visit. If the monitor had stopped working, they would have had to rely on the built-in battery. That lasted for only a certain amount of time…

'Ah, so you guys didn't get to light some candles and make the place all romantic and cosy?' The grin spreading over his face was exhausting, and Zara reached over the table to swat her friend on the arm.

'Dear Lord, is that all we're ever going to talk about? How my teenage crush lives in the cottage behind my house now? I say my house, but, of course, it is *also* her house, seeing as their parents gave them each half.' That was just another layer to the ever-complicating relationship she found herself in now.

'Well, technically Tess and Helly share ownership of the house,' Matt replied, even though Zara didn't need the reminder. Not that she was angry about any of this. Thankfully she and Sabrina had taken care of all the paperwork as her pregnancy had progressed.

'I'll admit, Tess showing up here wasn't on my bingo card,' Zara said, covering her face with her hands and muffling her exhausted groan. She'd barely slept even when she hadn't been monitoring Noel, her mind replaying their conversation on a loop until it had meshed into an unintelligible tangle of words.

'It's been two months now. Things haven't settled down between you two?'

Zara paused, giving the question consideration, and

then she shook her head. 'We did get to a point of peaceful co-existence both around the property and in the clinic. I mean, we had to because, as much as I don't trust her, I do want Helly to have her aunt in her life.'

But the truth was, *peaceful co-existence* had come with conditions. Silent rules neither of them acknowledged out loud. Don't linger too long in the same room. Don't talk about the past. Don't touch.

The last was one they found themselves in violation of the most. The touches were all innocent. A brush of fingers as they handed each other something, or a squeeze of the arm as they spoke. Nothing anyone could read into, except for them. With Tess everything meant something else.

Somehow, over two months of sidestepping and second-guessing, that old magnetic pull had crept back in. What had once been a teenage infatuation now felt like a low-level hum under her skin—persistent and impossible to ignore.

Zara's own behaviour and choices didn't help with any of it. After having to work late again the other week, she'd left her spare key on the counter with a tiny note directed at Tess to take it. Just in case she needed it. The subtext had been clear: *let yourself in.* And Tess had. Not often, but enough to trigger a dormant sense inside Zara, making her so much more aware of her presence.

She didn't know why she'd given her a key. A part of her clung to the excuse of practicality, but she knew it wasn't true. She'd given her the key because she wanted Tess in her space, even if she couldn't admit it.

Then there was last night, their palms pressing against each other for more than just comfort.

Matt leaned back in his chair and gave her a once-over. 'I sense a "but" oncoming.'

'She's only here temporarily, is she not? Tess will be out of work when the locum contract runs out and Tracey gets back. And then what? Just when Helly has had enough time to get used to her again, she'll be off chasing the next opportunity. Leaving me to deal with the aftermath. Again.'

That would be the third time Zara was responsible for holding things together while Tess pursued her own interests.

A part of Zara thought she was insane to give in as much as she had. Her gut warned her about Tess. And it was the cautious part of her that didn't want to acknowledge what she'd sensed between them. How *nice* it had been to simply talk to her, reminisce about some of the memories both shared about Sabrina. Or seeing Tess's face light up as she learned something new about her sister.

'Does she not seem sincere to you?' Matt asked, his eyes wandering over to Helly. 'She certainly left an impression on Helly. This morning, she asked about both you and "Auntie Tess". Are you really worried about her leaving?'

Zara dug into her own bowl of porridge, shovelling a few spoonfuls into her mouth before trusting herself to go on. 'I'm just not holding my breath for her permanence in my life. Like, I get what you're trying to say, but ignoring the very clear pattern this woman has displayed to me since I've known her doesn't do me any favours.'

Matt huffed out a laugh and looked at her from over the rim of his coffee mug. 'So, this isn't about Helly. It's about you.'

Zara's spoon clanged against the porcelain of the bowl. 'What? Of course this is about Helly. Tess wouldn't even be here if it wasn't for Helly and the only reason I'm tolerating her is because of Helly. She deserves a chance at an extended family, regardless of how likely I think this is to pan out,' she hissed in a low voice, glancing over at Helly, who sat at her own small table facing the window. Babbling away at the stuffie sitting on a tiny chair next to her, she was oblivious to their conversation.

By the smug look on Matt's face, she knew she wasn't going to like what he was about to throw her way. She'd warned him several times not to therapise her, but sometimes this man just couldn't help himself. 'Ah, but you said your life,' he pointed out, making Zara recall her words.

Her heart took a tumble inside her chest, but she pushed that feeling away. Something to deal with later. 'That's not the gotcha moment you think it is. Helly *is* my life right now. Having Tess in my life is unavoidable for having her in Helly's life.'

'Fair, but, for all the things you've shared, it sounds more like you are concerned about her leaving you and not her niece.'

This conversation was beginning to feel circular. 'No, that's you putting a weird romantic twist on things that aren't romantic at all.'

Matt shrugged, which only annoyed Zara more. 'Okay, fine. If Helly is your life, as you say, why do you still flinch when she calls you Mummy?'

Zara's spine stiffened the moment her brain processed the word. A familiar icy sensation swept through her, touching her everywhere—even the places she tried so hard to keep hidden. Safe. *That* conversation wasn't one she was prepared to have. Definitely not now, maybe not ever. 'I can't deal with this right now, Matt,' she said, pushing off her chair and onto her feet.

'Zara, let's talk about this.' His tone was pleading, and a quiet part of her knew she should. But she couldn't.

'She's just copying the other kids. She hears them calling their mothers and thinks that's what you call a female caregiver.' Zara hadn't really discouraged Helly from calling her Mummy. Because she was, and she knew what role she played in her girl's life. Helly was her daughter. But she couldn't stop the worry from sinking into her chest whenever she heard the word. Would other people take it the wrong way and believe she was erasing Sabrina? Would Tess think that?

Matt saw right through that reasoning without her even having to say something. 'Wouldn't she start calling Tess Mummy by that logic?' he asked, and Zara shook her head as she rounded the table to get to Helly.

'I'm trying to avoid any drama or misconceptions. I get it's how Helly feels and I'm not discouraging that. It's just…about how it might look. What people might think I'm trying to be.'

'Like who?'

Zara didn't answer. Because the answer was obvious. And sleeping in the cottage behind her house.

'Matt, I *can't* talk about this, okay? Definitely not now.' Her brain was already overwhelmed. Someone had promised her once that things got simpler after thirty. Whoever it was, she wanted to throttle them.

'Come, baby girl. Say goodbye to your uncle. We'll be on our way home now,' she said as she scooped Helly into her arms. The little girl gave a squeal, waving her arms at Matt, who'd come to stand next to her.

'Thanks for taking care of her,' Zara said, only shooting him a quick glance because she didn't want to deal with whatever she knew she'd see in his eyes. These were issues to be figured out at a later date.

One day, when Helly was older, the question might fall away on its own. She'd understand who Sabrina was. What Zara had stepped into. And maybe then, Zara wouldn't feel the need to defend something that already felt true: Helly called her Mummy because that was who she was. She just wasn't sure the rest of the world would see it that way.

A soft, irregular clanging of metal against metal filled the house when Zara pushed through the door. 'What is going on here?' she asked, looking at Helly, who shook her head.

Walking through the living room, she deposited Helly in her secured playpen and then followed the intermittent clanging sounds until she arrived in the kitchen.

The cupboard underneath the sink was open and Tess lay on the floor, half of her body inside it and an open toolbox next to her. The lights in the kitchen were off, except for the torchlight of Tess's phone illuminating the square of the cupboard as if it were some trophy case— with Tess framed right in the centre. Her sleeves were pushed up to her elbows, and Zara watched the muscles of her forearms bunch and relax as she worked on, well, whatever it was that was apparently wrong underneath her sink. Handiness didn't count as one of Zara's qualities. That was what she had neighbours for. Not Matt, though, he was just as useless.

Apparently, the same couldn't be said for Tess. A stark line sat between her brows as she scrutinised the pipes, her lips pressed into a thin line of concentration. Zara should look away or, better yet, make herself known. Lurking in the dark while watching Tess was definitely on the 'not do' list of all things concerning the other woman. Yet her heart kicked up a notch inside her, drumming against her sternum in an unsteady beat.

The picture unfolding in front of her was so...domestic. It should've felt out of place—because what did they have to feel domestic about? Sure, she'd given her the key so they could share more space, and Zara had to admit Tess hadn't been shy about fixing things or doing chores to make Zara's life a bit easier.

When had this quiet sense of intimacy settled in between them?

Zara could do nothing but stare, transfixed by the ripple of muscle underneath her skin. A long-dormant, almost unrecognisable feeling unfurled in the pit of her stomach and reached through her body with its long tendrils. The realisation of what it was—arousal—hit her so hard she let out a gasp.

Tess tilted her head, and their gazes collided just as a burst of heat reached her cheeks, and Zara had to fight the urge to feel her face and confirm the flush. Lucky for her, the other woman wouldn't be able to tell that she was blushing.

'Sorry, I didn't know how long you would be next door,' Tess said, then she went back to twist—or untwist, Zara really didn't know—something along the various pipes that made the inner lining of her sink, then she slid out from underneath it. She tossed the tool into the toolbox next to her, flipping the lid closed and then getting to her feet.

'What are you doing here?' Zara asked, her heart still hammering against her chest as she looked Tess up and down. Tess had always been the taller one between the two, but until now she'd not really noticed their difference in height.

'The pipes froze over at the cottage, so I came here to check if the same was true. Since I was here, I had a look around to see if there was any other storm damage.' Tess shrugged, as if that wasn't even a big deal. As if what she'd just said was a *good* explanation when really it left Zara more confused.

'But the dripping sink isn't from the storm. That's been there a while.' Zara's pulse took another tumble at not just the memory of Tess lying there but the entire gesture behind it. The storm had caused a problem in the cottage and her first thought had been to see if Zara's house was okay.

No, surely this wasn't about her. Tess must have wanted to make sure *Helly* had what she needed. And because Zara hadn't had someone in her life caring for her in any form, she'd instantly claimed that familial affection for herself. It was *not* for her, and, as she'd told Matt, she also didn't want it.

Tess, instead of noticing Zara's inner turmoil and replying to it, simply shrugged. *Shrugged* and then said, 'It was bugging me, so I fixed it.'

Zara could not hear the usual edge beneath her words. *I fixed it because you keep leaving half-damp tea towels in there and it smells.* Her tone was clear, and it would be so easy to fall into the back and forth they were so used to. But even though their last moments before coming home had been tense—and so had been the words Zara had said to Matt about Tess—she could hear something else resonating inside her words.

Figured it would make things easier for you.

That was why Tess had done it. Because she knew Zara didn't know how and, as far as worries were concerned, a dripping pipe below her sink was so far down her list, she probably wouldn't get to it until it progressed from drip to flood.

This was something Tess had done just for *her.* No matter how much she tried, Zara couldn't figure out how this might have been something for Helly, too. But she needed it to be so she could deflect those feelings and feel as though she wasn't getting sucked into something that she couldn't get out of.

Even after Zara had iced her out after talking about Sabrina, Tess had cared enough about her well-being to quickly fix something.

Not to mention there were other things Zara thought might be pretty nice if she dared to ask Tess to get on her knees in front of her. Like—

What the hell are those thoughts?

Zara's stomach clenched. She shouldn't be feeling any of those things. So she forced herself to remember the conversation from last night, the tension when she'd realised how openly Tess had admitted to leaving because it was simpler. Zara needed to remember that, at the core, this was what Tess was: unreliable. And Zara had enough unreliable people in her life. The whole reason she and Sabrina had grown so close had been because Zara's mother had often not bothered to come home—her tiny daughter more an inconvenience she needed to put up with.

Her spine stiffened when her defences snapped into place, and she squared her shoulders. Repairing random stuff in her house that, granted, needed repairing wasn't part of the deal. Maybe she'd made a mistake giving her the key. 'Thanks, but I had this covered. I don't need your help with fixing up this place.'

The unease slowly trickling through her paired with the flicker of hurt she saw pass over Tess's face told her she was being too harsh. Of course she was, but what else was she supposed to do in this situation where she felt this pesky attraction solidify and turn into something new and entirely unwanted?

The silence between them grew tenser the longer it went on until Tess let out a humourless laugh before stooping and picking up the toolbox. 'Noted,' was all she said before she walked past Zara, who moved closer to the counter to avoid both eye contact and accidentally touching her.

She only let out her breath when the door opened and closed, and Tess's presence vanished from her house.

Firm boundaries. This was what she wanted. Their lives were bound to intermingle but what Zara needed was fewer touch points. Outside Helly, she shouldn't want to see Tess, shouldn't want her in her space. Shouldn't think of Tess whenever her thoughts strayed. Yet she always landed with her—Tess.

And that was why she needed to be harsh. Tess was not hers to even consider, let alone keep. She was here for Helly and Helly alone. Because when Tess eventually left, Zara wanted to make sure that it had nothing to do with her.

Not again.

CHAPTER SEVEN

Tess couldn't recall the last time she'd been this eager about an evening shift. Probably because she'd simply *never* been excited for one. After spending evenings and nights in training, Tess knew every doctor believed their time was done in the undesirable time slots and let the more junior doctors take them. At least that was how it worked in more urban areas with a higher population density.

But tonight, the shift offered something else: distraction. An excuse not to be at the house, where everything between her and Zara hovered on the edge of too much.

'You're looking far too chipper for someone who's still here at this hour.' Tess looked up from where she'd been typing away at her notes for the evening walk-ins she'd looked at. Some patients were known to her, but others were new faces and whenever she looked them up on the system, they were almost always patients assigned to Zara.

Or in some rare instances, she saw Sabrina's name pop up. If a patient hadn't been to see them in several years, some still hadn't been updated and assigned to the newer doctors.

She smiled at Callum, the night nurse that had been

working alongside her for her first evening shift. Even though she'd spent her formative years in Invercaillie, it had taken her a few weeks to get used to the accent again. Strange what almost two decades away from here had done to her ability to both understand the natives and sound like one herself.

Maybe that was where this consistent buzz of *otherness* came from. Her already weak roots had become completely disentangled from her former home, making it much more of a challenge to find her way back.

'Just doing my part for the team,' she said, and was surprised by how much she meant it. When she'd first arrived, Zara had made it clear she didn't want Tess doing anything outside her contracted hours. No extras. No favours. No room to mess up. But that had been over two months ago.

Since then, things had thawed. Not completely, but enough. So when one of the A & E doctors had asked for additional support, it hadn't been the practice manager or a nurse who stepped in. It was Zara who'd turned to her and asked if she could take the evening shift.

And Tess had said yes—because she wanted to. Because it finally felt as if something real was shifting between them.

The friction was still there, but it had started to curl into something sharper. Less defensive. More…charged. Tess had caught herself wondering what it would be like to press Zara up against the kitchen counter. What her mouth would taste like now. Whether she'd still make that same noise in the back of her throat if someone touched her just right.

She knew better than to think like that. Especially

after the other night when Zara had told her to leave. But the wanting came anyway—sudden, hot, and bloody inconvenient.

'You settling in all right, lassie? Been nice having a semi-familiar face about the place,' Callum said, lowering himself into the chair beside her.

Tess understood what he meant, even if he didn't say it outright. Everyone here knew she was Sabrina's sister. Through quiet conversations with staff over the past weeks, she'd begun to piece together a fuller picture of who Sabrina had been—one coloured by grief, yes, but also affection.

Zara had been a big part of that. She had shared stories, offered little fragments, helping Tess see her sister more clearly. But then Tess had said too much, let something slip that hit the wrong nerve, and Zara had pulled away.

No wonder she'd told her to get lost the other night. Tess had all but admitted that she simply hadn't found the time to be a more active part of Sabrina's life, prioritising other things over a relationship with her sister. How could she have ever known she'd run out of time?

'Things are good,' she said, shaking off the heavy memories. There was no use dwelling on them now. 'It's quieter than I thought it would be.'

Callum nodded, the thick whiskers of his ginger beard twitching as he smiled at her. 'They told you it's mostly an on-call thing, right? Most we see here are drunk fools getting into fisticuffs and in need of stitches—and a good dressing-down.'

Tess laughed. 'That's what I have you for, right? Nothing scarier than a Nurse Ratched type to scare the young idiots straight.'

'Nurse Ratched? I'll have you know my bedside manners have won awards, Sinclair. You better watch that smart mouth of yours,' Callum replied with none of the menace his words implied.

Despite herself, she relaxed and let out another laugh. Callum mostly worked in A & E, so they didn't have as many touch points with her spending her time in the GP surgery. She'd seen the man occasionally when she picked up Helly from day care, but outside polite hellos they hadn't spoken. This week on the A & E evening shift had therefore been the first time she'd ever come into his orbit and to call this man a delight was selling him short by several magnitudes.

What was more surprising was the ease with which they had bonded, to the point where Tess thought she might have made a friend. For the first time since stepping foot in this clinic—in this village—she didn't feel like a visitor, but rather as though she belonged.

A dangerous, addicting feeling and a voice in the back of her head told her to be careful. She'd thought she belonged in the south of England with her spouse; had been so convinced of that despite the warning signs she'd put off returning here—reconnecting with her sister and her baby—because she'd been too busy fixing the ever-growing nightmare her place of belonging had become.

She lifted her hands in a defensive motion. 'I'm just saying, it seems only when you're on shift we get reports of people coming in after—how did you put it?—fisticuffing?'

Callum's laughter rumbled through the room, the sound warm and filling Tess's chest with something intangible. 'Why, you—I'd say you take right after your sister, but you're the older one, aren't you?'

Though Callum worked here now, he'd told her earlier in the week that he originally hailed from a village even further north and had come here after his trust had shut their little A & E down for lack of patient volume, forcing him to find a new vocation or to relocate. Which had landed him here.

'Yup, almost three years older. I was never quite sure if she'd come as a surprise to my parents or not. But I think because of that, they were much more critical of me than of her. Like somehow she was more precious to them.' She didn't know why she was volunteering this extra context except that it felt right. Or maybe it was because that exact question had been playing on her mind a lot since her conversation with Zara at Noel's place. Tess had never considered how different an impression Zara had made on her parents, who had doted on Sabrina and, by extension, her best friend.

Tess, meanwhile, had been held to rigorous standards in both her academic life and her private endeavours, her parents demanding excellence in everything she did. Maybe because they'd already had one daughter to pin all their misguided hopes and dreams on, they'd been happy enough to let the other one follow her whims.

Strange how they'd both ended up in the medical profession.

'You know, I think Sabrina suspected as much as well. She said she could see it wear you down only much later in life.' His voice lost some of his usual joviality when he spoke again, and Tess turned to him, eyes wide.

'Sabrina told you that?' Was Callum better friends with Sabrina than he'd let on?

But the nurse shook his head. 'Not to me. To a patient that came through here some years ago. A young woman struggling with more than just the thing that brought her to A & E on that day. Sabrina had sat with her long past her shift, trading stories, and this was one I'd overheard.'

Tess blinked several times, unsure what to do with that information. A part of her waited for the usual guilt to settle in the pit of her stomach whenever she got a reminder of Sabrina. Because even though she hungered to know more about her sister, that desire came at a price: the constant reminder that she'd wasted time that she could never get back now.

But it didn't come.

And for the first time, she felt like sharing a memory of her own. 'Sabrina couldn't stand inequality even from a young age. I remember once, as we were heading out of school, I was supposed to meet with my tutor. She was confused, asking why I had a tutor and she didn't. I just shrugged it off, thinking her more annoying than anything. At this point, I'd yet to see how different our parents treated us.' Tess paused, letting out a huff of genuine amusement. 'Instead of going home, she sat outside the tutor's classroom. By the time we'd come out, my mother was out of her mind with worry for Sabrina, who very calmly explained to our mother that she couldn't have me spend the afternoon alone while Sabrina herself idled at home.'

Callum burst out laughing, and Tess joined in, cheeks hurting by the end of it. She couldn't even remember the last time she'd laughed so freely. It must have been a few years at this point.

'That sounds like her. Just as smart a mouth as you have on you,' he said, smile dimming into something softer. 'We miss her something fierce around here.'

That took the breath out of her lungs, her stomach clenching. But again, it wasn't the usual guilt or shame. The hurt that bloomed at his words was just that—hurt. 'I miss her, too,' she said, voice brittle from the strain those words took.

Callum nodded, still smiling. 'She'd be glad you're here, you know? Getting to know her daughter and being a part of her life.'

Again, the nurse took her by surprise with his words. So far, Zara had been the only one to ever acknowledge her effort, and she'd done so begrudgingly. Somehow, after every step forward, she ended up two steps back again, making the rekindling of their relationship almost impossible.

No, not rekindling. Outside their teenage infatuation, she and Zara had never had a relationship. Now they were forced to find common ground for Helly's sake, but all they had to fall back on were those feelings of attraction that had been far too complicated for their teenage selves to unravel.

And after how things had ended on the morning after the storm, Tess wasn't entirely sure that the adult versions of themselves knew any better how to deal with things. If anything, the attraction only seemed to have grown in hibernation—the experiences that had shaped Tess's life making the idle fantasies of what things might be like now, even on a purely physical level, more vivid.

'I appreciate you saying that,' Tess replied, not sure what else to say. She hadn't expected to come out of her shift with this kind of emotional vulnerability.

'Well, don't let me chew your ear off. I know it's well past your shift.' Tess's eyes darted to the clock. She hadn't even noticed the time passing ever since Callum had sat down next to her.

Turning the computer off, she got to her feet and turned to the nurse with a smile. 'Pity there were no fisticuffs tonight.'

The barking laugh that answered her quip sent a familiar warmth radiating through her. 'The week isn't over yet, Sinclair.'

'See you tomorrow, Cal.'

Something stirred at the edge of Zara's awareness, pulling her out of sleep. It was Helly—babbling softly, the kind of sound that usually meant a nightmare was brewing.

Sleep clung to Zara like a weighted blanket, and she struggled against it, each blink bringing her bedroom more into focus until her mind was ready to let go of sleep. At least enough for her to listen to the sounds coming from Helly's room.

When Zara had transitioned her to her own room, Helly had woken her at least once a night. A nightmare, some late-night hunger pangs or even 'nothing', according to her child. Just an excuse to not be alone, and it had taken months until Helly had been comfortable sleeping on her own. During that time, Zara had honed her ability to sleep with one ear listening to a ridiculous degree. Now even small sounds would rouse her.

The concerned parent in her wanted to leap out of bed and comfort Helly immediately. After everything, Zara couldn't bear the thought of adding to the abandonment Helly might one day carry. But the parenting books had warned her not to rush in every time. At this age, Helly was meant to start learning how to self-soothe. Zara just didn't know how to tell the difference between building resilience and leaving her alone when she needed someone.

So instead of jumping out of bed, Zara lay with her eyes closed and listened—and then sat up straight when she heard a low humming from the other room that couldn't possibly come from Helly.

Brow furrowed, she looked at the alarm clock on her nightstand. Just after midnight. This had to be—

Now fully awake, Zara slipped on the nightgown draped over the chair and crossed the corridor to Helly's room. As expected, Tess was there, sitting in the rocking chair beside the toddler bed, gently rubbing circles on Helly's back. The child was already asleep, her breathing slow and eyes fluttering, but Tess kept going, as if reluctant to break the moment.

Zara stood in the doorway, watching in silence. Just like that scene in the kitchen a few days earlier, this stirred something in her she didn't want to name but couldn't ignore. It wasn't just gratitude. It was longing. This quiet, shared caretaking was part of why she hadn't protested Tess staying. What unsettled her was the deeper yearning that surfaced each time she saw Tess like this—tender, steady, quietly present. A yearning that had lived deep inside her, unspoken and undisturbed, until now.

For a moment, she got lost in the thoughts of how a life like that might look. Until she remembered who that was in her fantasies and then she snapped out of it. 'How did you know she was stirring in her sleep?'

Tess must have been here already. Not that it was odd. Even after the confrontation following the storm, the other woman hadn't stopped coming over unannounced. Zara hadn't asked her to return her key, either, wanting against better judgement for her to have it. To feel welcome even though Zara knew for her own brewing feelings it would be better if she didn't. If they kept things as separate as possible between them.

Or was it already too late?

Tess looked up at her, the shock in her eyes telling Zara that she, too, was reminded of the parallel of a few days ago. Without answering, she dropped her gaze back down on the sleeping Helly, her hand rubbing a few more circles before she lifted it off the sleeping child.

'Sorry, I didn't mean to wake you. I forgot to grab the leftovers before I left for work. But when I came in, I heard Helly crying so I came up to check and settled her back down.'

'Ah…' The sound was sleepier than she intended it to be, and Tess seemed to notice, for she shot her a one-sided smile that even in her half-drowsy state hit Zara squarely in the chest. She stiffened, the rest of the sleepiness draining out of her. The picture in front of her slotted into place in a way that shouldn't feel the way it did. It looked like a vision of the future, something tangible that she maybe could have if she just reached out and grabbed it with both hands.

Another parental figure for Helly. A *real* family.

Someone to rely on. For her little found daughter. But maybe also for Zara herself?

No. She couldn't go there. It would be reckless and selfish and, in her current situation, she couldn't afford to be either. Not when she knew in the depths of her soul people tended to leave. That *Tess* had her own history of leaving when things got tough.

But she was here now, wasn't she?

'I ate the leftovers,' she blurted out when the silence stretched on for too long with only Helly's breaths floating around between them. 'Sorry, I thought since you left them, you didn't want them. When I got hungry, I ate the rest.'

Tess's eyebrows shot up, surprise clearly written on her face. Then, so slowly Zara could feel each stutter of her heart against her breastbone, a smile unfurled on Tess's face. It was small and subdued, yet the effect it had on Zara was as if it were a fully fledged silly grin. Because for Tess it might as well be. Unlike Sabrina, she'd never been expressive of her thoughts or emotions.

'You enjoyed it?' she asked, catching Zara off guard when she was already struggling with her composure.

She blinked several times, trying to decipher why Tess was even interested, but then she nodded. 'You must know your food is so much better than the ready meals I've been subsisting on. Sabrina was the one who...'

Zara's voice tapered off, turning into a sigh. Even though they'd discussed Sabrina a few times and had agreed that avoiding that topic wasn't healthy, it still wasn't easy. Half of the time, Zara could see the pain it caused in Tess to hear about her sister—feel the regrets she now knew lived in the other woman.

But it didn't happen this time. If anything, the smile tugging at the corners of Tess's pillowy lips grew brighter and—wait, why was Zara even noticing the quality of Tess's lips? Wondering if they'd feel as soft as they looked?

A growl of a stomach running out of patience sounded so loud, Zara actually started. Then she clamped her hand over her mouth to stifle the laugh bubbling up in her chest. And again, Tess surprised her by not scowling but rather struggling to contain her own laugh.

Taking a step back, Zara waved the woman out of the room and closed the door. There was something different about Tess today, a lightness that reminded her of the younger version she'd known far better so many years ago. And it was because of that sense of familiarity that she said, 'Let me make you something. It's only fair since I ate your food.'

'*You* want to make *me* something? Considering you've roped me into cooking for you the first chance you got, I didn't think you knew how.' Hearing a trace of the usual bite that had accompanied their verbal matches in the past perked Zara up. Not just because of the familiarity, but because of what she heard beneath them— or maybe woven into them? Something that used to be sharp was now soft.

'Listen, I'm not much of a cook, but even I know how to slap together a sandwich. Enough to tide you over until you can get started on that gourmet breakfast of yours,' Zara replied, leaning into what she heard from Tess before she could second-guess herself.

Sure, she'd been the one who had put on whatever brakes there were between them after they'd been snowed in together, but that didn't mean it hadn't sucked for her. This was comfortable. Easier. And more dangerous.

Tess huffed out a laugh. 'You call making your own porridge gourmet?'

'Well, I rip open a package and nuke whatever powder is in the sachet with some milk for my version of porridge. It definitely doesn't involve butter or cinnamon.' There was also no way Zara would wake up any earlier than she already did and remain sane. Sleep was a luxury she ranked way above food.

When they got to the kitchen, Tess turned, as if to escape to the cottage. Again, Zara acted without thinking, reaching out to the other woman and laying a hand on top of her arm to stop her. 'I was serious about the food. Let me fix you something before you starve.'

Tess looked back at her. The smile was gone, replaced with something else Zara couldn't name. It slithered along her skin, leaving streaks of heat. 'You don't have to do that. I can find something.'

'But I want to. Otherwise, I'll feel bad about eating leftovers in the fridge, always questioning whether I was even supposed to eat them.' She had no idea why she was insisting as much as she was, but a part of her simply didn't want Tess to walk out of that door right now. And she didn't want to explore *why* that might be.

Tess looked at her, eyes roaming over her face, and she got the impression the other woman's thoughts were following the same pattern—wondering why she was insisting. But then she turned around with a nod and followed Zara back into the kitchen, where she sat down at one of the barstools while Zara got to work pulling together all the ingredients she needed for a sandwich.

'Callum is on the night shift this month and we kept talking for a bit after my shift. That's why I'm only here now,' Tess said as Zara fiddled around with the toaster. When was the last time she even used that thing? Had she *ever*? Or was this one of Sabrina's artefacts?

'Oh yeah? How did you escape him?' Zara—like everyone else at the hospital—loved Callum to bits. But she could also acknowledge that he was the reason she'd been late to pick up Helly several times, getting an earful from the day-care staff whenever she did so.

'You know, I actually enjoyed a pleasant conversation with him. He was grateful for my help in the evenings this week.' Her voice grew quieter, making Zara look over her shoulder to see the lines around Tess's mouth soften. Again. It was becoming a theme tonight, this slow unravelling of Tess's defences. But Zara still didn't understand why it was happening. Especially when they'd left things so tense after their snowed-in night.

Turning back, Zara grabbed the bread and placed it on the cutting board. 'Sounds like you're enjoying the evening shift,' she said, trying not to sound surprised or even too curious.

Tess breathed out a low chuckle. 'Don't sound so astonished. I'm here to pull my weight and I said I'd do anything that's needed.'

Zara dug through her drawers on the hunt for the bread knife, which also gave her a convenient excuse not to reply straight away. She'd failed at keeping her tone bland, but Tess didn't seem bothered by that—or otherwise alerted by Zara's unusual interest in the other woman.

Once she found the knife, she shoved the drawer shut

and turned back to the cutting board. 'Not astonished, just…grateful. Invercaillie is pretty small, but the surrounding villages are even tinier. We're the only after-hours clinic people can get to, so it's important to me it's staffed. But I understand people have families and lives to get home to and it's not always convenient to work this late.' She paused, looking up to where she knew Helly was sleeping. 'I mean, you know our entire bedtime routine and even though it's elaborate, I'm bummed out on the nights I miss it.'

Wait, she hadn't meant to share all of that. Where had this all come from? With how far more involved Tess had become in her life with Helly, of course she'd become a part of their routines. But that didn't mean she had to volunteer how she felt about missing them. Any topic that came too close to talking about *feelings* was to be avoided.

Taking a deep breath, Zara set the knife on the bread, cutting off the first slice. Halfway down the second slice, Tess said, 'Sabrina and I weren't talking as much as we should have. When she started the IVF process and she sent the message asking me if we could talk, one thing that stuck with me was how excited she was to co-parent with you. There was no doubt in her mind what an amazing parent you would be to her child.'

The words sent a shock wave through Zara, setting her off balance. Of all the things Tess could have said, she hadn't expected hearing this about Sabrina—about *her*. Her grip on the knife tightened, and that was enough to force it through the bread with less control.

At first, Zara didn't notice the sting blooming in her thumb and radiating pain through the rest of her hand.

Not even when the knife clattered out of her hand did she react to it. It was as if her brain had received too many signals and was picking one thing to struggle over, leaving her body to deal with the rest.

An amazing parent. The one thing Zara had never had in her life. How could Sabrina have been so sure of her when Zara doubted every single decision she had to make with and about Helly?

'Zara, you're—' The metal chair legs scraped against the floor and then a moment later Tess was by her side, moving her away from the counter. Zara hissed when Tess pressed a tea towel against her thumb, and that was when the pain registered. Looking over at the knife, she saw a few specks of blood glistening on the blade.

Tess's words had rattled her so much she'd cut herself. But again, that wasn't why heat was bubbling through her body in an uncontrolled manner. No, because that warmth started somewhere at her side—right where Tess was gripping her as she navigated her towards the chair.

Zara barely registered the way Tess guided her into the chair, her grip firm but careful. The kitchen felt oddly quiet now, the only sound the rustling of the tea towel as Tess unwrapped it to inspect the cut.

'Not too deep,' Tess murmured, more to herself than Zara. She walked around the kitchen island to a specific drawer, pulling it open and retrieving the first-aid kit that Zara hadn't even known was there. How had Tess done this without pulling half of the cupboards open to check?

Because she used to live here, too. The thought came out of nowhere, settling down on Zara and trying its best to disperse the heat of Tess's touch. This house had been her childhood home. They'd sat together with Sabrina at this kitchen island, snacking on whatever fruit was in the fruit bowl while doing their homework.

Tess and Zara needling each other while Sabrina rolled her eyes.

Simpler times. Could she have it back in some form if she just reached out and grabbed it?

Zara forced herself to look away, fixing her gaze on the half-made sandwich still sitting on the counter. 'It's just a cut. I can do it myself.'

Tess ignored her. She swiped an antiseptic wipe over Zara's skin, her fingers brushing feather-light against her palm, and it was ridiculous how much *that* set off a reaction in her more than the sting of the alcohol.

'Hold still,' Tess said softly, her tone absent of its usual sharpness. She pressed a plaster over the cut, smoothing it down with her thumb. Then her fingers lingered there, still pressing down when they both knew the adhesive was firmly in place.

There was no need for Tess to hold onto her hand like that. Absolutely no reason for her fingers to brush over the back of Zara's hand in the suggestion of a caress. She told herself to pull back. Commanded her brain to engage her muscles and take her hand out of Tess's. Why was she lingering?

Because even though the brush of Tess's fingers was so soft she could barely feel it, she *could*—feel it. It sent her pulse pumping higher and her breath hitched in her throat as the moment dragged on. As *something* co-alesced between them. Zara's first instinct was to push down on it.

Then Tess moved, somehow both slow and fast. Her

grip around Zara's hand tightened and then she dipped her head down to where their hands were clasped, brushing her lips against the inside of Zara's palm—right below where the plaster sat.

The kiss—because it was a kiss, right?—lasted the fraction of a second, yet it seared through Zara with an intensity as if she had just cut herself again. Her fingers flexed, tightening around Tess's hand, but the other woman wound out of her grip and straightened up.

Seconds ticked over in which they just stared at each other, and Zara's heart hammered so intensely in her chest she couldn't hear her own thoughts. Couldn't process what had just happened.

Tess—

Tess's eyes widened, as if she herself had just caught up with everything or had somehow experienced this as an out-of-body moment. An impulse poorly controlled. She stiffened, her spine going straight, and then her hand fell away from Zara's and she took a step back.

'I should…' She didn't finish the sentence. Instead, she took another step back, looking around while avoiding Zara's gaze. And then she was gone from the kitchen, leaving Zara alone to stare at the open first-aid kit sitting on the marble countertop.

And the two slices of bread, sitting on the cutting board. 'Wait,' she began, getting to her feet, but it was already too late. The door closed with a *thunk* and Zara was alone.

CHAPTER EIGHT

TESS HAD GONE almost the entire day without seeing Zara at the clinic.

She just wasn't sure who was doing the avoiding: her or Zara. Probably an unhealthy dose of both. Tess could recall at least one time today when she'd waited to open her door and call her next patient in until she'd heard the other woman retreat back into her exam room.

It was cowardly, Tess knew that. A well-rounded adult capable of self-regulating their feelings would pull themselves together and *talk* with the other person about what had happened. Tess knew herself well enough to know she wasn't that. And judging by how perfectly timed Zara's disappearances remained with Tess's schedule, she had the small satisfaction of knowing at least she wasn't the only one struggling.

Why on earth had Tess done that?

The moment in the kitchen had replayed in her mind over and over again. Seeing Zara hurt—even with such a small cut—had rattled Tess, making her act before she could even think about. Well, that wasn't entirely accurate. Disinfecting a wound and putting a bandage on it was one thing. Kissing the place on her body where she'd hurt herself? That wasn't something they'd taught her in medical school.

No, that had been all on Tess and her poor impulse control finally breaking. That had been only a matter of time, though she was reluctant to admit that. She'd come back to Invercaillie with the goal of getting to know her niece and processing the grief still clinging to her.

And she had achieved that, only not in the way she'd thought she would. Instead of moving on in some intellectual way she'd found something odd. Belonging.

It had taken Tess a minute to understand why Callum talking about Sabrina hadn't upset her. Or why she had then talked about her sister to Zara. Without meaning to, she'd found a spot of comfort right back in her home town, and so slowly she hadn't even noticed the tight coil of grief wrapped around her ever since Sabrina's funeral had loosened and fallen away.

Leaving her susceptible to the ancient feelings that lay buried beneath, now free to spread through her and whisper to her about possibilities Tess wasn't sure were real. She'd had an infatuation with this woman twenty years ago. Except for that one kiss, nothing had ever happened.

How could that still be a thing? Or was the forced proximity leading her to false conclusions? Would everything simply dissipate if she stopped living near her?

Tess sighed, clicking the patient file closed and resting her head against the wall. That was another thing she needed to deal with but didn't know how: her impending loss of employment. In one month, Tess's locum contract would run out with Dr Frazier ready to come back from parental leave.

When Tess had come up here, she hadn't thought this far ahead. She'd needed to escape her old life and finally deal with her sister's death by becoming a part of her niece's life. But she had spent little time thinking beyond that three-month window of her contract.

But somewhere along the last two months she'd realised she wanted to rebuild her life here. She hadn't planned anything beyond the initial contract, but she'd also never truly imagined leaving. Somewhere along the way, this place had started to settle into her bones.

Though what hadn't settled was the cottage. Or Zara. The proximity was becoming a problem. Maybe they'd fallen into too much familiarity with each other. Tess's heart had squeezed inside her chest when she'd found the spare key and Zara's handwritten note to let herself in. And she had, over and over again. First to see Helly and make food, but then also because she wanted to see Zara. Wanted to fix the broken things around the house. Wanted to be a part of her life.

This line of thinking had led to her poor impulse control last night.

Pushing off her chair, Tess stored her endless rumination in the back of her mind and opened the door to call her next patient. The sound of frantic footsteps snapped Tess's attention away from the waiting room as a woman burst through the entrance, her face etched with terror. She had a small boy clutched to her chest, eyes closed and head lolling against her chest.

'He—he can't breathe!' the woman yelled, though Tess had already reached that conclusion from the grey tinge to his lips. But why was she here and not in A &

E next door? No matter, she was here now, and her boy needed help.

'Bring him in here, quick!' Tess moved forward, guiding the woman towards the examination room. She reached out to touch the child's shoulder, feeling a pang in her chest when he gasped for air in shallow, ragged breaths, lips parted.

The mother thrust a familiar blue inhaler towards Tess, her hand shaking. 'His inhaler—it's not working. Please, you have to—'

'We've got this, Tanvi,' Zara said firmly from behind her, appearing as if summoned by the urgency in Tess's voice. 'I just saw Ravi this morning, and his chest was clear. He was responding well to his inhaler earlier, but clearly, things have worsened rapidly.'

They laid the boy down on the examination table. Tess reached for the oxygen mask, placing it over his small face, and smoothed back sweat-damp hair. 'Hey there, sweetheart. You're doing really well, okay? We're going to help you breathe easier. Just hold on for me.'

Zara moved, already setting up the nebuliser. 'Let's give him nebulised salbutamol, see how he responds.'

Tess nodded and stepped aside to let her work. Their movements fell into rhythm with surprising ease, even with so much still unspoken between them. She pulled her attention back to the mother hovering in the doorway.

'Tanvi, was it?' Tess approached the fretting mother, laying a hand on her arm. Then she made eye contact with the receptionist, who jumped from her seat and hurried over, picking up on Tess's non-verbal communication, and led Tanvi away. Zara had recognised both patient and his mother, so they wouldn't need any information while treating Ravi. Even if they did, Tanvi would be right outside.

As she stepped back into the room, Tess's eyes shot to the vital signs monitor. Her stomach tightened as she registered the numbers blinking back at her: the boy's oxygen saturation was hovering dangerously low at 86%. His heart rate was climbing, now at 140 bpm.

'His oxygen levels aren't improving, and his heart rate is climbing fast. Let's start him on IV steroids.'

Zara glanced at the monitor, her brow furrowing as she considered. 'Let's give the nebuliser another minute. He responded well earlier, but I've seen it take some time with him before. He's got a suppressed immune system already. Steroids would only aggravate that.'

Opening the cupboard, Tess grabbed an IV cannulation kit and set it down on the small tray table next to the exam bed. The whirring of the nebuliser filled the room, making each second ticking more tense. She shot a glance at Zara, who kept staring at Ravi's vital signs with the line between her brows growing starker. This wasn't about what had happened between them?

No, impossible. Their relationship might be in a state of constant change, but Zara would never let that influence anything with a patient. She didn't want to push steroids because she thought that was the best approach to treatment. Tess had to trust her, yet the words came out anyway. 'Risking a compromised immune system is better than not getting any air to his lungs.'

A muscle in Zara's jaw ticced, but she said nothing, her eyes glued to the display. Her lips started moving in a silent chant Tess was all too familiar with from her days training at the hospital before going into a private GP practice.

Come on, come on, come on.

The heart rate ticked over, the number lowering, but not fast enough for Tess's taste. She moved towards the tray table, her hand half extended towards the IV cannulation kit, when Ravi let out a soft cough. Then the vital sign monitor beeped and, with a lungful of air, the oxygen saturation jumped up.

The salbutamol worked.

'He's stable,' Zara said and moved closer to the bed with her stethoscope in her ears. 'Breath sounds are improving. There's still a mild wheezing, but that should subside in the next few hours. We need to get him transported to A & E so they can decide how long he needs to stay for observation.'

Tess nodded but didn't move, her gaze fixed on Zara. For all their rocky beginnings and the occasional disagreement, they'd found a rhythm. They worked well together—better than she'd expected. But it wouldn't last. Her contract was nearly up, and soon she'd have to figure out what came next.

She would have thought, at this time, there would be myriad ideas floating around in her head. Recruiters had been sending her a steady stream of other locum positions to consider all over the United Kingdom. But none of the locations, none of the jobs, sparked the need to explore. All Tess wanted was…this. Right here. Working together with Zara day in, day out. Going home with her and—

What was she doing? This vision forming against a distant horizon in her mind wasn't real. Would *never* be real, because how could it? Tess had made her move on Zara, and the reaction to that hint of intimacy had been clear enough.

That tiny indiscretion was more than the fragile *something* they'd built between them could stomach.

'You'll update the mother since she's your patient? I'll call up to A & E and see that they send someone round to transport Ravi.' Zara nodded, and Tess could see that there was something else she wanted to say. Only Tess wasn't sure if she was in the right mindset to hear it. So instead she turned around, hurrying out of the exam room and to the office next door to make that call.

Zara's nerves were still on edge by the time she finished writing all her notes and cleaned up her office. She'd already called ahead at the day care to let them know Matt would be picking Helly up today and had told him to have a sleep over with Helly. A favour her friend had thankfully granted and one she grew more relieved over as the minutes ticked on.

The emergency with Ravi had rattled her far more than it normally would, and she wasn't sure why. No, that wasn't quite truthful. She knew why, she just didn't want to acknowledge it. Didn't want to deal with the fact she hadn't known a single moment of peace ever since Tess Sinclair had walked back into her life.

Now she lived with this constant buzz of electricity coursing through her, jumping between her and Tess whenever they got too close. Like last night.

That moment hadn't left her, keeping her up all night with its constant replay loop. And not just the visual of Tess bending over and her lips pressing against the heel of her hand. But also the sensation. The softness of her lips, the soft caress of Tess's exhale skating down her skin and the press of her fingertips against Zara's hand, holding it in place with such care.

Zara didn't know how to feel about this entire moment. Her own reaction was all over the place and even when she tried to take each feeling and categorise it, she failed. Once upon a time, Zara had wanted nothing more than the attention of Tess in the way she was getting it now. She *wanted* to receive her kisses, let her take care of her wounds and rely on her through the difficulties of life.

Maybe not exactly in those terms, given her feelings of infatuation had been the ones of a teenager. But even then, the sense of *for ever* had been present.

Now she was living a completely different version of that for ever. One where Sabrina was gone and Tess was *right there*, making it so much harder to breathe, to think, to…stay steady on the path she'd chosen. A path that had consistently led her away from any romantic options with Tess. Hadn't Zara taken all her cues from Tess when it came to the amount of distance living between them? If Tess hadn't chosen to cut herself off from her family, maybe they would have remained friendly. Maybe this ancient tension would have eased into something else.

A knock on the door ripped her out of her thoughts and she knew who it would be even before she said, 'Come in,' and Tess walked through that door.

She closed the door behind her, then leaned against it as she looked at Zara. 'I was about to leave when I saw you were still in there. A & E just called with an update. They won't keep Ravi for much longer, thankfully. No prolonged overnight stay if they can swing it.'

Zara scanned Tess's face and, even though so many years had passed between them, she could see the girl she used to fancy. Could still feel her, too, lying right there woven into the sharp words and verbal volleys they couldn't help but toss at each other.

Something flickered over Tess's expression when Zara remained silent—the same scrutiny with which Zara was looking at her. Was she seeing it, too? Feeling it? Had last night's innocent kiss broken down some fragile barrier between the present and the past, giving those feelings free access to mingle with each other?

This couldn't happen, and Zara had told herself that over and over again. Yet Zara seemed powerless to stop her eyes from darting down to Tess's mouth, watching those lips and letting herself imagine all the things she wanted her to do with them.

Tess was feeling this tension—this want—too, wasn't she? She had to, since kissing Zara's hand had been all her doing; the entire reason why Zara had been spiralling with her own thoughts all day.

'Just say what you want to say,' Tess said.

Zara had no idea what she'd wanted the other woman to say in this situation. But she knew *that* wasn't it. *Say what you want to say?* When Zara hadn't even been the one to cross that very thin line they'd been dancing around for months. Now *she* was supposed to not just have an opinion, but share it first?

The confusing tension and heat inside her formed into the familiar sharpness of anger, and she grabbed at it for lack of any other options. 'Are you serious right now? You think after everything—not just today, but all the weeks ever since you arrived—you can just come in here and demand that *I* kick this off?'

Tess didn't move, though her eyes narrowed and a muscle in her jaw jumped when she clenched it. A few seconds ticked by in tense silence before she responded. 'What the hell is your problem? You got your way with the treatment earlier today.'

'My problem?' The tether that had kept everything inside Zara tied down snapped when she jumped to her feet. '*You.* You're my problem.' Every muscle in her body went taut as Zara gave those raging feelings inside her an outlet. She stalked closer to where Tess stood leaning against the door, peering up at her.

'You come back into my life just like that—scrambling my brain and making me believe you might actually stick around this time. But why do I believe that? You've left before. Repeatedly. Yet I'm here, struggling to come up with a version of my life where you're not around.' The words came tumbling out of her in a way even Zara hadn't expected. Because she'd spent the last few weeks pushing all those thoughts away into the depths of her mind, intent on ignoring them. Because letting them float out in the open was too terrifying to contemplate. What if it all fell apart again?

What if it didn't?

Tess's eyes flared, her lips parting in a sigh Zara couldn't parse. She blinked several times, just staring at her, and the longer the silence stretched, the heavier the regret grew at having spilled all her thoughts into the open. Then Zara saw something shift—something sharp light up behind Tess's eyes—and her heart skipped a beat. It was the same intensity she'd just channelled to get those words out.

'You think I'm doing this to mess with you? That I'm just here to play around for as long as I care? *That's* what you think about me? I'm not bailing, if you can even call it that, considering I don't know what *this* is.' She lifted her hands to the side, indicating their surroundings.

What this was? They were… Zara's breath stuttered out of her, but she didn't back down. 'You're telling me you're not planning your exit right this moment? You don't know how to stick around. At the first opportunity you got, you left Sabrina behind. You left m—'

Her breath caught just at the right time before she could form the word *me*. This was too vulnerable, too real for her to say. Even though it lay at the root of everything, all the struggles that were clawing their way up her throat unbidden.

Tess didn't need her to say the word to hear it. Her hands dropped down to her sides, her head tilted backwards and her gaze focused on some point behind her on the ceiling. Zara looked down, watching as Tess's hands balled into fists before relaxing again in a steady rhythm.

'Zara, this isn't…' She flinched at the tenderness with which Tess said her name. That tone was new and the squishy part inside her—the one where the yearning had lived all these years—leaned towards Tess, gaining confidence from that tone of voice. She could have it if she reached out and grabbed. She *could*, right?

'I told you about my regrets. About the things I wish I could take back but know I can't. They are mine to live with for the rest of my life. But I'm here now. And

I'm not going anywhere.' Tess's voice was low, lulling Zara into a sense of security she didn't know how to accept. Was it really that easy? She said she wasn't about to leave and that was the end of it?

'You make me want to believe you.' And she did. She wanted to believe it with everything she had. But how could she, when past experiences told her it would be foolish to do that? Hadn't Tess said that before only to disappear? Zara had to admit she couldn't remember if they'd actually had a conversation like that or if the last few years of loneliness had spawned memories all of their own making.

Her heart stuttered in her chest when Tess's warm hands came up to her cheeks, framing her face. Tess tilted Zara's face up, their eyes meeting, and a tremble skittered down Zara's spine at the fire she saw in the other woman's eyes. There was no sharpness—no softness, either. Something new, a steely determination, but determined about what? What was she—?

Zara's thoughts ground to a halt when Tess moved both her thumbs over Zara's cheekbones, each arch sending sparks flying right underneath her skin. Then Tess bent down towards her, their noses touching for the briefest moment before Tess's lips were on hers.

Then the world stopped spinning. That was the only way Zara could describe the measure of force thundering through her body as Tess's mouth slid over hers, drawing her into a kiss that she had dreamed about for far too many years of her life—never believing it could happen.

Now that it was real, Zara's knees buckled, and she had to brace herself against Tess. Or maybe it was the snap of tension finally breaking that unleashed the wave of need cresting through her, forcing her to eliminate every speck of space between their bodies. She buried her hands in the fabric of Tess's shirt, hauling the woman closer to her. A needy moan escaped Tess's throat—or was that her own?—that lit her ablaze from the inside.

This couldn't last. It was too good, too hot, too...everything for her to trust it. Yet, it was also the only thing she'd thought about ever since that night when Tess had made her food. Despite her less than enthusiastic welcome of Tess, the other woman had seen her struggle with such a simple thing as nutrition. And even though she hadn't needed to do anything, she'd cooked for her. She'd found ways around Zara's pride, quietly slipping back into her life through food.

Had fixed the tiny things in the house Zara had been too busy to deal with.

Had looked after her wound when she'd cut herself.

There were so many more times in the last few weeks that came rushing back at Zara as they deepened their kiss where Tess could have bailed on her. Or could have done the bare minimum. She was here for Helly, after all, not for Zara. Yet she hadn't hesitated to be there for both. Tess had stuck around.

And Zara? She had spent far too much energy pushing and insisting on the past still being true today.

Tess's arms came around her, pressing her closer until their hips were locked, shooting a delicious friction through her that lasted for all but a second before Tess wrenched her mouth away from her. The sudden loss of her lips against hers left Zara gasping for air, her hands winding even tighter into Tess's shirt.

'I'm not leaving. You got it? Not as long as you want me here.' Tess's voice was low and airy, vibrating over Zara's skin in a hair-raising tease.

'Okay,' she replied, more automatic than actually acknowledging her words because all she could think about was how quickly she could get Tess's mouth back onto hers. Or on other parts of her body. Because Zara really needed—

'Say it for me, Zara,' Tess said, making Zara blink several times in an effort to get her brain working again.

'What?' Apparently a few blinks weren't quite enough for that.

'Tell me you want me here. Because if you don't, I'm not forcing it. But if you want this—' Tess's hand pressed against Zara's heaving chest for a moment before she put it on her own in emphasis '—then I'm here to stay.'

There it was—the moment of choice. Or was it? Maybe that fork in the road had come and gone long ago, and she just hadn't had the courage to admit it. Because now, standing here, Zara felt no hesitation. Her whole body buzzed with certainty, every nerve pointing her towards the woman in front of her.

'I want you.'

CHAPTER NINE

TESS DIDN'T HESITATE to follow Zara inside as the woman unlocked the front door. But she didn't give her any time to shed her several layers of clothes before she was on her, pressing Zara against the door in a mirror image of what she'd done at the clinic. Tess needed her closer, needed to feel their skin against each other, needed—

Zara's lips parted, inviting her in and deepening the kiss the moment it began.

Tess's hands roamed over Zara's body, gripping her waist and pulling her even closer as they kissed. She could feel Zara's heart pounding through her chest, matching the wild rhythm of her own.

How long had she imagined doing this? Definitely since she'd started hanging out at the main house more often. Her offer to make food had been a genuine one and not some misguided attempt at getting back into Zara's life. Or getting on the other woman's radar on a romantic level. No, Tess had believed that possibility long since gone, though that hadn't stopped a small part of her heart from wanting differently, from hoping against hope that they could find their way to each other—that maybe the second time would be the charm.

Feeling Zara's body yielding beneath hers, Tess was

intoxicated by the thrill of finally having what she'd craved for so long. Her hands roamed over Zara's front, finding zips and buttons to peel her layer by layer. Zara was doing the same to her between kisses that had turned from exploring and tentative in the clinic to frantic and blazing here at home.

Their home.

Tess let out a throaty groan when her fingers slipped under the hem of Zara's shirt and found smooth skin there. Warmth darted from the place she was touching up her arm, ratcheting up the heat and igniting tiny fires all along her body. Touching Zara like this, feeling the curve of her stomach as she slipped her hand further up—it was like a revelation. The thoughts seventeen-year-old Tess had entertained about her crush didn't compare to this moment, twenty years later.

Zara gulped in a breath when Tess left her mouth to trace a trail of kisses along her jawbone and down her neck, where she pressed her nose into the riot of curls and took a deep breath.

'You smell amazing right now,' Tess mumbled into her neck, punctuating each word with a kiss. With her hands still working their way up Zara's body, she felt the other woman's tremor run through her.

'Is the implication here that I normally don't smell nice?' Zara pressed out, air suffusing her words, and the sound alone was enough to drive a spear of need through Tess—pooling heat right where she needed it.

Where she needed Zara.

Searching for friction, she pressed her hips against Zara's in a mirror gesture of the one at the clinic. Zara reacted to her movements as if she knew all of them, knew *her* and as if this weren't their first time together but one of many occasions imagined that had now finally come to pass.

Was that what it was like for Zara, too? Because Tess had imagined this moment so many times, the memories of those dreams already frayed at the edges.

Zara's legs fell open as she leaned her entire weight against the door, trusting Tess to keep her upright. She did that by slipping her leg between Zara's and the other woman let out a groan when she pressed against the right place.

'Of course you would look for the insult instead of taking the compliment as it is,' Tess replied, then pressed a kiss right behind Zara's ear that made her squirm.

'Because *we* don't do compliments. Not the way other people do,' Zara shot back, but the fire in her voice quivered as Tess traced her collarbone with her lips.

Tess smiled into her skin, feeling Zara arch towards her touch and pull her even closer. There was nothing she wouldn't do to keep them wrapped around each other like this for ever. It was a fleeting thought, brought to her by the heat of the moment, but one that left an impact on her all the same.

Because it was true. She was here now and wouldn't allow Zara to have these kinds of doubts ever again. For as long as Zara wanted her, Tess would be right here.

'All right, what do you want from me, then?' Tess breathed, pulling back to look at her. She still couldn't believe this was happening. That Zara wanted this, too. Wanted *her*.

Zara met her gaze with a dark, smouldering look and reached for the hem of Tess's shirt, pulling it up and over her head with one swift tug. 'At the moment? Your clothes off. All of them.'

Tess laughed—a tangle of nerves and relief—and eagerly obliged. For a few beats, they were an uncoordinated mess of flailing limbs and too many buttons until they stood in front of each other wearing nothing but their underwear.

Tess's breath caught at the sight of Zara like this, her already damp skin glistening in the sparse moonlight finding its way inside through the half-drawn blinds. She reached out to touch Zara, skating her finger along the edge of the bra and tracing the swell of her breast. Just like Zara, Tess had worn nothing fancy underneath her clothes. Hadn't expected they would land in this situation, after all.

The sheer white fabric was still enough to get Tess's knees to buckle. She traced it further, then palmed Zara's breast and swiped her thumb over a peaked nipple.

Zara's reaction threw fuel on the rising fire within Tess. She arched her back, pressing into Tess's arm and grinding her hip against Tess. Both sensations were almost too much for Tess, and she had to stop herself from rushing in. She wanted to devour Zara right here on the spot, but she *needed* to savour every second.

'Keep going,' Tess said, her voice rough and low. 'What else?'

Instead of answering, Zara slid her hand around Tess's neck and hauled her onto her mouth, searing her with an open-mouthed kiss that had her stomach buzzing with butterflies. When Tess went to deepen the kiss, Zara snapped her head back. 'How about we move this to a more comfortable place?'

'Bedroom?' Tess forced herself to step back, even though everything inside her screamed at her to grab Zara and never let go of her. Ever.

She grabbed Zara's hand and tugged her towards the bedroom, but then the other woman stopped dead in her tracks. When Tess whirled around to face her, she was met by a hungry pair of lips dragging her into another mind-bending kiss that had her gasping for air—and grappling with reality because how could one woman feel this good? How could their bodies fit together like this—as if Zara had always been meant for her? As if kissing were the only thing Tess was supposed to do with her life and, for some insane reason, she'd waited until now to do it again?

Zara broke away and gave her a look that was a mix of amused and carnal, sending a shiver up Tess's spine. 'Might not make it to the bedroom,' she said, eyes dancing with mischief. Her hand slipped under the band of Tess's underwear, sending a thrill shooting through her, then she hooked two fingers there and pulled her closer. Another slow kiss, deep and searching, had Tess losing all sense of where they even were.

Was it the second time they'd kissed or the thousandth? Each felt like both.

'Here is good,' Zara gasped into Tess's mouth when their lips finally drifted apart again and then she pushed Tess against the couch. 'We can always try again later.'

'Here is good,' Tess repeated because her brain couldn't really deal with making new words. Not when Zara moved to straddle her, her soft, lush thighs bracketing her own. She needed all her attention on the woman above her.

Her hands came down on Zara's waist, then swept upwards until she reached the band of her bra. The cups fell forward when she undid the hooks on the back, and with one flick of her arm, Zara threw the bra away.

Tess's heart slammed against her chest at the sight of Zara's naked body. Over the last few weeks, she'd imagined what she would look like often enough—even though she wasn't really keen on admitting how much her lonely brain had focused on the other woman.

I want you.

Now she was all hers, and the reality was so much better than anything she'd ever conjured up in her brain.

Unable to contain herself any longer, Tess reached out and traced a finger over one of Zara's nipples, feeling it stiffen even more beneath her touch.

'Beautiful,' she whispered, leaning in closer to taste the soft skin just above Zara's collarbone. Her hands roamed down Zara's sides, skimming over the smooth flesh, and she huffed out a laugh when she sensed a quiver of anticipation run through Zara's body.

'I knew you would be soft, but this…' Tess's voice trailed off as her hands did another sweep up her sides, nails trailing over sensitive skin until Zara let out a throaty groan.

Tess buried her face in the valley of Zara's breasts, taking a deep inhale. 'And your scent. It's been driving me wild every time I spend time in the house. But this close, it's overwhelming.'

She placed an open-mouthed kiss on Zara's heated skin, then licked along the curve of her breast. Zara's taste on her tongue was intoxicating, stoking the hungry flames inside her even higher.

Tess needed to know what she tasted like *everywhere*. Needed to absorb that knowledge and add it to the growing library of things she knew about Zara.

Dragging her lips over Zara's breast, Tess caught her nipple with her tongue first before closing her mouth over it. Zara slumped forward, her forehead coming to rest on top of Tess's head. Even here she forced herself to go slow, despite the need infusing her, pushing her to use not just her tongue but her teeth to make Zara scream.

She felt a tremble run through Zara when she released it with a soft pop and moved on to the other breast. Zara's fingers dug into her shoulders, the short nails finding enough traction to slice into her skin. Not that Tess cared. The edge of that pain was exquisite, telling her that what she was doing was working.

So was the moisture that slicked Tess's skin when Zara rolled her hips against her. She was *so* wet, so ready that it almost pushed Tess over the edge right there. Her self-restraint had reached the end, unravelling and then disappearing like a burning wick.

Tess slid her hand between them, caressing Zara's round stomach and relishing the softness there before dipping even lower and finding the spot she wanted to be at. The spot where Zara wanted her too, going by her reaction.

She only grazed her fingers over Zara, coating her fingers in the other woman's wetness, but the small touch was enough to elicit a big reaction. Zara moaned, her thighs squeezing together enough that Tess could feel the friction in her own core.

'Zara, this is so—' She didn't finish her sentence because Zara lifted her head and slid her mouth over her in a hungry kiss that was all tongues and teeth and swallowed moans.

Then Zara's hand slipped beneath Tess's underwear, following her lead, and the move was so sudden and un-expected, she didn't have time to brace herself—or to even contemplate how *right* it would feel to have Zara's hand right there, stroking her.

She pressed her mouth to Zara's chest, using her teeth this time and delighting in the way she arched against her, pinning her harder to the couch. Her grip on Tess sharpened and turned greedy, as did the way her fingers moved between Tess's legs. It was relentless and per-fect and stealing away every coherent thought Tess had.

Every single one except Zara.

Her mind was filled only with her now—Zara's body above her, Zara's taste on her lips, Zara's touch push-ing her higher and higher. She could feel herself com-ing apart at the seams, a tangle of nerves and need and wanting. So much wanting she didn't know if she could survive it.

'I've wanted you for so long,' Tess gasped into Zara's skin again, then pulled back to look up at her.

The words seemed to set something off in both of them. The air between them crackled with it, electric-ity poised to arc from one to the other. Tess's hand slid up, finding Zara's nipple and twisting just as she thrust two fingers deep into her.

Zara cried out, the sound so rich it was almost a laugh, and then she was moving against Tess with wild abandon. Their bodies locked together, every movement pushing their pleasure higher until it was hard to tell where one of them ended and the other began.

When Tess felt herself teetering on the very edge of oblivion, she sank her teeth into Zara's shoulder and let go, her whole world turning white with sensation.

The orgasm hit like a lightning strike, her body arching and shuddering under Zara as she came. Zara followed seconds after, hips grinding down as her own release tore through her and left them both trembling and breathless.

Tess collapsed back against the couch with a ragged laugh, pulling Zara down with her. She wrapped her arms around the other woman's body—her beautiful, soft body—and held her close. Their chests heaved together, sweat-slicked and utterly spent.

'Think you might have killed me,' Zara said into the quiet of her living room.

They'd both stretched out post-orgasm, heated skin cooling from the exposure to the chilly air of the early evening. Zara had tucked her head under Tess's chin and wrapped her arms around her, holding the woman closer. Both because she wasn't ready to let go of the closeness and to avoid eye contact because, well, she wasn't sure she could deal with any post-sex regret she might find in them.

'I'm still breathing,' Tess said, her fingers tracing lazy circles on Zara's back. She shivered at the gentle touch, some of the cloudy thoughts scattering. 'Barely.'

'Good to know,' Zara mumbled, smiling against Tess's chest and trying to come up with something else to say. Where were they supposed to go from here?

She had just slept with Tess Sinclair, her teenage

crush of many years. The one who got away, if she could even call her that when they'd never dated.

Was that what they were doing now? Dating? The thought sent her heart thrumming through her chest, excitement warring with unease. It was what she wanted, right? Having Tess by her side—both as a team member at the clinic and as a co-parent to Helly—had felt *right* to a degree Zara was almost too scared to consider. But when she'd let out those fears, Tess had told her what she'd needed to hear. Not just that, she'd shown her over the last few weeks the truth of those words.

She hadn't left. And despite her contract coming to an end soon, Tess also hadn't made any plans to leave. She was here. For good.

As long as you want me.

Zara took a breath, the air feeling heavy as it filled her lungs. She lifted her head and met Tess's gaze, an unexpected tenderness staring back at her. 'I—this was...' Her words petered off. What was she trying to say? The words were right there, at the tip of her tongue, bubbling up like champagne bubbles that burst before they reached the surface.

The vulnerability this situation required didn't come easy to her. It went against every single instinct she'd honed through the years of rejection and missed opportunities. First with her mother, when she'd left her days on end without any supervision. Then with Sabrina, who had promised her they would do this—*life*—together, only to leave her.

And Tess herself had left Zara behind, too. It had reinforced the idea in her mind that, outside Sabrina, all the relationships in her life had been transactional. That people left whenever they got their end of the bargain.

Below her, Tess shifted, and her hand stopped drawing their lazy circles on her back. Instead, she pulled Zara closer, slipping one hand under her chin so she was looking at those deep brown eyes.

'I meant everything I said at the clinic. I'm here to stay because I'm—I want to be with you. I want to… give this a try.' Tess paused, an uncharacteristic flash of insecurity rippling over her face.

And it clicked within Zara why all of this was only happening now. Because Tess, too, wasn't good at the vulnerability that a moment like this required.

The question of compatibility popped into her mind unbidden, and she almost instantly pushed it away. Tess saw it play out on her face anyway. But she didn't react the way Zara thought she would—offended that she would even doubt her when she'd not given her a reason ever since coming back to Invercaillie.

No, instead she leaned towards her and brushed a tender kiss over her lips that sent sparks flying through Zara's body again. 'I don't just mean to tell you I'm sticking around and for you to take my word for it. Let me show you, okay?'

Zara looked up at her, heart in her throat. Tess had read her with such ease. How was she supposed to keep her heart safe from this woman? 'Show me how?'

Tess pushed her hands against Zara, lifting her enough so she could slip out from underneath her. Zara watched, eyes wide as Tess climbed off the couch and stood up. She was still in her underwear. In the heat of the moment, neither of them had taken the time to get rid of more than the bare minimum. With only the dim light of a small tableside lamp illuminating the living room, Tess's pale skin stood at a stark contrast to their dark environment.

Something warm—an awareness that had been slumbering beneath the surface for a long time—unfurled within her when Tess turned around, stretching her hand out in an invitation. Zara stared at it, at the promise this hand represented, and then, with her heart beating wildly against her chest as if it were trying to escape, she grabbed Tess's hand. A spark came alive where their palms met, then Tess tugged her up and off the couch.

'However I need to. Every day,' Tess said, then grasped her hand tightly and pulled her along until they reached the bedroom.

CHAPTER TEN

THE IDEA OF a blood drive had started as a joke—how much blood did a tiny hospital in the middle of nowhere really need?—but by the looks of the crowded halls, everyone in town was in on it. A poster reading *Give Life, Give Blood* greeted Tess as she pushed through the double doors and into the lively chaos. Volunteers buzzed around the community room like a cloud of hummingbirds, coordinating patients, staff and guests.

What took her by surprise was how often people raised their hands to wave at her, some of them even stopping her for a quick exchange of words.

How are things with Helly?

I heard Silvano broke his hip, poor dear.

Take this jar of jam with you when you go home, all right?

They were small snippets of casual conversation in a community—words Tess had heard people exchange with each other every day. Except now she was on the receiving end of it and not standing outside looking in. Over the last few weeks, this had changed, but Tess couldn't point out when *exactly* it had all shifted. When she'd become one of them.

Which was odd the longer she thought about it. She

was from here, after all. Yet this was the first time that she felt as if she had a place to be. As a child and adolescent, she had spent too much time pursuing academic excellence under the watchful eyes of both her parents—to a degree that had been suffocating. That they hadn't had the same standards for Sabrina as they'd had for herself hadn't made the sibling relationship easier.

Had Tess, at some point, come to associate the pressure from her parents with the town itself? It was a plausible theory considering she'd packed her things and left the moment she'd been accepted on a medical course in the south of England. She hadn't even taken a second to look back or consider her options. All she remembered was wanting to get out of this place. Find her belonging, her people, elsewhere.

How strange that coming back here had given her exactly that.

Tess turned her head when Zara's laugh rang through the room where they'd set up for the blood drive, and Tess couldn't help but smile at the woman. At how much more *she'd* given her. She couldn't look at her without her heart speeding up, drumming against her sternum as if plotting its escape.

Things hadn't slowed down between them in the weeks that had gone by since their first night together. Quite the opposite. They'd been glued to each other's side at home, barely able to keep their hands from each other. It was as though they were trying to recreate the teenage romance they'd never got the chance to experience, with how often they sneaked a make-out session in between patients behind closed doors.

Tess also hadn't slept back in the cottage since that

night. She'd offered more than once to give Zara her space back, to take things slow and see where they were going with this relationship. After their initial conversation, they hadn't really talked about what it all meant and what might be on the horizon for them.

Most nights, they fell asleep tangled together on the sofa, TV forgotten, Helly's toys scattered across the floor like breadcrumbs marking the life they were slipping into. Tess had started brushing her teeth in Zara's bathroom without thinking about it. Folding her laundry because it was there. None of it had been discussed. It had just…happened.

But was it necessary? Tess understood the need to cling to definitions and labels as an adolescent. When she'd first realised that she was interested in girls the way most of her peers seemed to be interested in boys, she'd found the labels helpful. They'd given her some guard rails within which to explore what it meant to her to be gay.

But now? All she wanted was Zara for the rest of her life. Anything else simply wouldn't do. She knew that in the depths of her being, and she wanted to let her know. Tonight. Even if it meant leaning into the lesbian cliché she kept pretending she'd outgrown. Lesbians showing up to the third date with a moving van was so universally recognisable in her community, Tess actually cringed away from it.

Only it was true here. She was in love with Zara. Had been carrying a torch for her for so long, ever wondering how her life would have been if she'd stayed. Or if she'd just told Zara how she felt, despite her friendship with her sister. Could they have had twenty years together?

Or had it all been necessary to get them both to this point in time where they now fitted together as if made for each other?

When Tess approached Zara, she looked up from her clipboard and the smile she gave her turned Tess's knees into rubber.

'Did you give blood yourself? You look a bit unsteady.' Zara's gaze swept over Tess from head to toe, and Tess tried to ignore the sensation that crawled through her body. A simple look from this woman was enough to make her forget herself and turn her into someone that was there just to worship Zara.

'I didn't. It must be the effect you're having on me— commanding my blood into other parts of my body.' Tess's voice was low and filled with the intentions she had for later tonight.

Zara reached out, fingers grazing Tess's arm before she seemed to catch herself. She pulled back in a sudden movement, and Tess pretended not to notice. But something inside her shifted, the blood now draining out of her body completely.

Was she not allowed to touch her? Or was this about *what* she'd said? A part within Tess urged her to reach out and grab Zara's hand. Brush a kiss against her cheek. But a sense of uncertainty kept her frozen in place, worried she'd overstepped. They hadn't really talked about what they were for each other in public, and Tess had thought it unnecessary, but now…

'Did you get to chat with some people? Seems like the entire village turned up today, plus some people from surrounding areas.' The tone Zara struck with this question didn't reassure Tess either. Quite the opposite.

She sensed herself tense at how airy she sounded. What was that edge in her voice? Discomfort?

'I did, yeah. Funny to see how many people remember me from my younger years when I haven't been around for almost two decades,' Tess said, trying to bring some lightness back between them even though she wasn't sure how. 'I think I've agreed to a jam subscription.'

She held up the jar of jam when Zara tilted her head in question. A smile tugged on her lips as she examined the jar and its gelatinous red content, and the pressure on Tess's chest eased at that.

'Told you they would, didn't I? Your family name still carries weight here.' Zara's voice was warm, but there it was again—a distance that hadn't been between them since…since when?

She was making things up. For once, things were going well and because she was so used to disaster and pressure and things just feeling slightly off, she was looking for these things when there were none.

Right?

'Is everything okay?' Tess asked, despite not wanting to go there. This wouldn't lead to any real conversation, but something inside her urged her to ask anyway.

Zara's eyes flicked back to the clipboard, her expression unreadable. Which was another sign of trouble because the last time she'd seen her this guarded had been when Tess had first arrived here.

Zara cleared her throat and then looked at a point over Tess's shoulder. 'What? Oh—yes, of course. Never better.' She paused for just a moment too long. 'You know, if you have time, maybe check in on Callum? Looks like he could use some help.'

The words landed like a cold splash of water, and Tess struggled to keep her smile as steady as she wanted it to be. She gave a short nod and backed away. 'Sure. I'll go do that.'

Tess weaved through the room, which was brimming with people and chatter. For a moment, she hesitated, glancing back towards Zara. But Zara had already turned to speak with someone else.

Maybe Tess was imagining things. Paranoid, even. She was so wrapped up in this new life they were building any slight variation felt like a seismic shift. She found Callum by one of the donation stations, his smile wide beneath his mop of dark red hair.

'Impressive, isn't it?' the nurse said as he nodded towards the line still waiting to donate blood. 'We'll be able to supply some of the smaller clinics in the area as well.'

She matched his smile the best she could. Out of all the people she'd reconnected with or newly met in Invercaillie, Callum had to be her favourite. His older-brother energy never failed to make her day whenever they worked together. 'Do we even have enough storage space for all the bags?'

Callum shrugged. 'If we don't, we'll all just take a bag home.'

'You know blood has to be kept in quite a specific way? You can't just wedge a bag of blood between the carrots and cabbage in your crisper drawer.'

'Ah, I think those rules don't count for us rural people. Of course you'd follow the big city protocol.' He nudged Tess playfully, but something in his words threw her back into the pit her strange interaction with Zara had thrown her into. How he'd said *us people* had suspiciously sounded as though he didn't include her.

And as if Callum were reading her mind—or maybe the day had just decided to be one of *those* days—he leaned in, lowering his voice to a conspiratorial whisper. 'So, how long are we keeping you before you run off to your next fancy job?'

Run off? Was that what people thought of her? That she was flighty? Maybe that was a fair thing to think for people who'd seen her leave Invercaillie almost two decades ago. But how could Callum have gained the same impression from her? She'd spent so much time with him on shift, talking about patient care, about her old life, about things both significant and trivial. How had any of these conversations left the impression that she had one foot out of the door?

Tess's gaze drifted over to where Zara stood, but, with all the people milling around the space, she could only see the top of her head.

'Fancy job? I don't have anything lined up,' she said when the silence stretched for too long, mustering a smile that she hoped didn't look as icy as it felt.

Callum gave a rumbling chuckle, his large hand coming down on her shoulder to give it a squeeze. 'No worries. I'm sure you'll find something more exciting than this little village hospital. After your time here, I can tell you are missing the big city life.'

He could? Tess blinked several times to steady herself, thrown for a loop by his words. Wait, was that why Zara was putting distance between them? Because she thought now that Tess's contract was running out at the end of the month, she would be off on her next assignment, turning her back on Zara and Helly?

No, that wasn't possible. They'd talked about this. Tess had said she was here to stay no matter what. That she wouldn't leave again, not unless...

Not as long as you want me here.

A cold shiver ran down her spine. What if that was what the distance was about? Zara had changed her mind and didn't want her to stick around. And from what Callum had told her, neither did the people of Invercaillie. Despite all the interactions, all the conversations and the mysterious jars of jam exchanged, they were all seeing her as a temporary fixture. Here to do her job and then leave the moment something more exciting came along.

Could Tess really blame them for thinking that? The people living here looked out for their own, and by leaving not just once but twice—leaving her sister to struggle with the aftermath of their parents' death on her own—Tess had shown them she was someone who left.

Of course, they would all wait for her to do it again. Even Zara, who she'd spent the last few weeks with, drifting on a cloud. Even she thought Tess was flighty, no matter how much time she'd spent with her; no matter what she'd said.

Were they right?

Even though the blood drive had been more of a spontaneous idea rather than a plan thought through well in advance, the results had been great. The entire village had come together, either to donate blood or to support the event with food, drinks and company.

With only so many staff at the hospital available to actually draw blood, Tess didn't have time to dwell on her thoughts. The uneasy feeling however had remained and accompanied her throughout the rest of the day. It clung to her now as she came into the living room where Zara sat with Helly on the floor.

'Again! Again!' Helly demanded, her voice full of toddler insistence.

Tess set her bag down and joined them, ruffling Helly's hair and letting herself breathe out the knot of tension that had been there all day. 'This little munchkin still full of energy?'

'I think the people at the blood drive were sneaking the kids sweets. The sugar coma is going to hit her any moment,' Zara said, the amusement in her voice such a stark departure from how she'd behaved towards Tess in the clinic, it settled the unease deeper into Tess's bones.

Was she a secret to Zara? Good to have fun with, but nowhere near ready for an official debut around the town? The thought stung.

'Maybe she should have run around a little more at the event. Got rid of some of that sugar,' Tess teased, trying to sound light.

She watched Zara set Helly back on her feet, wondering if the distance she'd felt had only been in her head. It seemed impossible to imagine when she saw them like this: Helly clinging to Zara's legs, Zara trying and failing to keep a straight face as she pretended to shake the girl off. This closeness made Tess's heart lurch with both hope and fear.

It didn't help that when Zara shifted her eyes towards Tess now, they were filled with an affectionate spark that ran through Tess's body with a seductive warmth that made her want to disregard all her worries.

If there even was anything to worry about. Tess wasn't entirely convinced that she wasn't making these things up in her head. After spending so much time trying to save a marriage doomed to fail and regretting it, she knew she had ghosts she still wrestled with.

So when Zara stretched out her hand, Tess took it and let her lead her to the couch, where they snuggled up with Helly wedged between them.

Helly pointed at one of the books strewn across the floor. 'Story! Story!' she chanted.

'Which one this time?' Tess asked, already knowing the answer.

'Duck! *Quack!*'

'Is that the one?' Zara feigned surprise. 'Are you sure?'

Helly nodded so vigorously Tess thought she might fall over while sitting down.

'You heard the boss,' Tess said, reaching for the book. '*Quack* it is.'

They took turns reading, each doing different voices that made Helly giggle. With every page turned, Tess let herself relax. This, right here, was the kind of night she used to dream about without realising it. Warmth, noise, love all wrapped around her like a second skin. And Zara—Zara pressed in close, steady and soft and hers, even if the word had never been spoken.

Once Helly was asleep, Tess would tell Zara how she felt. That she loved her and that their future together was so clear in front of her mental eye she didn't know how to *not* live that life now.

As long as Zara wanted her. It was the eventuality where it all fell apart. With her actions during the blood drive contradicting what she did at home, Tess didn't know where to look—what to believe.

Zara seemed at peace, unworried and unfazed by the fear that shadowed Tess—which didn't help Tess in figuring out how much of this was in her head. Helly eventually tired herself out, and her eyelids drooped with sleep. As they reached the last page, Zara lifted the little girl into her arms and carried her to bed. Tess watched them disappear down the hallway, a tightness growing in her chest. The life she wanted, the life she had nearly convinced herself she had, felt achingly close. Close enough to hurt.

Zara returned to the living room, and they settled together on the sofa. Tess leaned into her warmth, seeking the reassurance Zara didn't even know she needed. The words were on the tip of her tongue. She just needed to open her mouth and say them.

What was so hard about that?

'Finally, some peace,' Zara murmured, resting her head on Tess's shoulder.

'Helly's going to sleep well tonight. I might follow her lead,' Tess said, forcing herself to sound playful rather than afraid. She felt Zara's breath against her skin, relaxing into the softness of their shared space. It was supposed to feel good. It *did* feel good—but not enough to drown out the uncertainty still simmering underneath.

Zara's hand slid down Tess's arm and laced their fingers together, a simple gesture that thundered through Tess. 'I was hoping we could steal a little time for ourselves,' Zara whispered, the words low and intimate.

Tess wanted that more than anything, so why did she freeze? Why couldn't she just be here without always wondering when it would end? She twisted her body towards Zara, trying hard to let herself fall into the moment. 'Yeah?'

Zara nodded and trailed a line of kisses from Tess's shoulder up her neck. Her exhales skittered across Tess's skin that was heating under her touch by the second, eroding all the thoughts that had weighed her down throughout the day—along with the resolve to speak those thoughts aloud. She needed to address what was inside her, right? The reason they were here now, so many years and missed opportunities later, was that neither of them had said anything when they'd still had the chance.

'Zara...' Her hands tightened around Zara's shoulders, the soft skin meeting her there sending a renewed wave of heat through her.

But Zara didn't pick up on the pleading tone underneath her words. Or maybe she did, but she didn't realise what Tess was asking her for was a moment to breathe. Some time to understand where they stood—what they were to each other. Because next week Tess would be out of work and that was fine, if there was a future here for her. One where they were a couple for real and looking after Helly together.

'I've been thinking about doing this to you all day,' Zara whispered, her lips connecting just below Tess's ear and sending shivers down her spine. Tess took a steadying breath—or tried to but ended up with a lung full of Zara's scent instead, further scrambling her brain.

She'd been thinking about her all day? So had Tess,

though, from what Zara intended to do with her now, their thoughts were quite different. And even though she wanted to sink into the warmth and softness and euphoria that Zara's probing hands promised, she couldn't stop thinking about the day.

'You didn't like it when I made that suggestion earlier,' Tess forced herself to say, because if she didn't say it now, she was certain she never would. She'd go on ignoring her gut feeling, giving it a life of its own inside her until it would eventually come back and explode on her.

It was what had happened with Giulia. She'd known something wasn't right in their relationship, but instead of digging into it, she'd ignored it and willed it to go away.

Zara's hands froze, their explorations stopping just above Tess's waistband. Then they fell away altogether, sending a cold shiver through Tess at the loss of contact. When Zara sat up and looked at Tess, her face was inscrutable.

'What do you mean?' The question came out with hesitance. Was that because she really didn't know what Tess was alluding to or had she too been ignoring the weird sense of tension between them?

'Earlier today during the blood drive. I got flirty with you, but when I reached out, you flinched back.' That moment had replayed in her mind for the rest of the day, even though Tess herself had found hundreds of excuses for that little twitch. Maybe she'd surprised Zara. Or Zara hadn't been sure if Tess had washed her hands recently. What if she had misinterpreted her gesture as something else?

And then there was the one thought she couldn't let go of. The one that had stuck its thorns inside her so hard that she needed Zara to remove it. That or…

'We can't be making out at work. It's not proper.' The thorns catching along Tess's insides dug deeper at those words, and she forced another deep breath into her lungs.

'I wasn't about to kiss you. I'd just reached out to touch your arm. An innocent enough gesture for anyone looking. Though I guess you're more concerned about that than I am.'

It was the conclusion her mind had reached after a few hours of stewing on it, even though she'd refused to follow this thread all the way down to where it led. But she was there now, needing to clear things up because if she didn't, how could that possibly end? Would Zara insist on them keeping things secret for the foreseeable future? Or was this simply a casual thing for her and meanwhile Tess had made the mistake of letting those old feelings reform into something new? An adoration underpinned by memories of the past.

She was in love with Zara. And from the way Zara stared back at her now, Tess feared the same wasn't true for Zara.

'Tess, you caught me by surprise,' Zara began, backing off until there was some space between them on the couch. 'We haven't discussed anything, and I didn't know…'

'Is there much to discuss between us? I thought I made my feelings for you quite clear throughout the weeks I've spent right here in this house. And more recently in *your* bed.' So that was what it boiled down to?

Tess had been far too comfortable living on this sex-fu-elled cloud, convincing herself that they were heading in the same direction—*felt* the same way. But meanwhile, this had been nothing more than a casual thing for Zara. Something to finally tick off her to-do list after so many years of wondering what it would be like.

'So, what? You think you can just spring public affection on me? At our place of work?' Tess saw Zara tense up and familiar defences snapping into place between them. As she stared at her now, it was so hard to read her mind when over the past few days—*weeks*—she'd been an open book to Tess. Though now she thought she'd been kidding herself with that. How much did she really know about Zara if she'd felt comfortable touching her in public when it seemed to revolt her?

'We were in the building where we worked, but we were not *at work*. I would not be so unprofessional. We were both volunteering for the blood drive, not looking after patients in our capacity as GPs.' Tess knew it was a flimsy excuse that fell apart under the most basic of scrutiny. Instead of telling her the truth, Zara was holding onto these things to shield herself. Which could only mean...

'This doesn't mean anything to you, does it?' The words came out low and monotone, her mind too busy grappling with the meaning of the words to find the proper inflection to use.

Zara's eyes went wide at her declaration, mouth falling open for a moment before snapping shut again. Tense seconds ticked by between them, where Tess braced herself for the devastating answer she knew would come from Zara. She was about to confirm the one thing Tess had been denying throughout the day, because... What was she supposed to do with all that fullness within her that Zara had brought out in her? With all those feelings?

'No, Tess—' Zara shook her head, trying to find the right words. 'You're wrong.'

Tess hated how her heart fluttered at those words, hope rushing into her system when she'd spent all day telling herself she shouldn't. 'What am I wrong about, Zara?'

'I didn't mean it like that. Of course, this means something. I care about you.'

'But not enough to be with me openly?' Tess said, her voice harder than she'd planned. But if they were going there, they might as well go all the way.

'It's just...complicated.' Zara's gaze dropped to her lap, where her hands were wringing together.

'Complicated?' Tess repeated, the word slicing through her. 'I see.'

'It's not what you think it is,' Zara insisted, eyes darting up again.

'I think I do. It's too complicated to be with me. Still.' Tess's voice came out far more brittle than she intended, but what was she supposed to do when the thing she'd been yearning for was falling apart in front of her eyes? 'I guess it does mean something to you, but just something *different*. A good lay maybe?'

Zara stiffened, defensiveness clouding her features. 'You're twisting this into something it's not. I don't want our personal life under scrutiny by the entire village when *we* haven't even spoken about it.'

Tess paused at that, willing her galloping heart to slow. 'Let's talk about it, then. I thought "I want you" was as clear as it was going to get. But if all that's holding you back is a conversation, then let's have it.'

Silence spread between them again, though this time lacking the easy-going comfort it usually had. They'd spent hours in the quiet in the last few weeks, each one just enjoying the other one's presence. Apparently they should have been talking instead.

On a deeper level, Tess knew that. But she'd also let herself believe that her action would go so much further in speaking than words ever could.

Zara stood abruptly, pacing a few steps away. 'Now you want to talk? *Now?* Twenty years later, you've finally grown up enough that you're considering settling down? Coming back and making amends when the worst is already over. How do I know you won't leave again?' She uttered those words with a quiet intensity, but they landed with Tess as if she had shouted them.

Getting to her feet herself, Tess backed away from the couch—drawn to the entrance. So that was it? The real issue—the crux of everything. Despite her declarations and actions, Zara wasn't any closer to trusting her than she'd been when she'd first arrived back in Invercaillie.

'Is it not enough that I'm here now?' she asked, though she knew the answer already. Still, Tess had resolved to tell Zara how she felt and she would do that. 'It's not enough that I love you?'

Something intangible rippled over Zara's expression, and then her entire body stilled. Eyes unblinking, she stared at Tess as the seconds stretched on.

'No,' Zara said, her voice raw, reaching out and then dropping her hand to her side. 'Please don't say that.'

Tess felt a sharp dagger hollowing in her chest. She

forced herself to stay in place, though every nerve screamed at her to retreat further. 'Why not? If that's what you want to hurl at me, you should at least know the truth.'

Zara took a stuttering breath, her lips moving without any words coming out. When she finally shook her head, Tess's chest caved in on itself and she knew she'd lost. She'd put herself out there, laying it all bare for Zara to see—and she hadn't wanted it.

'I don't know how to do this, Tess. Not at the speed that you're forcing me to go. Can't we just—?' Her voice cracking interrupted her mid-sentence. 'Things were fine right now. We can continue to figure things out.'

Tess shook her head, even though she wanted nothing more than to say yes. But where would that leave them? What if she spent years chasing something that didn't exist again? Where would that leave her?

'We are figuring it out. This *is* figuring it out.' It was figuring out that they didn't work together, but Tess wasn't sure she could say those words that bluntly. It might just tear her apart if she did.

They stood across from each other, the distance both shrinking and stretching in unbearable waves. Tess felt her world narrowing down to Zara's pained eyes and the breathless pause of everything in between them. She had to get out.

'I can't be around you if you won't even see me,' Tess said, the words breaking something open within her. 'If you don't trust me to take care of you.'

Zara's hand lifted, reaching for Tess with a desperation that struck Tess like a blow. 'You said you would be here.' Zara's voice wavered, pleading and raw. 'Stay.'

Tess felt herself teetering on a knife's edge, every part of her wanting to fall back into Zara's arms and pretend this conversation had never happened. But what then?

'I'm not leaving, and I'm saying that out loud because I want my intentions to be clear. You're the one who doesn't want to figure out how to move us forward.' Her heart twisted painfully as she moved to the back door leading to the cottage. Zara's eyes filled with silver, but they were beyond a point where she could turn back. She couldn't stay on maybe and might-be. Not any more.

Turned out she'd been wrong about their third chance in life. Earning back Zara's trust had been an effort doomed to fail from the start. Zara would never see her as anything else than the woman that fled twice. No matter how much Tess showed her she'd changed. At some point, she had to realise that Zara simply didn't want to see her in a different light.

That the connection was always meant to be fleeting. Maybe that was the reason they'd never found their way to each other until now.

The door closed behind her with a resounding click, her path cut off by the finality of that sound.

CHAPTER ELEVEN

The usual flurries of snow had turned into a steady rain over the last four weeks, turning the roads into a muddy mess. One that reflected Zara's mood with an accuracy that was downright scary.

Ever since that conversation with Tess—now almost a month ago—she'd been a wandering storm cloud to the great annoyance of Matt, who'd also become her dumping ground for any Tess-related rants she needed to get off her chest.

After their break-up—could she even call it a break-up when they hadn't agreed to anything formal?—she'd confided in her friend. Okay, maybe *confide* was a strong word. She'd rambled at him at an unintelligible pace and, because Matt was a nice person, he'd nodded and sneakily placed a new biscuit in her hand whenever the one before disappeared.

That had only been one evening. After that, Zara had vowed to snap back to her usual self and get on with life. Because any day now, Tess would disappear from her life as she pulled another vanishing act. It was what she did best. Her reaction to hearing Tess confess her love had *nothing* to do with her 'inability to let people take care of you' as Matt had put it.

What did he even know? Never mind that one of the last things Tess had told her had been exactly those words. *I can't be around you if you won't even see me. If you don't trust me to take care of you.*

The words stung far more than Zara was willing to admit, even in front of Matt. Because it wasn't true, was it? Zara was strong, dependable, steady. Those were the things she *had* to be because of how she'd grown up. With her parents' struggle to get a regular job and their general lack of interest in being parents, she'd relied on herself to keep moving forward. Even when the Sinclair family had all but adopted her, she still hadn't ever let go of that sense of self-reliance.

It was a good skill to have, was it not? Especially when she knew Tess was different—far more interested in her own situation than in being someone dependable. More like her parents.

Except that idea fell apart as Zara pushed the door to the house open and found the light in the kitchen still on. Just as she'd found it the last seven days as she'd worked the late shift in the surgery. Because Tess was still living in the cottage behind her house and had, for the duration of Zara's late shift, taken care of Helly.

Hanging her coat and toeing out of her shoes, she padded down the corridor and even though she'd found Tess in the exact same place every night she'd come home, she still wasn't prepared to see her. The breath rushed out of her lungs as she looked at Tess, her pale skin glowing under the dimmed light above them.

This part of their relationship hadn't changed. Tess had remained in Helly's life, helping Zara out whenever she needed and staying out of her way when she didn't.

Zara saw less of her, the handovers timed to perfection. Whenever Tess wanted to see Helly, Zara would make herself scarce, even though the protective part of her wanted to hover.

She was waiting for a sign that Tess was leaving, breaking Helly's heart the way she'd always suspected. As the weeks ticked by, she wasn't so sure any more the day would come.

'Hey,' Zara said, and, like every other night, her voice quavered enough that a flush crawled up her neck. She shouldn't feel this way in her own house, yet she did. The five minutes it took for Tess to get out after watching Helly for Zara was agony on repeat.

The decision to end things with Tess before they had gone too far hadn't made Tess any less beautiful. Even in her baggy plaid lounge trousers, an oversized shirt and her hair piled into a messy bun at the top of her head, she was still ravishing.

Tess looked up from her book, her face a carefully blank arrangement. Zara knew that because she, too, had practised this composed expression in front of the mirror since that evening a month ago.

They'd seen each other on the last day of Tess's contract, but other than that, she'd kept to herself. No more unannounced visits. Things had been awkward at work as well when Zara had been forced to introduce her to Tracey, who also didn't seem too happy to be back. Halfway through her shift, she'd found her colleague in the staff restroom bawling her eyes out because she missed her son.

Another thing to worry about on top of everything else.

The memory faded as Tess shut her book with a soft

thump. 'Helly's fast asleep.' Her tone was casual but held a breath of tenderness that always caused Zara to clench her hands to stop them from trembling.

'Thanks. I...appreciate you doing this.' That wasn't what she'd wanted to say, but those were safe words. Words that stayed as far away as possible from how she felt—what she really wanted to say to Tess.

Her eyes darted down to Tess's mouth, watching for the slight twitch of her lips that showed her amusement. But those intoxicating lips stayed pressed into a tight line. 'Nothing to thank me for. I enjoy any time I can get with Helly.'

That had been the state they'd lived in ever since Tess's contract had run out. Zara had thought the other woman would be on her way to her next job in a matter of days. With how there were far more open GP positions than people to fill them, she knew Tess had her pick of roles. But she'd remained in that cottage, texting her every day to arrange a time to see Helly.

'So does she,' Zara replied, and her traitorous little heart gave such a big leap when those words earned her a smile from Tess. A small one, like the ones she used to share with her whenever the three of them did story time on the couch.

Why was she still longing for those moments? Zara didn't know, but she was. Dear God, every time she caught Tess's lingering scent in the air, the memories from the weeks when things had been okay between them came rushing back at her.

Along with the knowledge that she couldn't have it. Not when Tess had one foot out of the door already.

Had she though? That thought had become harder

and harder to shake as the weeks went on and Tess remained rooted in that cottage. She'd not been to Tess's place, but she'd been observing her from a distance, trying to glean what Tess might have been up to. A part of her had expected to see boxes or suitcases stacking up as she readied to leave. But none of that had come to pass. To the point where she felt more than a bit weird about how she was manifesting this outcome.

Was she trying too hard to see something that was not there?

Tess picked up her book and stood. 'I guess I should get out of your hair,' she said with a glance towards the door, and was that resignation in her voice or something else? Whatever it was, it tugged at a place inside Zara's chest, yanking the next words out of her without her input.

'Stay.' The word echoed through the kitchen, settling between them. Why had she just asked her that? Judging by the crease deepening between Tess's brows, she had the same question. 'You just made yourself some tea, right? Don't hurry on my account. Enjoy it.'

Silence stretched again—something that, to her chagrin, had become far more normal between them than ever before—and Tess kept eyeing her long enough that the flush crawling up her neck spread further up, driving the heat to her cheeks.

Then, ever so slowly, Tess sat back down and curled her fingers through the handle of the mug. 'Thanks.'

Zara's heart was beating in her throat and her fingers picked at the seam of her T-shirt as she looked for an outlet for all the nervous energy bubbling up within her. She hadn't thought this scenario through. Hell, she hadn't even meant to ask Tess to stay when a different part of her brain had taken over and overwritten her will, leaving her stranded with the consequences of that impulsive action.

Not knowing what else to do, Zara wandered over to the fridge, her hand reaching for some yoghurt pouches she knew were in there. Her hand froze mid-grab when her eyes landed on the oven dish inside the fridge. Condensation had gathered on the cling film, but beneath it she could see the mouth-watering crust of a lasagne. Her stomach gave an instant growl at the sight.

'Oh wow,' Tess said.

At the same time as Zara pleaded, 'Please pretend you didn't hear that.'

Behind her, Tess chuckled, and Zara had to grip the handle of the fridge tighter as that sound rippled through her in all its warmth and familiarity. Being able to just be around her, maybe even joke around like this, should be what Zara strived for. Especially since Tess seemed determined to be a part of her life through Helly.

But if that was the case, why wouldn't they be together?

'Let me heat it up for you,' Tess said, pushing off her chair again and grabbing the lasagne out of the fridge.

'No, it's okay. I can do it.' Zara moved to intercept Tess, who gave her a sceptical look.

'I don't trust you, even with the microwave.'

'I'm not that hopeless,' Zara said as Tess slid the dish from her grip and set it on the counter. 'Not entirely, anyway.'

'It's not a problem.' Tess removed the cling film and turned to set the timer. Zara watched her, the easy way she plated the food, the tilt of her head as she fiddled with the microwave settings. It was like watching a memory in motion, those moments when they'd been so effortlessly in sync.

Yearning hit her right in the chest as the life she might have had with Tess manifested in front of her eyes. It looked exactly like what she glimpsed right this moment, with her coming home and finding Tess here.

But she couldn't have that. It wasn't real. Couldn't be because Tess…well, she hadn't left.

No, she was still here. And that small kernel of *something* at the back of her mind that had grown louder and more insistent as the weeks had gone on without Tess vanishing as Zara had expected was now screaming in her mind.

What if you were wrong?

Wrong that she would bail again. Wrong about pushing her away. Wrong about not trusting her.

'Really, I've got it,' Zara insisted, knowing full well how weak her protest sounded.

'Sit down, Ellis. I'm heating this up for you and then I'll be out of your way. Helly and I made this earlier, and she liked it so much, she was excited for her mum to try it.'

'Don't call me that.' The words left Zara's mouth before she could stop them, automatic and sharp. And the moment they landed, she regretted it.

Tess turned around to face her, leaning against the kitchen counter as the microwave buzzed behind her and the plate kept spinning. 'Why do you say that? You don't like it?'

Zara didn't answer. Not right away. Because the truth was more complicated than she could explain in one clean sentence. She didn't flinch when Helly called her

Mummy any more. Not really. What made her flinch was the idea that someone else might hear it and think she'd claimed something that wasn't hers.

'It's not that,' Zara mumbled. 'It's…it's how it might sound to someone else. Like I've overwritten Sabrina. That people will think I'm taking something that was hers.'

Zara stared down at the stone countertop of the kitchen island, splaying her hand on top of it. The polish had chipped away as her nails grew out, and she picked at the loose flakes as she sorted through all the thoughts tumbling inside her brain. All the while, Tess stood there in silence, only her taking a sip of tea occasionally breaking through the quiet.

'I know I'm her mother. Like…we had it all planned out. Both of our love lives had been such a disaster we'd decided to move on with our life plans as friends—platonic life partners. We both wanted more than one child, so we decided she would go first, and I would have Helly's sibling from the same donor.' Zara didn't know why she was telling all of this to Tess when not even Matt knew about this. She'd always thought it didn't matter because those plans were gone. How could she possibly have another child all by herself when she already felt guilty every time she needed to drop Helly off at Matt's or ask the day-care staff to keep her longer?

Maybe it had something to do with the fact that, over the last few months, Tess had been here whenever Zara had needed help from a second parental figure. She'd stepped up so often without Zara even having to ask for it in *so many* ways.

The mug clinked as Tess set it down on the counter. 'Were you planning on each being in the other child's life? I must admit, I don't know how platonic life-part-nerships work.'

Heat rushed to Zara's face as Tess repeated her words back at her. 'It's a real thing for some people. For us, it was more…something we saw on TikTok that just made sense. It fitted how we felt about each other, so we started using it.'

Tess simply nodded, her face not revealing any of her thoughts. It was silly to latch onto something like that, but her acceptance of what other people would have derided as *not a real thing* soothed something inside Zara. A wound that had never quite healed over ever since Sabrina's death. And it was because of this that she continued, 'And yes, we thought why not cut out all the volatility of romantic love and just co-parent our children together?'

That had been the plan until Sabrina had landed in the hospital. Zara still remembered the call from Callum, urging her to rush in. Her best friend hadn't been the only one to die that day. All their plans—the child Zara had wanted to carry—had faded away with Sabrina's last breath.

Tess's voice was low, but steady. 'That doesn't change the fact that you're the one who stayed. Who raised her. You've always been her mum. She's just finally saying it out loud.'

The words sat in Zara's chest like a warm stone, heavy but grounding. She looked up at Tess, and for one brief, dangerous second, she let herself wonder.

What if…?

What if she stopped resisting? What if she was wrong about Tess? What if there was something worth salvaging underneath all the years of tension and regret?

Zara wasn't sure if it was something in her expression, but Tess let out a trembling breath. She shook her head, as if to clear it, and before Zara could stop herself, she asked, 'What?'

'I...was hoping we could talk, but I hadn't expected this conversation to go this way. Last thing I want is to pile on.'

Zara's pulse quickened; she was unsure what the other woman was referring to. She wanted to talk? 'About what?'

'I...' Tess's lips thinned into a line, her eyes darting down to her cup. When she looked back up, the vulnerability in her eyes made Zara's breath stutter out of her. 'I still want this. Living beside you—parallel to you—has been torture for me. And I wonder if it's been the same for you. Or is it all in my head and I just need to find a way to move on?'

Zara blinked, the sudden pressure behind her eyes overwhelming. This wasn't a conversation she could have in the state she was in. Not when she herself had been so close to asking the same question—moving into the same space.

Except she couldn't. Nothing had changed since Zara had asked Tess to leave. They were the same people, were they not? Zara always waiting with bated breath for the moment Tess decided she was done here and...

She was still here, though.

Something in Zara's chest went brittle. She stood up too fast. 'Tess...'

'Just listen—'

'No,' Zara said, backing away. 'You don't get to bring this up again. We agreed—' She caught her breath, the edges of it frayed.

'We didn't agree on anything. You told me to leave and I left because I respect your choice. But if you would just listen to me…'

In the depths of her mind, she knew Tess had a point. She'd asked her to leave—had pushed her away, because she hadn't wanted to deal with the fallout she knew was waiting for her at the end of this relationship. Even though, for a few heartbreaking weeks, she'd let herself believe she could have it all.

'I can't do this any more.'

Zara stilled. 'Do what?'

'Stay in the back of this house, staring at you through windows, through walls, while my heart is breaking. While I'm begging you to let me in and you keep pretending you don't hear me.' Tess's voice cracked, but she kept going. 'It's not fair to me or you.'

The words hit Zara in a soft spot inside her. The proof of what Zara had been afraid of all this time smacking her right in the face. 'You're leaving? After promising to stay put?'

'I promised to stick around for as long as you wanted me. But you don't *want* me, Zara.' Tess pressed those words out through clenched teeth, the hurt underpinning them spearing right through Zara. 'You can't tell me you would stick around in the backyard of the woman you are desperately in love with, waiting for her to change her mind. You must know how cruel that would be.'

There they were again. The words that had been fluttering around her head—her heart—for the last month ever since Tess had first said them. She hadn't known what to do with that back then. Didn't know how to deal with it now, either.

'This…isn't about me. Or us. It's about Helly. You came here to be in her life and what? You'll just abandon her because of…' Zara couldn't finish the sentence because wasn't she as much to blame if Helly lost her aunt again? Because she didn't have a grip on her feelings, Helly would now suffer yet another loss.

'I'm not walking out of her life. As painful as it is to be around you, I'm never going to abandon my niece ever again. But I can't stay here looking at you from afar—wishing things were different. We need some distance.'

Zara shook her head, even though she knew that wasn't the whole truth. 'I don't. Things can stay exactly like this with you—'

'Fine, then *I* need some distance. Okay? Guess you were right about me and I can't be around you all this time without…' Tess shook her head, then grabbed her phone and stuffed it in the front pocket of her hoodie. 'It's slowly killing me to be around you and not touch you, not kiss you. I *can't* do it right now.'

Zara's breath stuttered out of her as her mind held onto Tess's words. Her body's reaction was visceral, her muscles clenching and all her hair standing on end. With legs that had developed a mind of their own, she took one step towards Tess, putting her right in the other woman's personal space.

Tess tilted her head to look down at her, and they were so close her breath swept over Zara's face. She could close the distance by standing on her toes and grabbing what she knew would be a world-shattering kiss.

Tess was never going to stay.

That thought sobered Zara. She jerked back from Tess, whose lips had been only a few centimetres away from hers. Taking a few extra steps back, she swallowed a trembling breath and reminded herself that this exact moment had been the reason why she'd decided to end it when she had.

Tess was *never* going to stay.

'You should go.' She forced the words out around the growing lump in her throat because she knew how close she was to abandoning them altogether. That was the effect Tess had on her even now, with her heart broken into pieces.

'We have to—no, you're right. I'll leave.' Tess skirted around the kitchen island towards the back entrance of the house. Her hand hovered over the handle, fingers grasping at the air above it. 'I'm determined to be a part of Helly's life regardless of how we might feel about each other.'

Zara nodded, not trusting herself to say any more, and then watched—again—as Tess retreated from her and left the house. Behind her, the microwave pinged, and she spun around to look at it, the sudden reminder of Tess's presence staring at her in the form of a small piece of lasagne.

It was for the best. That was what Zara told herself as she grabbed a fork with shaky fingers and dug in, ignoring how each bite reminded her of Tess and their future that had come crumbling down around her.

CHAPTER TWELVE

A FEW PEOPLE sat in the waiting area of A & E when Tess stepped through the doors. Even though the GP clinic was at the other end of the building, the familiarity of it hit her right in the chest. It hadn't been that long since she'd stopped working as the GP in Invercaillie, just over a month, yet the space still felt like a second home to her.

People nodded at her with open smiles as she crossed the waiting room to access the staffroom where Callum had asked her to meet. Tess wasn't sure why she'd come. Or why the nurse wanted to talk to her, though she had a pretty good idea what it might be about. And that she didn't want to talk about it.

Tess found a place one village over available in a few weeks. She'd have preferred to stay in Invercaillie, but there were no available places. It was close enough so she could still see Helly whenever she wanted. Things with Zara had become untenable and though she wasn't sure how they would navigate things in the future, she would find a way to make it work. After interviewing over the last few weeks, she'd received an offer from a tele-health company to be a part of a virtual GP surgery app.

The way the conversation had gone with Zara—her final attempt at mending fences rejected—she needed to leave the cottage. Even though it hurt to step away, Tess needed some distance to consider her feelings—to rebuild the thing inside her that had caved in when Zara had pushed her away.

Callum looked up from the notepad he'd been scribbling on when Tess walked in, greeting her with a warm smile that was like a punch in the gut. God, she would miss this goofy man that had become her friend. Would miss this building and the people who worked here. She'd even miss Silvano's weekly calls, even though the conversations always went the same way when it came to his brother's condition. But he cared, and Tess didn't mind repeating herself as she reassured him.

Things would be much lonelier working in front of her computer all day.

'Good to see you, lass. Have a seat.' He kicked the opposite chair out from under the desk, and Tess laughed because such a graceless invitation was so quintessentially Callum.

Taking the offered seat, she leaned back to watch him. 'You want your own personal goodbye? I'm not moving *that* far.'

She'd told the nurse the news last week, the day after she and Zara had another falling out, and, until this moment, he'd pretended he hadn't heard anything. Even in his message today, he'd not acknowledged the reason he'd asked her to meet, but it could only be about one thing.

'You know when I asked you about whether you already had a new fancy job lined up, that wasn't meant as an encouragement,' he said as he set down the pen.

Tess snorted, not letting the sinking feeling inside her take root. God, how she hated goodbyes. Leaving was so much simpler when no one would miss you.

That wasn't the case here. Tess had bonded with people, even made friends in the case of Callum.

Had found love and then lost it.

'It was bound to happen. My position at the clinic was only to cover Tracey's parental leave,' she said, trying too hard to sound casual. By the way Callum's lips pulled downward, she already knew she hadn't convinced him.

Fair enough. She'd barely convinced herself. Only problem with that was that it left her exposed to whatever Callum had cooked up to get her to stay. Because she knew the only reason he'd asked her to come here was because he wanted her to stay.

'So, what are you running from this time?'

'I'm not—wait, this time?' Tess didn't know why that was the part her brain clung to. Maybe because, unlike the other part, she hadn't expected it.

'I mean, you've been through the wringer, I'll give you that. It's understandable that you'd want some time to yourself. But I thought that was why you'd hidden away in the cottage for the last month.' His words stood in dizzying contrast to his gentle tone and calming smile.

'I-I don't understand what you expect me to do. I certainly can't live in that little cottage for the rest of my days. That's not fair to either of us. Zara wants to move on and I need to give her that space.' She'd expected Callum to ask her to stay, to find any and all arguments he could cobble together to change her mind. But these were…accusations?

'Ah, finding a position didn't seem so hard, considering you've already lined up something that lets you work remotely.' Callum waved his hand in front of his face dismissively. 'Did you even consider staying put?'

Tess didn't answer. The string tying itself around her chest cut off the air she needed to form words.

The truth was, she hadn't needed to move at all. The job didn't require relocation—it was entirely remote. She could've stayed in the cottage. Kept walking the same paths to the clinic, the little coffee shop she'd come to enjoy, the house she still caught herself calling home.

But staying on Zara's property, seeing her across the garden every morning, hearing her laugh echo through the walls—that had felt impossible. Staying would've meant waiting. And Tess wasn't sure what she was waiting for any more.

Callum raised an eyebrow. 'So you found a job that lets you live anywhere and chose to move one village over.'

Tess let out a sigh, head drooping forward. 'With all that has happened, I don't know—maybe some space will be good for both of us. You know? This thing between us has been brewing for so long, maybe we just needed to try it. Now that we have and we've realised it doesn't work, I think I need to be elsewhere to…reset.'

It all sounded so plausible. Sensible.

Cowardly.

'I'm not in the business of telling you how you should feel. What?' Callum widened his eyes when Tess shot him an incredulous look that he waved off with a laugh. 'Okay, fine. I'm all in people's business. Sue me.'

'At least you can admit it,' Tess muttered, though she was grateful to have someone to confide in.

Since they'd never done anything couple-y in public, no one in the village had any clue what had happened between them. That was until Callum had confronted her one evening, sharing his suspicion with her. Tess had lasted only a few minutes before she'd spilled her guts in a cathartic rant. It had only been afterwards that she'd realised she had really needed that.

'Anyway, since I am in everyone's business, I know exactly that what you're doing now is what you *always* do. And I think no one has ever called you out on it. So let me be the first.' His voice was still gentle, though Callum's expression had morphed into a rather smug one.

'You told yourself this would never work because she'd push you away, and the moment it got hard, you let her,' he continued when Tess remained quiet.

'She did push me away!' Tess shot back, then closed her eyes. In a smaller voice, she added: 'Again.'

'And you're running. Again.'

Tess felt the words ripple through her, undeniable and brutal in their truth. He was right, of course, but she couldn't just admit that. Something inside her refused. What was she supposed to do when the woman she loved didn't love her back? 'I'm not running,' she said, even though it was barely a whisper.

Callum shook his head, holding her gaze with an intensity that made it impossible to look away. 'Sabrina told me about you two. What it was like growing up with her sister and her best friend making goo-goo eyes at each other.'

'Goo-goo eyes? That's not a real expression.'

He waved her words away. 'She said when she was younger she hadn't really understood you. Hadn't understood how differently your parents had treated you. And so when she saw your interest in Zara, her instinct was to be defensive. You got all the attention from your parents. Why couldn't she have something for herself?'

Tess stiffened at that thought, her own defences clicking into place the way they always did when her parents came up. 'I could have done without that attention. Nothing good has ever come from it. Their pressure was the reason I left Invercaillie behind.'

Callum nodded. 'She got there, even if it took her some time. But what I know through these conversations is that she cared about you, and she regretted not supporting you earlier.'

Pressure increased all around Tess to where every breath became a struggle to swallow. That was what Sabrina had thought? She struggled to believe it. No, that wasn't it. As one of the few friends she'd made in town, Callum wouldn't lie to her or sell her some fiction to make her feel better. If he was telling her about her sister's thoughts, then it was because Sabrina had confided in him.

But why hadn't Zara told her that? They had spoken about Sabrina, but…

'I'm not sure Zara ever knew this about her,' Callum said, reading her thoughts off her face. 'You all carry some guilt around for how things have turned out, and that was true for Sabrina as well. She wished she'd been more supportive of you two, but I don't think she knew how to express that to Zara with how things had progressed ever since your parents' funeral.'

'You are way too well informed about my life for how little *I* told you about it,' Tess mumbled, clinging onto that thread so she didn't have to look at the others as her insides unravelled.

Callum gave a gruff laugh. 'When you work in health care in such a small village, people start to talk really fast to fill the air. You'd be surprised about the things I know.'

He took a sip of his tea before continuing. 'So, what's the harm in giving it a shot? It seems to me like you've never really tried. Not fully.'

Tess was still reeling from all the things he'd just told her. She shook her head, then stopped and nodded as she let herself consider what he'd said. Was she running? Had she stood her ground or let Zara push her away, grabbing at the first excuse to give up?

'Fine,' she breathed, barely audible. 'Maybe I do run.'

Callum waited, his silence more patient than she could bear. She shook her head, wishing it were as easy to shake loose the thoughts tangling inside her mind. 'But Zara pushed me away first. She doesn't want me here.'

The nurse leaned forward, clasping his hands together as he studied her with that gentle, unwavering look she'd grown to appreciate. And dread. 'Did she? Because from where I'm standing, Zara doesn't push away anyone she doesn't care about. She pushes people away because she cares too much. You know better than anyone how much she's lost. But she's steadfast. She had to be because there was no other choice for her.'

The words struck Tess like a physical blow, each syllable unravelling another carefully constructed lie she'd told herself. Zara had never fled—she had stayed in Invercaillie through every storm life had thrown at her. Stayed for Helly, stayed for Sabrina's memory, stayed *with* Tess, even when it had hurt them both.

And if Tess left now, she'd be the one turning her back on all of it, forfeiting any chance they had left. The realisation sank deep, settling cold and heavy in the pit of her stomach.

'I can't leave,' she whispered finally, the truth heavy on her tongue. 'Not like this. Not without really trying.' She met Callum's eyes, feeling both relief and terror at the clarity of her admission. 'Zara means too much.'

A slow, knowing smile spread across Callum's face. 'About bloody time you realised it.'

Zara moved around the kitchen on autopilot, washing the dishes she'd already cleaned twice, reorganising mugs that hadn't moved a centimetre since yesterday, doing anything to avoid meeting Matt's probing gaze. He sat at the kitchen island as silence stretched between them, watching her pointless routine. His quiet scrutiny prickled against her skin, an uncomfortable reminder that she was fooling exactly no one.

'Okay, I feel like I have to say something,' he finally said, and Zara paused her pointless pottering to glare at him over her shoulder.

'You don't *have to*. What you mean is you can't help yourself butting into something I told you to stay away from.' They'd had a conversation similar to this one every time they'd seen each other since her and Tess's second big fight. Actually, thinking back now, she realised Matt had been going on about this for a solid month. 'Who died and made you the king of the Tara fan club?'

Zara didn't like the smirk tugging at Matt's lips one bit. 'We've decided on the ship name Zess and not Tara.'

That was absurd enough that it got Zara's attention. Letting go of the mug she'd been about to stuff at the back of the cupboard, she turned around fully. '*Zess?* Are you for real? When Tara was right there?'

Matt shrugged. 'It's what the club decided.'

'This joke has gone far enough that I feel compelled to ask: there's no fan club, right?' Matt's ensuing laugh was less than reassuring. After keeping quiet for the last month, Zara had finally given in to the need to talk to someone about her situation with Tess and had spilled her guts to Matt. Not only because he was her friend but also to get advice. Because even though Tess had reacted the way Zara had always suspected she would by leaving, she'd hit on an important thing within Zara that she was finally ready to talk about.

That she was Helly's mother. And that she now understood people would never judge her for that or think she was taking something that wasn't hers. Because Helly was her child and had been since the moment she'd been born. It had taken her far too long to get comfortable with the idea, but she was ready now. Matt's enthusiasm and support in taking that conscious step had helped her get her head straight.

Almost straight. There was still the matter of Tess. Or rather, the matter of Matt not shutting up about her when Zara was ready to move on.

'There's me and Callum—'

'Okay, that's fair enough,' Zara mumbled.

'—and the knitting circle that meets at Mabel's cafe on Saturdays.'

'What?' Zara gaped at Matt, who gave her yet another casual shrug.

'What can I tell you? You two might have thought you were being subtle, but anyone with eyes could see the sparks flying between you. People *without* eyes might have even noticed if they came close enough to you two.'

Zara plopped down on the chair next to Matt, grabbing the mug of tea he was offering. She stared down at the milky contents of the mug, tracing the steam curling through the air. So what he was telling her was that… 'Everyone knows? About me and Tess?'

If Matt was surprised by the quiver in her voice, he didn't show it. 'I don't think they *knew*. They kind of filled in the blanks in between some moments people witnessed around you two. Don't worry about it too much. The fan club was cheering you on. Which is why it breaks my heart that I'll have to tell them it's all over.'

'I'm really sorry for this burden I hoisted upon you, Matt.' Zara rolled her eyes, though she couldn't deny the sting the words caused inside her.

The night of their conversation had left her reeling. Tess had stood there—heart in her throat, voice shaking—offering one more chance for something real. And Zara had said nothing. Pulled away.

She'd wanted to reach back. To say she'd made a mistake. That she loved her. That she was finally ready to stop running. Except Tess had dropped the bomb right at her feet. She was moving out. Needed some distance between them.

Two days later, Callum had mentioned at the clinic that Tess had found a place one village over, though he hadn't been clear on her moving date. Tess hadn't told her directly. Hadn't explained anything or followed up.

And that had felt like confirmation. Not that Tess was leaving Invercaillie—just that she was leaving her.

'I mean, you could try a little bit harder. Who knows what would happen then?' Matt said, though his tone wasn't quite as glib as his words.

She looked up from her tea with narrowed eyes. 'Try a little harder? Matt, *she's* leaving.'

'After *you* told her to leave.' The calmness in his voice sent her tumbling from annoyance to fury.

'You know that's not how it is. What you're suggesting is that she only decided to leave once we broke things off, but that's not how it happened. She...' Zara's voice trailed off, the thread she'd been following inside her head ending in a tangled mess. She had no idea how things had gone down any more at this point. Zara had asked Tess to leave. That was true. But Tess... 'She's been planning her exit ever since she got here.'

Matt shook his head. 'How can you say that with such a certainty? Didn't she tell you she'd be here for as long as you wanted her? Then you telling her you didn't want her could be interpreted as a clear signal for her to move on—potentially to another place.'

Her fingers closed around the mug, pressing against it as if that were going to solve all her problems. When had their conversation taken this turn? Zara couldn't even remember asking Matt to stick around. He'd brought a sleeping Helly over, and after she'd settled her down in her bed, she'd come back into the kitchen to find Matt fixing them some tea.

'Why are you ambushing me?' This was the last thing she needed right now when the shock of Tess's actions still ran so deep. When she could still remember how close she'd been to taking it all back and telling her about her feelings. What a mistake that would have been, knowing what she knew now.

Matt let out a sigh. Silence stretched between them and then she felt his hand come down between her shoulder blades with his thumb drawing a soothing circle. 'I'm sorry. It wasn't my intention to ambush you. What I'm trying to do is talk about this before it's too late.'

'Too late?' What did he mean? It was already too late. They were done.

A frown appeared on Matt's face as he said, 'Tess hasn't left yet.'

Zara let out a shaky breath, trying to wrestle down the stubborn knot forming in her throat. 'You weren't there, Matt. I've seen her pack her things. She's ready to get out.'

'And did you ask her why?' Matt asked, unrelenting but kind. 'Did you give her a chance to explain herself?'

'I—' The denial died on her lips as the conversation replayed in her mind. 'Tess said she needed some space. She told me she needed to leave. I would have been content keeping things the way they were—might have even…'

Zara let out a groan from deep inside her bones, letting go of the mug and covering her face with her hands instead. She couldn't answer his questions truthfully.

Not without exposing parts of her she'd rather keep hidden away. It was easier that way. If she didn't acknowledge things, they couldn't hurt her. Tess couldn't hurt her if Zara refused to rely on her.

Except hadn't she tried to have it both ways? Keep her distance enough so she still felt in control but also have Tess close enough for her to get her support and affection. Her love.

'She told me she loves me.' Zara wasn't sure how relevant this was to their conversation, but the words just popped out. As if she needed someone else to witness them and acknowledge the depth of this thing. How far Zara had let it run without intervening.

'What do you think about that?' Matt asked. Of course he would, even though she'd much rather he tell her how she should feel. But her friend was also a psychologist and he would make her work for this, even though she wasn't sure what *this* was.

Zara took several breaths, thoughts twisting and turning inside her, but all of them spinning around one axis. One truth that she hadn't admitted to herself out loud or in the privacy of her own head. But even without her explicit acknowledgement, the thought was there and her stubborn refusal to accept it wasn't changing the fact that—

'I love her, too.'

Silence spread between them with nothing but the gentle wind rattling against the windows now and then. Zara held her breath, waiting for the heaviness to settle in as it had in the entire month since she and Tess had their falling out. But the opposite happened now. A calmness washed over her as those words settled into their supposed place inside her.

They felt so *right* that even the thought of saying them out loud to Tess couldn't frighten her. No, that wasn't entirely true. She was scared of putting herself out there and voluntarily giving someone this power over her. But hadn't she already given that piece of her to Tess in the last few months when they'd grown closer? How many times had Tess told her she would be there as long as Zara wanted her?

She'd been the one to tell her they needed to break things off before they got too serious. And now she was blaming Tess when all she'd done was act on the signals she'd got from Zara. Really, all of this had started with Zara.

Would she be able to end it, too?

'I don't want to lose her,' Zara said, the words coming out so much quieter than intended.

'Then don't,' Matt said, as if it were that simple.

'I told her she should go. I can't take that back,' Zara said, picking up the mug with shaky hands and taking a sip.

Matt gave her a long, unyielding look. 'The Zara I know is not afraid to try—even when things feel impossible.' He placed his hand on the side of her arm, a gentle touch of reassurance, and she didn't flinch away from it this time.

A decision was forming inside her chest, loosening in small, determined breaths. She'd been so afraid of losing Tess that she hadn't even dared to fight for her. 'What if her decision to leave is final?' Zara asked, but there was less defeat in the question now. 'What if she doesn't want me back?'

'Then at least you'll know you did everything possible.'

Zara nodded, setting her mug down with finality. The shaking stopped as the decision solidified in her mind. Matt was right. She couldn't—shouldn't— have stepped away from Tess without giving her a proper shot at this. Instead of keeping her mind open to how different things were not just between them but in life in general, she'd focused on a small snapshot of time that confirmed a behaviour in Tess that Zara had wanted to avoid. Except this had been a purely self-preserving instinct. If she didn't let the picture of Tess change in her mind, she could keep herself safe.

Being safe wasn't what Zara wanted any more. Because how had it served her life? It had taken her this long to accept her role in Helly's life when her little girl had been expressing herself so well—calling her Mummy.

And Tess had done the same. She'd told her she loved her, and, rather than embrace it, Zara had pushed her away.

'I have to talk to her. You're right,' Zara said, and this time there was something else in her voice. A strength and determination that hadn't been there in their conversation until now. 'Will you hang around here while I go talk to her?'

She glanced over to the cottage as she said that, watching Tess's shadow move around behind the drawn curtains. Zara had to speak to her before she lost her nerve. Before she could think of just how many ways this might blow up in her face.

'Of course. Take your time,' Matt said with a smile, letting go of her arm.

Zara stood up, hovering around her friend for a moment before throwing her arms around him and pulling him into a quick but tight hug. Then she was out of the door, not bothering with her coat or anything else to keep her warm. She'd be back in a warm place soon enough. The only question was, would it be in her own home or Tess's cottage?

CHAPTER THIRTEEN

SHOULD SHE UNPACK the boxes now or keep them as they were just in case? Ever since Tess had got back to the cottage, she'd stared at the few cardboard boxes stacked in the corner of her home. A part of her was impressed that she even had accumulated enough stuff here in Invercaillie to fill these many boxes.

She should unpack them, right? It would be tempting fate to keep them all packed up, even if she hadn't spoken to Zara yet. Or was it tempting fate to unpack them so brazenly when she didn't even know if the other woman wanted her in her life still? She wouldn't blame Zara if she held her temporary flight against her.

Tess shook her head, then stepped up to the tower of boxes and tore the top of the first one open. No, she was staying, regardless of whether Zara wanted her or not. Maybe not as a couple. That was still up in the air. But she'd stay for Helly. She would be part of her family, full stop.

She was halfway through the second box, piling up clothes, books, and some kitchen utensils she'd acquired over the last few months, when a knock came on the door.

Tess froze into place, the item in her hand forgotten.

Her heart lurched into her throat, getting stuck there for several beats. No one had knocked on her door since, well, when she moved in some months ago, really. Whenever Zara had needed something from her, she'd texted her since she didn't like leaving Helly by herself for even the few moments it took to get here.

Tess placed the spatula on the pile of clothes and straightened, her limbs moving as if through a thick fog. She took a bracing breath and walked to the door, hoping yet terrified of finding precisely who she thought she'd find on the other side. Only why was she here?

She saw Zara through the glass door before she opened it and even though she'd known it could only be her, the shock still rippled through her when their eyes met. Zara stood there, her expression not letting Tess glimpse the reason for her appearance.

'Zara,' Tess breathed out, barely above a whisper.

'Hey.' She stood at the doorstep, short sleeves exposing her arms enough that Tess could see the goosebumps trailing up. Her eyes drifted over Zara's shoulder to the house, where the lights in the kitchen were still on.

'Is Helly okay?' Something urgent must have happened if she'd left Helly by herself.

'What?' Zara followed her gaze, her expression now slipping into flustered, and then she shook her head. 'Oh yeah, she is fine. Matt is at the house.'

'Oh.' Tess's relief lasted only a moment before she looked back at Zara, the question around why the other woman was standing in the freezing cold without even a coat on.

'Can I...?' Zara shivered, and that was enough to shake Tess out of her stupor.

'Of course, yeah.' She stepped aside, waving her in and then closing the door behind her.

Turning around, she opened her mouth to ask why Zara had come, but paused when she saw Zara pick up the spatula she'd just put down. She weighed the utensil in her hand, slapping the rubber end against her open palm. Then, with much more speed than Tess had anticipated, Zara whirled around.

'You're all packed up and ready to leave?' There was an edge to her voice, the words reminiscent of the fight they'd had the other night. But the tone… Something wasn't right. This wasn't an accusation, but rather— panic?

No. Was it?

Tess's heart took a stumble at the thought. 'Well, no. Actually, I was…unpacking?' Her inflection went up at the last word, turning it into a question. Because it *was* a question, right? Not whether she should be unpacking, because Tess had already decided she was here to stay, no matter what. No, the question was how Zara felt about that.

'Unpacking?' Zara looked down at the spatula and then back up at Tess, making her wish she could read her expression. But too many conflicting signals were coming at her, and Tess was *so desperate* to see that one thing in Zara's eyes she was hoping for against hope that she wasn't sure she wouldn't make it up at the slightest sign of affection.

'Yeah, I was going to talk to you about it. Though I hadn't decided when, since I just came to the conclusion today.' Tess paused, unsure if this was how she wanted to say it. Only a few hours had passed between her conversation with Callum and this moment, most of which she'd spent agonising over whether she should unpack her boxes. Now that she stood in front of Zara with nothing to say, she realised she should have thought about how to share all her news with the other woman.

Especially since Zara asked in a shaky voice, 'Talk to me about what?'

A lump appeared in Tess's throat, partly because of how she'd navigated herself into this spot, but also...was that a glimmer of hope she heard in Zara's voice? Or was she projecting the thing she really wanted onto her?

She took a deep breath, selecting the right words in her head and then immediately forgetting about them the second she opened her mouth. 'About unpacking. And staying here. I don't want to—that is, I'm not leaving. But only if—'

The rest of her sentence disappeared—right into Zara's mouth as she pressed her lips on Tess's. The kiss rocked through Tess, and would have knocked her off her feet if Zara hadn't wound her hands into her shirt and hauled her close.

Tess stiffened in shock, her brain needing a few seconds to catch up. When she did, her hands came around Zara to press her closer, her mouth opening as she moved on instinct. A well-rehearsed dance her body knew how to respond to even without any of her active input. As if Zara was the other half and only when they were touching did she become the person she was meant to be.

Her heart thundered in her chest, drowning out any coherent thought. All that mattered was that Zara was here, with her, choosing her. The realisation made Tess's knees go weak, and she had to lean against Zara.

When they parted, Zara's eyes were wide, as if she couldn't believe what she'd just done either. Her hands still fisted into Tess's shirt, anchoring the two of them together as she searched Tess's expression. She must have found what she was looking for, because the look on her face softened.

'I want you to stay.' Her voice came out breathy and so reminiscent of how she sounded right after waking up.

Tess swallowed against the storm of emotions inside her conjured up by those words. A part of her still wasn't sure if she hadn't made up the entire episode in her head and that loneliness had hit her so hard, this was all just some very strange dream.

But then Zara leaned forward and planted another kiss on her mouth, softer this time than the impulsive one from a few seconds ago. When she withdrew, Zara looked at her and all the wild and untamed emotions tumbling through Tess were reflected in the other woman's eyes.

'I came here to ask you to stay. To tell you that I was an idiot for even suspecting you of bailing when you've shown me time and again that you wanted to stay. That you *wanted* to be with me.' Tess stepped forward, sliding her hand over Zara's cheek and pulling her closer, but Zara shook her head. 'Sorry, I didn't mean to ambush you. When I heard you say you wanted to talk to me about staying...'

Zara took a deep breath and Tess had to stop herself from sliding her mouth over those lush lips again. She knew this conversation was important, but the primal part of her that had missed *touching* this woman screamed at her to back her against the wall and drop onto her knees so she could worship her until she screamed.

'That's what I meant,' Tess said, forcing her gaze away from Zara's mouth. 'This. Us.'

Zara let go of the breath she'd been holding, the warm air skating over Tess's skin. 'You forgive me for not seeing what was right in front of me? I hope you know this was *all* my fault. I was the one carrying around these old insecurities about having to go through everything on my own. With my parents never being around and then Sabrina…'

Zara's voice tapered off into a watery laugh that had Tess wrapping her into a tight embrace until there wasn't a millimetre of space between them. 'There's nothing to forgive, Zara. I *did* run. Making my presence in your life contingent on how much you wanted me wasn't fair. I should have stayed here because *I* wanted it and because you are worth any fight. But I'm not going anywhere. Because I—'

Zara surged forward, interrupting her with another kiss. When her mouth opened and her taste flooded over Tess's tongue, she shuddered as need pooled deep inside her core. That was the effect Zara had on her and even two decades apart hadn't changed that. She was as crazy about her now as she'd ever been.

When Zara wrenched her mouth away from hers, she felt the absence of her grab at her bones. 'I love you, Tess. I've been in love with you for a while now and I'm sorry it took me so long to say it. You too are worth any fight and I— Stay. With me and Helly. For good.'

Tess's heart slammed against her ribcage so fiercely

she felt dizzy. Those words—words she'd dreamed about hearing—now hung in the air, bright and undeniable. Her hands tightened against Zara's back, fingers clutching the fabric as she held onto her, anchoring herself in this perfect moment.

'You mean it?' Tess whispered. She searched Zara's eyes, desperate for confirmation, even though everything in Zara's expression already told her the truth.

'I do,' Zara replied. Her voice wavered, eyes shining with unshed tears. 'I was so scared, Tess. Scared of losing you, scared of trusting someone enough to let them stay. But I'm done running from it. I want you with me. Always.'

Relief and joy coursed through Tess, spreading warmth into every part of her body. She leaned in again, brushing her lips against Zara's. 'I love you too,' she breathed between kisses, pouring everything she felt into each touch. 'Always have. Always will.'

Zara let out a small, shaky laugh, the tension finally leaving her body as she melted into Tess's embrace. 'Good. Because I have a feeling Helly's already pretty attached to you too. It would be a shame to disappoint her.'

Tess laughed, pressing her forehead against Zara's as happiness bubbled within her, pure and overwhelming. 'I'll never let either of you down again. I promise.'

'I believe you,' Zara said, and the quiet strength in her words made Tess's heart swell.

They stood there for a long moment, locked in each other's embrace, the quiet around them a soothing balm after weeks of uncertainty and pain. When Zara finally drew back slightly, her eyes sparkled with gentle humour. 'But if you're staying, maybe we should get these boxes unpacked?'

Tess chuckled, pressing a kiss to Zara's temple. 'Maybe later. I have a different idea first.'

Zara's eyebrows rose, a smile curving her lips. 'Oh?'

Tess traced her fingers gently along Zara's jaw, drawing her towards the bedroom. 'Let me show you exactly how happy I am about staying.'

CHAPTER FOURTEEN

One year later

SUNLIGHT SPILLED THROUGH the lace curtains, casting golden patterns across the worn wooden tabletop. Tess poured steaming coffee into mismatched ceramic mugs, the rich aroma blending with the comforting scent of freshly toasted bread Zara had prepared. Helly, perched in her chair, swung her legs, chattering about her up-coming birthday between mouthfuls of jam-smeared toast.

'Auntie!' Helly squealed, reaching out to tug on Tess's sleeve, her eyes bright and wide with anticipation.

'Yes, sweetheart?' Tess bent down to match the girl's earnest gaze.

'Can we have cake? A big one with chocolate and sprinkles?'

Tess laughed, glancing over at Zara, who was already smiling into the mug Tess had put in front of her. 'I think we can manage that, don't you?'

Zara nodded, amusement sparkling in her eyes. 'Anything for our little birthday girl.'

Helly giggled, seemingly satisfied as she returned to her breakfast, humming as she spread more jam onto her toast. Tess's heart swelled at the ease of it all—their quiet, domestic morning had become a cherished routine, a comforting confirmation of the life they'd built together.

When she'd returned to Invercaillie a year ago, she hadn't expected her life to look this way. She'd returned here with her pride bruised and her shoulders weighed down by the unresolved feelings that had haunted her ever since her sister's death. All she'd looked for in those days had been a connection to Helly and a place to stay as she figured out how to put her life back together.

What she hadn't expected was Zara to breeze into her life and upend everything in it.

'I've already ordered the cake. Can you pick it up? I promised I'd stay a bit longer after work and help Callum plan the blood drive.' Zara leaned against Tess's side as she stepped closer, her arm coming around Zara's shoulder.

'You know I suggested the blood drive as a joke, yes? There's no way our little hospital needs so much blood.' Callum had also tried to rope Tess back into planning this thing, but she had declined. She was still doing remote work for the virtual clinic she had signed up with. As it had turned out, that gave her plenty of time between patients to look after Helly while Zara was at work. She sometimes missed being around people, though for those occasions she'd joined the Saturday knitting circle, which had a new gossip focus now that she and Zara were officially an item.

'Yeah, but everyone had loads of fun baking cookies. Plus, the blood centre in Inverness got in touch asking if we were doing it again. Apparently, we have quite a few

AB-positive people in our little village.' Zara smiled at her and even though Tess had woken up to this smile for the last year, she still wasn't used to it. Knew she would never get tired of it for the rest of her life.

Tess leaned down, pressing a gentle kiss against Zara's temple, lingering for just a moment to breathe her in. Zara relaxed further against her side, letting out a contented sigh that felt like a promise.

'Chocolate cake with sprinkles and an oversized village blood drive,' Tess teased, laughing against Zara's hair. 'Who knew this would be my life?'

Zara looked up at her, eyes sparkling. 'Happy with your choices?'

Tess didn't hesitate, her heart full and sure in a way she'd never thought possible. 'Happiest I've ever been.'

Helly interrupted their quiet moment, waving a sticky hand in the air, jam smeared across her fingers. 'More toast, Auntie!'

They both laughed, and as Tess reached for another slice of bread, she felt Zara's hand slip into hers beneath the table. She gave it a squeeze, soaking in the warmth of the moment—the easy laughter, the simple comfort of a shared breakfast. The bright future stretched out in front of them.

She had found home, she realised. Not in Invercaillie itself, not even in the cosy kitchen filled with morning sunlight—but with Zara and Helly. Exactly where she belonged.

* * * * *

If you enjoyed this story, check out these other great reads from Luana DaRosa

Faking It with the Doctor Prince
Falling for Her Miami Rival
Hot Nights with the Arctic Doc
Pregnancy Surprise with the Greek Surgeon

All available now!

A FLING WITH THE ER DOC

SUE MacKAY

MILLS & BOON

CHAPTER ONE

'SHAUN, I NEED you here. Now.' Emergency doctor Nikki Marlow didn't wait for a reply, if there was one coming. Instead, she got on with making an incision to insert a tube into the chest of the woman writhing in agony on the board in front her. 'Pneumothorax. I concur with the paramedic's diagnosis of fractured ribs being the cause.'

'Tell me when you're ready and I'll insert the tube,' Dr Shaun Elliott said as he joined Nikki. Running a hand down the woman's right side to her pelvis and lower to her hips, he reported back. 'More injuries here.'

'I'm making the incision between the third and fourth ribs.' As she cut in, a nurse swabbed the site. Then it was done, and she held the incision open and nodded at Shaun.

'Here we go.' His fingers firmly pushed the tube through the incision, then stopped. He turned the tube further to the right, pressed again, and it went into place. 'I'll hold it while you stitch it.'

Nikki took a threaded needle from the nurse standing opposite her. 'Thanks, Georgie.' As she worked, she asked Shaun, 'Do you think there're more fractures elsewhere?'

'Her pelvis feels soft, as if it's been shattered, plus I'm not sure her hip's in much better shape.'

'I'll call radiology as soon as I'm done here, and also

let the surgical unit know the first patient's ready and needs to be taken to Theatre to deal with the pneumothorax before anything else.'

'Want me here, or should I attend the patient who's being placed on the next bed? He's got fractured femurs and abdominal injuries.'

The second victim had arrived. Two down, five to come, and those were only the seriously injured. Nikki shuddered at the thought of a bus careering into pedestrians on a crossing. An image that kept her awake many nights flicked across her mind. A small boy running away from his mum onto a busy city road right in front of a speeding car. Hideous. Terrifying. 'Yes, Shaun, you go to him. Take Sarah with you.' The junior doctor looked pale but determined to deal with whatever was required in the coming hours. 'Sarah, do as Shaun says and you'll be fine.'

Sarah flicked her a tight look. 'Of course.'

Shaun gave them both a smile. 'We've got this.'

'I know we have.' Nikki ignored the stunning smile that the new doctor turned on easily and focused on her patient, leaving the other two to get on with theirs. The woman's abdomen was swollen, probably from an internal haemorrhage. 'I need a phone—'

'I'm here.' A surgeon spoke from right behind her. 'Pneumothorax, I heard. Fill me in on everything.'

Nikki gave him a relieved smile. 'Unconfirmed fractured ribs, punctured lungs. Haven't had time to arrange radiology. The pelvis appears badly fractured, as does her hip. Her abdomen's swollen.'

The surgeon was checking the monitor, assessing the low oxygen levels and increased heart rate. 'Leave her with me. I'll get her into Theatre and arrange radiology. You've got plenty going on without this one.'

They sure did. 'Thanks, Jack.' Nikki looked around and saw paramedics wheeling in another patient with an ED doctor on hand. The department was filling up fast. It seemed only minutes ago she'd informed the staff about what was coming, and everyone had been quick to prepare. Radiology and Theatre had also been warned. The unfortunate patients who'd come to the emergency department prior to the call saying to expect numerous code-five patients could be sitting in the waiting room for hours to come. They might be ill, but serious impact injuries came before most other cases. As far as she knew, no one out there was a code five. The triage nurse would've told her.

Leaving Jack with the woman, Nikki crossed over to Shaun and his patient. 'Fill me in.'

'Not good.' Shaun glanced up at her, anguish filling his eyes, before turning back to the heart monitor.

Dark blue eyes, Nikki suddenly noted. She shook her head. Out of order. She was in the middle of an emergency. What did it matter what colour his eyes were? 'Tell me more.'

'He arrested on the way in. The paramedics revived him. Then he had a second event here as he was being rolled out of the ambulance. His heart rate's so low, I'm surprised it's beating at all.'

'Serious head injury.' She carefully touched the man's scalp. 'Blunt force trauma.' She shook her head. This was awful. What had the bus driver been doing to not stop for people on a controlled crossing?

'Here we go again,' Shaun said as the heart monitor flatlined. 'Stand back.' After quickly checking everyone had moved out of touch of the bed and patient, he gave the man an electric shock.

Nikki held her breath, her eyes fixed on the monitor. The line wobbled, returned to flat.

'Again.' Shaun looked determined this man was going to make it no matter what, like he was going to personally ensure the man's heart restarted and stayed beating.

Something she understood too well. After saving that little boy, Jordie, who tore out onto the road, she knew too well how fragile life could be. 'Go, Shaun,' she muttered under her breath.

'Doing all I can.'

So much for thinking she'd spoken to herself. Sometimes in this job it didn't hurt to let people know how you felt about their work though. Everyone would be pulling out all stops to get the best results for the people being brought in from the accident, but she'd never seen someone quite so determined as Shaun to get a stopped heart beating. A bad experience in his past? Staring at the screen, she saw when the next shock slammed into the man's body. Saw the green line move in the right directions—up, then down. Up, then down. 'Phew.' As she glanced around the department, her relief disappeared. More ambulance gurneys were being pushed into the room. Numerous paramedics were talking to other doctors and nurses about their patients. 'Kennedy,' she called to one of the doctors. 'Can you prioritise? Shaun needs another pair of hands here.' Prioritising was her role, but Kennedy wasn't new to it.

'No problem.'

Shaun said, 'Nikki, can you deal with the head injury while I look after the heart problem and check out the cause of massive bruising in his groin?' He didn't wait for an answer. 'Sarah, the left knee appears dislocated.'

The list of injuries seemed endless. Nikki checked

the man's skull and his neck. 'I'm calling for a neurologist. These head injuries are critical.' She felt her heart squeeze for the people who'd been so badly injured by the bus that hadn't stopped for a red light. If it was true. That had been what the first paramedics bringing in a victim had told them, but it might not be exactly right. Here, though, the cause was irrelevant. It was the injuries that mattered.

'Where's my son?' a woman on a trolley coming in from the ambulance bay shouted. 'To hell with my leg. I want my son here. You have to make sure he's all right. He's more important. He was hit by the bus. Where is he?'

'Go, Nikki. Sarah and I've got this covered,' Shaun said.

'There's serious trauma on the right side of the man's head. Bleeding on the brain a real possibility,' she said. 'I'll call the neurology department before anything else.'

Crossing to the distressed woman minutes later she noted the paramedic dealing with a bone protrusion from the patient's lower leg. 'Who do we have here?'

'Carol Tipping, thirty-one, fractured tibia, knock to chin and some front teeth missing.'

Add in two black eyes. 'Hello, Carol. I'm Dr Nikki Marlow. We're going to get you onto a bed and check you over. I understand you're very worried about your son. I'm sure he's being brought in here by ambulance.' She glanced at the paramedic, one eyebrow raised.

'A policewoman's bringing Sammy in. He's got lots of bruising to his arms and legs but otherwise appears to have escaped any serious injuries. Of course an X-ray will confirm that.'

'I don't care,' Carol cried. 'I want him checked out by a doctor.'

Ouch. Paramedics were very good at their jobs. They faced trauma most days. 'Carol, take a deep breath.' The woman was in shock, and the fact her son had been hurt even mildly would add to the stress going on in her head. 'The paramedics know what they're doing just as well as the doctors in here. If this man says your lad has dodged serious injuries, then you can believe him.'

Carol stared at her with wide eyes. 'I'm so worried,' she said more quietly. 'It's freaking me out that Sammy's with strangers and not me.'

'What about his father? Has someone been in touch with him?' There might not be a father on the scene. 'Or another family member?'

'The cops got hold of Carol's husband, and he's on his way in,' the paramedic answered.

'There you go,' Nikki said to Carol. 'Please try to relax and let the doctors and nurses look after you.' As Carol opened her mouth to reply, Nikki placed a hand on her arm. 'I know it's not easy, but everything possible is being done to make sure your son's all right.'

The woman slumped back onto the trolley. 'I'm sorry. It's so terrifying what happened.'

'I bet it was.' Even now, the moment when she was hit by a vehicle racing closer by the second when she leapt onto the road to save the little boy running from his mother was a vivid memory. Drawing a breath to quieten her mind on that subject, she looked around again, saw all but one patient being dealt with by doctors or nurses and the paramedics who were handing over responsibility for their patients. Jacqui was heading her way. 'Can you take this one, Jacqui? She's got a fractured tibia and other mild injuries, but is more worried about her young son who's being brought in by a policewoman.'

Jacqui was a doctor in her forties and very calm with distressed patients. 'The poor woman. I'm on to her.'

'Thanks.' Nikki crossed to the patient still without a doctor in attendance. 'Ash, what have we got?'

The ambulance officer looked up from the teenage girl. 'This is Katie, fifteen. Fractures in both legs caused by the bus running over her, dislocated right shoulder. She's been unconscious since we found her. Injury to the back of her scalp and a deep abrasion on the right cheek, where I understand she skidded across the tarmac.'

Nikki shuddered. It wasn't getting any better. 'She's the last of the serious cases?' Seven was what she'd been told when the 111 operator called, but she also knew the numbers could change once the scene was under control and panic had settled.

'Yes,' Ash said.

'Thank goodness for something. Bring her through to a cubicle. Georgie, you free?'

'Yes. Coming. '

'Good. Let's get Katie hooked up to oxygen and monitors so Ash can get on the road again.' To bring them someone else, hopefully not quite so badly injured.

Nikki began a thorough check of the teen, recalling the pain when the car slammed into her. Her hand automatically rubbed her thigh where it had been fractured.

'Want me here or with someone else?' Shaun appeared at the end of the bed. 'My patient's on his way to Theatre with the neurosurgeon and an orthopaedic specialist.'

'I could do with you here.'

Shaun had only started in the department on Monday, but so far he'd been impeccable. Confident and careful. Along with everyone else, she was glad to have him on the team, especially today with all the carnage around them. She wasn't thinking how attractive he was or what a distraction his steady blue gaze could be. 'From the little the paramedics know, Katie's been unconscious since being run over by the bus. Her legs bore the brunt of that, but the back of her head has a blunt force injury, and her face has deep abrasions.'

'Theatre's opening up more room as the few surgeries underway when the call came in are being finished and others have been postponed,' Shaun said as he read the monitor. 'I'll look at the head injury when you're ready to roll Katie onto her side.'

'Let's re-strap the shin so it doesn't move when we do that.' The bandage in place to hold the protruding tibia wasn't firm enough in her book. Creating more problems with the injury was not an option. 'We need splints on both legs.'

'I've got them.' Georgie handed her one and began to put the other on the opposite leg.

Shaun muttered, 'This cheek is open right through into the mouth. She's going to need a plastic surgeon after the others have done their work. It isn't as urgent, though sutures are required to help stem the bleeding. Plus we don't want her ending up with major scars on her face.'

Nikki huffed out a breath and gave him a wobbly smile. 'Welcome to Christchurch General.' It felt good working alongside Shaun. He made her feel comfortable about her efforts with their patients, even though she knew she was more than competent. It was only that sometimes her father's derogatory remarks throughout her life about her lack of ability to do anything properly sometimes made her pause and wonder if she could do better. *Not today, Dad. I know what I'm doing, and I'm doing it well.*

'You know how to put my skills to the test,' Shaun said with a wonky smile that had her looking at him twice. It was genuine and showed he wasn't afraid to admit his feelings, which was a surprise as so far he'd been a little remote with everyone apart from that smile. Could be part of the process of settling in to a new job, or today was catching up with him, as it was her. 'I've never been involved in a situation quite like this one.'

She had, in an Auckland ED a few years ago after a multiple car pile-up on the Southern Motorway. 'You don't appear too frazzled by it all.' He was handling the situation like the professional he was.

'I imagine that'll come later.' He was wiping away blood and bits of gravel from Katie's face so gently that Nikki got goose bumps. He was good.

Katie groaned.

Everyone stopped what they were doing and watched her. Her eyes opened, closed instantly. Another groan.

Nikki leant closer. 'Katie? Can you hear me? You're in hospital.'

Katie opened her eyes again, held them open for a few seconds. Closed them.

'She's coming round, and she's going to need analgesics. The pain level will be high,' Shaun commented quietly.

'First I'll find out how long before one of the surgeons can see her, though I doubt there's a space in Theatre right now.' She had no idea how long it had been since the first patient had been taken into Theatre. Time meant nothing. Hopefully *all* the previous surgeries that were underway when this nightmare began had been completed. Picking up the phone, she looked around the department. Every single staff member was doing their utmost to help patients. Her heart swelled with pride. They were a good crew. Including the new doc on the block. Shaun Elliott had slid into place as though he'd been here for years and not just days. Yeah, he was a good dude.

Hours later—Nikki had no idea how many—the department quietened. She looked around and smiled tiredly. 'We're done? No more accident victims?' She should've known, but she'd been too involved with the young boy whose mother had been so stressed.

Turned out Sammy had fractures in his hand and elbow on one side, and had taken a slight knock to the head. Thankfully that had no repercussions. He'd returned from the plaster room and was sitting in a wheelchair beside his mum and dad, smiling at his cast where she and other staff had signed it.

'Not a one,' Shaun told her with a smile.

That smile tipped her off centre; it was wide and encouraging. Pulling on her straight face, she said, 'So we're done.' Except for all she knew, their shift mightn't be over, plus the waiting room would be overflowing with other patients requiring help. Glancing at her watch for the first time since all this started, she gasped. 'Three thirty-five. It feels later than that.'

'Time flies when you're having fun.' Shaun was still smiling.

How did he manage that when everyone else looked exhausted?

'Okay, everyone, the next shift is already seeing to the patients that were sidelined earlier.' Paul, the man in charge of ED, had stepped up beside Nikki. Wasn't he meant to be on leave this week? 'We've already seen to some of them. All of you get out of here while you can. But first, thank you for your dedication. You're amazing.'

The afternoon/evening staff began clapping, soon joined by some patients who'd been brought through from the waiting room.

Nikki squirmed. They'd only done what they always did, whether they had one patient with trauma injuries or numerous, putting everything they had into helping sick or injured people.

Shaun nudged her with his shoulder. 'Make the most of it. We don't get applauded often.'

Glancing at him, she gave in and smiled. They *had* done a great job. 'You're right.' Turning back to the room, she raised her voice. 'Thanks, everyone. Sorry to leave you with a heavy shift, but I'm ready for a shower and a hot coffee.'

Paul lifted his hand. 'Which has been catered for in the cafeteria. They've made sandwiches for you all. No showers there though.' He laughed. 'Go and unwind. And—' His countenance became serious. 'When you leave the hospital, go out one of the side doors. The media are all over the front entrance. If any of them ask you questions, you know not to answer them.'

A gentle reminder to keep their mouths shut. Nikki shivered. It could go badly when someone spoke up about a patient they'd dealt with after something as serious and public as this morning's bus accident would no doubt already be. After she'd saved Jordie in October last year, the media had hung out at the hospital in the quest for any information about her and the boy she'd snatched out of harm's way. Two reporters managed to get onto the ward she was in after surgery on her fractured hip, which infuriated her. She'd had little to say, preferring to keep her life private. Not that it was exciting enough for people to want to read about. Of course the reporters had had other ideas until a woman was murdered at a horse race meet two days later. Even then, she struggled not to regularly glance over her shoulder once she was back on her feet.

'Thanks, Paul. Come on, everyone. Let's change out of our grubby scrubs and go eat.' She'd prefer to go home for the shower her tired muscles were crying out for, but as head doctor on the shift, she would be there for the team.

As the day staff headed away to the changing rooms, Nikki lingered to go over some finer points with Paul, only to be told he had everything under control.

'I'm sure you have,' she agreed. 'I'm just finding it hard to switch off.'

'Perfectly normal,' said Shaun from behind her. 'One moment we're going non-stop crazy with desperate cases, and then suddenly there's nothing to do. I get it. I'm feeling the same. I suspect everyone is.'

Paul nodded. 'They will be. Go on, Nikki. Get out of here and start unwinding.'

'Yes, Boss.'

'Too right I am.' The man she'd known for years gave her a quick hug. 'You were amazing. And yes, I was keeping up to date with everything as I drove back from Nelson, where I'd gone for my grandmother's ninetieth birthday.'

'You're missing that?'

'I'm heading back up there tomorrow afternoon for the party. Stop dithering and go, will you?'

Shaun nudged her lightly, as he had earlier during the day. 'Sandwiches and coffee sound good.' His voice was low and gravelly, not something she'd noticed since he'd started working here at the beginning of the week. But then, she hadn't been quite so wound up before today either.

'All right. Give me five to put on some clean clothes.' She'd work hard at not racing outside and heading home. She'd rather deal with days like this one on her own at home, surrounded by the photos she took of birds and other wildlife. Photography had become her escape as a teenager when life got difficult facing new schools far too often. She had become very good at integrating herself with groups of popular girls, but the day always came when her father said they were moving. She'd have to cope with leaving her new friends, so out would come the camera she'd saved hard for. Far easier to rely on herself to get through whatever life threw her way. Her father had never given her or her brother, Ross, any attention or any of his precious time, and their mother had been too busy pleasing their dad to be bothered with her children. Thankfully she'd always had Ross at her side for understanding and the occasional hug. Then there'd been Brett, her husband and the love of her life, who turned out not to be the man she'd believed in but a piece of scum who had another woman on the side.

Life hurt at times, she thought as a yawn gripped her. Yes, she was exhausted, but she wouldn't be the only one. Everyone had given their all for hours, and the toll was exhaustion. She wasn't thinking about her busy mind that would go on during the night, replaying everything. That was for later.

Shaun watched Nikki drag herself off to the women's changing room and smiled. Talk about a dynamo with patients. She hadn't stopped once, making sure all the victims of the bus encounter were being dealt with as well as looking out for the doctors and nurses as they too did everything within their ability to help the victims of a hideous accident.

Accident. The word reverberated around his head. The bus driver wouldn't have meant to mow down all those people. At least, Shaun hoped he hadn't. But was it an accident when the guy hadn't seen the light was red? He shuddered. Whatever the answer, the guilt would be colossal.

'You need to get to the cafeteria too,' Paul said.

'I know.'

'But you're wondering how you're going to get through the hours to come.'

He'd been deliberately avoiding that. 'Not quite. Though I'm sure it's not going to be a picnic.' He hadn't been on a picnic since he was a kid in shorts.

Paul nudged him. 'Follow Nikki's example. She's one strong lady when the going gets tough.' He'd been working with Paul when his life imploded four years ago, so the guy knew his history and understood how he struggled to cope with major incidents like today's. The good thing about today was they hadn't lost anyone. It had been touch and go with the man whose heart gave out for the third time, but Shaun'd been determined he wasn't going to die and gave everything he had to make sure of it. And he'd been successful.

If only he could've said that after his mate Liam's heart failed, but some things turn out to be impossible. Doing compressions when squashed into the tiny cabin of a Cessna plane five thousand feet above ground was one of those things. Throw in the fact he knew next to nothing about flying apart from the little Liam had taught him on previous flights, and it was the day from hell. Liam died before he'd had time to radio for help, so getting them down to the ground in one piece became his priority. At least he was able to keep the plane flying straight and steady until a flying instructor in the control tower talked him down, keeping him calm and focused until the wheels hit the grass runway. The plane bounced in the air, came down harder the next time and finally crashed. His guilt from that day was still with him, though quieter than it used to be.

'You still with me?' Paul asked.

Sort of. He'd been more than impressed with how Nikki handled the situation from the moment they first heard they were going to be overwhelmed with multiple seriously injured patients. The downside to having only one major public hospital in the city was needing to take all the cases, but Christchurch had faced some horrendous times before and came through well.

Likewise Nikki Marlow. He'd seen her on the news nearly a year ago when she'd raced onto a busy road to save a three-year-old boy who'd run in front of an approaching car. From all accounts, she'd been focused and determined then too, hadn't hesitated for even a second.

What he hadn't expected was to feel cdgy around her. She made him look at her more than once. Many times more. Even in scrubs, it was obvious she had a stunning figure. Then there were those sapphire-blue eyes that seemed to see right inside him, which was the more unsettling of the things about her that got to him. He wasn't looking for a woman to become part of his life until he'd settled down in one place permanently. He was setting out to do that here on home turf with family nearby. In the meantime, he only did flings, and lately even those happened less often. He did want to find love one day, but not until he knew for certain he wouldn't move on yet again. Something he did every few months. A habit or still the past shaking him up, he wasn't sure, but he was now ready to do something about it.

'Coming, Shaun?' Nikki stood in front of him, a quizzical smile on that lovely mouth. She'd changed into fitted trousers and a floral blouse, looking so good it was difficult not to reach out and touch her.

Instead he concentrated on answering her. 'I'll be right behind you.' He hadn't ditched the scrubs yet.

'See you upstairs.' She headed away, leaving him to watch those shapely legs eat up the distance to the elevator.

Might be an idea to go home and put some space between them until his head quietened down. Except then he'd be letting down the team. When Paul announced there was food waiting for them, he'd sensed Nikki wasn't in a rush to join everyone either, but she was doing it. Therefore, so would he. It was important to be a part of the team, especially if at all possible this was to be a long-term job, not one that lasted only weeks or months. He'd made the decision to let go of the pain that had held him in limbo for so long. Shying away from something as simple as joining his colleagues for a quick—he hoped it'd be quick—get-together letting go of the day was not the way to begin. He would make this work. He would.

Five minutes later, dressed in jeans and an open-neck shirt, he headed to the cafeteria, where coffee and sandwiches waited. 'I'm starving,' he said as he took the chair beside Georgie after ordering a cappuccino.

'Given the way those sandwiches are disappearing, I think we all are.' Georgie nodded.

Opposite him, Nikki was chomping into one with a smile on her face.

'Good?' he asked.

'Delicious,' she agreed. 'Mind you, I could probably eat dog food roll right now and say the same.'

'Fried or cold?'

'Whichever.'

Leaning back, he looked around at everyone. They were a good bunch. Today had been his fourth day on the job, and he already felt comfortable. But that wasn't unusual. It was further into his time at a new job when he began to get itchy feet and started looking for other positions available in emergency departments across the country. New Zealand had a shortage of doctors at the moment, so he never had any difficulty getting a new job. Yet something about how everyone had worked together today had him feeling he belonged here more than anywhere else he'd been lately. Probably rushing things, he admitted. It was early days, and the hard ones were yet to come.

'Regretting coming to work here now?' Georgie asked through a tired smile.

'No, I was thinking the opposite. Today's been hell, yet I'm glad I was here to help those people.' He glanced across to Nikki and saw her nod.

'You fitted in so well,' she told him. 'It's as though you've worked here for a while.'

'Most EDs are the same. It's the people you work with who make the difference.' Something he hadn't acknowledged for a long time because to do so meant admitting he'd been lonely. After losing his mate, he wasn't in a hurry to make new friends. It wasn't fun being on his own all the time either, but here in Christchurch, he'd pick up with those he'd left behind.

'I think you're right.' Nikki sipped her coffee, suddenly looking a bit withdrawn.

Because she was head of shift and therefore had to remain a little removed from everyone? Or didn't she mix with people easily? Something to learn about her as time went on. He did want to know more about Nikki Marlow, which was unusual for him. He couldn't find it in himself to pretend he wasn't interested in her. Not that he understood why, and for some inexplicable reason, he didn't care. He was, and that was enough. 'I've worked in this ED before,' he said suddenly. 'I left three and a half years ago.'

Nikki's eyebrows rose. 'So you knew Paul when you applied this time?'

'Yes.'

'He never mentioned it.'

Knowing Paul, he'd have left it to him to decide what he told people about his past and why he'd left. At the time, he'd barely been coping with losing Liam and then breaking up with Amy, his wife, four months later. That had hurt more than losing Liam, and he'd carried some guilt over letting Amy down too. With the state he'd been in, he'd needed to get away from here before he made a horrendous mistake at work. He'd found having short-term contracts helped him get through the worst because he was always preparing to move on again. 'I imagine I did okay last time, so Paul saw no reason to mention it.'

Nikki's smile was wry. 'Fair enough.'

That was it? She wasn't digging for more info? Again he wondered if she'd been hurt in the past and kept things close to her chest. That could explain why she didn't pry into other people's lives.

* * *

'Damn and blast,' Nikki muttered half an hour later as she stepped through the door Shaun held open to go outside. 'I thought they were hanging out at the front.'

'They've probably seen others leave through the side door and figured you'd come this way too.'

A crowd of reporters stood around the side entrance, and their faces lit up with expectation when they saw Nikki.

'Dr Marlow, how many people died in the accident?'

'Nikki, did you work with the survivors?'

'Doctor, how serious are their injuries?'

Nikki balked, and colour drained from her face.

Shaun stepped up beside her. He wasn't leaving her on her own to deal with this lot. 'You know Dr Marlow can't answer any of those questions.'

Nikki gave him a quick look, surprise and possibly gratitude filling her eyes.

'Come on, we're allowed to know what the injuries are,' a woman at the front retorted. 'That's not revealing any secrets.'

Nikki stood tall and spoke coolly. 'I am not giving out any information about the patients we've seen today. It isn't right.'

As the journalists began shouting over each other to have their questions answered, others came flying around the side of the building, obviously suddenly aware someone of interest was here.

'Nikki, you know we find out everything in the end,' a male at the back called out. 'Like we did last time,' he added with a laugh.

She glared at the man. 'But you didn't learn anything important from me. The same goes for today.'

She was tough, though now resentment was taking over. He presumed last time had been when she'd saved the little boy. The media would've been all over the scene, and therefore Nikki. They were wolves, with no thought for the people they were chasing for info. Or the people whose details they wanted. He knew all too well about that after the death of his friend and how *he'd* had to land the plane with no real experience to fall back on. The media had had a field day as he hadn't been in any condition to deal with them. He hadn't forgiven them either. The pain over his loss and the fact he hadn't been able to save Liam had been huge, and it was like the reporters were rubbing salt into his wounds. At least they'd never learned that he'd lost his wife, Liam's sister, that day too.

It had taken a few months for their marriage to combust as they were both numb with grief, and he'd carried the extra weight of guilt. If he'd saved Liam, his friend wouldn't have missed out on so much living. No one ever blamed him for what happened—instead, they'd been grateful he'd survived—but that didn't stop the guilt. Amy struggled with her grief and how despondent he became. He'd struggled with having to face her every day, knowing her brother was gone. Finally they agreed to go their separate ways. Amy had found someone who made her happy again and had remarried last year, whereas he was still tottering from one place to another, looking for who knew what. Except this was the final move. He was stopping here, making a new life in old surroundings with family and friends nearby. Say it often enough and he'd come to believe it, right?

Shaun was suddenly aware he had been asked a question. 'Sorry, didn't hear what you asked,' he said to the crowd in general.

'Who are you? Another doctor? Or a friend of Dr Marlow's?'

Oh, great. 'I'm an emergency doctor.' Hopefully no one recognised him. He didn't need his past mentioned now. There was enough going on without that.

'Will you answer our questions? Who were the people who were injured? Were there any kids hurt?'

'I'm sorry, but I won't be telling you any details either. Now, if you'll excuse us, we've had a busy day and would like to get away from here.'

Voices rose as more questions were fired at them, but no one stopped them from leaving. Something to be grateful for, he supposed.

Until one man stepped in front of them, preventing them from going further. 'Do you know what Nikki Marlow did to save a young boy's life, Dr Elliott?'

Damn and blast. It'd been too much to expect to get away unrecognised. 'Yes, I do.'

'She's quite something, isn't she?' The man was ogling Nikki. 'Of course, you must be interested in her.'

Bile rose in Shaun's mouth. Punching the man's smug face would be too good for him. 'You obviously haven't a clue what you're talking about.'

'Excuse us, we need to get through.' Nikki had moved closer to him, not away. Tension tightened her face.

Totally agree. Shaun took Nikki's elbow and stepped towards the man. 'If you don't mind.' *Don't you dare mention the incident involving Liam and me.*

Just then, a photographer grabbed the man's arm. 'Leave them alone, will you? They're the good guys.'

Giving the photographer a quick nod of thanks, he kept moving with Nikki's elbow firmly in his grip. Her limp had become more obvious than usual. He'd read that her leg had been broken when the car hit her and noted she had a slight limp, but today being on her feet non-stop seemed to have taken a toll.

'Thanks, Shaun. That was creepy,' she acknowledged when they reached the sidewalk and were finally alone. 'Though I could've dealt to him.'

He bet she could've, but it was in his nature to protect women, especially one who intrigued him as much as this one was starting to. He'd noticed her the moment he first walked into the ED on Monday, tall with curves in all the right places. Not that she was the first woman he'd known to have a lovely figure, but there was something else about Nikki that teased him. He hadn't yet been able to put a finger on it. After today, he knew she was tough and kind all wrapped in one, there was a lot more that piqued his interest. 'I know, but I don't do standing aside when someone's behaving like that to a woman I respect. Or anyone else, come to that.'

She glanced at him, confusion overtaking the tension. Didn't she think he'd respect her? 'Still, thank you for sticking up for me.'

His eyebrows lifted. 'Why wouldn't I? You were amazing, the way you handled today's crisis in the ED. That has little to do with your doctoring skills, though they're top-level. It's about you as a person.' *Shut up, Shaun.* It was hard to stop yabbering on when Nikki looked so intriguing, thereby further ramping up his interest.

'Stop now or you'll embarrass me.'

Not used to compliments? Interesting. There was more to this woman than the doctor he worked with and the woman who leapt into traffic to grab a small boy as he ran amok on the road. 'Do you blush when you're embarrassed?'

Her eyes widened. 'Sometimes.' Then she spun around. 'I'll get going before any more reporters come looking for answers to their questions.'

'Did you drive to work?' He had no idea where she lived.

'I walked.'

'Then I'll give you a lift. My car's in the staff park.'

'Thanks, but the walk'll do me good.'

He doubted that with her limp, but he didn't argue. It was hard to accept this particular lady was walking away. 'See you tomorrow,' he called after her.

'Will do.' She waved over her shoulder as she strode away, eating up the metres like she was in a hurry to get away from him, the limp becoming even more pronounced.

Suddenly he laughed. What the heck had he been thinking? He and Nikki were doctors working alongside each other, nothing else. Besides, he was here long-term, not for a few months. He couldn't afford to upset his plan by letting Nikki in under his skin. When that had run its course, they'd still have to get along, and that could make working together awkward. *So turn around and stop watching her as she heads away.* Hauling air into his lungs, he did manage to turn away, not because he didn't want to watch her but because it could be interpreted as creepy, and he didn't do creepy.

He hadn't done long-term anything for years. Yet now he was setting out to do just that. He intended buying a home and maybe getting a dog, plus spending time with his family, with the idea of seeing how he coped. To get into a relationship with a woman and then find he couldn't do permanent would only lead to heartbreak. He'd struggled to settle anywhere after he lost Liam and then Amy, and knew he couldn't face losing someone else. At the same time, he was ready to give all he had to getting back on track with his life and maybe fulfilling those dreams of love and family he'd once had.

Spits of rain landed on his face. Would Nikki change her mind about accepting a lift home now?

He headed to his SUV feeling more optimistic. Only one way to find out.

CHAPTER TWO

NIKKI FOUGHT THE urge to turn back and accept Shaun's offer of a ride if he was still around. She was aching from head to toe after the crazy busy day, and the muscles in her right thigh where the femur had been fractured were tighter than normal. That would get worse before it came right. The sooner she got home and into a hot shower the better. On the other hand, she wasn't acknowledging the fact Shaun had a way about him that drew her in and made her want to know him better. He was an enigma she'd like to unravel, which wasn't something she'd felt when it came to men in a while.

But then she wasn't good at long-term relationships. Having to start over with new friends at all the schools she went to, she'd learned to be friendly while holding back a little. She did have two close friends from those years, and loved them for sticking by her throughout the turbulent times when she moved around so much. Other than Molly and Collette, and her brother, it seemed she wasn't made to be with someone forever, either a friend or lover. For her it all went back to her father and how he kept getting asked to leave a school because he bullied his pupils, demanding perfection. Her way of dealing with her father being the nasty teacher was to get onside with everyone else and be a great friend.

Then there was Brett. She'd fallen for him hard and fast, and he'd loved her back just as much, making her believe miracles did happen. She'd finally found the stability she'd wanted all her life. Their marriage had been wonderful, warm and happy. She'd no longer dreaded going home at the end of a busy day as she had with her parents, where her father was always waiting to put her down over something, or her case was on the bed waiting to be packed. Instead she'd gone home to throw her arms around the man she adored, and been hugged back just as strongly. Until she miscarried at fourteen weeks pregnant. That day changed everything. Brett wasn't there for her so often. She supported him through his grief but got little back, which was nothing like the man she believed she'd married. Then things got worse. One night he came home to tell her he was leaving and going to live with his girlfriend, who he'd been having an affair with for eight months. The woman was six months pregnant, and now that Nikki wasn't, he felt his loyalties lay elsewhere.

When she'd burst into tears and asked why he'd had an affair, his answer was blunt and cruel. He didn't believe half of what she'd told him about her upbringing and thought she was a needy woman who no one could please. Look how she had behaved when she had lost their baby. As though she was the only one suffering. Well, he had been too, but he had another opportunity to have a family with someone else that he wasn't giving up.

It was clear he'd felt that if he stayed with her, chances were she might lose the next baby too, and that wasn't happening to him. Had she ever been right in believing he was so wonderful? Had she worn blinkers when it came to Brett, looking too hard for happiness? Or hadn't she been good enough for him all along? The worst was that he'd been so loving even in the midst of his affair. Moving past the hurt and disbelief had been impossible at first. If not for her brother and two best friends, she doubted she'd have got to where she was—comfortable with her lifestyle and finally beginning to wonder if there might be a man out there she could let into her heart.

Now Shaun was getting to her in unexpected ways. Working alongside him earlier, she'd felt his intense focus on the patient he was helping and thought he was wonderful. Whether it was the man with the serious head injury or the young girl with broken legs, he gave his all. He was thorough while taking the time to make sure the patient was taken care of, even when unconscious. Fast but careful. Surely a man like that would be the same with his family and friends?

He'd stood up for her when that reporter tried to harass her. The guy wouldn't have had a chance against her, but with Shaun telling him where to go, she'd felt truly protected and liked it. Too much.

A reporter had recognised Shaun. Why? What from? And when asked by a reporter if he knew what she'd done for Jordie, Shaun had answered in the affirmative.

Damned reporters. She hated them after being continually approached with questions about Jordie and her role in his life now. A few weeks after she'd snatched Jordie off the road, his parents asked her to be their son's surrogate aunt, making her weep with heartfelt joy, but when the media heard of it, it became a nightmare. Especially for the wee boy, as everyone wanted a part of the news and his life. In the end Nikki had told his mum and dad it might be best if she stepped back until everything quietened down. It eventually did, though when she'd met them for coffee and orange juice at a mall a couple of

Saturday mornings ago, they were photographed by a reporter. Nothing major came of it, but it'd been a reminder they were still news when nothing else was going on.

Thunder blasted through the sky, followed by a flash of lightning. Next Nikki was doused in heavy rain that looked close to becoming hail. 'Should've taken the offer of a ride,' she muttered under her breath. She was already nearly soaked through, and home was twenty minutes away.

Toot, toot.

'Ready to change your mind?' Shaun called from a black SUV that'd pulled onto the kerb in front of her.

She didn't answer, merely went to the passenger door and opened it to flop into the seat. 'I didn't see that coming.'

'Miles away thinking about your day?' Shaun nodded as he pulled back out onto the road.

'Something like that.' It wasn't a lie. Shaun had been part of the day.

'Where am I headed?'

'Fendalton.' She named the street where her small cottage was. 'Number five.' Then she wondered how well he knew the city. 'Do you need directions?'

'No. I grew up around here.'

'So you're a local.' She leaned back into the seat and rubbed her cheek, thinking how much more she'd like to know Shaun. The rain had cooled the air, and she shivered. Wet clothes didn't help.

'Want the heater on?'

'No, thanks.' They'd be at her place shortly. Then what? Did she invite Shaun in for another coffee out of politeness? Probably best to say thanks and head inside alone. They'd catch up tomorrow in the department. He was being helpful. Giving her a lift wasn't a date. A date? With Shaun? Where did that come from? She was obviously more exhausted than she'd realised.

He pulled into her drive and drove right up to the front door. 'Home sweet home.'

'It is.' She was proud of her house. Eighty years old, it had been well-looked-after by the previous owners, something she worked hard to keep up with.

'How long have you been here?' Shaun asked as he gazed through the window at the building, then her gardens.

'Nearly two years. I bought it when I moved back from Auckland.'

'So you've lived in Christchurch before? When you were growing up?'

'Only briefly.' Like all the places her family had moved to, it had been a short stop. Less than eighteen months for that one. 'Now I'm here to stay.'

'Family in the area?'

'My brother.' Her mother remained in Auckland when their father died and wasn't budging. With the past still hanging between the three of them, she and Ross had little contact with her, mainly brief phone calls for Christmas and birthdays. Mum wasn't interested in their lives, while she and Ross had moved on. She opened the door. No talking about herself. It wasn't something she did. 'Thank you for not driving off and leaving me to walk home.'

'I'd never do that.'

'Would you like another coffee?' The question spilled from her mouth.

'I should go home and get cleaned up.'

Should? Or would? 'I understand. I need to get out of these wet clothes and have a shower.'

'I'll make the coffee while you do that.' He was out of the car before she'd taken in what he'd said.

Shoving the door wider, she got out and slammed it shut. Now she was stuck with Shaun coming inside her house and sitting around drinking coffee. Perhaps she could stay under the shower until the water ran cold, by which time he'd have given up and left. Except then she'd be disappointed. She did like him. He was a puzzle, and she liked puzzles. No matter the source, they always had her trying to fathom the answers. Shaun certainly rattled her, even annoyed her, and then made her want to laugh and throw her arms around him—very odd. 'Come on. Let's get inside.' The rain was bucketing down. 'I hope it's not going to last too long.'

'This is lovely,' he said as he closed the front door behind them and glanced around. 'Did you do the decorating?'

Drops of water sprayed everywhere from her hair when she shook her head. 'I wouldn't know where to start. The house came all done up, and I only changed the purple velvet curtains. I mean, purple velvet? Really?'

He grinned. 'I'm affronted.'

'Sure thing. They're your favourite style.'

His shudder was exaggerated. 'Might be all right for lining the dog kennel, I guess.'

'You have a dog?'

His smile slipped away. 'No, but I might get one now that I'm intending to buy a house and stay in Christchurch for a while.'

So he wasn't moving on like he'd done with previous positions? She'd heard from one of the doctors who knew him that he rarely stopped in one place for more than four months since something had happened that changed him forever. Something to do with why the reporter recognised him? She was yet to find out what that had been. 'With Christchurch being familiar territory, I'm guessing you've returned home for a while.'

'Being all over the place with different jobs, I missed my family.' He turned away to look around the lounge they'd entered on the way to the kitchen. 'This is nice.'

Okay, he didn't want to talk about himself. Something she understood. 'It gets a bit chilly in winter due to the lack of insulation in houses built so long ago, but I love it.'

'Show me where the coffee is and go take that shower you mentioned, then put on some warm clothes. You're shivering.' So he wasn't one for dragging out a conversation for the sake of it.

'Through here.' In the ultra-modern kitchen installed by the previous owners, she showed him where everything he needed was, and once he'd assured her he could manage the coffee maker, she left him to it and went to get clean and warm.

If Shaun hadn't been here, she'd have stayed under the shower for ages washing away the day, but good manners won out. She was soon back in the kitchen, dressed in jeans and a sweatshirt and sniffing the coffee-scented air. 'Smells better than the cafeteria coffee.'

'I hope so.' Shaun was parked on a stool at the counter, holding a mug between both hands as though they were cold. He hadn't been drenched in the rain, but the house wasn't warm right now.

She switched on the wall heater and sank onto a stool at the other end of the counter, putting space between them. Couldn't have Shaun thinking she was interested in him other than as a doctor. Because she wasn't, right? 'You okay?'

'The day's catching up. It got a bit grim for a while. Kind of reminds me no one's invulnerable.'

Surprised he was admitting that, she agreed. 'True. Thankfully we didn't lose anyone.' Always a good outcome, though some of the patients were in for a long haul to get back on their feet.

'What do you do to move on from something like that?'

'Go walking in the hills.' Hiking was one of her loves, along with photography. Both helped divert her mind when she was overthinking horrific scenarios. 'In fact, I'm going walking with a friend on Mount Richardson on Saturday.'

'Perfect timing.'

'It is.' The weather was supposed to be fine and not too cold, though even if it turned out to be windy and chilly, she'd still keep the date. Right now she needed to get out there and let go of the tension brought on earlier. She knew from past experience she'd be on edge for days if she didn't do something physically challenging.

Shaun drained his coffee. 'I'm having another.' He wasn't asking.

'Go for it.' *Then leave me to get on with doing nothing.* She'd watch something trivial on TV or do a crossword or something else inane while trying to shove aside thoughts about the day, which included the man taking up space in her pristine kitchen. 'Another coffee addict, I see.'

'How else did we get through those night shifts without falling asleep when we were training?'

'True.' She pictured him sprawled over a bed on his back, out for the count, that broad chest rising and falling in a perfect rhythm. Why was Shaun Elliott taking over her mind like this? She wasn't immune to a hot man, but she rarely let them get to her. She wasn't letting Shaun, she realised. He was managing it all by himself. He'd piqued her interest while they were completely focused on seriously injured patients. That said a lot, because nothing, nobody, ever did that to her. Well, he could finish his next coffee and head away—get out of her house and out of her mind. He might be waking her up in ways she hadn't known in years, but she would not be following through. She'd learned the hard way how that ended, and she wasn't ever going to be put aside again. It had happened all her life by her parents and then Brett. Never again.

Her life was now about permanency, staying settled, keeping friends and not leaving town. She was done with moving from town to village to city, from one school to another, from meeting new people only to be hauled away somewhere else. She was in Christchurch to stay. If she ever found a man she could trust to love her for who she was and who didn't want to walk away when the going got tough, then she might take a chance on her heart, but for now she was happy as things were. Ross was here. Molly and Collette were here. She had the ideal job. A lovely home. What more could she want?

Her eyes shifted to Shaun. It would be wonderful to have a man at her side, one she loved beyond reason and who loved her equally. But was it going to happen? With a man she could rely on not to break her heart? There were no answers, and she wasn't about to make a fool of herself by finding out.

Her phone vibrated on the counter. Molly's name appeared on the screen. 'Sorry, I'd better take this.' Molly probably wanted to set up a time for going hiking on Saturday. 'Hey, how's your day been?'

'Pretty rubbish, if you really want to know. Which is why I'm calling. About Saturday. I can't make it. I'm sorry.'

Nikki felt her heart sink. She really needed to get out there and slog up and down a few hills. 'What's happened?'

'My sidekick quit. Right in the middle of a fraud investigation. I'm doing my best to fill in the gaps.' Molly was an accountant working for the police fraud squad.

'Fair enough. You do what you've got to do. I'll walk around Hagley Park fifty times.' Hiking alone in the hills was not a safe thing to do, even when there'd likely be others on the trail. *Likely* being the operative word. The tracks would be slippery after all the recent rain. If no one else was about and she fell and injured herself, she'd be in trouble in more ways than one. Putting her phone down, she got up to make another coffee. So much for getting out in the fresh air.

'What's up?'

For a moment, she'd forgotten Shaun was here. 'My friend can't make the walk.'

Looking thoughtful, Shaun took his mug to the sink, where he rinsed it out. Then he turned around and said, 'I'll go with you. I could do with stretching my legs.' He headed towards the front door before stopping and asking, 'What time?'

'Seven.'

'I'll pick you up then.'

She hadn't said she agreed to him coming. But it was too late. The front door snipped shut, and he was gone. She could run after him and say no, but she desperately wanted to get out in the hills and exert herself. Whether she wanted to do it with Shaun was another question. One she didn't have a definite answer to, and she wasn't going to waste time working it out.

Nikki didn't look pleased with him, Shaun thought as he drove away from her house. It had been a sudden decision to go hiking with her and if he'd taken the time to think about it, he wouldn't have run with the idea. But he had, and he wasn't going to regret it. It would be good to get out in the hills, and especially good doing it with Nikki. There was so much more to her than the exceptional doctor she was. Which was the case with most doctors, but for some reason he wasn't prepared to dig into, Nikki seemed to have more going for her than most. In his eyes, anyway.

The car surged forward as his foot pressed harder on the accelerator. 'Easy, man.' It'd been a reflex action to the thought that Nikki might be waking him up in ways he wasn't ready for. Returning to Christchurch to live long-term was a big enough deal to cope with without letting a woman into his life. A fling here or there was fine, but somehow he didn't think that would work with Nikki. She didn't appear to be your one-night-stand kind of girl. He wasn't ready for anyone else, not even this woman winding him up too easily. But he could do friendship. Walks in the hills. Maybe a coffee in town, even a meal together. Nothing deep and meaningful about that, just comfortable.

His fingers tapped the steering wheel. So he was going hiking on the weekend. Unless Nikki cancelled on him. It wouldn't surprise him after her stunned expression when he said he'd go with her. On the other hand, she hadn't instantly said no to the idea. Not that he'd given her much of a chance. After saying he'd pick her up, he'd got out of there fast.

They still had tomorrow working together in the department, which'd give her plenty of opportunity to say he wasn't welcome to join her. If she did, he'd be more than disappointed when he should be relieved. Coming home was hard enough. Taking on his first permanent position in more than three years was a challenge that he'd see through come hell or high water. The flat he was renting temporarily was pokey and cold, so he'd got on with looking at houses on the market in the two weeks before he started at the department. So far nothing had excited him. The most likely reason was that buying a home would tie him down when his instincts would soon be crying out to move on. Nothing new there.

He couldn't move again. The time had come when the past had to be laid to rest. Liam was gone. He was never coming home. He would not want Shaun to continue on the solitary road he'd started down the day he died. Slowly he was coming to see that for himself. He wanted a real life, not the lonely one he'd got used to.

Like other things in life, Liam's heart failure had come out of the blue. Or so he'd thought, until Liam's fiancée told him Liam had complained a couple of times about chest pain and done nothing about it despite her pleading with him to see a doctor. Since he was super fit, he hadn't believed there was anything seriously wrong. If he'd got wind of it, Shaun would've tied him to a bed until he'd been checked out. He still hadn't quite forgiven Liam for not mentioning the chest pain, but he was getting there. All part of letting go and starting afresh here.

Hopefully one day he'd find the life he used to believe

was there for the taking. The one that included a family of his own, which meant the woman of his dreams. Amy had been that woman. They'd loved each other so much, but it hadn't been strong enough to see them through their grief and his guilt over not saving Liam despite knowing he wasn't at fault.

His phone rang.

'Hey, Mum, how's things?'

'I'm good. Heard the news and figured you were probably involved with those poor people hit by the bus. You must be exhausted, so drop whatever you're doing and come here. Dinner's on, and your father will be home shortly.' *Click.* She was gone.

'Thanks, Mum,' he said to the silent phone. She knew when to turn on the love, and neither she nor Dad would question him about what had happened to those people she mentioned. He'd be able to chill out and pretend nothing had been too hard at the department that day. Bring it on.

CHAPTER THREE

NIKKI DRAINED A glass of water as she swallowed pain meds before turning out the bedside lamp. Her thigh was giving her hell. Switching the light back on, she reached for her phone. Yep, the alarm was set. Off with the light. She stared up through the darkness towards the ceiling, desperate for sleep to push aside the chaos in her mind. Images of the teenage girl with her legs at impossible angles, the little boy who wanted his mum and his mum screaming to look after him and never mind her, tormented Nikki.

She concentrated on the breathing technique she'd learned when first working in an emergency department as she trained to qualify as an ED specialist. Low, slow breaths in through the nose, out through the mouth. Uncurling her fingers, closing her eyes, breathing slowly. She deliberately thought about Shaun. He made it easier than dealing with the other images forcing themselves into her mind.

When he started on Monday, they'd been busy so she hadn't taken a lot of notice of him other than giving him details of who were the priorities, though his height and firm build had been obvious even then.

They'd worked together intermittently over the days since, and it was his deep, raspy laugh that had her turning her head to check him out when she wasn't focused on a patient. Sexy as all being, that laugh. But no, she wasn't interested in getting to know him beyond work. What about Saturday and going hiking with him? She'd deal with that tomorrow. Cancel the walk, find something else to do to fill in the day. *But* a walk was the best thing to do when she was uptight about work. Scenarios like today's reminded her how fragile life could be. She rolled over, pulled the pillow around her neck. She'd make a decision tomorrow. Shaun was a nice guy.

More than nice, Nikki. He's gorgeous.

Shaun sauntered across her mind as she drifted into sleep.

Blood and more blood. Broken bones. Screams. Pain. Nikki pressed her joined hands down hard on the man's chest, fighting to make his heart start. A monitor beeped. Another doctor held the pads as the current got up to speed. Someone shouted. A mother screamed, 'Jordie.' Car wheels screeched on the road. Nikki leapt off the footpath in front of the car. Snatched up the wee boy, held him tight against her chest. The car came straight at her. *Thud.* She flew through the air, still holding the boy. Banged down hard on her side. Pain overtook everything except the boy in her arms. Pain. Bleeding. More pain. Oblivion.

Nikki sat bolt upright, gripping the bedcover to her chest, panting hard. Sweat poured down her face, her neck, between her breasts. Her thigh ached, her elbow hurt. All part of the familiar nightmare, with more drama from the bus accident thrown in. When would they stop? Ten months since she'd rescued Jordie, and right now it felt like today.

After swinging her legs over the edge of the bed, she stood up slowly, fighting the shakiness threatening to undermine her stability. So much for being a strong woman who coped with anything. Being a doctor had its ups and downs. Helping people when they were ill or injured was what it was all about, but it wasn't always easy to put aside the images of pain and trauma.

A cup of tea would calm her. That and reading a chapter or two of the novel she'd begun the night before. Hopefully she'd finally get some dreamless sleep before the alarm went off. It usually worked, so fingers crossed. She could try thinking about Shaun to deflect other pictures filling her head, but he wasn't meant to be that important. His role in her life was as a doctor in the emergency department, and nothing more.

Except a hiking companion on Saturday.

No, not happening. She'd pull out of that in the morning.

'You looked whacked,' Shaun said as he crossed the parking lot towards Nikki first thing next day. 'Didn't get a lot of sleep?' There were dark shadows under her eyes, and the sparkly sapphire shade was dull. She was still limping badly.

'Not enough, that's for sure.'

'Is there such a thing?' The urge to reach out and hug her had him shoving his hands in his pockets as they headed for the hospital's main entrance. 'Should we go in the side door?'

'You're thinking about reporters? I'm presuming

they're more interested in other staff now those patients are on the wards.'

'I hope you're right.' The way Nikki looked would have reporters making up reasons for why she appeared so shattered. 'Let's go for the side door anyway.' He took her elbow to underline his point, and was relieved when she went with him.

'What did you do last night?'

'Had dinner with the parents. They'd heard about the accident and knew where the injured people would've been taken, so Mum doubled the casserole and told me to get my backside around there.'

'She sounds lovely.' Was that longing in Nikki's voice?

'Even better, Mum and Dad know when not to ask questions about my day.'

Nikki glanced at him. 'You're so lucky. Most people want all the details even when they know you don't want to share.'

'True. Your family included?'

'My brother's a firefighter so totally gets why I hate talking about the bad days.'

Of course doctors weren't meant to talk about their patients, but there were times they needed to get things off their chest, and usually that was with someone they could trust to keep their mouth shut. 'If you want to go over anything from yesterday, I'm available.' No barriers between them when it came to work-related subjects.

Another glance came his way, this time with a frown. 'Thank you, but I'll be all right.'

'I'm sure you will, but it never hurts to share.' Not that he'd ever been good about sharing the pain he went through when Liam died, nor when Amy left. Nothing had been the same since.

'If only it was that easy.'

They were on the same page. 'Okay, we can share coffee and talk about the weather for tomorrow's hike. That way no one will get upset.' He was going for relaxed when he felt anything but. Nikki was lovely. He'd also seen a hint of vulnerability when she'd glanced at him. Before she'd pulled down the shutters.

'About tomorrow.' She paused. She would change her mind, cancel on him. It was there in her set mouth, in the now determined look in her tired eyes. Then she shook her head. 'Forget it.'

Despite what she'd told him, he'd bet Nikki hadn't slept a wink last night. 'Forgotten already.' He wasn't going to let her off the hook too easily. He wanted to go hiking with her, spend time away from here getting to know more about what made her tick.

Thankfully they'd reached the ED. Time to get changed into scrubs and find out what was happening in the department and put private conversation aside. 'It's quiet in here,' he noted.

'Long may that last,' Nikki gave him a small smile that inexplicably tugged at his heartstrings. 'I'm not asking for a slow day with nothing serious because that'd definitely tempt trouble, but I can hope for a quiet hour or two to start with.'

'I'm with you.' He swallowed. With her in more ways than he'd have believed possible given how he wasn't ready for a woman to come into his life. Went to show how Nikki had edged in under his skin with her calm, strong manner during yesterday's mayhem. She'd been professional as well as compassionate. Admirable and downright nice. Qualities that were important to him. *Not looking, eh?* He *was* remaining single for a long time yet. There were other things he needed to concentrate on before contemplating looking for a woman to share his life with. Settling down permanently was top of that list. Having a woman in his life meant risking his heart. It didn't need a battering when it was only now recovering from his losses.

'Hello, you two,' Michaela called from the hub. 'Looks like you could do with a few more hours sleep.'

'Thanks, Doc,' Shaun quipped. 'How was your night?'

'Not too bad for a Thursday. The usual drunks with broken noses and twisted ankles, a cardiac arrest around midnight, an appendicitis, and so on. Nothing as horrific as yesterday.' Michaela stood up, stretching her back. 'We did have a reporter sneak in with a patient, hoping to get some answers to questions about the victims of the bus incident. Security dealt with him fast.'

Nikki shook her head. 'Seriously? He believed he'd learn something titillating at that time of the night?' The loathing was strong in her voice. 'Some reporters don't give a toss for the people they upset.' She'd know after saving that boy.

As did he from his experience of landing the Cessna with Liam aboard. 'They're not all bad, but some are loathsome.'

'Right. I'm getting changed,' Nikki said. 'Then having coffee before we get started.'

He watched her limp away, head high, back straight as though no one should notice her uneven walk. Those tight, light blue jeans emphasised her shapely legs and firm muscles. Nothing like long legs to turn up the heat in his body. Was Nikki still hiking tomorrow? She had to be in pain to be walking like that. Was that why she'd been going to cancel? If so, now he'd accept that maybe she should.

'Her leg plays up whenever she spends too much time on it,' Michaela commented matter-of-factly.

'We never stopped yesterday, and I imagine bending over beds doesn't help either.'

'Don't say a word if you want a peaceful day.' Michaela grinned.

No surprise there. 'Got you.' Seemed Nikki didn't go for sympathy. He presumed the limp was a result of the injury where that car hit her. There'd been mention of a fracture in some of the articles about her grabbing the kid, but if he wanted to find out more, he'd ask Nikki, no one else. He headed for the men's changing room. The thought of coffee to go with the egg roll he'd bought on the way in was making him salivate.

Nikki swallowed coffee and light analgesics as she watched Shaun decimate his egg roll. 'That looks yummy.' Her apricot croissant was tasty, but for some reason, his breakfast looked better. Nothing to do with the long fingers that picked up the roll. Nothing at all.

'Wish I'd bought two,' he said as he screwed up the paper bag it came in. 'That's not a bad café over the road.'

'Suzie's?'

He nodded.

'Everyone's favourite. Most of the hospital staff go there.'

'So you drove today.'

'Can't trust the weather at the moment.' Her leg wasn't in the mood for striding out the kilometres from home, which was a concern if she didn't cancel tomorrow. Except she was desperate to get out in the hills. Walking with Shaun would be a bonus if she stopped thinking of reasons to avoid him. Maybe she wouldn't cancel on him. Sitting here, she felt a little wound up and warm. Even in shapeless scrubs, his body appeared sexy. There was a light stubble on his chin, which made her palms itch. He was too unsettling when she wasn't concentrating on anything else. Scary. It was so unlike her to get rattled around any man, good-looking or not. 'Anyway, I'm going shopping after work.' The new filter she'd ordered for her camera had arrived, and she wanted to use it tomorrow.

His smile said he knew she wasn't being totally honest, and that he didn't care. Kind of a new experience for her. 'From what I saw when I looked up the forecast, today's meant to be fine all day,' he said.

So was tomorrow. She'd checked when looking for an excuse not to go hiking with him. Her leg would hurt like crazy until she warmed up, but her head would hurt worse if she didn't get out in the air and quieten down all the noise going on in there. Those were things she would not tell Shaun. She didn't do sharing personal concerns. The last thing she wanted was sympathy.

'Hey, mind if I join you?' Michaela sank onto a chair between them.

Michaela was the distraction she needed. 'Go for it.' No more taking sneak peeks at Shaun and wondering what lay behind his doctor façade.

'Want coffee?' the man filling her head asked Michaela.

'Love one.'

'Nikki, another?'

'Please.' His husky voice sent a shiver down her spine. She needed to get working and find something that required total concentration so she could put Shaun out of her head except when it came to patients. Easy to think, harder to make happen.

A couple of hours later, Shaun stood at the end of the counter where she was requesting an online prescription for a little girl with an infection in both ears. 'Can you take a look at my patient when you've got a moment, Nikki?'

'Sure. What's up?'

'Josie Lane, fifty-four, mild concussion after falling off a ladder, fractured ulna and radius, right side.'

Nikki looked up at Shaun. 'But?'

'You're on to it.' Concern filled his face. 'The wounds occurred three days ago. Her husband brought her into the department then. He was the one who filled in the triage nurse and follow-up doctor on what had happened.'

'Who saw her?'

'Jack. He's tagged her notes with a caution—says he wasn't sure if the husband was being truthful about a fall from a ladder or covering up some abuse. Not a lot he could do when Josie insisted on going home after her arm was put in a cast.'

'I hate these cases. My heart goes out to anyone who might be abused. The trouble is that we can't be certain that's what's happening unless the victim says so, and most times they refuse to do that.'

'For fear of more abuse once they leave here.' Shaun sat at the computer next to her and brought up Josie's notes. 'I'm going to get her arm X-rayed again to make sure it hasn't got worse. I've seen fresh bruises on her abdomen. She was quick to pull her top down when she realised I'd noticed them.'

'Is the husband with her?'

'He's gone to the pharmacy to collect the script I ordered. I told them to take their time so I could talk to you.'

'I'll see her now.' Nikki pushed up from her chair.

'Hopefully she might be a little more open speaking with a female doctor.'

Glad he'd noticed. Nikki bit down on her bottom lip to keep that to herself. 'I'll see what I can do. No promises.'

'Nikki? I get it. These cases are the most difficult when it comes to learning what truly happened. Cubicle ten,' he added.

She headed down the line of cubicles until she reached number ten. The woman looked on edge. 'Hello, Josie. I'm Dr Marlow. Call me Nikki. I hear you had a fall a few days ago.'

'Yes.' Her fingers were scratching at the bedcover. She lowered her head so as not to meet Nikki face-on.

'So what brings you back here today? Another fall?'

The woman was clothed from neck to feet. It must've been a fluke that her top rode up when Shaun was with her.

'Sort of. I slipped down the stairs during the night while going to the bathroom.' She was talking too fast, as though trying to get everything out of the way.

Nikki closed the curtains and nodded at Georgie standing on the other side of the bed. 'I think we should give you a full check over to make sure you haven't got any other serious injuries. Is that all right?'

'No. The other doctor checked my arm, said I need an X-ray again. I don't need anything else.'

'Did you bump your head this time?' Nikki carefully felt around Josie's skull.

'No.'

'It feels all right. Now can I check your tummy?' To

see the bruises Shaun mentioned. It was an area often struck by an abusive partner because it could be kept hidden.

'Why?'

'I like to be thorough. Can't send you home without being certain there're no other injuries that need attention.'

Josie loosely wrapped her arms around her waist. 'I only came because my arm's still hurting. Nothing else is wrong.'

Nikki sat on the edge of the bed. 'Josie, did you truly fall off a ladder the other day?'

No reply.

'Do you want to tell me what happened?'

Blink, blink. Those fingers tightened.

'We can get you help. Also, we can prevent your husband from coming in here while you talk to someone.'

Josie swung her head back and forth vigorously. 'No.'

No surprise there. 'Have you talked to anyone about what's going on?'

'Nothing to tell.'

'Hey, mate, another doctor's with Josie. Come and wait here until she's finished.' By the sound of it, Shaun wasn't far away and was warning her the husband was back while trying to keep him away until she'd finished talking to Josie.

The curtain was flung aside. 'Hey, babe. I've got your meds. Let's get outta here.'

'Not so fast.' Shaun was right behind him. 'Josie's going to have her arm X-rayed before you go anywhere.'

'Nah, she's not. The arm's good. Just takes time for the pain to stop. Come on, babe.'

Josie was sliding off the bed to stand up, not looking at anybody. 'Okay.'

'Josie, you need another X-ray so we can tell if the bones are healing,' Nikki told her quietly. It wasn't usual to do that, but then, neither was an abusive relationship.

'I'm good to go.' This time the distressed woman looked Nikki right in the eye. 'Thanks for your help.'

She hadn't achieved a thing. Her stomach knotted. How she hated these cases. It would be easy to turn around and berate the smug-looking man reaching for Josie's other arm, but that'd only make matters worse for Josie. In the end, the decision to get help was Josie's. All Nikki could do was put it out there that help was available when she was ready, if she found the courage to follow through.

Nikki swallowed the bile in her mouth. Her father had abused her mother mentally non-stop. Ignoring her unless he wanted something *now*. Not coming home on time for dinner, then demanding a fresh meal, not what had been waiting in the oven. His temper was fast and furious and over in an instant, to be followed by ignoring everyone around him. He never struck out physically, but then, he hadn't needed to. His verbal bullying worked perfectly. He got whatever he wanted whenever he demanded it. Except at the schools where he taught. There they quickly lost patience and asked him to leave, and once more the family would be on the road as he searched for a new position. Growing up, Nikki and her brother had never lived anywhere, merely existed. Which was why they were both settled in Christchurch with no intention of moving away. Here was home. Christchurch was where they'd both made friends who'd stayed in touch from then on. It had been a no-brainer to come back when she broke up with Brett.

'That was a fail,' she muttered as she watched Josie drag herself away with her partner holding her hard against him.

'You tried. It's all we can do,' Shaun said beside her.

She flicked around. 'It's not enough.'

'I get that, but short of causing a scene, what else could you have done?'

Her shoulders slumped. 'Nothing.' It wasn't the first time she'd tried to help a woman in a violent relationship, and the result had always been the same. The woman did what her man told her. Just like her mother in her abusive relationship. 'At least being an emergency doctor, I do get to fix people physically.'

'That's not to be taken lightly.'

Nikki walked away before she said anything else. She'd already talked too much about how she felt. 'Who's next?' she asked the first nurse she saw.

Laurie smiled. 'A wee tot named Michelle. She's so cute.'

Nikki tried not to laugh. Laurie was enamoured with little girls now she was pregnant with one of her own. 'Why's Michelle here?'

The smile disappeared. 'She's got a peanut stuck in her ear.' Laurie leaned closer, said quietly, 'Why do parents leave dangerous items lying around?'

'I think you have a lot to learn about parenting, Laurie. From what I've seen in EDs, kids manage to find all sorts of things Mum and Dad think are out of reach. Which cubicle?'

'Two. Come on. I'm with you.'

When they walked into the small space, Shaun was already there, talking softly to the little girl and at the same time calming a distraught woman, presumably the mother.

'Here's another doctor to make you better,' Shaun told Michelle. 'Say hello to Dr Nikki.' While he was talking, he was carefully examining the ear where the peanut must be.

'Oww.' Michelle jerked her head away. 'Hurt.'

Nikki sat on the bed beside her. 'Hello, Michelle. That's a pretty top you've got on. A pink elephant, is it?'

'Pretty.' Michelle nodded, earning Nikki a wry smile from Shaun.

'Oops. Keep your head still while Dr Shaun looks at your ear. I think pink must be your favourite colour. I like your pink trousers.'

'Everything's pink at the moment,' said her mother. 'Even your sheets, aren't they, sweetheart?'

'Yes, pink. Oww. Hurt again.' Michelle glared at Shaun, who had a pair of forceps in hand. He worked deftly to remove the object blocking the earhole.

'It won't hurt again. Here's the bad peanut, Michelle. Except it's a pink bead. Now your ear's going to be better.'

Michelle looked at the bead. 'I don't like it now.'

'What do you say to Dr Shaun?' her mother said.

'Thank you.'

'That's all right, Miss Pinky. Just don't go putting anything in your ears again, will you?'

'No. Naughty peanut.' She slapped at Shaun's hand. Everyone laughed.

'I'll give you some antibiotic cream to rub in twice a day just in case she's scratched the skin,' Shaun told her mother as he grinned at his little patient with a look of something like yearning in his eyes. 'Otherwise you're good to go.'

Nikki understood that yearning. She mightn't be prepared to risk falling in love only to find the man was like her father or Brett, but it was her dream to become a mother. But to do that, she wanted a partner to be there for her child too, to be the loving dad she'd always dreamed of for herself.

'Nikki, the paramedics are bringing in a seventy-year-old woman with a probable fractured thigh,' Nurse Cameron called from the hub. 'They'll be here in five.'

'Put her in the trauma bay. What happened, do you know?'

'Slipped down the outside steps at home, apparently.'

'Okay, let me know when she's here.' Nikki headed to the hub feeling good despite worrying about Josie. Was that anything to do with Shaun? She couldn't see how. He did tickle her interest, but surely not to such an extent that she was waking up to possibilities about anything more than working together?

And going hiking tomorrow. Hmm. So much for cancelling. It wasn't too late. But something held her back, suggesting she should go for it and have a day out with a gorgeous man. Anything to blot out the nightmares she'd had last night.

'See you in the morning,' Shaun said as they left the department together at knock-off time.

'About that.' She paused, drew a breath. 'I'm looking forward to it.'

Shaun exhaled sharply. Knock him down, why didn't she? So much for thinking she was going to pull out of the walk. Instead she was looking forward to hitting the hills with him. 'Me too.'

He truly was. Nothing better than getting out in the

fresh air and pushing his body hard. Could be even better doing so with a lovely woman who was definitely snagging his attention, whether she meant to or not. It was becoming impossible to ignore the warmth that enveloped him when around Nikki. She intrigued him with her smarts and her vulnerability.

'It wouldn't be much fun if you weren't,' she quipped.

'You think?'

'I can't stand gloomy people when I'm out doing what I love best. Can't stand them any time, in fact.'

'Hopefully I don't fit into that category.' Except when it came to sharing himself too much with a woman. Then he wasn't gloomy, more wary so not as much fun as he could be. Might have to put his fun hat on tomorrow to prove he wasn't too dull to be around. There was one thing he had to ask though. 'You're still limping quite a bit. Will your leg be all right?'

'It had better be. I'm going, no matter how it feels.'

'No surprise there.' He grinned, pleased with her reply. 'Seven still suit for pick-up?'

'Perfect.'

He was hoping for a perfect day in every way. Weather, the hike he hadn't done for a long time, and the company, though he already had no doubts that Nikki would be fun to be with. He enjoyed working with her, so why wouldn't hiking be the same? Sharing lunch on a hilltop as they took in the views beyond? His chest rose and fell a little too quickly. He was excited. Damn it.

CHAPTER FOUR

BANG ON SEVEN the next morning, there was a knock on her front door. Nikki shook her head. She'd over-slept—something she never did—and now she was flap-ping around like a bee in a jar getting ready. Just as well she'd put everything she required into her backpack last night. 'Morning, Shaun. Come in. I'm having a coffee. Want one?'

'I never say no to coffee.'

'Even when we're meant to leave at seven?' she teased.

He smiled. 'I can take it with me.'

Her stomach knotted while her head felt light. That smile would do it for her every time. There hadn't been many in her life that could trip her up, but Shaun's did far too easily. 'Leaving five minutes later than planned won't change a thing.' The idea of sitting in the SUV be-side him suddenly felt like it could get awkward if she fell into his smiles without thought. She wanted more, but receiving a Shaun smile was unlikely to change how she looked at life. She'd no doubt be in for a big disap-pointment if she didn't keep her sensible hat on.

'I take it you carry first-aid gear when you go hiking?' Shaun asked as he sipped the coffee she handed him.

'Of course.' Not only for herself but for anyone she might come across on the walk who needed medical attention. It had happened a couple of times in the past. Broken ankles on both occasions. 'Don't you?'

'Yes. I'm being careful, that's all.'

'I also carry an ELB.' Emergency locator beacons were the best piece of equipment any hiker could take when in the hills. Weather could change rapidly, causing people to become disorientated. Accidents also happened when least expected, and the best way to get help was to use the beacon.

'Me too.'

'Then we're well equipped if something goes wrong.' They could leave one of everything here, but somehow she doubted Shaun would. As the gear didn't add much weight to her pack, she wouldn't either. After draining her mug, she put it in the dishwasher. 'Let's go stretch our legs.'

'From what I remember of this walk, it will be more than a stretch.'

'How much hiking have you done recently?'

'Very little, but I do keep fit by running daily.'

Glancing down, she noted his trousers were like hers in that the bottom half of the legs could be unzipped to make the pants into shorts. If the day turned out warm, he might do that, and she'd get to ogle his muscles. Showed how boring her life had got if that was a turn-on. 'Do you mind stopping at a bakery on the way out of town? I haven't got any lunch.'

'Already on the agenda.'

'Cool.' Grabbing her camera from the hall table, she locked the door and followed Shaun to his vehicle.

'That's a serious camera,' he said as he started the SUV. 'Photography your go-to?'

'Totally. I'm in another world when I'm taking photos.

It becomes me and whatever has my total focus. I'm into birds more than anything.'

'Glad I don't have wings.'

'You don't like having your photo taken?' She smirked. Then felt disappointed. It would've been good to get a snap of Dr Sexy. No, it wouldn't. That would be weird when she wasn't interested in him more than as a colleague—and a hiking partner. It also wouldn't be difficult to take the odd snap when he was concentrating on something else.

'Not fussed one way or the other.'

Maybe she could take a picture without getting growled at.

'Have you heard how our patients from the bus incident are getting on?' Shaun asked as he drove away from her house.

A change of subject to keep her off the topic of photographs? She'd oblige for now. 'The four who were sent to ICU after surgery are still there. All except the man with head injuries are making progress. He had another operation late yesterday afternoon after a second brain haemorrhage.'

'Not good.' Shaun's hands tightened on the steering wheel. 'It freaks me out how someone can get up in the morning to go about their normal day only to have it turn to disaster through no fault of their own.'

Wow. That was quite a speech for this man. It was sounding more and more like something awful had happened to him in the past. Something that was behind his usual reticence to talk about himself? 'I admit I often feel the same. We see the repercussions from those situations, don't we?' After saving Jordie, she knew exactly what it felt like to have a normal day turned upside down through no fault of her own. It had been an instinctive reaction. If she'd hesitated to think about it then she'd have been too late. Would she do it again? Definitely.

'Yes, a lot of them. They don't go away easily either.' There was a new tightness in Shaun's voice.

She'd swear he *had* faced something horrific at some point of his life. As a consequence, had he lost someone close or been badly injured himself? Not her place to ask when they didn't know each other very well. Perhaps Shaun, like her, had learned to hold in pain and not share it with anyone. It didn't matter how often she'd been pulled out of one school to be dumped into another where she knew no one. She never got used to it. She learned not to complain. Otherwise her father would lecture her about how he was the money earner and she'd put up with whatever he chose to do. So when the man she'd believed to be the love of her life walked away after saying the *other* woman needed him more, she wondered if she'd ever be free of her doubts when it came to relationships. She trusted Ross and her closest friends, but she wasn't in a hurry to be too accepting of anyone else. Especially if it meant handing over her heart. Of course she was asking a lot of life, but that's how it was.

'Where have you gone?' Shaun asked.

'Nowhere important.' Not to him, anyway. 'Thanks for offering to drive. I'll fix you up for fuel.' He hadn't offered, just said he was picking her up, but she could play nice.

'That won't be necessary. I'm glad to be getting out and about after the week we've had.'

'Apart from Thursday, how are you finding working with us?' He might've taken up a permanent position and had talked about buying a house, but he was known to move around a lot. Chances were he mightn't be in Christchurch that long. Something to remain wary about. She wasn't getting involved with a man who could pack his bags and move on without a thought for anyone else. Right, Dad? Brett?

'Can't complain.' He glanced across and smiled that devastating smile. 'You wouldn't listen.'

'Maybe not today.' Relaxing into the seat, she decided to drop any talk about work and go with the flow. Except with Shaun, that meant a lot of silence. He wasn't into talking for the sake of it any more than she was. She didn't mind. It was a comfortable silence, though the noise in her head built up as she thought about him. He was unlike most men she knew in that he didn't try to impress her, or show how wonderful he was, or talk for the sake of it. Yes, he was interesting—to the point she couldn't wait to arrive at their destination and get her boots on to hit the hills, so she'd have something else to focus on. He was quite a diversion when she wasn't looking for one.

He interrupted her thoughts. 'Where did you live in Christchurch as a child?'

'Halswell.' A rental property with no yard and little space inside. Her father wasn't into saving his teacher's salary, preferred to spend it on high-end motorcycles and showy clothes. The meagre wages her mother made working in shops went to feeding them. 'How about you?'

'Merivale. My parents are still there, though they've handed over the gardening and upkeep of the property to experts. They're in their seventies and tell everyone their spare time's now for fun. The real reason is Mum was a very keen gardener, but arthritis prevents her from continuing, and she doesn't like the place looking in the least messy because it never did when she looked after it.'

Merivale was high-end, unlike Halswell. 'Your father's not interested.'

'No way. Gardens are for looking at, not for spending hours on your hands and knees, pulling weeds.'

'I agree with him. There's nothing like a well-designed garden to make me smile, but I'm no gardener. I tried but got frustrated when I put in plants and all looked good. Then they started growing, and the heights were all over the place, and nothing looked right.' That had been during the first year in her house. Since then she paid someone to maintain a simple garden while she stuck to mowing the lawns. 'What about you? Are you into gardens?'

'Never given it a go. Guess I'll find out when I get around to buying my own home.'

'Doesn't sound like you're in a hurry.'

'I'm looking, but so far nothing's appealed.'

She opened her mouth to ask more about him staying permanently, then noticed his hands tighten on the steering wheel again, and closed it. The last thing she wanted was to get offside with Shaun today. Instead she stared at the passing scenery and tried not to wonder what made him tick.

As if that was possible in the confined space. Every time she breathed in, she smelled spicy aftershave. Each time she shifted her head to the right, she noted firm trouser-covered thighs. It didn't matter what she did. She was totally aware of Shaun. Did that make her feel good? She winced. She wasn't sure. She hadn't done getting to know men well since Brett turned out to be a liar and so cruel. It was still hard to believe she hadn't sensed something was off in their relationship when he was having the affair. Her fault? Or his? She'd never really know, which made her wonder if she could ever trust a man to love her honestly. But it might be time to stop blaming herself for all that went wrong. It took two to make a happy couple, and Brett had been the one to play around. Not her.

'This the turn-off?' Shaun asked as he slowed down.

'Yes. You haven't been here?'

'Once a few years back, but I wasn't a hundred per cent certain I had it right. My mate and I used to do a bit of hiking when we had time.' Again his hands tightened on the steering wheel.

What was bothering him? He sometimes seemed to say things he instantly regretted. Odd. Could be he was like her and not used to talking too much about himself to someone he didn't really know, so he struggled with saying things he didn't normally. 'There a problem?'

'No.'

Okay. 'Molly and I started hiking when I was specialising and she'd joined the fraud squad. We both needed to get away from unpleasant cases for a few hours as a reminder that life wasn't all bad.'

'We all need that at times, hence today.'

'Agreed.'

'So Molly's a cop?' He was good at abrupt changes in conversations.

'She studied to become an accountant and is now a detective investigating shady businesses. We and another friend shared a house when we were studying in Auckland. I said I was moving to Christchurch, and they came too. Molly's from around here. We were pals when I was here as a kid. As for Collette, she's from Auckland and couldn't wait to get away from there.'

'Too big?'

'Something like that.' An abusive boyfriend who followed her wherever she went in the city was the main reason.

'Not many people on the track at the moment,' Shaun commented as he parked on the grass near two vehicles at the beginning of the walk.

'Just how I prefer it.'

Shaun grinned. 'You wouldn't be a bit of a loner, by any chance?'

He didn't realise what he was asking. A loner? Or plain lonely? Both at times. Though not so much these days. 'I can be.' It was true. There were plenty of moments when the past came back to knock at her confidence and she'd withdraw from people, afraid of getting hurt again.

The grin disappeared. 'Why? You appear very outgoing, especially when you're telling reporters to go away.'

He was too shrewd for her liking. He'd have her spilling everything about her past if she wasn't careful. 'It's how I am.'

'And when you're helping patients, there's no holding you back.' This time his grin was gentle, as though he understood what she wasn't saying.

'You know how to win me over, don't you?' He could turn out to be too much if she wanted to remain a little aloof. The barriers were already crumbling, and she wasn't sure she could take whatever lay behind them, be it wonderful or bad, because mostly wonderful turned to bad anyway.

'I say it as I see it. Let's get our boots on and hit the dirt. I've been looking forward to this.'

'Me, too. And Shaun, I'm pleased you're here. I do prefer walking with someone else, and this will give us a chance to get to know each other better.' Did she want that? Yes, she did. What's more, she refused to regret it.

She liked him a lot. She was coming to accept he might be on the same page as her when it came to getting to know someone more than as a colleague. Wary but interested.

'You talk too much, Nikki.' His grin was broad as he stuffed his foot into a boot.

'Smart alec.' She liked him teasing her. It made friendship real. Boots on and laced up, Nikki swung her day pack over her shoulders, her camera around her neck, and started for the track. Shaun was right behind her, making her more aware of him than ever. At least she'd put on fitted trousers that would flatter her behind. A laugh rolled over her tongue. Being concerned about how a man might see her physically was so unlike her it was funny.

'What's amusing you?'

'Nothing.'

'In other words, you're not sharing.'

'Damn right I'm not.' She laughed again and looked up at the clear sky. 'Looks like the weather's gotten over its wet mood and giving us a good day for a change.' She'd checked the forecast again when she got up and knew they weren't going to be rained off.

'Bet you came prepared for anything.'

'Not quite. I figured it's not likely to snow.' Not that it did out here. She concentrated on the track and setting her pace, hopefully one that suited Shaun. He appeared to be fit, so she figured he wouldn't want to dawdle, but he might think she was too slow for his liking.

Shaun followed Nikki, keeping space between them so she didn't feel crowded, something he sensed she might easily do. She hadn't denied she was a bit of a loner, though she hadn't come across as such with him except for that moment when he'd made the comment about being on her own. He had a feeling that, like him, she didn't get too close to many people, though probably not for the same reason. He had some great friends, but after Liam died, he kept them at a distance.

Amy had moved on and fallen in love with a decent guy she'd married in a quiet ceremony last year with only family and a few close friends, including him, attending. He suspected it was Amy's way of showing him he could move on too. He'd agreed that he should, but knowing it was time to leave the past behind was one thing. Making it happen was not so straightforward.

But now he had started. He was in Christchurch with his family and friends nearby. He'd got a permanent job for the first time in years. Though it was too early for him to be restless, that would happen, and he would deal with it. He'd make sure of it.

As he looked ahead, his mouth dried. Was Nikki going to be a step in the process? As in the woman who could make him happy again? He stumbled, got his balance back to find Nikki had turned to see what was going on.

'Are you all right?' she asked, concern darkening her beautiful eyes.

'Absolutely. My mind wasn't on where I was going.' Actually, that's exactly where it was, just not on the track.

'Really?' Sounded like she didn't believe him.

'Really.' He wouldn't enlighten her about his thoughts. *He* needed enlightening first, and for the life of him, he had no idea where he and Nikki were headed. Except he liked her a lot. Anyway, what was wrong with having some fun and stepping out of his comfort zone along the way? It might help him settle into this new life he was determined to make work. 'Want me to go ahead?' He knew she wouldn't, but anything to get her turning away and moving on.

'If you want to.'

So he was hopeless at reading her. 'No, keep going. You set a good pace. I'm enjoying it.' What he was enjoying, he wasn't about to say. Those firm thighs in fitted khaki trousers were a sight to behold. So was Nikki's backside. Maybe he should've gone in front. 'How far to the top?' He couldn't remember the exact lay of the land.

'Roughly another hour and a half.'

They'd been walking around that long already. 'Not bad.' They were ahead of the time on the sign back at the beginning, but then, those signs usually gave a longer estimate so as not to send people on a walk they mightn't be able to manage safely in the suggested time frame.

Nikki paused, focused on a weka running along the track a couple of metres in front of them. Her camera was already in her hands as she waited patiently for the bird to stop. When it turned back, she focused the lens. 'They're not shy birds,' she said quietly.

No, they were cheeky and had no problem with strutting up to a person and taking a bite of their food if possible.

Click. Click. Click.

Nikki straightened. 'I am a bit OTT when it comes to taking photos, so expect the occasional delay if we come across something interesting.'

'No problem. What do you do with all the photos?'

'I had a calendar made last year using photos I'd taken of a variety of birds.'

'Did you sell the calendars?' Another side to Dr Marlow he hadn't known about. Along with just about everything else.

She smiled happily. 'I sold heaps of them. Couldn't quite believe it when the retailer rang to say she'd run out, and could I get another print run done ASAP.' The passion was gleaming in her eyes. 'It was great having my photos accepted by so many people.'

'Got any left?' It was over halfway through the year, but he'd like to have one.

She blinked. 'Yes, I still have a few. Do you want one?'

'You bet I do.' He meant it. He wasn't playing nice to get onside with Nikki.

'Remind me when you drop me off.'

He didn't believe for a moment that she'd forget. She was testing him to see if he truly wanted one or was only being polite. 'Will do,' he agreed.

Nikki started walking, her camera still in her hand, no doubt looking for another photo opportunity. There were always thrushes and blackbirds about, if nothing else. Though being cautious creatures, they wouldn't sit around waiting for Nikki to do her thing.

As they continued up the track, he thought about other times he'd gone hiking, mostly with Liam. They'd often done overnight trips and bunked down in a hut for the night, which he'd missed doing over the past years. Now he'd found someone else to do it with, someone he was getting on with. Hopefully Nikki might be open to other walks with him. Maybe even an overnight one at some point. *Don't go there.* That was getting a little intense even when lots of hikers did it. He wasn't ready to share a hut with Nikki, unless there were thirty other people there at the same time, and then it would be noisy with everyone talking and moving about, nothing like being in the bush with quiet surroundings to relax in.

'At last,' Nikki said when they crested the hill and began tugging her pack off.

Shaun stepped close and took it from her. 'There you go.'

She rolled her shoulders. 'That feels good.' Glugging at her water bottle, she looked out over the valley below. 'This is wonderful.'

'Not bad, is it? Wonder what everyone else is doing?'

'No sign of the people from those other vehicles,' she said.

'The track continues down the other side of the hill and around the bottom back to the beginning where we set out. It's a lot longer distance.'

'I haven't done it, and I don't think I want to today.'

'Good answer.' He wasn't keen to go much further. His legs were letting him know they were out of practice, and they still had to return to the car park.

Her eyes crinkled at the corners as she laughed. 'Thank goodness.' Opening her pack, she pulled out the chicken and salad rolls she'd bought at the bakery. 'Help yourself.'

'Thanks.' He dug out the berry muffins and cheese scones he hadn't been able to choose between. His plan to make a bacon and egg pie the other night had fizzled out.

'How often do you do walks like this?' he asked.

'About once a month, depending on what Molly's up to and my shifts.'

'Do you still lose any sleep over the accident where you saved that little boy?'

Nikki coughed, staring at him as though he'd asked the worst possible question. Then she rubbed her lips with the back of her hand and set down the roll. 'You think I lost sleep?'

'I can't imagine you didn't have at least the occasional nightmare.'

She nodded slowly. 'Did you know what happened before Thursday when those reporters spoke about it?'

'It did make the national news. More than once,' he added bluntly. Did she really think he wouldn't have recognised her after her face had been on TV and the news apps for days less than a year ago? Had she recognised him from four years back when he'd made the news for landing the Cessna in one piece? She hadn't given any indication that she had, but she wasn't always easy to read. 'When I got the job at Christchurch General, I asked if you still worked there.'

'Why?'

She'd intrigued him with her determination not to let the media make a big deal about her. Not everyone who'd done a heroic act wanted to avoid letting the world find out. 'I like to know who I'm working with.'

She didn't look convinced. 'What happened that day hasn't affected my work in any way.'

He hadn't said anything like that, but he let it go. 'What about your sleep?'

She shivered. 'Sometimes.'

'It's understandable. Did dealing with those victims of the bus incident bring everything back?'

'Yes.' She picked up the chicken roll again and took a bite. Her way of saying *no more questions*?

He understood, but for once he didn't feel like playing nice. He knew too well how those nightmares went, having had them screw with his life far too often. 'Have you seen anyone about the nightmares?'

'No. They're occurring less often, so I must be getting

on top of them.' She shivered, which told him she wasn't being entirely honest.

He didn't push it any further. It was a long drive back to the city if he fell out with her. 'Those people who were injured in the bus incident will have their problems getting through what happened, and I'm not talking only about their physical injuries.'

'I can't see any of them rushing up to a pedestrian crossing any time soon. They were all lucky not to have been injured worse. Even the worst cases got through, though some have a long road to recovery ahead.'

'I agree.' Here they were sitting looking out over some stunning scenery, and they were back at Thursday's carnage. Not great. They were meant to be letting it go. He changed the subject. 'Have you walked the Milford Track?'

'No. It's on my bucket list, except these days you have to be quick when they open the site for bookings, and I figure it'll be crowded, so I'd rather do some other ones instead. What about you?'

'Did it a couple of years ago, and it was amazing, but even then it was busy. Like you, I prefer fewer people and more quiet. What about the Heaphy Track? That's another good one.'

'Molly and I did it last year and loved every moment. Each day the terrain was so different to the previous one. We started at the Collingwood end and came out at Karamea, where we spent a couple of days wandering around the area.' A soft sigh escaped her lips. 'It was whitebait season, so we made the most of that, eating fritters every night.'

'Can't beat a whitebait fritter. I tried whitebaiting as a kid but was too impatient to sit waiting to collect enough in the net to make it worthwhile.' He laughed. 'Far easier to pay a small fortune for some at the takeaway shop.'

Nikki returned his laugh. 'Not a patient man?'

'I've improved with age, though doubt I'd like white-baiting any more these days than I did back then.'

'Take a good book with you and the time will fly by.'

'You think?' She might have a point.

'No idea.' She grinned and sent his stomach into a riot of need.

Standing up, Shaun downed half a bottle of water. Time to focus on walking and not the hot woman with him. 'Guess we'd better not hang around too long. There're some dark clouds on the horizon.' Not what had been forecast, but then, meteorologists weren't per-fect. Though right now, he was almost grateful the fore-cast might be wrong as it was a good excuse to get going. This time he'd take the lead so he didn't have a view that had him thinking of sex.

Somehow he doubted it was going to be that easy to stop thinking about Nikki at all. She was gorgeous.

CHAPTER FIVE

NIKKI COULDN'T BELIEVE how relaxed she felt when Shaun pulled into her driveway hours later. 'It's been a great day.' She'd definitely sleep without interruptions from nightmares tonight. Despite them talking briefly about the horrors of Thursday, she was okay again, which was better than she'd hoped. Shaun had been quick to get them off the subject of work and onto more interesting topics. 'Would you like to come in for a drink of anything?'

He put the gear in Park and leaned back, regarding her with a softness he hadn't shown before. Nor was it what she was used to from a man she didn't know well. 'I've a better idea. How about we go for a meal later on?'

It was a lovely thought even though it meant something more personal than walking in the hills. Or did it? Was she overreacting to a simple invitation to have dinner together? Probably, but then, that's what she did. 'I'd like that. A lot,' she added without thought, and didn't regret it for a moment. It would be fun to go out with a man who had her heating up one moment, then cooling off the next as reality set in. Shaun was opening her eyes to a new world, and whatever the outcome, she was going to grab the moments they had together and make the most of whatever was on offer. Where the heck did that come from? Dinner was dinner, no more, no less. It could be a lot more. *Stop it. You've said yes, so make the most of it and see where this new friendship goes from here.*

Shaun was laughing softly, as though she'd made a joke. Maybe he'd read her mind. Not likely. She was good at keeping her thoughts to herself. 'What's funny?'

'I can't believe we're spending so much time together and how much I'm enjoying it.'

That was honest—if she could trust him. She had to. It was time to let go of some of her fears. He did seem to be thinking the same about their day. Somehow that made it easier to accept she was getting closer to him and more interested in who he was behind that sometimes withdrawn expression. 'So am I.' Opening the door, she reached for her pack. 'Where shall we go?'

'Leave that to me. I'll pick you up at seven if it suits.'

Plenty of time to soak in the bath and find the right outfit to wear, plus have a small wine for Dutch courage in case she suddenly got cold feet thinking of all the reasons she shouldn't be going out with Dr Elliott. Such as she worked with him, and he could make her happy, then walk away without a care in the world. Or he could turn out to be the one who got her back on track for the life she dreamed of. 'Perfect.'

'Anything you don't like to eat?'

'Very little.'

'Good. See you later.'

Nikki watched Shaun drive away with a growing warmth that was new. She hadn't felt excited about a date in so long. Strange considering she'd only met Shaun on Monday. Or was that how these things went? They'd worked well together, which had garnered a certain amount of respect and trust, and today's hike added to that. They got along like they'd known each other for months. Yes, he was waking her up in all sorts of ways. Usually that would make her hesitant about going out with him, but for once she didn't want to let the chance go by. She'd begun to feel she was ready to try to find love again, but every time she'd felt that since Brett left her, she'd got over it fast, not wanting to face heartache again. But if she didn't keep at it, then the future was already decided. A solitary one she wanted less and less by the day.

She wanted to love and be loved by a special man. She dreamed of having children to adore and watch over as they grew into adults and beyond. To share a home and time and holidays and problems. The only way to find that was to take risks and step out into the fray that was dating. Starting tonight.

Shaun smiled all the way home. He had a date with Nikki. He had to pinch himself to believe she'd agreed to go with him, though why he was surprised he had no idea. Only that Nikki was taking over his sane mind and turning it into mush whenever she came near. Of course he shouldn't have asked her out to dinner, but how could he not? She'd been sitting beside him all the way back to town, filling the air with the scent of the outdoors, reminding him what a great time they'd had and thinking how special she was.

Very special. Scary and exciting. He was home for good. It was exhilarating. He had to stick to his guns and not be sidetracked by memories of the fateful day that changed his life forever. His mate would've been the first person to tell him to grab whatever opportunities came along so his dreams became real. 'Yes, well, pal, I'm doing my best.' So far it was better than good. But he had to go slowly on the romance thing. That was the riskiest of everything he'd set out to achieve.

Where to go for dinner? Shaun pressed the call button for his brother on the car phone. 'Hey, Archie, where's a good place to go for dinner around here?'

'Depends what you're wanting. If you're trying to impress a woman, then I'd say the Blue House, but if it's a casual kind of night, then the Fish Box is ideal. They're both in Merivale.'

Not too far from home, or Nikki's place, for that matter. 'I'll check them out when I get home. How's your day been?'

'If you like watching seven-year-olds playing soccer, then great.'

'I'll come next week.' He'd been to his nephew Thomas's game the previous weekend and laughed the whole time. The kids were cute, running around after the ball, being very earnest as they attempted to kick it in the right direction. 'I've been hiking. It was good to get out in the hills and forget everything else for a while.'

'Go with anyone?'

'One of the doctors from work.' *And that's all I'm saying, because you'll have fun going on about me with a woman.*

'Not who you're going to dinner with, by any chance?'

Showed where his mind was. He hadn't given it any thought when he'd called Archie. 'One and the same,' he admitted. Since he'd returned home for good, he might as well involve his brother in some of what he was up to. 'Anyway, got to go. Thanks for those suggestions. Talk tomorrow.' He hit off and pulled away as the traffic light changed to green.

It was good being back among his family. They teased

him about the itinerant lifestyle he'd been following, but deep down, they knew how much he'd been hurting. They'd supported him through his grief, and now he owed it to them to settle into a meaningful life. The life he'd once dreamed of and could have if he remained focused on now and not the past. Funny how his smile remained firmly in place. He *was* happy. What more could he want right now? Nothing. Everything felt good.

His phone pinged with an incoming text. At the next set of traffic lights, he glanced at it and groaned.

Don't forget condoms.

Brothers. Sometimes his was the best, and sometimes he was a pain in the butt.

Not bothering to reply, Shaun continued toward his flat, deliberately ignoring the pharmacy at the mall he passed. He didn't need to stock up on condoms. There were a couple in his wallet just in case. Anyway, he and Nikki were having dinner to finish off a great day as friends. Getting into bed together would only complicate things.

Unfortunately.

She was one hot lady. And interesting. He still knew very little about what made her tick, and wanted to know more before getting in too deep. Hard to do when she wasn't very forthcoming about herself. Not that he could complain when he was reticent talking about his past. He didn't need Nikki feeling sorry for him. He'd done enough of that himself and was finally letting go, accepting the fact there'd been nothing he could've done that day to change the outcome. Sometimes life was a bitch.

Amy had moved on, showing it was possible. Now it was time he did.

When Nikki opened her door to him later, he admitted he might've started. 'You look beautiful,' he said around the lump in his throat. Yes, Nikki was attractive, but tonight in a sapphire-blue dress that barely reached her knees and showed a cleavage to dream about, she was something else. Her short black jacket emphasised the curve of her waist and tightened his groin when it was the last thing he needed right now. *Friends, remember.*

'Why, thank you.' She looked stunned as she stepped back, putting space between them. 'Want to come in?'

He shook his head. 'We might as well head to the restaurant.' It'd be easier to maintain control over his feelings when surrounded by other people.

'Then I'll grab my bag and be right with you.' She was gone.

Waiting on the doorstep, he drew steadying breaths. That woman was not Dr Marlow. That was Nikki, the woman starting to wake him up in many ways. Too many? *Bring it on*, his mind retorted. He laughed.

'Share the joke,' Nikki said as she came out the door and closed it behind her.

Quick. Come up with something sensible. 'After our walk, I'm feeling more energetic than I have in a while. Thought I'd be complaining of muscles aching in places I didn't know I had any.'

'It's the fresh air getting to you.' She grinned over her shoulder as she got into the SUV. 'You need to get outside more often.'

That wouldn't be difficult if Nikki was happy to go on other hikes with him. As he backed out of her drive, he asked, 'Have you done any of the walks around Governors Bay?'

'Most of them. Thinking you'd like to give some a go?'

'I'm keen to. Today reminded me why I used to like hiking.'

'Strange how we sometimes stop doing something we enjoy, isn't it?'

Was she asking why he'd stopped? If so, he wasn't telling her his story, but he could open up a little. Somehow he didn't think Nikki was the type to start digging for more info so she could say she knew more about him. 'I used to hike with my best mate. He died a few years ago, and I sort of drifted away from doing it.' He'd gone once with some other friends, but it wasn't the same, like something was missing. Which it was, only it wasn't some*thing*, it was Liam. Another reminder of what had happened. Yet today he hadn't once felt that way.

'I'm sorry to hear that. I'm glad you came. I needed to get out there, and I won't go alone on long walks. If it helped you find your mojo for hiking again, then that's a bonus.'

'You're right, it is.' He hadn't hesitated to suggest he'd go with her when her friend pulled out, which said more about how comfortable he felt around Nikki than anything else. The fact she didn't delve into why his friend had died added to that. It was usually the first question people asked when they heard Liam was killed. 'Anytime you want to go hiking and your friend isn't available, give me a call.'

Her smile was open and friendly. 'Can do.'

See, as easy as that. Caution had taken a back seat, making him happier. Life was looking better by the day. Seemed he was already making serious changes, though getting close to a wonderful woman wasn't on the list. That wasn't because he wanted to remain single forever, but more because he was still afraid of falling for someone and then losing her as he had Amy. For a man who used to take risks about most things, he really had become a hermit when it came to sharing his heart. Now there was a lightness in his chest he hadn't known in a long time. *Bring it on.*

Nikki placed her fork on the empty dessert plate and leaned back in the chair. 'That was delicious.' Almost as yummy as the sight before her.

The dark blue shirt Shaun wore matched his eyes perfectly, drawing her gaze to the vee pointing down his chest. His blond hair fell in light waves over the back of his neck, and her fingers itched to run through it, to feel the silkiness. It had been a while since she'd wanted to be intimate with a man, yet it hadn't taken much to feel that way about Shaun. He was a hunk. Kind and generous to go with that. Serious when he had to be, light-hearted when he didn't. Not that he talked much about himself, something she normally didn't mind, but she longed to learn more. She mightn't be willing to hand over her heart, but she could have fun while getting to know Shaun.

He put down his spoon. 'I agree.'

If he knew what else she'd been thinking, he probably wouldn't. 'I didn't know about this restaurant. I'm coming again.' Who with? She shrugged. She wasn't going to worry about that right now.

'Something else you can give me a call about.' Shaun grinned.

'You're on,' she said without thinking. But then, why

not? They'd got on well throughout the day and over a wonderful dinner. She was realising how much she'd missed having someone in her life to do the things she enjoyed with. Not since Brett had she been overly keen on a man, and now Shaun was knocking at her door far too easily. Was he someone she could trust not to hurt her? Brett had been the opposite to her father, not aloof or selfish in the least. Or so she'd thought until the day he told her he was leaving her for the pregnant woman he'd been in a relationship with on the side. Call her a fool, but she doubted Shaun was the type to go behind his partner's back and have an affair. Not that she knew why she thought so, only that he came across as sincere about everything he did. He didn't talk a lot about himself and try to impress her with things he'd done. Quite the opposite. Of course, she could be wrong. Brett hadn't appeared to be a liar or selfish either. The problem was that if she wanted to find love, then she had to start trusting men more often. Maybe this one.

'I'm going to have to give you my number, aren't I?' He was still grinning. Another surprise, because he didn't do that often.

'That'd save me looking it up at work.' She grinned back. This was getting silly. They were like teenagers on their first date. Well, it was their first date. 'Time to go?'

'Unless you'd like a nightcap?'

'No, thanks. It'd keep me awake half the night.' She suspected images of Shaun were going to do that anyway.

Shaun stood up. 'Thanks for a good time. It's been a while since I had such a lovely evening.'

He didn't date? Come on. He was good-looking and hot. There must be a queue of women wanting to go out with him. 'You're out of practice?'

His laugh made her skin tingle. 'No, but it's not often I enjoy myself so much.'

She blinked. Seriously? Shaun said that? She'd take it as a compliment. 'Maybe there are some good things to come from that bus incident.'

'Could be. It struck us both hard, and now we're working on getting over it.' He pulled his wallet from his jacket pocket. 'Together.'

She was lost for words. For a man who rarely said anything personal, he seemed to be getting carried away. Not what she'd expected, but she liked it. The trust barrier was not going up tonight. She would continue having fun until he dropped her off at home. Unless— She swallowed hard. Unless nothing. Their day together was about to finish. Nothing else was happening. So why was disappointment filling her? Life was too short for procrastination. Look at those people they'd helped in ED on Thursday. When they left home that morning, not one of them knew how their life would change so abruptly. She knew what it was like to have everything change without warning—from losing her baby and Brett to leaping in front of a moving car.

Yet it felt like the time had come to let go and take some risks.

When he pulled up at Nikki's, Shaun turned off the motor and turned to face her. 'Thanks for an awesome day. Like I said, I've really enjoyed it.'

'You and me both.'

Hauling her into his arms and kissing her blind might not go down well, but it was hard not to. Nikki was temptation on amazing legs. Shoving his door wide, he got out before he made an idiot of himself. They had to work together, and if she wasn't on the same page, life in the department would be hell.

But it was impossible to ignore the longing for someone special in his life. If he didn't ignore it, he had to start taking chances on *everything*, and put the brake on thinking about how abruptly things could change without any input from himself. Thursday had been a shocking reminder of that, which was a good reason not to follow through on the longing heating his body right now.

Opening the passenger door, he offered Nikki his hand to help her out of the car. She took it, and he kept it there as they walked up to her front door, momentarily savouring her warmth through the sleeve of her jacket, pretending the need Nikki created within him wasn't real. So much for friendship. He had to be careful. He didn't think getting too close to Nikki could end comfortably. If they started something intimate, then he suspected he might not want it to end, and he wasn't ready for that.

Opening her door, Nikki turned to him. 'I haven't had such a good time in ages.' Her eyes widened as she watched him. 'It's true.'

'Nor have I,' he said softly, forgetting the warnings he'd given himself. His hand was on her arm, and he was reluctant to pull away. He could feel her muscles tighten, then soften.

Then she was leaning close, her scent teasing him, her breath whispering across the skin on his neck. Her lips brushed across his so lightly it felt like a feather. But it wasn't. It was Nikki, her lips, her mouth, her body suddenly pressing up against his.

His arms were around her, pulling her nearer so he could feel her breasts against his chest, her firm thighs meeting his. Opening his mouth, he covered her tantalising lips, tasted her, felt her heat, wanted more. Pulling his head back, he looked into her gaze. 'Nikki?'

Her nod was abrupt as she tugged him inside and slammed the door shut behind them. Then her arms were around his neck, and his mouth again covered by hers. Warmth filled him, hunger and longing following fast. Nikki was beyond wonderful. Deepening his kiss, he drank in her taste and her heat. So much for behaving. It was impossible.

His hands found her buttocks and gripped them, pulling her up against his arousal.

Nikki groaned, long and low, driving him crazy with need. Pulling back, he looked at her. 'Nikki? Are you sure?'

Her eyes widened, and those luscious lips curved upward. 'Oh, yes.' Then she grabbed his shoulders and lifted her legs up around his waist. 'Oh, yes.'

He was throbbing with need, and when he touched her heat, he found the same reaction. Wet, hot, wanting. His fingers rubbed her. She bucked against him. This would be over before they started if they didn't slow down.

'Shaun, please. Take me.'

He was more than happy to oblige.

'One moment. I need to remove my trousers *and* find my wallet to get a condom.'

Nikki slid to the floor and waited impatiently until he'd removed his pants, then reached for him, leaning down and licking him.

'Nikki, please. I won't be able to wait if you do that.'

She snatched the condom from his fingers and tore the packet open.

Her face lit up. 'Good.'

Placing his hand under her chin, he held her still. 'No, we do this together.'

'I intend to.' Her eyes were wide with heat and a need identical to his.

He took the condom from her and deftly slid it over his throbbing erection. Lifting her back up into his arms, he turned so she was against the wall. When her legs went around his waist, he touched her centre, moving back and forward until she cried out, and then he dived into that heat. Then pulled back to repeat the move, again and again.

Nikki cried out. Louder this time as she tightened around him. He let go all restraint and dove in as deep as possible, feeling her enclose him, suck his need into hers.

How long he stood there, Nikki's legs still tight around him, he hadn't a clue, but eventually she moved, and he lowered her to stand in front of him. Her face was pink, her eyes filled with passion, and her exquisite mouth tilted into a soft smile. 'Wow.'

Leaning in, he brushed a kiss over her swollen lips. 'Yes, wow.'

She took his hand and led him to a bedroom. Hers, he presumed since the furnishings were blue and pink. More importantly, the bed was large. And soft and cosy when they lay under the covers, their clothes on the floor, and Nikki's legs wound around his.

Placing a kiss on her forehead, he sighed. 'So much for dropping you off and heading home.'

She tensed. 'You're regretting this?'

'No, I am not.' He should have been, but he wasn't going there when he felt happy beyond reason. 'That was amazing.'

The tension left Nikki as quickly as it had come. 'Good, because we're not finished yet.'

He'd barely got his breath back, but so what? Reaching for Nikki, he rose above her and set out to discover every inch of her beautiful body. Kissing and touching warm velvety skin from her face to her toes and everything in between, he couldn't stop. She was wonderful.

Nikki's hands were on his back, his thighs, his chest, his erection, heating him throughout. Turning him on as fast as the first time. He reached for his wallet, glad for a second condom or this wouldn't be happening.

'Let me.' The foil packet was gone, and Nikki was dealing with the condom.

Then he was being covered.

Taking Nikki in his hands, he slid her beneath him and gazed into her eyes, falling into her warmth and heat and sex. Knowing nothing but this. Being intimate with Nikki. Giving her more of himself than he'd thought possible.

CHAPTER SIX

'WHAT HAVE I DONE?' Nikki groaned the next morning as she rolled over in the twisted sheets.

Shaun had left a short while after they'd made love for the second time. She'd been tucked up beside him, savouring the moment with him, his hand rubbing light circles on her back. She'd known it wasn't forever but had been happy with what she got. When he hauled himself out of bed and shrugged into his clothes, she'd wanted to beg him to stay longer but instead enjoyed the view for the brief moments before he was fully dressed.

He'd leaned down to kiss her cheek. 'Again, thank you for an amazing day.'

'And night,' she'd whispered.

He'd nodded. 'You're right there. But I think I'd better be going so we don't overdo things and live to regret it in the daylight.'

He was right even though she hated to admit it. 'I agree.'

'Bye.' Then he was gone.

She'd got up to check the door was locked behind him before crawling back into bed filled with wonder and a deep longing for more of what they'd shared all day and night.

She'd been getting ahead of herself. They'd barely met and she was thinking of the future. So unlike her. Usually her way was to think more about the person than the effects he had on her. But then she hadn't had such intense desire for a man since Brett and had believed it might never happen again.

Rolling over, she'd tucked the covers up around her neck to keep warm, believing she'd lie awake most of what was left of the night.

Got that wrong, hadn't she? She couldn't remember much at all after that. Now she was wide awake, she wasn't feeling quite so relaxed about having made out with Shaun. Not once but twice, and she'd been the instigator, kissing him when he was about to leave. Not that he'd been far behind her when it came to getting turned on and ready for sex.

But reality was kicking in. They were workmates who'd spent a day together hiking and enjoying a meal. That should've been it. Friends, not lovers.

But they'd had sex. Twice. Mind-blowing sex that she wasn't going to forget in a hurry. He was good. Sexy and hot, and very satisfying. It wouldn't be easy to forget how good whenever she saw him and that would be often in the ED when rostered on the same shift. He'd been right to go when he did, but part of her regretted it. They'd been great together.

She had to focus on the fact Shaun had a history of taking short-term positions and that while his current one was supposedly permanent, the odds were stacked against him staying for long. He'd said something about buying a house and maybe getting a dog, but had he seriously started along that track, or had he been a bit casual about the houses he'd looked at? He'd mentioned doing more walks with her, but how long would he stay here? After her childhood spent regularly moving from place to place, she intended staying put. Even if she fell in love with a man who had other ideas about where he wanted to live permanently. That was the word that mattered to her. *Permanently.* At the moment, she didn't think Shaun was capable of that.

She had no idea where that thought came from. It was too soon for her to ask him if he was serious about settling down. Whatever the circumstances of his friend's death, they might be behind his inability to have settled so far. If only he'd share a bit more with her. Of course she was out of line, considering she didn't like talking about Brett and how he'd left her for the other woman, leaving her feeling unworthy and wary of taking a risk, of being hurt again.

Her phone rang. Molly. Not in the mood to talk about Shaun to her friend, who would ask about the hike, she ignored it.

Everyone needed a best buddy to share certain things with, but not when she was still working through her feelings about having slept with Shaun.

Nikki didn't want to be cautious whenever she saw him, but she knew so little about him. Believing she could trust him not to hurt her was all very well. Been there, done that. But if she loosened up, maybe she could have it all. Greedy? Why not? Other people had it all. Maybe it was her turn.

Her phone rang again. No doubt Molly trying again. But no, it was Ross.

'Hey, Nikki, got anything planned for today?'

'Not a thing.' She wasn't calling Shaun to see if he'd like to go for another walk. That would appear too eager. She was going to take things quietly—for today anyway. That was kind of what they'd agreed on when he left last night.

'Good. Haul on some warm clothes and meet us at

Hagley Park. Logan wants to see Auntie Nikki and go for burgers and chips afterwards.'

'Catch you shortly.' Excellent. Something to keep her mind busy so she couldn't keep rerunning last night and that amazing sex. She was starting to see there couldn't be a repeat. It just wouldn't work. They couldn't have a relationship while working together.

Other staff did.

It could get awkward if something went wrong between them. Looking for trouble? Or looking out for her heart? Last night she was willing to take a risk. Not so much this morning. Reality was a wake-up call. Chances were Shaun wouldn't want to be obvious about their day out around other staff members either. He might've thought about what they'd done and decided it wasn't for him. One night was enough. Was that the real reason he'd left? Even knowing it had probably been for the best, she hoped not. She was coming up with so many reasons it was doing her head in.

This was ridiculous. She leapt out of bed and went to turn on the coffee machine before showering away the scents of last night and giving her hair a good wash. Time to get out and about, and stop overthinking everything. That only spoilt those amazing memories, which was the last thing she wanted right now. She really didn't know if she was coming or going with this so-called relationship.

On Monday morning, Nikki walked into the ED feeling uncomfortable. Would Shaun be okay around her? She worried he'd have been busy overthinking everything too and would want nothing more to do with her. That'd be awkward around the other staff.

'Morning, Nikki. How was your weekend?' Paul asked.

'Great. Went for a hike on Saturday, gave the muscles a good stretch. What about you?'

'We went up to Kaikoura for a friend's birthday and stayed the night.'

'It's a lovely spot for a break, isn't it?'

'Sure is. Right, let me run through what's going on before I head home for a shower and sleep.'

'It seems quite busy for this early on a Monday morning,' Shaun said from behind Nikki.

The clock read six forty. 'Can't always predict what's going to happen.'

Shaun gave her an open smile. 'I know, but no harm in wishing for a quiet start.'

The worry rattling in her chest subsided. He didn't appear to have any problems about their weekend. 'Right, let's get this underway.'

Other staff were beginning to appear, and soon everyone was listening to Paul's summary of patients and what had been arranged about treatment.

The bell at the ambulance bay rang loudly, cutting through the discussion going on.

'That'll be the woman involved in a car accident at Hillmorton,' Paul said.

'I'll take it.' Shaun looked to Nikki for agreement.

'All yours. Georgie, go with him.' Sipping coffee, Nikki concentrated on allocating patients to everyone else. No such thing as too much caffeine early in the morning. Especially this morning after tossing and turning for hours before finally dropping into a restless sleep around midnight. Shaun had been in her head all the time. Could they have a relationship or a long fling, or should they quit while they were ahead so neither of them got hurt?

'Morning, Nikki. I hear there's a girl needing an appendectomy waiting for me.'

She glanced up at Jack. 'Cubicle one. Jenny Brown. Fourteen.' She'd just finished reading the notes on screen. 'Have a good weekend?'

'I was on call. It was busy. You?'

'No complaints.' The phone was ringing. 'I'll be with you in a minute.' Picking up the phone she said, 'Emergency Department, Dr Marlow speaking.'

'Morning, Nikki. It's Darren. Can you send your patient up to Radiology now? We're all set to take his X-rays.' *Click.* The man was gone.

Nikki shrugged. She was used to Darren's abrupt manner. Pressing the number for the orderlies, she arranged for one to come along right away.

A trolley pushed by paramedics came past with Shaun walking at the side, watching the woman lying on top. 'Meredith, can you hear me?'

She groaned.

'You're in the hospital emergency department. I'm Shaun, a doctor.'

Another groan.

Nikki got up to follow in case she was needed.

'The paramedics think you banged your head on the steering wheel. Do you know if that's right?'

The woman dipped her head slightly.

'We need Radiology on alert. Right arm's fractured. Internal swelling in the lower abdomen.' Shaun flicked Nikki a glance. 'She wasn't wearing her seat belt.'

Grand. When would people learn not to takes risks behind the wheel? 'What did she impact into?'

'Power pole,' one of the paramedics answered. 'She ended up twisted around the steering wheel and half in the foot bay. According to a bystander, she was unconscious for about ten minutes.'

'Want a hand, Shaun?'

'If you've got a few moments, that'd be good. I'll take the head injury if you can check out Meredith's abdomen.' He was already focusing on the head, feeling for skull fractures.

Pulling on gloves, Nikki, with Georgie's help, slid Meredith's trousers down to expose the abdomen.

Behind her, a paramedic continued filling them in on details. 'The right thigh is tender to the touch, as is her right shoulder.'

'Did the car spin into the pole?' All the injuries seemed to be on one side, as though she'd been flung sideways.

'According to a bystander, yes.'

Glancing at Shaun, she found him looking at her. 'Makes sense?'

'It's the right side of her head that's taken the impact,' he agreed.

'Want me to alert the neurology department?'

'Yes, along with Radiology for X-rays and a CT scan. Orthopaedics too.' He returned to checking Meredith's head and neck.

'There's swelling at the top of the colon,' she told him as she ripped the gloves off. 'I'll be back shortly.' Getting specialists on the job was the priority.

Shaun sighed as Nikki strode away. She was the loveliest woman he'd encountered in a long time. Spending time with her during the weekend had been wonderful, and as for the sex—out of this world.

'Meredith, I'm going to check your shoulder. It's possibly dislocated, and this might hurt. Tell me if it's too much.' He didn't wait for an answer, got on with feeling the bones to see if they were in the right place. 'Not dislocated,' he said moments later. 'More likely a fracture.' Which meant another operation ahead.

He moved down the bed to Meredith's exposed abdomen and within moments agreed with Nikki. Now they needed to find the cause of the swelling. The upper bowel seemed fine. Then he touched the pancreas. Meredith cried out, making him feel bad. 'I'm sorry. Your pancreas appears to have ruptured. We'll know more after an X-ray of the abdominal area.'

Nikki was back, all professional and organised. Back straight, serious face on, organised to a T. Except he had his own special memories that were quite the opposite. Nikki all hot with her hair mussy as it spilled over the pillows. Her mouth soft and sensual as she tracked over his hot skin with her tongue. He reminded himself to concentrate as she said in a professional voice with a hint of a smile for him, 'An orderly's coming to take Meredith to Radiology as soon as the neurologist has been, and he's on his way down now. Someone from Orthopaedics will be along after Meredith's back from Radiology.'

'Thanks.' He'd wondered how she'd react towards him today. She seemed to like to keep her personal life to herself, and even being overly friendly might be going too far. At the moment, all was good. She wasn't making a big deal out of their time together, but neither was she ignoring him. A relief, really, because he liked her and didn't want to return to being only a colleague. He was settling down, and that meant making permanent friends. Friends like Nikki.

Looking around, he spied her talking to a little boy holding his arm hard against his chest. She was crouched down looking at the kid, touching his arm and asking questions, and the kid was answering her. She was good with the little ones. No doubt she'd make a great mother if that's what she wanted. He knew almost nothing about her. It was quite exciting in an odd way. Getting to know Nikki Marlow better would mean stepping outside his comfort zone. He could do it.

'Is this the patient with a head injury?' Charlie, a neurologist, asked from behind him.

Spinning around, Shaun nodded. 'Yes, Charlie, meet Meredith. She's been in a car accident where her right side seems to have taken the brunt of the impact.' He went on to describe the head injuries he'd found, all thoughts of Nikki on the back burner.

But she returned the moment he sent Meredith to Radiology with an orderly. 'Shaun, can you see to the elderly gentleman in cubicle six? He had a fall down some stairs during the night and couldn't move to get help. It was his grandson calling in on the way to school who found him and called 111.'

'A fall or a stroke?' Shaun wondered aloud as he headed for the cubicle.

'The paramedic thinks stroke. His speech is indistinct,' Nikki said from behind him. 'His name's Jason.'

'Hello, Jason. I'm Shaun, a doctor. I hear you got yourself into a bit of bother.' Shaun watched for the man's reactions.

'Y-yes.'

'Do you remember what happened?'

Jason moved his head awkwardly to one side. 'N-no.' His words were slurred. A stroke was a likely possibility.

'Okay, don't try to move at the moment. I'm going to touch your arm, then fingers and further down your body. If you feel me do that just say yes.' Shaun slipped up the sleeve of Jason's pyjama top and touched his bicep.

No reaction.

Same when he touched his wrist, then fingers. Whether that was because he hadn't felt anything or because he hadn't understood what Shaun had said didn't matter. He was going with the diagnosis of a stroke. 'We need oxygen. His breathing's shallow. I'll see if we've got a medical history for him.'

'The paramedic seemed to know him, which suggests he's been here before, though what for I've no idea,' Georgie answered. 'I'll fetch the oxygen and get that going.'

At the desk, Shaun looked up his patient and found he had been on blood thinners but had stopped taking them a month ago. 'Why?' There was no answer in the notes. Now he'd have to go back on them fast. There'd be clots in the man's blood system causing the stroke.

'Why what?' Nikki sat down at the computer next to him.

'The man stopped taking his dabigatran. It's in the notes but not the reason. His idea or the GP's?'

'I doubt it would've been his doctor's.'

'So do I.' Suddenly the air had a floral scent. Nikki's scent. Damn it. Now he'd smell her all day long, and with that would be the memories of what it had been like to get up close and personal to her satin-like skin. How was he going to get through the week if this was what she did to him within the first hour on duty?

She began filling in a prescription on the screen like she had no difficulty being near him.

He'd follow her example—because he didn't mind being near her. 'What's up with the little boy?'

Her smile illuminated the already well-lit area. 'Billy.

He put his hand down a drain hole. When he tried to pull out, it was stuck, so he banged the drain with a stone to break it, and broke a bone in his wrist instead. It's not funny, but the kid is quite a character, saying he is going to be a plumber like his dad one day and was practising removing dirt from the drain.'

'He didn't seem too upset when he was talking to you.'

'No, the upset one would be Billy's mother. She was shaking her head at him with worry in her eyes all the time he was telling me his story. I think she's got her hands full keeping an eye out for him.'

'Better than sitting glaring at a phone all day, I reckon.' Shaun stood up to return to Jason.

'Couldn't agree more.' Nikki went back to her screen, the smile still on her lips.

Thank goodness scrubs aren't tight-fitting was what he thought as he walked away. If that's all it took to make him start hardening, might be an idea to wear a bigger size from now on.

'Home sweet home,' Nikki muttered as she dropped her shoulder bag and the groceries she'd bought onto the bench and pulled the band off her ponytail. Shaking her hair about so it fell over her shoulders, she groaned. The day had gone on forever, and that wasn't only because of the number of patients that came into the ED.

Shaun had caught her attention from the moment he'd walked up behind her that morning and hadn't left her head since. It didn't help that they were often at the department hub at the same time, where she could not avoid noticing him, seeing that body filling out the scrubs and knowing exactly what they covered. As for the spicy aftershave smell, she was a goner. It'd been hard not to reach across and run her palm over the light bristle on his chin. She hadn't been a beard girl before, but the light one on Shaun's face stole the air out of her lungs. It was gorgeous and emphasised his good looks.

It was only Monday. Thankfully they'd got along fine. She'd been worried he might be overly friendly towards her, but there'd been no mention of the weekend, for which she was grateful. She didn't need other doctors or nurses knowing they'd spent time together. She'd also been concerned he might be a bit aloof if he didn't want to continue seeing her outside of work, but he hadn't. Seemed that they would carry on as they had last week until Saturday. All work and no play. Perfect.

Or it would be if she could ignore how happy she was whenever he was nearby. And warm in a special kind of way. And hot whenever she looked at his beard or smelled the aftershave.

Time for a wine. She'd earned it. The flow of patients hadn't slowed all day, mainly non-urgent cases but still needing total concentration. That was the only way she dealt with patients. It's what they deserved and what she loved giving them.

Laughter bubbled up as she thought about Billy. He was a right little man, cheeky and determined to be a plumber when he grew up, or way before then if today was anything to go by. If she had kids, she'd want them to be like that, confident and cute all in one. Like Shaun.

The wine sloshed over the side of the glass as she poured. Shaun was not cute. He was too much of a man to be that. How about good-looking and sexy? Definitely. She'd been saying it to herself all day and needed to back off. There hadn't been any blips in their work relationship throughout the shift, but she couldn't start looking for more to what they had than was really there. It had been a good day hiking followed by a wonderful dinner and awesome sex. That did not mean there was more to come.

Did she want more? Taking a sip of her drink, she mulled it over. It would be wonderful to find a man who loved her for who she was and wouldn't leave her on a whim, or expect her to be obedient and do as she was told all the time like her father had. Whether Shaun was that man, she had no idea. All she knew was that she more than liked him. He intrigued her with his ability not to rave on about himself or ask questions of her that were too deep and personal to answer until she knew him better. More than that, he made her feel comfortable, plus intrigued about him. The fact she'd kissed him without thought on Saturday night and followed up with intense sex said a lot about where she was at, because she wasn't one for leaping into bed with just any man. She might've wanted to, but rarely had she followed through. Yet with Shaun, once she leaned in to kiss him, she hadn't considered pulling back at all and hadn't had a single regret since.

Except for worrying about working with him and if he'd make it awkward around other staff.

Okay, she wasn't totally comfortable with everything, but then, wasn't that normal when starting a new relationship? Was this already a relationship? She didn't think so but couldn't find another word to describe what they had going, or even if it would continue or had been a one-off, which was more likely. Shaun didn't seem in awe of her, she laughed sadly.

Time to stop this and do something practical. Like download the photos she'd taken on the hike and see if any of them were worth keeping.

As the lasagne she'd bought at the deli heated in the

oven, she downloaded the photos onto her computer and studied them, looking for imperfections. There were plenty. The photos were good but not perfect, and she was a bit of a perfectionist when it came to her photography. It was why she'd won an award for one she took of a tui in some bushes by a beach last year.

She clicked through the photos, deleting some as she went. Her hand stopped as one appeared on the screen. Shaun stood on top of the hill where they'd had lunch, staring out over the valley, looking completely at ease with himself. Something, she realised, he didn't often appear to be. She'd known he enjoyed the walk but hadn't seen how truly relaxed he'd been. Why wasn't he like that more often? What had happened that kept him on edge? He had said his best friend had died, but not how or where. She was probably looking for something that wasn't there.

She couldn't drag her eyes away from the photo. No denying he was getting to her, and that she wasn't unhappy about it.

'Feel like a meal at the pub and then going to see a movie?' Nikki asked Shaun on Wednesday as they were making their way out to the car park at the end of shift. No matter how hard she'd tried, she hadn't been able to put last Saturday behind her and pretend she wanted nothing more to do with him. She named the movie she wanted to see.

Shaun didn't even hesitate. 'Beats grocery shopping any day. Add in how I'd thought about seeing that movie and you're on.'

Relief filled her. 'Great. Thought we'd go to the Jolly Roger pub. Shall I pick you up?'

'I'll meet you there. I've got to drop off some shoes for my nephews that my brother asked me to pick up.'

'So grocery shopping wasn't your plan?' She laughed, though it wasn't quite how she'd hoped to set up the evening. She'd still get to sit by him throughout the film and breathe in that aftershave that she enjoyed so much.

'Actually, I do need to get a few things, but they won't take long. See you at the pub around six?'

'Will do.' That gave her plenty of time for a long soak under the shower and finding the perfect shirt and jacket to wear with her new jeans. *Call me OTT, but I'm loving this dating stuff*, Nikki laughed to herself as she headed home with a skip in her step. Who'd have thought she'd be so relaxed about asking Shaun to go out for a meal with her? That feeling stayed with her throughout the evening.

'Those fish and chips were delicious.' Shaun pushed the plate aside and drained the last mouthful from his glass of beer.

'Not bad at all,' she agreed. 'Have you looked at any more houses lately?'

'A couple, but neither got me excited. It's harder to find what I like than I thought it would be.'

'You're not picky by any chance?' She grinned to show she didn't mean anything off by that.

'If wanting everything for nothing is picky, then I guess I am.' He chuckled. 'Seriously, I hadn't thought too much about what I might prefer. A house is a house, or so I thought.'

'When I decided to buy my own, I thought I wanted modern with little upkeep. Then one day I was heading over to Molly's when I saw an open home sign and on a whim stopped to look at the house. I was sold from the moment I walked inside.' The ambiance had grabbed her heartstrings. She probably paid too much, but nothing was stopping her buying the house.

'I have a feeling that's what I'm hoping for. A place I'll know immediately is my home.' Shaun checked his watch. 'We'd better get a wiggle on if we're not going to miss the beginning of the movie.'

She picked up the tab. 'My turn, and don't bother arguing.'

Shaun laughed. 'Me? Argue with you? I don't think so.'

'The movie was better than I'd expected,' Nikki said as they walked to their cars afterwards.

'I thought it was a bit drawn out, frankly.'

It was hard walking beside him and not grabbing his hand, but she managed. It was a casual date, and she was being careful not to set herself up for a fall. When they reached their vehicles, she said as casually as she could manage, 'See you tomorrow, bright and early.' No going back to her place for hot sexercise.

Shaun reached for her and placed a gentle kiss on her cheek. 'Early, maybe not so bright. Thanks for a lovely time.' He waited until she was in her car before he went to his. A true gentleman.

He didn't follow her home though. She should've been grateful but a part of her felt disappointed.

Then her phone lit up. Shaun. 'Hey.'

'How about a walk out Governors Bay way sometime over the weekend?'

'You're on.'

'Good. Sort details tomorrow. Bye.'

She did a wriggle in her seat. Woo-hoo. Another date with Shaun. Yes, they were dating. As friends or more, she didn't know, but she'd take what was on offer and enjoy every moment.

CHAPTER SEVEN

FRIDAY AT LAST and the end of shift. Shaun was looking forward to going hiking with Nikki again if she was still keen. Wednesday night at the pub and movies had been good, friendly without getting too intense. They hadn't returned to her bed for a repeat of the other night, which had to be for the best, for now, anyway. But he couldn't deny he could do with more time like that with her.

She was sitting in the hub, signing off for the day, looking as lovely as ever.

'Hey, Shaun, you got anything on tomorrow night?' Charlie, the neurologist, stepped in front of him.

'Nothing planned.' Though he had thought he'd ask Nikki to dinner if she was willing.

'How about coming to my place for dinner? I know it's short notice, but there's a small group of us who get together every month or so at one or other's house to relax and put work behind us for a while. You could get to know us a bit better without scrubs on.'

'Sounds good. What do I bring?'

'Whatever you like to drink. We take turns in either cooking or ordering in food. It's all very casual.'

'I'm in. Where do you live?' Who else would be there? Nikki?

'Give me your number and I'll text the address. Glad

you've agreed to join us. Bring your partner if you've got one.' His eyebrow rose in a question mark.

'Nope. Just me.' At the moment. He'd ask Nikki if she wasn't already going, but that might be awkward when it was a group of colleagues getting together.

'No problem.'

It usually wasn't, but right now, he felt sad. He could ask Nikki if she was going and offer to pick her up. Or he could turn up alone. 'Here's my number,' he told Charlie.

'Thanks. See you tomorrow night, Nikki,' Charlie called out.

'Looking forward to it.'

His question answered, there was a lightness in Shaun's step as he made his way to the changing room. He was going to dinner at Charlie's, and Nikki would be there too. He was beginning to accept he wanted to spend time with her as friends, and maybe as more than that.

When Charlie's text with the address popped up on his phone, he saw Nikki lived only a couple of streets away from the neurosurgeon's. When he drove towards Charlie's on Saturday evening and saw Nikki walking along the street, he pulled over and opened the passenger window. 'Like a lift?'

'It would be rude to say no.'

Leaning across, he opened the door. 'That bag looks heavy.'

'Wine and books. Simone and I swap books all the time. She's Charlie's wife, in case you didn't know.'

'I didn't. I don't even know who else's going to be there.'

She turned to look at him and quickly filled him in. 'You've probably met them all apart from their other halves.'

Those drop-dead gorgeous eyes drew him in like an open fire on a cold winter's day. It was getting harder to stick to the friends idea. Even friends with benefits didn't quite gel. Time to let go and take a chance at happiness? It could be.

'Shaun? Hello?'

He shook his head and turned to face the front. He needed to get back on the road. 'Sorry. I was miles away. But I heard what you said,' he added quickly.

'That I don't like dogs?'

'You didn't say that?' Had she? 'No, you said you like them when I mentioned I might get one once I've bought a house.'

Her laugh teased him. 'Just jibbing you because you looked so far away for a moment.'

He'd been right here with her. 'Let's go.' He wasn't getting any deeper into this quagmire than he already was. She'd think he was crazy and want to get out of the car to start walking again.

'First street on the left.'

'I've got it. Used to spend quite a bit of time around here when I was at high school as some of my mates lived in this area.' Liam for one. He could picture the dude giving him the thumbs-up for spending more time with Nikki.

'What's it like returning home after years away? Are your friends still around, or have they moved away?'

So much for thinking she wouldn't ask personal questions, though to be fair, it wasn't a deep one. 'A couple are here. Others have gone for their work or to their partners' towns. Most importantly, my family's here. I missed them more than anyone when I was away.' Now who was getting a little deeper into his background? 'It doesn't seem to matter where I am or what I'm doing. They're always a part of my life, even if it's to tell me I'm making a mistake about something I've done.'

'That's families, I guess.' There was a longing in her voice.

'Not like yours?'

'My brother, definitely. Mum, not so much.'

He wanted to ask about her father, but she was closing down, and that was the last thing he needed. No, actually, they were friends. He could ask. 'What about your father?'

'He died a few years ago. He wasn't the best dad out there.'

There was so much he wanted to know, but the pain in her voice put the dampener on that. 'Which station does your brother work out of?'

'Christchurch Central.'

'That must keep him busy.'

'It does, but not so much that he's not there for his family. They come first, no matter what.'

Turning into Charlie's street, he looked along the road. 'We're headed where all those cars are parked?'

'You're on to it.' Nikki rolled her shoulders. 'Thanks for this.'

'It's cold out there. I'll take you home afterwards.'

'I could get to like you.' She laughed.

'You don't already?'

'Yeah, okay, like you even more.'

'That's better.' It was silly talk, but she was lightening up again, and that made him happy.

'What about going for that walk you mentioned tomorrow morning?' she asked as he parked on the side of the road.

The one he hadn't done anything about because caution had won—for a while at least. 'I guess we could.'

But was it a good idea if he wanted to stay safe from temptation? *Come on. Get over your hang-ups.* Time with Nikki was always wonderful.

'Fine. Obviously you're not keen anymore.' She opened her door.

He reached for her arm, held her lightly. 'Sorry, I'd like to go for one.' The kids, sports. Damn. 'I'm going to watch my nephews play soccer at ten. Want to join me, and then we could do a shorter walk after?'

'What?' Her eyes widened in surprise.

He felt the same. He'd just asked her to meet his family. That was left field, if ever anything was, and totally out of sync with being cautious. 'If you can put up with two toe-rags giving you cheek, that is.'

'That's a challenge I can't refuse.'

'So I figured.' He hadn't thought that at all, but hey, she was going with him, so all was good. Better than he'd planned on.

Nikki pinched herself. Did Shaun really suggest she join him with his nephews in the morning? He was beginning to open up to her. He wasn't withdrawing as she'd been thinking. Woo-hoo. Bring it on. These past weeks, she'd done little but think about Shaun and how he made her feel special without even trying. Despite all the warnings going off in her head about how Brett had also once made her feel special, she knew the time had come to take some risks. She did not want to look back and regret a missed opportunity at happiness. If she was getting carried away with the idea, then so be it. Right now it was hard to deny how comfortable she was with Shaun. Even knowing he was right to leave her place last Saturday night, she couldn't stop feeling this going well.

He walked into Charlie's house beside her. 'I'm looking forward to this.'

'Good, because everyone's great company.' As she glanced at Shaun, her heart moved. Yes, he was special. Hopefully she could come to be special for him too.

Charlie spotted them instantly. 'Hi, you two. Come through and meet everyone, Shaun. I think you've met everyone except Sheree. She's a radiologist. Nikki, Simone's in the wine cellar looking for some Pinot Gris that's supposedly better than the one I brought up.'

'I'll go help her.' When she found what she was looking for, Simone wouldn't bring only one or two bottles up from the chiller. Never mind that everyone usually brought a bottle with them. She liked being generous. 'You got this, Shaun?'

'You bet.' He gave her the cheeky smile that did nothing to calm her.

Instead it fired up the hormones he'd wreaked havoc with two weeks ago. Grand. They'd been here barely two minutes and already she was in a mess over him. She placed her bag on the hall table before disappearing down the stairs to the cellar. Here she breathed, hoping to calm her hormones. 'Hey, Simone, I hear you're looking for a certain wine.'

The walk-in chiller was open, and Simone was inside, reading labels on numerous bottles. 'Not having much luck, I'm afraid. Must've finished it when the family were here for my birthday last month.'

'Doesn't matter. I've brought Pinot Gris and Chardonnay.' Not all for her.

'Thanks. I so wanted you all to try that particular one.

Never mind, let's get back upstairs and join in the fun. Charlie says he invited Shaun Elliott from ED along.'

She nodded. 'He started with us three weeks ago.'

'How's he doing?'

'He's great. Just who we needed.' Surely her cheeks weren't warming in the cool air of the chiller? How embarrassing.

'You like him.'

More than embarrassing. 'Of course.'

'I don't mean as a colleague. It does happen, you know. Doctors fall for other doctors or nurses all the time. Take Charlie and me, for example. We met at Wellington Hospital nine years ago and haven't been apart since.' Simone was an obstetrician.

'Steady up. You know I'm ultra-cautious when it comes to men and relationships.'

Simone gave her a quick hug. 'Maybe it's time to have some fun and fall in love along the way.'

'You're an old nag.'

'But a good one. Come on, let's grab a glass of wine, and I can suss out this guy who makes you blush far too easily.'

She had no answer to that. 'Bring on the wine.' Nothing else.

It wasn't easy to avoid Shaun when the moment she stepped into the lounge he smiled directly at her, once more tightening her insides. Those blue eyes were always drawing her in and making her feel a part of him. He really was a problem—a good problem, she admitted. Seeing Shaun so relaxed, she pictured a little boy looking just like him. 'Where're the wine glasses?' she demanded of Simone.

'Got it that bad, huh?'

'Oh, shut up.' She really was letting Shaun get to her in far too many ways.

Simone laughed out loud, which had everyone looking their way. 'Which would you like? Pinot Gris or Chardonnay?'

Both. Pour me a bucketful. 'Chardonnay, thanks.'

'I'll get those.' Shaun was right there. 'I'm Shaun, by the way.' He held his hand out to Simone. 'Charlie's wife?'

'That's me. I'm glad you've joined us. I'm sure you'll have a lovely night.' At least she didn't look at Nikki when she said it.

Nikki sighed. There was no getting away from Simone, so she'd concentrate on talking about boring subjects, and hopefully she'd back off.

Shaun handed Nikki her Chardonnay and a Pinot Gris to Simone, then raised his glass. 'Cheers. Here's to a great evening. It's already turning out to be fun. Everyone's so relaxed and easy to talk to.'

'What did you expect?'

'From past experience, sometimes there can be a bit of one-upmanship at these dos.'

She'd never struck that. 'Might be you're out of practice.'

'True. It helps me feel like I'm starting to fit in, something I haven't bothered with too much lately. When I was only ever in any place for a few months, I never put a lot of effort into getting to know my colleagues out of work.'

'Sounds lonely.' He could be congenial with everyone and yet cautious about mixing with people as well. Other than her. He seemed keen to spend time with her. She didn't think the walking was all about keeping fit. He didn't need her for that, but she understood the loneliness.

'I won't lie. It was at times. Part of returning home means finding friends.'

What about me? She swallowed a big mouthful of wine and started coughing.

Shaun instantly patted her back hard enough to ease the coughing. 'Easy, girl.'

She laughed. 'Girl? Not for a while now.'

He laughed too. 'You think?'

'Hey, you two. Get over here and tell us what's so funny,' Paul called across the room.

'I was pointing out to Nikki she shouldn't be wearing high heels when she's racing down stairs. It's not a good look to land head first at the bottom.'

'Careful, man. She'll have you on the floor with a judo hold in a flash if you're not careful.'

Shaun spun around to stare at her. 'You do judo?'

She burst out laughing. As if she was going to spend time getting thrown to the floor or returning the favour with someone else. 'Welcome to the group, Shaun.'

He grinned. 'Guess I got that one wrong. Let me know if you ever want to find out what it's like to be dropped to the mat in a bundle.'

She gaped at him. 'What belt have you got?'

'A faded green one.' His grin was still in place, wreaking havoc with her head and heart. 'I gave up when I left school to go to university. Far more interesting things to discover there.'

'Beer and girls,' Charlie agreed.

'You're on to it.' Shaun wandered closer to the others, at the same time making sure she came with him. 'Nikki dragged me out on one of the tracks on Mount Richardson a couple of weekends ago. It was good to do something else I haven't done in ages.'

So much for not letting people know they'd seen each other outside work. No one looked surprised, or even shocked. More like they were pleased that she and Shaun had done something together. That rocked her. While some of them were brutally honest about their thoughts on her not dating more often, she wouldn't have expected them to think she should go out with the new doctor in the department. 'His boots were very dusty.'

'We're thinking about heading up to Hanmer Springs for a weekend next month,' Simone said. 'Those of us who aren't on call, that is. There're walks around there if you're interested, Shaun.'

'I could be, depending on the roster and when you decide to go.'

'We'll keep you posted.'

He'd been accepted into the group. Nikki wasn't sure if that was good for her or not. Fine while they were getting on, not so much if they fell out. There again, she was trying to move forward with this, and thinking about things going wrong wasn't the way to do it. 'Better polish those boots,' she said with a laugh.

'Done that already.'

'Dinner's ready in five if anyone needs to top up their glass beforehand,' Simone said.

Nikki, along with Sheree and Mallory, Paul's wife, headed for the kitchen to give her a hand putting food on serving dishes and taking them to the long table in the dining room. This was a normal evening with friends, and yet she felt a new buzz in her veins. Shaun. He had a way about him that lifted her concerns regarding her future that she couldn't ignore. He was special.

'Stop smiling so much.' Simone grinned. 'You'll have everyone thinking he's already had his way with you.'

Heat scorched her cheeks.

'Oh, oh. I see. Well done, girlfriend.'

'Simone, shut up.'

She laughed. 'Okay.' She returned to plating up the broccoli and pecan salad.

Mallory and Sheree were grinning too. No secrets with this lot.

Then Nikki found herself laughing. She'd had some lovely times with Shaun and felt lighter in spirit for them. 'What the heck?'

'What's mentioned at dinner stays at dinner,' Sheree said.

'You know he's worked in Christchurch ED before?' Mallory asked.

'I heard that. Why did he leave?' Was he restless back then too?

'Do you remember when a pilot of a small plane died while in the air and his passenger landed the plane with no flying experience? It was about four years ago.'

'Vaguely. I was in Auckland back then.' Was Mallory talking about Shaun?

'Well, Shaun was the man who brought the plane down. Amazing feat considering. His friend had had a fatal heart attack.'

Nikki's heart slumped. The mate who'd died. 'Oh.' She was lost for words.

Mallory nudged her. 'You haven't heard it from me, okay? I don't normally gossip, but I wanted to give you the facts, brief as they are.'

'Thanks, Mallory. It explains a few things.'

'Stop frowning. You'll get wrinkles on your forehead.'

'Come on, let's eat,' Simone said and carried the last platters into the dining room.

'Nikki, how's your glass?' Shaun asked the moment she entered the dining room.

'Almost empty.' Normally she wouldn't have more than one drink, but right now it seemed like a good idea to have another. She finished the wine and handed Shaun the glass. 'Thanks.'

Of course Simone made sure she and Shaun were sitting together at the table. If asked, they'd probably say that was because the two of them were on their own, so it was the natural thing to do, but Nikki knew there was some stirring going on. At least everyone was okay about her and Shaun being together and not looking for trouble. Another thing to be grateful for.

'Would you like some gurnard?' Shaun held a platter with baked fish towards her.

'You bet. What about you? Like seafood?'

'Can't get enough of it.'

'You into fishing by any chance?' Paul asked. 'None of these morons like getting smelly handling the bait.'

'Anytime you need someone to go out with you, give me a call.'

'You're on.'

He look so relaxed and happy, Nikki couldn't help smiling. It wasn't as though he was a surly man, more that he didn't often open up around people. She was beginning to understand why. He'd been through hell. That made her feel closer to him and hope there'd be more occasions for him to enjoy, some with her. She wanted Shaun to stay in Christchurch permanently. She really and truly did. He was showing her she could let go of her fears and enjoy life more than she had since breaking up with her ex. Hopefully she might be able to return the favour.

* * *

Hours later, Shaun pulled into Nikki's driveway and cut the motor. Should he stay a while? Or would it be wiser to head home before they got too involved? Except he wanted to spend more time with Nikki. Lots more, scary as that might be. 'That was a great night.'

'Certainly was,' Nikki responded with a smile. 'They're a good bunch. It's fun seeing a side to them that's got nothing to do with sick or injured people.'

'Reminds you that you're more than a doctor?' He got that in spades. Being a medic was a serious job, though there were light moments when patients cracked jokes or could finally get out of bed and walk by themselves once more. But to be able to fully relax and not think about the consequences of being himself with other people who understood was great. 'How long have you been a part of the group?'

'From when I came to Christchurch. After I split up with my husband.'

So Nikki had been married before. 'You're divorced?'

'Yes.' The word ground out through her teeth before she turned to look at him. 'I had a miscarriage. Brett left to live with his girlfriend who was also pregnant and needed his support, since I was no longer having a baby. Unbeknown to me, they'd been having an affair for many months. He's a GP with a practice in Auckland, and she was a nurse working for him. All those nights he told me he was seeing patients, he was actually having sex with her.' That beautiful smile was gone.

He reached over and wrapped her in his arms. 'How did you cope? I mean, how could he leave you when you'd be grieving for your baby? I don't get it.'

'Seems I didn't know him as well as I thought.'

'Nikki, my heart's breaking for you. How did you get out of bed every morning?'

'Slowly.'

'I bet.' But she had got up. No surprise there. 'Did you seek help? Talk to anyone?'

Lifting her head, she stared at him for a long moment. 'Yes.'

'That man had better not come visiting any time or there'll be trouble.'

'No, there won't. You'd be there for anyone you believed needed you, but you'd never do what you're implying.'

The air whooshed out of his lungs. Nikki had just said something amazing to him, about him. He wouldn't have expected that in a million years. 'Thanks,' he croaked.

'Come on. Let's go inside.' That wasn't an invitation, more of an insistence with a small smile thrown in.

One he was happy to comply with. 'Thought you'd never ask.' She wanted done with this conversation, and he'd comply. Having her drag up any more painful memories wouldn't be fun.

'Coffee, wine or me?' she asked as she closed the door behind them.

He looked at her, saw the amazing, strong woman she was along with the doubt in her eyes. He still had no idea where he was going with this and didn't want to get in so deep he couldn't get out, but neither did he want to ignore her doubt. She needed him at the moment. He enfolded her in his arms. 'You.'

They stood there embracing each other for a long, quiet moment before he swept her up and strode to her bedroom to place her on the bed, then knelt down to kiss her smile. Followed by her chin, neck and down the wonderful cleavage he knew was behind the cream blouse. All the time her fingers were working hot, sexy magic on his skin, arousing him way too fast. 'Stop,' he said, panting.

'Soon,' she whispered.

'Soon will be too late.'

'You think?'

'I know.'

Then there was no thinking going on. Their bodies melded into each other as their mouths met. Clothes flew through the air as they hurriedly undressed. And then Nikki was as naked as it was possible to be.

He drank in the beautiful sight. She really was something else. He could fall in love if he wasn't careful. But he was always careful, so he was safe, despite how his heart was beating hard and erratically.

'Shaun?' Doubt was creeping into her face.

'Coming.' Lying on the bed, he wrapped her in his arms and legs. 'I meant—'

'You're coming.' The doubt was replaced by a sexy-as-hell twinkle in her eyes. 'Me too.'

They didn't say anything else. Their bodies took over their minds and led them on an amazing ride.

Sometime later, Shaun woke to find Nikki curled up against him, her arm tight around his waist. The sense of belonging was strong. They got along so well he could accept his plans for coming home might all work out.

Nikki had been hurt by that low-life of a husband. How could he have an affair, especially when she'd been carrying his child? He'd got the other woman pregnant too. Nikki deserved so much better. Hearing why her marriage ended made Shaun seethe. She must feel so vulnerable now. Was that why she didn't talk about her past and her feelings? Like him not talking about his. They were both protecting their hearts. Was that why she agreed with him when he'd said he was going home the other night? She didn't want to be hurt again.

Gazing at her sleeping against him, he felt a longing he hadn't known since Amy begin to spread throughout him and raise his protective instincts for Nikki. Which said he might be getting too close, too soon. Although he thought the world of her and did want a proper relationship further down the track, he did not want to rush things. It was time to go home, put space between them. Staying through till morning suggested he'd like more than a brief get-together in bed, and he didn't want to give Nikki the wrong idea about where he stood at the moment. That could hurt her, and that wasn't happening as far as he was concerned.

Slowly and quietly he slipped out of bed, doing his damnedest not to wake her. Once dressed he made for the door, then turned back. No way could he walk out of the room without placing a tender kiss on her soft lips. Leaning over, he did just that, holding his breath, still not wanting to wake her.

'Shaun?' she croaked, one eye dragging open.

'Shh, go back to sleep. See you later,' he whispered. 'I promise,' he added so she knew he wasn't running away from what they were sharing.

Her eye closed, and she snuggled into her pillow. Gorgeous. As tempting as it was to climb back in with her, he headed away. Time to be play sensible. For a while anyway.

'Shh, go back to sleep,' Shaun had whispered in her ear during the night.

Now he wasn't here.

Nikki stretched full-length in her bed. She'd slept in.

The sun was streaming in around the edges of the curtains where she hadn't closed them completely. After walking around the park yesterday morning plus an entertaining evening with her friends and then making out with Shaun, she'd been tired. Throw in the busy week, and it was no wonder she hadn't woken at her usual time.

'Why did you go home, Shaun?' They could've had breakfast together before watching the boys play soccer. Then again, they weren't partners or in a relationship of any kind, other than a few outings together and amazing sex. But she liked him more than a lot and wanted to spend more time with him.

So it was just as well he'd gone home. He mightn't be keen while she was getting too keen. She'd reached a point where she felt ready to take a chance on settling down with a man if she loved him, yet she still worried about being hurt. Moving on from Brett had been hard. She'd loved him so much. After her childhood never living in one place for long, a man who said he loved her and wanted to live with her forever in one place was a keeper. Putting him behind her and getting back out dating when she understood that people made promises they had no intention of keeping had been a struggle.

Yet along came Shaun, and the barriers around her heart began dropping away fast. *Too fast, Nikki.* That was the problem. Because she wanted to let him in, at least enough to get to know him for real, and be certain he was the right man for her before making a big mistake.

Tossing the duvet aside, she clambered out of bed and grinned at the new aches. Her body had had quite a workout, showing how out of practice she was. Yes, this was definitely going well, and she could relax about him disappearing after they had sex. He was probably protecting himself as much as she was herself.

A long, hot shower put her on top of the world again. Add a strong coffee and marmalade-covered toast and she was ready for just about anything. Looking outside, she sighed. 'Darn, the lawns need cutting.' Not her favourite pastime for sure.

The phone rang. 'Saved.'

Shaun. 'Nikki, did you sleep in?'

'I did. How about you?' It would've been bliss snuggled up to that hot body as she came awake.

'No, I've been for a run. The boys' soccer's been cancelled. They're going to a birthday party instead. But I was wondering if you'd do something else with me. Not the walk.'

'I was looking forward to meeting your family.'

'I need to look at an open home and wondered if you'd come with me. I saw the house on Thursday and liked it a lot, but I want another opinion if you're up for it.'

She wasn't going to meet his family? That stung, even when there was a good reason not to. She'd felt like he'd been opening a door for her, and now it had been slammed shut again. But then, he wanted her to look at a house he was interested in. Could he be taking their friendship another step? He hadn't mentioned anything about looking at houses last night. She could give him some leeway and see where it led. 'Beats mowing the lawns any time.'

His laughter warmed her through and through. 'I'm not picking you up for a few hours. You've got plenty of time.'

'Spoil-sport.' He was right, though, and now she was going to see him later, it didn't seem so much of a hassle to get the mower out and do the job. 'See you soon.'

She almost skipped around the lawn. It had never been so quick to mow the lawns. After shoving the mower back into the corner of the garage, she locked the door and went inside for another shower. Not that she really needed one but she liked to be ready in case they got all hot and close again.

'Where's this house?' Nikki asked when Shaun arrived to pick her up.

'Merivale. Perfect for work and not far from family.' His fingers were tapping the steering wheel. 'The owners are moving up to Napier for family reasons and are looking for a quick sale.' There was a lightness in his voice that suggested he was keener than he'd let on.

'Is it in good nick? Or is there work to be done?'

'It's perfect. Just walk in and get on with life.'

Interesting. So he *was* staying, or at least working at making it happen. That looked good for the future. In lots of ways, not only because she was starting to let him in but because he might finally find what he was looking for. It was hard to accept when she was afraid of being left behind. Or being dragged from town to city to town. She'd put her own roots down here, but if she fell in love, then those roots might amount to nothing, and that frightened her.

He hadn't finished. 'I'd change the décor, though. It's all white, and I find that quite sterile. But I'm getting ahead of myself. This second viewing might reveal things I won't like about the property.'

'Then there's my opinion to consider,' she said with a laugh.

'There is that.'

'Seriously, you're not to listen to me if you think it's the house for you.'

'I won't.'

So why had he asked her to come along and give her opinion? Was it a kind of date? 'You know I'll be honest about what I think?'

'Exactly why I'm taking you with me.' He chuckled. 'I thought I'd like someone to look at it and know what I might be letting myself in for. Buying a house is part of my plan for returning home.'

'You are determined to stay.'

'Why wouldn't I be?' he asked tightly. 'It's time to settle down in one place, and besides, my family is here.'

Ouch. Seemed that she'd touched a subject he didn't want to talk about. Was this to do with losing his friend years back? If so, she did feel bad for upsetting him. 'I imagine it won't be easy to stop moving around on a regular basis. Before you ask, I did hear that you'd been working in quite a few different locations lately.'

'I take it that Paul told you.'

'When I asked where you'd been working, all he said was that you'd been on the move a bit since leaving Christchurch General a few years ago. Nothing else. It was a normal question to ask about a new doctor coming on board.' Any minute now, he'd turn around and take her back home. 'I wasn't trying to pry.' After that reaction, she wasn't mentioning the loss of his friend. 'Nor was Paul speaking out of turn. He'd never blab about someone.'

Turning to face her, he said, 'I know. Sorry I overreacted.'

It wasn't like the Shaun she was coming to know, though she guessed she didn't really know him well at all. She was intrigued to find out what type of house piqued his interest. 'I've already forgotten what you said.'

Silence fell between them. It was the first time she'd felt uncomfortable with him, and she didn't like it. It wasn't as though she'd asked something deep and meaningful, surely? Whatever the reason, he didn't have to go quiet on her. She wasn't looking for trouble. Trouble was one thing she tried hard to avoid. Along with falling in love. Often the two went hand in hand.

When Shaun pulled into the driveway of a very modern-looking house with a large for-sale sign at the front, Nikki gasped. 'It's stunning.' Obviously someone had spent a small fortune to have an architect draw up the plans; the house hadn't been one of a building company's array of fast builds. 'The black framework highlights all those windows.'

'Which look directly onto the street,' Shaun commented. 'Though the current owners have planted a lot of shrubs that are beginning to break the view so that people walking past won't be able to peek in as much.'

'I can't wait to see inside.'

'Then let's do it. I'm liking your positive vibes so far.' Shaun was smiling again.

The tension gripping her faded away. 'You couldn't have more different taste in houses than me.' Nothing like her little old cottage, but she'd never expected to fall in love with it either.

A well-dressed woman, presumably the real estate agent, stepped out onto the terrace. 'Hello, Shaun. The owners have gone for a coffee while you have a look around. I'll stay here, out of your way.'

'Thanks. This is my friend, Nikki Marlow.'

Nikki shook the woman's hand. 'I'm looking forward to this.'

'Take your time. I'm not in a hurry to be anywhere else.' The agent left them to wander inside on their own.

Looking around as she followed Shaun, Nikki shook her head. 'It's wonderful. Though I do agree there's too much white.'

'Easily fixed.'

'Do you really think grey?' She felt more colour was needed, but then, she could be way out of tune with the latest fashion in house decorations.

'I haven't come up with an answer to that yet. That's for when—if—I buy the place.'

'Fair enough.' A warm green came to mind. She'd keep that to herself. This wasn't going to be her home, even if she and Shaun were getting along just fine. They weren't likely to become more than friends with benefits for a long while, if at all. Too hard to let go the restraints she'd put on herself when he didn't have a good reputation for settling down. He might be looking to buy a house, but that didn't mean he was staying put from now on. He could always rent it out.

'What do you think?" Shaun asked after they'd had a thorough look around inside and out.

'I really like it. There's a certain wow factor about the whole property that kind of sucks me in a bit.'

'I know what you mean. Which is why I'm going to put in an offer.'

Nikki spun around to high-five him. 'Go you.' It was a step towards staying in Christchurch permanently, and she wouldn't be discouraging that even if she did have doubts about him staying long-term. It was her past and her father's continual moving from place to place that made her reluctant to believe Shaun could be different, not Shaun himself. She wanted to believe in him, wanted to think he was different and ready to change his lifestyle.

His smile was huge. 'Thanks for your support. It means a lot.'

She was grateful he hadn't been able to read her thoughts. 'Why don't you go discuss things with the agent, and I'll find my own way home.' She wasn't going to hang around while he got down and serious about his offer with the agent and how he was going to pay for it. That was his business and nothing to do with her.

'I can drop you home first.'

'No need. I'll walk over to the mall to get some film for my camera and then grab a taxi.'

'That seems unfair considering I asked you to come along to tell me what you thought about the property.'

'Go talk to the agent. I'm a big girl and can look after myself.' Leaning in, she placed a light kiss on his raspy chin. 'Good luck. Keep me posted.' She headed away before he could say anything else. But as she walked out of the drive, she peeked over her shoulder and found he was watching her, his finger touching his cheek where she'd kissed him. Warmth stole through her. He was special. And despite everything Brett had done, wakening her to all sorts of possibilities.

CHAPTER EIGHT

'HAVE YOU HEARD anything about how the legalities are going on your contract to buy the house?' Nikki asked as she looked hungrily at the eggs Benedict the server had just put before her. They looked yummy. When Shaun suggested breakfast over the road from the hospital at Suzie's when they came off night shift, she'd all but grabbed his hand and run across, she was that hungry.

He handed her the pepper grinder. 'Not a lot. The lawyer's still waiting for the council's building report. Apparently it usually takes at least a week so can't be far off.'

'Have you started looking at furniture yet?' He'd said he didn't have any, so it was going to be a big buy-up at some point.

'I had a wander around one of the big furniture stores. There was so much selection it was mind-blowing. I didn't know where to start, so I walked out.' He looked embarrassed.

'Not as easy as dealing with a drunk teen with a broken leg then?' That had been one of his patients last night.

He grimaced. 'Put it like that and I sound hopeless.'

'Not at all. If you need a hand, give me a call. I have a thing about good furniture.'

'I might just do that.'

Really? If she had any doubts, that'd show how well

they were getting on. She took a mouthful of eggs and sighed contentedly. Perfect. 'Just what the doctor ordered.'

'Not bad, are they?'

'What are you are up to today? Other than grabbing some sleep?'

'Having a round of golf with Dad. He's determined to make me improve my score, which is pretty bad, I admit. But I haven't had much practice at it.'

'Do you enjoy playing?' Somehow she wouldn't have thought golf was his thing.

'So-so. But it means I spend time with Dad, so I'm up for it, along with the ribbing I get about my lack of style.'

From the little he'd said, family meant a lot to Shaun. As Ross did to her. Not so much her parents, but that was history, and she wasn't wasting time wishing she could change it. 'Make the most of it,' she said.

Shaun nodded. 'I am.'

'Good.' A wave of sadness caught her. She and Ross had missed out on so much growing up. She grabbed her coffee and took a gulp. But Ross had got his act together and was a wonderful father. She could do the same if she ever was lucky enough to have children. Glancing at Shaun, she felt flustered. She was stepping outside her barriers, and it was so darned scary. There was a lot to lose—or a lot to gain. Plastering a smile on her face before he noticed she was at odds with herself, she said, 'I can't imagine swinging a club at a ball and getting it to land in a tiny hole.'

'You want to try?'

'No, thanks.' Would he offer to show her how it's done? She'd turn him down on that one.

'Fair enough.' Shaun pushed his empty plate aside. 'So, what's on your agenda today?'

'Not a lot.' She hadn't made any plans. 'Might take the camera to Hagley Park and get some shots of the Avon River flowing through the greenery.' Actually, that's exactly what she'd do. Then she'd stop worrying about everything else.

'Another calendar in the making?' He'd been impressed with the one of birds she'd given him after their first walk.

'Who knows? It could be.' Anything was possible. *Get that, Nikki? Anything's possible.* She smiled. *Here's hoping.*

The following Friday, Shaun stared at the papers his lawyer handed him.

'Here you go,' she said. 'Sign these and the house is yours.'

Really? As in, he really had bought a house? The papers shook in his hand. Had he seriously ticked off another box on his list? There weren't many to go. Only one major one. The one he was not ready for, but getting closer.

'Shaun? You okay?'

He nodded. 'Yes.' Damn it, he truly was. This was the most exciting thing he'd done in forever, and his body was humming. With a firm hand, he signed on the line. 'I've bought a house. My own home. If I seem a little stunned, it's because I'm still absorbing what's happened.'

'I've seen it all before. There's something special about buying your first house.'

It wasn't his first. He and Amy had bought one on the other side of Christchurch when they got married. A little doer-upper that they'd enjoyed because it was *their* home. Once they decided to go their separate ways, neither of them wanted it—too many memories—so sold it. That had been a sad day for both of them. Now he had a new property to make his home. Life was looking up big-time. 'As long as I'm not getting ahead of myself,' he muttered.

If only Nikki was here to share this moment with him. He'd like that even if he was expecting too much when they weren't that close. Getting there, but they had a way to go—if he allowed it to happen. Right now, despite how happy he was, he wasn't sure what he felt about Nikki other than he seemed to be falling for her a little more as each week passed.

He needed to share his news with someone, and the first name to pop into his head was Nikki's. What about his parents? Or brother, or sister? No, the urge to call Nikki was stronger. So much for keeping her at arm's length.

Once outside the lawyer's office, he pulled his phone from his pocket and pressed her number.

'Hey, Shaun, what's up?'

Her voice thrilled him. Soft and caring all in one. He paused, wanting to drag out the moment, enjoying every second. This was so exciting.

Nikki waited.

The words burst out. 'The house is mine.'

'Woo-hoo. That's wonderful news.'

'Honestly, Nikki, I am thrilled. It's a wonderful property, and I can't wait to take over.'

'When's that likely to happen?'

'Two weeks from today. The current owners have already started packing as they're desperate to get to Napier.' Two weeks and he'd be moving into his own home. 'I've got a lot of shopping to do before then.' When he and Amy bought their place, they'd had to be cautious about what they spent. He'd put a lot of money away since then, always on the move and not filling any apartment with furniture he'd have to move whenever he headed to the next job. He'd also earned good wages with the shortage of doctors currently a problem for most health boards in the country. This was so much fun.

'Right. Unless you already have plans, I'm taking you out to dinner tonight to celebrate your news.'

His heart squeezed. Awesome. 'I'd like that more than anything else.' Now wasn't the time to keep Nikki at a distance. He couldn't. He was so happy to have bought a home and added a massive tick to his list that he could share the fun with someone special. Yes, Nikki was special, and becoming more so all the time. Another squeeze under his ribs. Right now he was a very happy man. Such a new feeling, and he was going to make the most of it. 'What time?'

'I'll pick you up just before seven.'

'I can pick *you* up.'

'No. It's your celebration, and you might want an extra drink or two. See you later.' Click. She was gone.

Five minutes later, he got a text from her. What's your address?

Laughing, he sent the details, ignoring the temptation to say now he had to pick *her* up. No point in stirring up trouble. Not that he believed she'd get cross, but still. Best to play fair and keep onside. Who knew how they might fill in the rest of the evening after dinner. Though he had a darned good idea of how he'd like to. No denying Nikki was beautiful and sexy and downright cool to be with. What was it about her that had him thinking like that? No woman since Amy had interested him half as much. He hadn't wanted them to, yet Nikki just wandered into his head and took over. Even his heart sometimes got a bit soft around her. Scary. Exciting. He truly was settling down and moving forward.

The evening was better than good. It was perfect. 'Dinner was amazing,' he told Nikki as they strolled hand in hand along the Avon River afterwards, wrapped in warm jackets. It was chilly, but the night sky was clear and full of twinkling stars. 'I've always enjoyed Spanish cuisine, but that was way beyond anything I've had before.'

'Glad you liked it. I wasn't sure if you would and did think of calling to ask, then decided to hell with it. If you didn't like Spanish food, then tough.' She laughed.

He paused and pulled her to a stop before drawing that delightful body in against his. 'Thanks for a great ending to a great day.'

'We had to celebrate. It's not every day you do something as important and exciting as buying a house.' She sounded almost as excited for him as he was.

'It's a big step.' He grinned. 'One I'm pleased I've made.' He was getting on with his plans. It *was* good, he told himself. So now he'd make the most of any time spent with Nikki and possibly grow the relationship further. Enjoying each other's company wasn't something to be tossed aside like a banana skin.

Leaning back in his arms, she locked her eyes with his. 'You mean that, don't you?'

It was a serious question he hadn't expected. 'Yes, Nikki, I do. I am determined to settle down here.'

After staring at him for a long moment, she placed her mouth on his. 'Good.' Then she kissed him hard.

He responded just as hard. She was hot and tasty, and other parts of him were hardening too. Jerking his head back, he growled, 'Nikki, can we go back to your place? Now?'

Her eyes widened as she gave him a wicked grin. 'What a good idea.'

It was hard to focus on driving with Shaun sitting next to her, Nikki thought. His hand on her thigh sent warm tremors throughout her, waking her body up and filling her with eager anticipation. Making love with Shaun had become her favourite pastime, and she couldn't get enough. There was a large hotel up ahead. It'd be too easy to pull in and grab a room for the night. Even though they were only ten minutes from her house, it would be fun going to a hotel with Shaun for a couple of hours.

'Pull in there.' Shaun nodded towards the hotel.

On the same page as her? A trickle of excitement raced down her spine. He was awesome. Indicating a right turn, Nikki crossed the road and pulled up outside the entrance, where the doorman opened Shaun's door.

'Good evening, sir. Do you have a booking with us? Or would you like to make one?'

'I'm going to see if a room is available.' Shaun hadn't leapt out of the car, was instead trying to adjust his trousers without being obvious.

Nikki giggled. 'I'll go in.'

'No, I'll take care of this.'

'There're rooms available.' The doorman spoke very politely, not a hint of a laugh anywhere on his face. He was probably used to couples turning up and being in a hurry for a bed. As they didn't have bags, it would be obvious what this was about, and for once she couldn't care less what the man thought. 'I'll park your car in the basement, madam.'

'Thank you.' Nikki got out and went around to Shaun. 'Ready?' She grinned.

'As I'll ever be.' He grinned back, standing up.

She winked. His situation wasn't quite so obvious as it had been. Could be that talking to the doorman had been a little like ice on his need. Something for her to rectify the moment they were behind closed doors. Melt the ice.

Within minutes Shaun was holding open the door to their room, waving her inside with a very sexy smile that she could not resist. As he let the door shut behind him, she took his hand and tugged him into the centre of the room. Then she began to strip. First her earrings. Then the silver chain from around her neck. Followed by her jacket.

Shaun stood watching her, his tongue circling his lips.

Her dress was next. Lifting it slowly up to reveal her butt, then her stomach and breasts, she did a little wiggle and danced in her heels.

Shaun's eyes widened.

As she seductively slipped the dress over her head, her hips moved in a circle, toward Shaun, away from him.

His hands tightened against his sides. His need pushed out the front of his trousers. He wouldn't be able to wait much longer.

Spinning around on her high heels, she blew him a kiss. Then she unhooked her bra and swung it in the air above her head. Not that Shaun saw that. His focus was entirely on her naked breasts.

'Nikki,' he groaned. His fingers were now fumbling with the buttons on his shirt.

'Shaun.' How was she going to get out of her nylons without falling over and making an idiot of herself?

Then she was being swung up into his arms and laid on the bed.

Shaun's kiss was deep and long and sent the level of her desire off the scale.

She couldn't tell him to make love to her now because his mouth wasn't leaving hers at all.

At the same time he removed her shoes, then got busy sliding her nylons down over her hips, his hot, firm palms ramping up her need even further. Then he was on her thighs, before going lower to her ankles, and finally the nylons were gone. Then Shaun was tugging his clothes off in haste, no finesse going on. When his erection sprang free, she reached for him, held his penis and rubbed it, up and down.

'Nikki, wait.' He had a condom in his hand.

She took it and slid it over his heat. 'I'm ready.'

Then they were together, as one, bringing each other to the peak. And falling over the precipice into oblivion.

Shaun woke to find himself wrapped around Nikki and smiled happily. Not getting out of bed and leaving her in the middle of the night was a plus. This part of time together was as wonderful as everything else. More so. He felt they'd taken another step forward in their relationship. He hugged her tighter. She was so warm and sexy and good and a load more. What a night they'd shared. A superb dinner at a top-notch restaurant followed by mind-blowing sex more than once at the hotel. He couldn't think of a better way to celebrate his new house. Home.

Nikki hadn't been surprised when he'd told her to pull in to the hotel. It was as though she might've had the same idea. They did appear to think along the same lines about quite a few things, which was good and helped this feel like the beginning of more than a friendship, more like the start of a relationship. If they both were ready for that. He wasn't there yet, but he wasn't averse to the idea anymore.

When Nikki had mentioned her marriage, he'd suspected she wasn't fully over the repercussions. There might be trust issues when it came to believing in a man again. He mightn't have trust problems, but he did struggle to believe he wouldn't again lose someone he loved. Yet Amy had taken the chance and was happy. So why couldn't he give it a try? Because trying wasn't good enough. It had to be for sure or not at all. Though there were never any guarantees about what lay ahead. Knowing it and accepting it were two different aspects of the future he was working towards.

'Morning,' Nikki murmured against his arm lying over her waist.

He brushed a kiss on the back of her neck. 'Morning, Nikki.'

Rolling over, she studied him through sleepy eyes. 'Wow, what a night. I'm glad we stayed right through.'

'I'm not arguing.' He grinned. He hadn't woken this relaxed and in tune with himself in ages. 'Feel like breakfast in bed?' Suddenly he was starving, and for the first time since they'd come to this room, it was for food and not Nikki.

'Absolutely. Though I need a long soak in the shower first.'

'How about we order what we want for half an hour away and then soap each other off?'

Her eyes widened as she grinned. 'Better make that an hour. Sharing a shower might lead to complications. Good ones,' she added with a wicked twist to her grin.

'It's a deal.' He got out of bed to find a menu. He could

do sex followed by breakfast. Not a problem. In fact, there wasn't a lot that was a problem with Nikki.

'Have you got any plans for the rest of the day?' Nikki asked when they were finally dressing to leave the hotel.

He paused. Yes, he was going to see his family and tell them the good news. Did he invite Nikki along to meet them? No, she might think he was getting too involved with her, which was the last thing he wanted right now, even if it might be true. Sharing his monumental news with the family was not the same as watching the kids play soccer. 'I'm catching up with my brother and his family. And Mum and Dad.'

'Haven't you told them your news?'

'No. I got sidetracked.' He grinned at her. 'When I left the lawyer, I just had to tell you, and then—well, you know how the night unfolded.'

'I can't deny that.' She slipped her feet into those high heels that turned him on. 'You need to tell your family. They'll be thrilled.'

'They will. What about you? What are you going to do today?'

'I'm catching up with my friend, Molly, and then might drop in on my brother and his family.'

Stepping closer, he wound his arms around her waist. 'Nikki, I have had the most amazing time with you. I'm not walking away from that. We get on brilliantly.'

'But?'

'We haven't known each other very long, and I am not one to rush into things.' Not anymore. He'd done great so far with his plans to settle down here, but if he was going for a permanent relationship, then he had to know it was for real, not something he'd wake up to regret one day. 'I do want to spend more time with you. And with my family. I've missed a lot of time with them and am loving getting to know my nephews better.' He'd invited her to join his family for soccer before it had been cancelled a couple of weeks back. Did she hope he'd ask her along today? 'I would like you to meet my family at some point. I just don't want everyone to read too much into it. Me having bought a house might have them all wondering what else I'm up to.'

A wry smile came his way. 'I'm sorry. It's been an amazing time, and I don't want it to stop. But you're right. We do have separate lives outside this room.'

'We do, and we'll have more great times together.' That wasn't telling her he was looking at a future together, more that they'd see how everything went between them over the coming weeks and months. 'What I mean is that we—'

Her finger touched his lips. 'Stop, Shaun. I get it. I really do. I got carried away and didn't think past leaving the hotel. I am not one of those women who goes home and waits for her phone to ring with someone asking her to join them for the day.'

He couldn't help it. He laughed. 'You honestly think I thought that? You sitting around waiting for other people to bring your life to light? I don't think so.'

'Phew.' Nikki smiled, a little too tightly for his liking. 'Let's get cracking. I'm meeting Molly for coffee soon.'

Nikki was wonderful and becoming more important as the days went by. He wasn't ready to admit that to her, though, or even to himself most of the time. It was too soon. He'd bought a house, and work was going well. Neither had the itch to move on raised its head, which was a positive sign. Everything was working out, but finding a woman he could fall in love with was not to be rushed. Of course, he wanted to love and be loved again. But since meeting Nikki, whenever he thought about love and kids, he got scared. It would be too easy to be hurt if she didn't reciprocate. If she did and it still went wrong, she'd get hurt too, and she'd already been through a nasty divorce. Why was life so darned difficult?

Nikki ran her fingers through her hair in a vain attempt to not look like she'd spent most of the night being active in bed. It was pointless. They had no bags, no overnight gear. The reception staff would know exactly why they'd spent the night in the hotel. Did it matter?

She glanced at Shaun as the lift dropped to the ground floor. No, it didn't. She'd had an amazing night, and so what if other people knew? They didn't know her, weren't about to tell her friends. No, it was fine.

So was Shaun. Despite how he'd suddenly backed away when she'd asked about his plans for the rest of the day. He was right to point out they had lives beyond here that didn't involve them together, and he had told her what he was going to be doing. It was a reminder that they weren't a couple, and that she needed to keep protecting herself.

If only the thought didn't fill her with sadness. For the first time since Brett left, she'd begun to believe there might be a future for her that involved love and family. All because she'd met Shaun. It was still possible, just not this week. She shook her head. She really was rushing in with her eyes wide shut. There was so much she didn't know about this man setting her alight in ways that she'd forgotten were possible. 'Who's the oldest? You or your brother?'

'Me. By eighteen months.'

'That's close in age. Did you get on well or fight all the time?'

'Fought like tigers until we hit the teens, then became best buddies.' Shaun was staring at her. 'Why are you asking?'

Be honest. 'Because I know so little about you other than you're a superb doctor.'

'Only a doctor?' He grinned.

'You're not bad at walking up hills either.' She returned his grin, feeling better by the second.

'Seems I need more practice in certain fields.'

The lift bumped to a halt, and the doors began sliding open. An elderly couple rushed in as though afraid the lift would start moving before the doors closed.

Nikki gave Shaun a sexy wink. At least, she hoped it was sexy. 'Happy to help sometime.' She wasn't rushing him. She did need to look out for herself.

'I'm sure we can come up with something as entertaining as last night,' he said quiet enough so only she heard.

She blushed. That gravelly voice raised a myriad of memories about the entertainment he was alluding too. Heck, she didn't do blushing. That was for teenagers, not thirty-four-year-old medical specialists. Nudging Shaun with her elbow, she said, 'Get out of here.'

'Can I wait till the lift reaches the lobby?'

Did they have time to go back to the room for another round before checking out? She glanced at Shaun, and he shook his head.

'Afraid not.' His smile hit her in the gut, and she gasped.

This was getting out of hand, and while she was enjoying it, she had to pull the brakes on. They couldn't get too close too soon. It wouldn't be great to have her heart broken again.

CHAPTER NINE

'HOW IS IT that we're nearly always on the same shift?' Shaun commented to Nikki over coffee during a brief lull on Tuesday morning. 'We've hardly done any night or late afternoon ones either.'

'Careful or Paul will put you on nights for the next two months.' Nikki smirked. 'As for me, I did twelve weeks of late shifts when one of the doctors left suddenly, so I'm more than happy with what I'm doing.'

'That must've been exhausting.'

'It was, but I got used to it.' One plus to not having family to worry about or even a dog. 'According to the roster, we're both on late shift next week.' Part of her was pleased she'd still be working with Shaun. Another part worried she was getting too comfortable around him despite wanting to let go of her trust issues. But they worked well together, and frankly, that was good for the patients and other staff.

Michaela came into the tearoom and sat down. 'How was your weekend, Nikki? Go walking?'

'No, didn't get the boots on once. Kept pretty busy, though.' She wasn't looking at Shaun in case that annoying blush returned. Michaela wasn't stupid and would know straight away something was up if it did.

'Shaun?' Michaela asked.

'Spent time with the family, played soccer with the nephews in their backyard before filling them with burgers and chips and getting into trouble with their mum. What about you?'

'Not a lot. We were both tired after a busy week. My husband's a radiologist at the private hospital,' she told Shaun.

Georgie appeared in the doorway. 'Nikki, you're needed. A chopper's about to land with a woman on board who fell off the chairlift on Mount Arthur.'

'Coming.' Forget coffee and the banana muffin she hadn't managed to take a bite from yet. Welcome to their world. 'Anything about the injuries?'

'Suspected broken back,' Georgie informed her.

'Right.' Instantly her mind brought up what she had to do for her patient. It wasn't going to be fun. 'How does someone manage to fall out of a chairlift?'

'By fooling around? Or if the person securing the bar before they left the hut didn't do it correctly.' Shaun was right beside her. 'Though I thought the method was supposedly infallible.'

Nikki considered who to call to come to see the woman apart from Radiology. Hopefully Charlie was on duty. He was a superb neurosurgeon. 'How long before touchdown, Georgie?'

'Any minute. Sarah's gone up with Cameron to collect the woman, who's conscious, in pain, and can't feel her feet. The emergency doctor on board has got her fixed so she can't move.' Georgie was babbling, which was unlike her.

'You okay?' Nikki asked quietly.

'My best friend broke her back when she was fourteen. Hasn't walked since,' she replied in a strained voice.

Nikki wrapped her arm around Georgie's shoulders. 'You work with other patients, and Cameron can stay on this case. Unless you want to be there, that is.'

Georgie shook her head. 'Not really. It's the one situation I still struggle with. I was with Tracey when it happened, and I still haven't got all those images out of my head.'

'I'm not surprised.' She dropped her arm. 'Some things never leave us, do they?'

'Seems not. Thanks, Nikki.'

For what? She was only doing what she'd want if faced with a similar situation. 'No problem.'

'You're very understanding,' Shaun muttered as they made their way into the emergency cubicle where their patient would be brought.

'Of course I am,' she snapped. Then felt contrite. 'Sorry. But I know what it's like being reminded of that day I grabbed Jordie from in front of the car, and that was nothing compared to seeing a friend lose her ability to ever walk again.'

'You know because you've been there, faced something horrific.' A shadow was forming in his eyes, as though he also knew was it was like.

'You have too.' Would he say anything about that?

Shaun straightened abruptly and changed the subject. 'Want me to phone Radiology?'

Okay, don't go there. 'Yes, please.' It was starting to irk that he wouldn't talk about the day he had to bring his friend down in the plane. Maybe he never talked about what was important to him, might never open up to her about himself even if they did spend more time together. If so, then she had to keep him at arm's length too. An equal footing, which didn't bode well. So much for getting closer.

They weren't. She went to scrub up and prepare for the woman, all the time wondering how Shaun had dealt with the aftermath of that horrendous time he'd gone through.

'Radiology's gearing up for our patient, and someone will be here shortly.' Shaun was back. He looked around. 'Where is this woman?'

'Patience, man.' Nikki said. It was like tiptoeing around on eggshells waiting for someone who was seriously injured to arrive. All ready to go and no one to work on.

'Me? Patient? Not happening.'

Said the man she'd seen to be very patient in tricky situations with people in agony. 'Yeah, right.'

The lift doors slid open. Two men in rescue orange overalls pulled a trolley into the department, followed by Sarah and Cameron.

'Here we go,' Nikki said and crossed over to join them. 'Hello, everyone. How far did our patient fall?'

'About twenty metres is the estimate,' answered the doctor from the helicopter. 'She landed on rocks. She's in and out of consciousness and has lost all feeling from her ankles down.'

Nikki winced. That wasn't good. 'Who is she?'

'Angela Dane, twenty-four, champion skier.'

She recognised the name. 'Let's hope this isn't as serious as it seems.'

'I imagine we'll have another sparring match with the media once this gets out,' Shaun said.

Her shoulders drooped. Hauling them back in place again, she said, 'We'll deal with that later. In here.' She indicated the room they were using. 'Cameron, I want you to stay. Sarah, too. What meds have you given Angela?' she asked the doctor.

He named the painkillers and handed her the notes he'd written on the way in. 'All here. If there's nothing more you need, we've got to get on our way. There's another woman waiting to be brought in who was in the same chairlift. They're friends and were leaning over the bar looking at some skiers when the lock holding the bar in place gave way. The other woman appears to have got off lightly, possible fractured arm and light concussion. As the second chopper is out on another recovery, we're going back to Mount Arthur for her.'

'See you in a bit.' Nikki was already focusing on Angela, who'd opened her eyes. 'Hello, Angela. You're in hospital. I'm Nikki, an emergency doctor.' She named the rest of the team, but whether Angela took it all in, she wasn't sure.

'I can't feel my feet,' the woman murmured. 'This can't be real. I'm a professional skier. I need my feet.' So she was aware of what was going on around her.

'Angela, I've been told that, but I'd like to check myself.'

'Good. Two opinions are better than one.'

Not if they're the same bad one. Nikki lifted away the blanket covering Angela. 'Tell me if you feel anything on your soles.'

As she pressed her fingertips against one of Angela's heels, then toes and inner foot, the silence was heavy, and upsetting. 'This foot?' The same result. 'What about your ankles?' Again, no reaction. Nikki didn't get any reaction until she touched Angela's knees.

'Yes, I can feel that. Try my feet again.'

Nikki obliged, knowing the result would be the same as before. 'Right, the first thing to be done is have your spine X-rayed. Are you in any pain?' She'd had analgesics, but Nikki needed to know what Angela was feeling now.

'My head hurts. My right arm is agony to move. My back's sore and hurts a lot when I move. But I can't move because the doctor made sure I couldn't.'

'That's so you don't do any more damage while we find out what injuries you have sustained.'

Shaun was examining Angela's elbow and lower arm. 'Multiple fractures here. Did you land on your right side, Angela?'

'Think it was my back, and my arm was under me.'

'That would explain both areas of injuries,' Shaun said.

'There's a deep gouge on her right hip,' Sarah told them.

'Go with her to Radiology, Cameron. We also need an EMI done.' Nikki picked up the phone to call Radiology.

Shaun and Sarah rechecked that Angela couldn't move at all, while Cameron continued monitoring BP, temperature, pulse and more. At one point Shaun looked up and met Nikki's eye. His face was grim. It wasn't looking good. Angela's competitive days were more than likely over.

Nikki's hand tightened around the phone as she talked to the specialist on the other end. She was supposed to be used to dealing with cases like this, but it didn't matter how often she saw a patient with horrific injuries. It never got any easier. From the look in Shaun's face, it didn't for him either. It didn't for any of them.

'Nikki, wait,' Shaun called after her as she left the department at the end of shift. 'I'll walk out with you.' There were bound to be reporters demanding to know what had happened to Angela Dane. Not so much her friend, who only skied for pleasure. No wonder he hardly ever read or listened to the news these days. It was more often than not one-sided, and exaggerated to boot.

Nikki had a grim smile on her face. 'You're going to get a reputation for always being at my side when the going gets rough.'

Yep, and he found it didn't bother him as much as it once would've. 'Too right I am.' He hoped his smile was a lot more relaxed than hers. 'To hell with journalists. We're doctors here to help people, not to indulge in too much talk.'

Nikki huffed out a breath. 'Did you drive to work? Because I walked, and don't feel like being followed through the park on my way home.'

'It's your lucky day. Why not go out the side door?'

'Because it rarely works when it comes to avoiding the reporters, and besides, I need to stare them down and ignore what they ask. There's no avoiding them, so I might as well get on with whatever they throw my way.'

Go, Nikki. 'Of course, they may not have heard about Angela Dane's accident.'

'You're kidding, right? Not only will they have heard she's injured, but they'll know that the chairlift failed. Even if that's an exaggeration, they'll know something went wrong with it. I wouldn't like to be the poor people on the ski field working the chairlifts right now. Though I suppose they stopped using them from the moment the women fell.'

'You're right. There'll be an enquiry.' Shaun suddenly realised he was holding Nikki's elbow. When had he done that? She wasn't pulling away. Because she needed his support? Or because, like him, she hadn't realised what he was doing? Whichever, he wasn't letting go while she was comfortable with his action. He liked being there for her, even though she didn't need his support. She was strong and could stare down anyone who got in her face. But that didn't mean he wasn't watching her back.

The hospital foyer was no different to most days, people coming and going, some looking stressed, others carrying bunches of flowers and talking non-stop to their companions.

'So far so good,' Nikki said.

As they walked outside and headed to his car, reporters began shouting questions at them, and he felt Nikki take a deep breath. 'Ignore them.'

'I intend to.'

'Shaun, are you all right?' a female reporter called.

Afraid the woman would mention Liam's story, he moved faster. It was not how he wanted Nikki to learn what had happened. 'Let's get out of here.'

She upped her pace. 'I'm with you all the way.'

The time was fast approaching when he'd have to talk to Nikki about his past. He didn't wanted her to hear about it from anyone else, but telling her wouldn't be easy. He'd be showing her how vulnerable he'd been, and maybe still was.

When they reached his SUV, she said, 'Thanks for that. I'd have stopped to say I couldn't tell them a thing, which would've got me nowhere.'

'Feel like going for a drink to let off steam?'

Finally a beautiful light-up-his-world smile came his way. 'Sounds perfect.' Then she got in his vehicle and buckled herself in. 'Where should we go?'

'There's great little bar in the centre of the city. It's quiet, and I doubt anyone will find us there.'

'Sounds ideal.'

Unless she began asking why that reporter knew him. Of course all she had to do was go online, and she'd soon learn what had happened. But was she that kind of person? Or would she wait until he told her his story? If he didn't tell her without prompting, what did that say about him, or where they were at? He had no idea at the moment, only understood he was beginning to fall for her, and the time was coming when he'd have to front up about his fears. In the meantime, he'd continue to try to go slowly, saviour the good moments. Except going slow wasn't working. He couldn't get enough of her, which was scaring the pants off him. Laughter tripped over his lips.

'Want to share the joke?'

Hell no. Then again, why not? 'I was thinking how quickly you manage to get me to remove my pants at times.'

'That's all up to me, is it?'

He laughed again. She knew how to make him relax and put aside the fears he carried. 'If you weren't with me, it wouldn't be happening.'

'Glad to hear it.' She grinned, looking relaxed again.

They were a good team, both at work and away from the department.

Later, after an early dinner, they went back to Nikki's and proved just that.

As soon as she finished work on Friday, Nikki headed straight to her favourite clothing shop that happened to be owned by Paul's wife. Shaun was taking her out to dinner again, and she wanted to look as good as she could. So much for backing off. She couldn't stay clear of him.

'Hello, Nikki. I haven't seen you in here in ages, so

you must have a hot date lined up. Who's the lucky man?' asked Mallory when she walked into the shop. 'Not Shaun Elliott by any chance?'

'You might be right.' Nikki laughed. Strange how she no longer wanted to keep quiet among her friends about the fact they were dating. How he'd feel about that was anyone's guess, but for once, she was comfortable with a relationship and wasn't going to hide it.

'Awesome. Everyone liked him at the dinner. Now, what are you looking for?'

'We're going to dinner, and I want to look a bit swish.' If that was possible. Hopefully she could turn out all right with a bit of help from Mallory.

'Any particular colour in mind? Style?'

'Not black or white. Fitting without showing the bumps.'

'What bumps? You've got a lovely figure.' Mallory was already at a rack of evening dresses and lifting a red dress off the rail. 'What do you think of this?'

Immediately she fell in love with it. The satin midi frock with a deep vee neckline was sleeveless. A wide waist band flowed into the floating skirt. 'Beautiful.' It had better fit perfectly or she'd be gutted. Since when did she get in such a fuss about an evening dress? Since she'd fallen for Shaun, that's when.

'Come on. Let's get you trying it on.' Mallory led the way to a fitting room. 'I can't wait to see you wearing it.'

'You're certain it'll fit, aren't you?'

'I know my job, Nikki, so don't prove me wrong.'

Within minutes Nikki was strolling around feeling like she'd touched down in Paradise. 'It's beautiful.' Hadn't she already said that?

'It's a perfect fit.' Mallory got serious. 'Right, shoes

next. You need a jacket too as it won't be warm tonight. Winter hasn't let its grip go yet.'

When Nikki walked out of the shop nearly an hour later, she was smiling so hard it almost hurt. When had she spent so much on clothes for one evening? Never was the answer.

Then Shaun walked in her front door and nearly tripped over his feet when he saw her. She knew it was worth every single cent.

'You look stunning. Wow. I mean—' He shoved his fingers through his hair, mussing it a little. 'I'm behaving like a horny teen, but seriously.'

She laughed. He knew how to make her feel good about herself. 'Seriously nothing. I felt like sprucing up a little.' Sometimes she did need to know she was attractive to a man. After Brett, she'd often doubted it, but tonight she'd made the grade.

'Hey, come here, my girl. You are beautiful—even dressed in scrubs.' Shaun kissed her lightly. 'I mean it.'

My girl? She'd take that as a positive. But as for the scrubs scenario, 'You might be going a bit far there.'

'Me? Never. Right, are you ready? We should hit the road or else we might not make dinner, and I don't really want to get you out of that dress yet.'

Picking up the small evening bag she'd added to her purchases, she grinned. 'Ready as I'll ever be.'

'Let's go.' There was a bounce in his step as they walked out to his SUV.

The bounce didn't dim all evening. Or all night for that matter.

Only in the morning when Nikki's alarm went off did Shaun suddenly turn serious. 'What time is it?'

'Seven thirty. I've got a hair appointment at ten.'

Shaun leapt out of bed. 'I'm meant to be meeting the kids at their soccer game at nine thirty, and it's out at Lyttelton. Before then, I have to pick up a present for my sister-in-law, Sandy. It's her birthday.'

'Slow down. You've got plenty of time.' What was the panic? Two hours was enough to do all that.

'You're right. I have.' He leaned across the bed and kissed her lightly. 'But I should go home and get tidied up first.'

'Fair enough. Will we catch up later?'

'Not today I'm afraid. I'm due at Sandy's birthday dinner at my brother's. But how about we go for a hike tomorrow? Try one around Lyttelton?'

'Sounds good to me.'

'I'll call later to arrange a pick-up time.'

'How about I drive up for a change?' She hadn't been inside where he currently lived. Then again, she had seen where he was moving to, so he wasn't keeping her at arm's length. It rubbed her up the wrong way whenever he kept things to himself now.

'Because I like driving.' He gave her a self-mocking smile. 'It's the male side of my personality looking out for you.'

'Get out of here. See you tomorrow.' She didn't want him to leave, but that was the nature of this relationship. They did spend more time together than she'd have believed a couple of weeks ago, and she was loving it, so she let it go for now.

'Bye.' Shaun disappeared out of the bedroom. Moments later, the front door banged shut.

Nikki pinched herself to make sure he really had been here and they'd had incredible sex more than once. No wonder she felt tired and ached in places. She hadn't had so much exercise in forever. She laughed. So where to from here? More sex for one. More walks and dinners. Dating was a lot of fun. For the first time since she'd found herself single again, she was making the most of every moment. Especially the ones spent with Shaun. She was happy when not querying everything he said and did, and not waiting for the clang when he said enough was enough and he was off to find someone more obliging and loving.

Shaun could still do that.

Yes, he might. Yet she wanted to believe he wouldn't. Probably setting herself up for a big fall, but having decided to start putting herself out there in an attempt to find true love, she wasn't backing off without good reason.

Throwing the bedcovers aside, she leapt out of bed and went to have a long, hot shower to ease the aches before getting ready to go to the hairdresser. Maybe she could ask for a different style. She'd kept her hair long and straight for years and suddenly felt like a change. A bit like that dress she bought yesterday. It'd been stunning and more revealing than her norm, and she'd enjoyed every moment wearing it. Especially the gleam it brought to Shaun's eyes. Oh yes. Thinking about him made her grin. Except she really had no idea what was going on with both of them.

Standing in the driveway of his house, Shaun tossed the keys to the front door in the air and caught them again. Toss, catch. Toss, catch. The previous owners had moved out early and were happy for him to have the keys before the takeover date. He'd been coming around here every day with the intention of making decisions about colour schemes for when it came to redecorating and what sort of furniture he'd like. He hadn't asked anyone to come with him to help with those decisions. Not even Nikki. They were choices he had to make himself because he was the one going to live here. As in he now really and truly owned a house in Christchurch where his family were. Life couldn't get much better.

It was the biggest decision he's made so far. What next? Yes, well, he was having a wonderful time dating Nikki. More than wonderful. She was everything he could wish for and more. Going out to dinner had been special, like every date they went on. As for that incredible dress she wore to dinner—it had lit up her eyes and made her look drop-dead gorgeous, out of this world. Followed by making out in her bed and staying throughout the night. Walking in the hills on Sunday had been a bonus as they'd gone for a meal in Lyttelton afterwards. Over the past week, they'd had another, less upmarket, meal together, and he'd stopped over at her place after.

Did this mean he was getting serious about where they were going with their relationship? He *was* falling for Nikki. She had his heart in her hand, but he was not prepared to accept that completely. There were moments when he had to step away and take a deep breath because he was still worried that he didn't deserve being happy when Liam couldn't. He still hadn't told Nikki about how he'd lost Liam and hence Amy. At times it still felt raw, though less since meeting Nikki. Did that mean she could wipe away his fears and become a permanent part of his life? He hoped so, and would work hard to make it possible.

Unfortunately he didn't know how Nikki felt about them. Was she happy with things as they were? Or was she wanting more, like the whole relationship thing? If she didn't, then he was setting himself up for more heart-ache. And he wasn't sure he could take that again.

'Hi there. Are you our new neighbour?' A middle-aged guy stood at the end of the driveway. 'I've seen you a couple of times over the past few days so figured you must be. I'm Colin.'

'Hey, Colin. I'm Shaun Elliott, and yes, your new neighbour.' He shook Colin's extended hand. 'I haven't moved in yet. Still haven't bought any furniture.' But he was heading to the furniture store shortly to start on selecting what he liked. He had given notice on the flat he was renting and was ready to move in once he had some furniture.

'It's always a hassle shifting house. Getting everything put in the right place and unpacking the millions of boxes of stuff you never use.'

Shaun laughed. 'I come very light. Very few cartons and at the moment no furniture.' Furnished flats had been his way since breaking up with Amy, and he wasn't a hoarder of junk.

'Obviously you don't have a wife then.'

No laugh this time. 'No, I don't.'

Colin looked contrite. 'I'll leave you to it. If you want a hand with anything like moving furniture when you get some, give me a shout. We're on your left.'

'Thanks. I will.' Only if to get back onside with the man. It didn't pay to upset neighbours. You never knew when you might need them. 'When I move in, come over and have a beer with me.'

Colin looked relieved. 'Sure will. See you around.'

Inside Shaun wandered from room to room, trying to soak up the feeling of being on track, except it wasn't happening. It was as though what Colin said had burst his bubble. Asking about a wife shouldn't tip everything askew in his mind. But he was off centre now. This was his permanent home. But looking around the bare lounge, he suddenly felt at a loss over how to cope. He'd never done anything like this on his own. Making decisions about colour schemes and furniture to suit himself was alien, and while it should have been exciting, he was confused.

Is that how he'd react if he did fall in love with Nikki? Be happy one day, messed up and out of it the next? Nikki, Nikki. She filled his mind so often it should be thrilling, except right now it was worrying.

Calm down. Take your time. Start with getting the house sorted before anything else.

He looked around, half expecting to see Liam in the doorway.

Of course he wasn't there. But those words remained. They were right. He had to get a grip and work his way through everything that needed doing piece by piece, not try to do it all at once. Easy said. Darn sight harder to do.

His phone rang. Nikki. To answer or not? Toughen up. 'Hey, how's things?'

'Can't complain. Wondered if you'd like to drop in for dinner later on? I've put together a venison casserole.'

'Venison, eh? You're not into hunting by any chance?'

'No way. But Ross is. My brother,' she added.

'Yes, you've mentioned him.' Often. They appeared to be close, unlike their parents. What had it been like to never settle in one place and be able to make permanent friends? Worse than the last years he'd spent on the move, he'd bet. Something to remember about Nikki. He did not want to be one of those people who upended her world to satisfy his own needs as her father had. That made the thought to take his time getting settled before deepening their relationship more important. So did he accept her invitation? It wasn't out of the blue. They were friends. In other words, yes, despite the tightness in his belly.

'Hello? You still there?'

'Sorry. I got sidetracked. Dinner would be great, venison being one of my favourite meats. I'll bring some wine.' Red would go well. 'But I might be a bit late as I'm going furniture shopping first.'

'Want some help with that? I love trying out lounge suites.' Her laugh nudged his mood upwards.

'Is there no stopping you? I'm heading to Furniture Central. See you there.'

Walking into the massive furniture store, he hesitated. This wasn't going to be easy. The range of lounge suites alone was mind-boggling. Where to start?

'There you are.' Nikki appeared in front of him.

'Where am I going to start?'

'What's most important to you? The lounge, kitchen dining room or your bedroom? Focus on one, and then everything else will fall into place.'

He shrugged. Made sense—if he knew which was the most important. 'My bedroom.' Then he'd have somewhere to sleep and could move in sooner than later. Hopefully selecting a bed would be straightforward compared with lounge furniture.

Nikki slid her arm through his. 'You look lost.'

'A little.' There were beds in all directions and headboards and bedside tables with every single one. 'I want a super king-size bed, and not one that you can raise the mattress.' Surely that would narrow the options a little.

Nikki wandered around for a few minutes. 'Guess we can't try them out,' she said, grinning.

The tension was back, harder than before. This wasn't how he wanted to do this. The furniture was for him. But he had agreed to Nikki coming along, so he'd have to suck it up. He could. He would.

'Shaun? Problem?' The grin had disappeared.

'I'm fine.'

'No, you're shutting down on me.'

True. 'You think?'

'I know.'

Deep breath. 'Sorry. Come on, let's find me a bed.'

Thirty minutes later, Shaun sighed with relief. He'd chosen a bed and bedside tables. 'One room done.'

'What's next?'

'Lounge suite, or maybe two reclining chairs. Preferably leather.'

As he followed Nikki he looked around the huge area and began to feel overwhelmed. This was getting serious. He'd bought a house and been thrilled, but choosing furniture made everything more real. This was permanent. It was going to be all right. Was it though?

For the first time since he'd arrived in Christchurch, the familiar itch was beginning to make itself felt deep in his gut, reminding him he couldn't stay in one place for long. Soon he'd have to move on.

'What colour do you prefer?' Nikki again.

He could do this. He was not moving away. He was not. 'Dark green.'

'Over there.'

He strode in the direction she pointed, his back tight, his gut getting in a tizz. *I am staying.* The reclining chairs were exactly what he liked. He sat down on one and pulled the lever to make it recline. Yes, it was comfortable, but he wasn't. This was serious, being here and looking to buy everything to make his life right, to make his house a home with Nikki watching.

Sitting up abruptly, Shaun got back on his feet and began walking away. This was wrong. He couldn't settle down. Not yet. Maybe never.

'What's wrong?' Nikki asked.

'I think I'll leave the rest for another day. I'll pay for the bedroom furniture now and organise a delivery time, then go.' He *was* staying, wasn't moving away. But first he was getting out of here.

To go to Nikki's for dinner. Oh hell. He couldn't. He didn't trust himself to remain calm, and not to tell her everything going on in his mind.

'Still on for dinner? Nikki asked.

He couldn't let her down. That wasn't right when she'd come here to help him with decisions about furniture. He hadn't asked her to. Damn it. He was between a rock and a hard place. Just what he'd spent years avoiding. 'I'll be right behind you.'

CHAPTER TEN

SHAUN SAT OPPOSITE Nikki at the table, each with a plate of casserole and rice in front of them. He'd hardly spoken since he'd got here, and he knew she was fed up about something. 'What's going on, Nikki?'

'Nothing.'

His mood had gone downhill fast in the furniture store as it sank in what he was doing. This was a permanent move, one he wanted more than anything, but suddenly reality had hit, making him feel scared. Now he longed to know what Nikki was thinking. 'Try again, Nikki.'

'Are you regretting buying the house by any chance?'

'Not at all.'

'You'd have preferred I hadn't joined you looking for furniture? Your mood changed big-time there.'

'No, I appreciated your help.' He really did.

'Then tell me what's bugging you. Is your past hindering you?'

Leaning back, he studied her, wondering where this was going. Did she know what had happened? Had Paul told her? He'd better not have. It was his to tell, no one else's.

'What?' she demanded. He hadn't been forthcoming about Liam or his marriage, and now he regretted that. He also wished she'd talked more about her past. He hadn't asked, knowing how hard it could be to do. But what if Nikki didn't trust him enough to share her story? His heart plummeted. That would break him.

'Nikki, neither of us have talked about our pasts. I know little about your marriage and how you feel about getting involved with another man. Do you trust men? Me?'

The fork she'd been holding dropped onto her plate with a clang. 'You want to know that now? What's it got to do with your mood swing?'

'I'm finding a few obstacles as I make this a permanent move, but don't ever doubt that I am here for good.' She still wasn't giving of herself.

'Trying to convince me or yourself?'

He sat upright. 'How about answering my question? I'd really like to know more about what makes you tick, Nikki.' So far she'd seemed happy to share her time with him, but it now seemed not who she really was. Her explanation about losing her baby and husband had been very brief, with little about how she'd coped and what she felt going forward. Did she even want another relationship? He had no idea.

'Sounds familiar,' she snapped. 'I know about how you brought down that Cessna with your friend on board. Why haven't you talked to me about that? About how it's affected you? I presume that's why you haven't been able to settle in one place since it happened.'

He said nothing.

Nikki drew a breath as she waited, hoping against hope he'd talk to her. He was right though. She hadn't talked about Brett and how broken she'd been over losing him and their baby for fear Shaun would think she was too needy and run for cover. She'd spent the intervening years since Brett left getting back on her feet, afraid of losing her way. She did want a second chance at love but had been afraid she didn't deserve it. If Brett could walk away so easily, so could the next man she gave her heart to. But she had to try. This was too important to give up on. Obviously Shaun wasn't about to open up, so she continued. 'Don't you trust me to understand how the loss of your friend would've affected you?'

Shaun shook his head, sadness filling his eyes. 'I could ask you the same question regarding your marriage, and about losing your baby, but I haven't because I hoped you'd tell me without prompting. Yes, I do understand how that feels.' Standing up, he looked at her with sorrow. 'I guess neither of us is ready to talk about ourselves. Which means neither of us is ready to go any further with this.' Then he walked out of the room to the front door, leaving her decimated.

She had no answer to that, because he was right. They weren't ready. But neither could they get there if he was gone.

He'd blown it. Shaun groaned as he got into the SUV. He should've kept a lid on his emotions, but they were roiling around his body, getting him into a tight knot that he couldn't find a way to unravel. Nikki had come to mean so much to him, yet he still couldn't tell her. He couldn't show her how vulnerable he felt after losing the two people he'd loved so much.

How long had she known about the Cessna incident? She'd probably always known. With major headlines on the TV and internet news coverage here and overseas, it would've been hard not to. To be fair, she understood too well what that was like and how it played with your head. She never talked about saving Jordie, though they had both admitted struggling to cope with the day in the department when those people were hit by the bus. He hadn't explained why he felt that way, nor had Nikki mentioned her story, presumably because he'd told a reporter he knew about it.

He banged his hand on the steering wheel. What a mess. So much for thinking he was on track with his plans for the future. But he was. So why had spending time in the house looking around thrown him off centre? The house was right for him. Was that the problem? For him, and not for anyone else to join him? When the neighbour mentioned a wife, he'd felt a weight come down on him. And when Nikki turned up at the furniture shop all bubbly and happy, nothing at all felt right.

Pressing the button to start the engine, he glanced towards Nikki's front door. She stood in the doorway, highlighted by the lights behind her long hair falling over her shoulders and her tight stance, no longer bubbly and happy. Neither was he. But this had to be a blip, nothing major to upset his determination to stay here. Because he was staying, no matter what.

Nikki watched Shaun accelerate away. Despite his change in demeanour at the furniture shop, he'd accepted her invitation for a meal and even said he'd bring wine. When he hadn't, she'd got out one of hers. No problem. Neither of them had finished their meal, had been merely pushing it around their plates with a fork. Nor had the wine been touched. Was this the end of what they'd had? It felt like it.

'What the heck is your problem, Shaun?' she asked

as his taillights disappeared round the corner. 'Why the mood change?' He'd been so thrilled to have bought the house, yet something had upset him. After going inside, she slammed the door shut and locked it before heading to the kitchen to drink her wine.

'Shaun Elliott, you owe me an explanation for walking away.' From the moment he'd put in an offer on that house, he'd been ecstatic and on tenterhooks until the deal was finalised. Now it seemed he'd come crashing down off the high. Did he have regrets about buying it? He'd said he was home for good. Was that it? He didn't want to stay after all?

It was the one thing she'd feared when she started falling for him. She couldn't stand the thought he'd move away, or want to keep moving time after time, yet she'd let him into her heart anyway. Because she couldn't stop him. She was ready to take a chance on love, all because she'd met Shaun. He'd been the tipping point, and she didn't regret it until tonight. She hadn't done anything wrong that she could see, and she thought she knew him well enough to think he'd have told her otherwise. But then, she wasn't great at understanding the men she came to care about. Look how badly she'd messed up by believing Brett loved her and only her.

You didn't explain how Brett had made you distrustful about loving someone again when he asked. You owe Shaun that as much as he needs to talk to you.

Taking a big sip of wine, she looked for her phone. They had to move beyond this, couldn't give up so easily. She pressed his number.

'Nikki.'

'Hi, Shaun. Are you okay?'

'I'm fine,' he snapped.

Which said to her he wasn't. 'Then why did you leave?'
Silence.

'Shaun, talk to me.'

'I'm pulling over.' A moment later he continued. 'I apologise for my behaviour. It's been a busy day, and I'm exhausted. Just want to get home and curl up for a good sleep.'

Just as well she hadn't put on her new sexy little number, because she didn't believe him, and it would've been demeaning if he'd reacted like she was a nuisance if she came on to him. 'You could've taken the time to tell me what was bothering you.'

'Yes, you're right, I probably should've, but I needed to get away and be on my own.'

That hurt. Big-time. 'I thought we were better than this.'

'Seems we both have problems talking about our pasts. I'll see you at shift changeover tomorrow.' He hung up.

Something was definitely wrong, and now she was more convinced it was to do with her. If he'd gone off her, all he had to do was say so and not accept her dinner invitation. He could've said he hadn't needed her to help select furniture. Everything had been going well. The nights together in bed, the meals they shared, working alongside each other. But still, she hadn't been very forthcoming about her past either.

Work. Great. How was she going to manage that comfortably if Shaun wasn't talking to her? Guess she'd find out soon enough.

Shaun rolled his shoulders and rubbed his lower back. He was tired beyond reason. He'd barely slept a wink since their argument thinking of Nikki and his house and ticking off that damned list. Why had he even drawn it up in his head? It was always going to lead to disaster.

'Doc, I think I'm going to be sick,' said the eighteen-year-old lying on the bed in front of him.

Shaun grabbed the bowl the nurse had placed on the cabinet. 'Use this.' The guy had been brought in with concussion after falling off a ladder in the storeroom where he worked. 'Vomiting's a normal reaction to hitting your head.'

'I've got this,' Georgie said. 'Paul wants you in emergency cubicle two.'

'I'll be back shortly.' Shaun went to see what was going on in the next cubicle. Except it was Nikki attending to the patient, not Paul. 'I hear I'm wanted.'

'This is Maria. She suffered severe chest pain while playing golf.'

'Cardiac arrest?'

'Yes. Lucky for her, help was right at the golf club.'

He got down to business, helping Nikki with the patient, not quite sure why he'd been called on.

When a cardiologist arrived, Shaun went back to see his other patient. 'How're you feeling?'

'Better now I've thrown up.'

'We'll keep you here for a couple of hours, and if nothing else goes wrong, you'll be free to head home.' He filled the guy in on what drugs he'd prescribe for the pain. 'Stay away from ladders for a while. Another knock on your head could have serious repercussions.'

'You on for a coffee break?' Georgie asked as they left the cubicle.

'Definitely.' Along with something to eat. He hadn't had more than one piece of toast for breakfast, and now his stomach was complaining.

Nikki was sitting at the table when they entered the staffroom and said, 'Maria's going up to ICU as I speak. She's in a bad way.'

'I'm not surprised. Her readings indicated a major cardiac event. She doesn't know how lucky she was not to arrest.' He poured a coffee from the plunger and went to sit on the opposite side of the table. Directly in line with Nikki's gaze. Damn it. He missed her like he couldn't believe. After her phone call as he drove away the other night, she'd been aloof towards him. He wasn't blaming her. He'd messed up. Would she give him a second chance? She could say what she liked. He'd listen and try to find a way through this mess they'd got into.

'Has Paul mentioned the group dinner next weekend?' Nikki asked, surprising him.

Maybe there was a chance. He shook his head. 'No, but he knows I won't be here.' He was sorry he'd miss getting together with them all. They were fun and friendly and added to his sense of belonging, which right now was headed out the window. All because everything had gone too well and frightened him.

'You're on holiday for the weekend?'

'For five days actually. To Adelaide.'

She pulled a face. 'You never mentioned it. But then, I don't suppose you had to tell me everything you're up to.'

Had, as in the past. He glanced around, but thankfully Georgie was nowhere to be seen. This was getting a little personal. Pain enveloped him. It wasn't what he wanted. He wanted to leap up and pull Nikki into his arms and hold on to her, but that wouldn't be right when he was so unsure of himself. 'Nikki, I'm sorry. I seem to have hit a wall and need to move around it before I know what I'm doing next.'

The mug moved back and forwards in her hands. She

watched him closely for a long moment. 'You know you can talk to me anytime you want.'

Surprised, he shook his head. 'Thanks, but I prefer working through my problems by myself.'

Her head jerked up, and her eyes widened with something like anger as she stared at him as though he was a complete stranger to her.

He waited to be blasted with criticism for being selfish. If only he had talked to her about the past when they were getting along. It would've been easier. Now every time he opened his mouth, he seemed to hurt her. Now it was too late. He'd hurt her when he'd been trying hard not to hurt either of them. She wouldn't forgive him for that. She held her heart tight and wasn't giving it away easily. He didn't want Nikki feeling sorry for him, or staying around because she thought he might feel worse if she dumped him.

'Fine.' She stood up, placed her mug in the dishwasher and strode out to the room with a very straight back and long strides.

The message was loud and clear. She was done with him, whether he changed his mind about how he felt or not.

One thing to come out of the days of going over everything countless times was that he had fallen for her. But that wasn't enough. He had to trust himself to stay around, had to believe his heart would be safe with her, had to know hers would be more than safe with him, and at the moment he was a bit wobbly where that was concerned. He couldn't trust himself to see through his plans to settle back here. Since buying the house, it had become clear how much harder it was to let go of the past than he'd thought. So much for thinking he was ready. Obviously he wasn't.

Maybe he should look for a new position in Adelaide while he was there for his sister's wedding.

* * *

When he finished his shift, Shaun went directly to his house as he'd had a message saying the store was delivering more furniture in the afternoon. He'd no sooner stepped inside when the sound of a truck backing up the drive had him walking out the front door.

A man hopped out of the passenger side of the delivery truck. 'Hey, mate. I've got a load for Shaun Elliott. That be you?'

'Sure is. What've you got?' He'd been back to the store and chosen more items in the hope it would quieten his concerns about staying. It hadn't worked, but he'd do anything to stick to the plan.

'A lounge suite and a table and chairs. There's more to come tomorrow morning if you're about.'

His house was becoming his home, yet he didn't feel right about it. Falling out with Nikki had killed a lot of his happiness and hope. Even work didn't feel as comfortable at the moment. Instead he was constantly questioning if he was doing the right thing by staying on.

He'd worked the evening shift when he overheard Kennedy saying his son was sick and he wanted to be with him. It meant he didn't have to rub shoulders with Nikki until he flew out to Adelaide. Time off to go to the wedding had been part of the deal when he signed up with the department. He hadn't mentioned it to Nikki out of habit. Another mistake, but it didn't matter now. She'd learned he was going away, and they weren't spending time together anyway.

'Show us where you want this stuff and we'll get on with the job, and then we can knock off for the day.'

'Come in.' He led the man inside and pointed out the rooms where the furniture was going. 'I'll give you a hand.'

'Thanks, but me and my offsider have got this. Though you could bring in the dining chairs.'

The lighter pieces. He supposed it made sense. These guys were used to hauling furniture around. He wasn't. It didn't take long for the three of them to unload everything. 'I can't even offer you a beer,' Shaun said as they finished up. 'The fridge hasn't arrived.' Along with the freezer and a new dishwasher since the one that had been here wasn't in great condition. Seemed strange they hadn't been delivered when the saleswoman had said they had some in stock. Then again, it didn't really matter. He wasn't living here yet.

'No problem, mate. See you in the morning with the next load.' They were gone, obviously in a hurry for that beer.

Shaun wished he did have a cold beer on hand so he could drink a toast to his house and maybe improve his mood, but knew it would take more than a beer to do that. There was more furniture to decide on, and his few books and other possessions to unpack, which hopefully would make everything feel right again. He imagined his nephews running around the lawn kicking the hell out of their soccer ball and yelling at each other just like he and his brother used to at that age. Kids. He'd always wanted a family. He and Amy talked about it often, coming up with names and how many they might have when they finally got around to it. They'd intended waiting until he'd specialised so he'd be on hand for the kids more, and he didn't want to miss out on too much time with them. Then it all went belly up.

It hurt, but nowhere near as much as usual. He had to believe he was moving on and getting used to the idea of a second chance, yet it wasn't true. He felt lonely and empty, longing for Nikki to be at his side again. But how to overcome this? Anything he said to Nikki could do more damage, not repair the hurt he'd caused. Love could be forgiving and wonderful, and sometimes it couldn't cope with life's atrocities.

Wandering through the house once more, he wondered if he wanted to share it with someone—with Nikki. Living here alone forever was not what he'd hoped for. Nor did he want just anyone here with him. Nikki would be the one if he did take that last step. Not ready. Not by a long way, despite caring about her so much it hurt. They couldn't even have a conversation about their pasts without getting wound up with each other. There was a lot they hadn't talked about. He didn't know how she felt about having children now that she'd lost one. Losing the baby and her husband within weeks of each other had to have cut deep. That man leaving her while she grieved could have well and truly put her off ever wanting to try for a family again.

He had tried asking Nikki about it, and look where that got him. Out in the cold, because he hadn't been able to talk about himself either.

It *was* time to open up about his past, to expose his fears, make himself vulnerable, if he wanted to achieve his dreams.

I'm not ready.

Nikki was in his heart. That didn't mean he was ready to step up and declare his love. Not by a long way. So much for thinking he was moving on. Especially when Nikki might still have issues with her past. She didn't need a man in her life who could wake up one morning and say it was time to move on to a new place and ask her to go with him. She'd made it perfectly clear she was settled and wasn't prepared to go somewhere else to start over with new friends when she obviously had a great circle of pals here already. No doubt for the first time in her life, if he'd understood how moving around as a child had affected her.

It was time to take a step back and think everything through properly. For both their sakes. He did not want to go through the pain he'd known when he lost both Liam and Amy. Nikki didn't need additional pain any more than he did.

He walked outside and around his home. Yes, his home. He'd get there. He had to for his sake if no one else's. But he wasn't taking that final step with Nikki until he was absolutely certain he could last the distance. Just thinking about Liam and Amy had his heart racing and the fear returning.

But he owed Nikki an apology for being blunt yesterday.

Tugging his phone from his pocket, he stared at her number.

He'd let her down.

Which would be worse? To apologise and possibly raise her hopes he wanted to get together again? Or to be honest and tell her he wasn't ready to commit to a relationship?

He slid the phone back into his pocket.

Nikki was still peeved over how Shaun had treated her. So much for thinking they got along well. He hadn't been forthcoming about himself, but she'd thought he'd slowly get over it and talk to her about why he didn't stay in one place for long and why this time he was determined to settle down.

But she was also angry with herself.

One thing that was very clear was she loved him. Not a little but completely. But she also wasn't going to be treated like she didn't matter. Either they were together or they weren't, and he'd gone for the second option. She needed to know why if she was going to be able to move on. *Move on.* The phrase that had haunted her since she lost her baby and then her husband. Yet after only a few weeks with Shaun, here she was thinking she could do it. No doubt she'd been reading too much into their dates and sex. It was no more than a fling, but since she'd finally loosened the knots around her heart, she'd found more to their relationship than was really there.

'Stuff you, Shaun. You've hurt me, and I need to know why.' Shoving her plate aside, she grabbed her laptop and began typing. She'd put off doing this to give him the opportunity to tell her and got nowhere. And yes, she did feel guilty for not talking about how Brett had decimated her with his infidelity. There had been a moment or two when she could've sucked up her fears and got on with explaining why she felt so vulnerable.

Shaun Elliott, NZ.

Ping. His name came up more than once, along with photos of him looking distraught.

'Shaun Elliott did all he could to save his friend's life in the skies over Christchurch.

Shaun Elliott, doctor, not a pilot, brought plane down, with dead friend.

Shaun Elliott refuses to talk to media.

On and on it went. Many details about Liam having a cardiac arrest while flying the plane and Shaun being unable to save him. How Shaun worked hard to bring his friend back to his family in one piece. How he hadn't been able to do CPR.

Nikki leaned back in her chair. Sweat broke out on her forehead. Her heart pounded. How did anyone move past that? Shaun definitely hadn't. He'd been caught in an impossible situation. It had been in the news for days. No wonder he'd been short with the reporters on the day the people hit by that bus came into ED. It also explained why he'd had her back the whole time. He definitely understood what it was like to be continuously hounded by the press.

Something they had in common. But she hadn't kept her feelings to herself when with friends. Talking to Molly and others had helped her get through the worst days. Did Shaun talk to his family about what happened that day? She'd listen without butting in every few minutes if he'd let her, but she knew he wouldn't let her anywhere near. It was time to let it all go, if that was possible, and leave it up to Shaun to decide if and when he was going to talk about his past. If she didn't, then she'd only end up bitter and angry with herself.

He hadn't even mentioned that he was going away for a few days at any time they'd been talking about places they liked to visit. Why was he going to Adelaide? Looking into a new job? But he'd bought a house here, had said he was staying, settling down to be near his family.

Her head throbbed with all the questions and no answers. Time to leave it alone. She needed to sleep, having had little last night because once again Shaun had been in her head all night long. Why had she been so stupid to let him into her heart?

Because she'd had no choice. One day she hadn't known him. Less than a week later he was setting her alight with need and a longing for the life she no longer believed possible. Now he was in her heart.

It was time to pull on her big girl pants and look out for herself.

But as she lay in bed waiting for sleep to take over, she couldn't stop thinking about Shaun and how it must've been in that plane that he couldn't fly with his friend dying at his feet. He had mentioned nightmares after the bus accident. Now she understood why he had them. Like hers with the car repeatedly racing towards Jordie and her.

The car that grew bigger and bigger the closer it got until the bonnet was in her face. Then the front was slamming into her legs. Jordie was screaming as they became airborne. Screaming and screaming. Both of them. Slam. Onto the road. Pain. Excruciating.

Nikki jerked awake, sat up fast. Sweat poured down her face. Damn it. When were these nightmares going to stop? Why tonight when she hadn't dealt with anything traumatic in the department? Other than Shaun's cold shoulder, and that shouldn't have brought on the nightmare.

Her heart was thumping, making her ribs ache. Her head felt full of air. Damn you, Shaun. He could take the blame since he'd messed up her heart. But she had to take the guilt she carried about not telling him about herself and explaining why she found it hard to talk about her vulnerability.

Climbing out of bed, she pulled on her thick bathrobe and went to make a cup of tea. And thought more about their last conversation here. He hadn't been forthcoming. But neither had she, instead turning it back on him. She hated exposing her pain over losing her baby, and then Brett, hated admitting how wrong she'd been about her ex. Talking about it only brought all the anger and hurt and disappointment roaring back, making her vulnerable all over again.

Exactly how Shaun must feel.

She'd let him down. She could admit it now. What next? He'd left work this afternoon, apparently going straight to the airport for his flight to Adelaide. Talking to him, apologising and telling him what he wanted to know, was going to have to wait until he got back. Whenever that was. It was going to seem like forever. Phoning wasn't right. She had to do it face-to-face. Hopefully then he might feel comfortable with talking about his problems. Because they both needed to be honest with each other.

On Saturday, Shaun stood beside Larry, one of his close friends, and watched his sister holding Larry's hands as they exchanged their vows. It brought tears to his eyes to see Joy so happy, something that had been missing in his bright, bubbly little sister for years. After an abusive relationship, she'd sworn she would never again set herself up to be vulnerable to any man, and here she was marrying his friend.

Larry was an emergency doctor at Adelaide Hospital. When Joy moved over here to get away from her ex, Shaun had set them up for a date. Voilà, here they stood, looking beyond happy.

'You could have it too,' Joy had said last night. 'If I can do it, then so can you. You just have to stop hanging on to the past so fiercely.'

'Yeah, right,' he'd retorted. But seeing these two so happy, the thought crossed his mind that maybe his sister had a point. He'd tried but had given in too quickly. Within weeks of returning to Christchurch, his life had started changing. The job was similar to most others, yet he felt he fitted in better at Christchurch General. He didn't spend his time looking for reasons to leave. Until it all went belly up with Nikki. Spending time with the family was awesome. Throw in the house and he'd made progress. All that was left to finish the list was Nikki. Not any woman. Nikki. She'd won him over without trying. His heart was hers to do with as she saw fit. She could break it in one move, or she could love him back and make him the happiest man on the planet.

If he let her. He had to. There was no other way.

'Ladies and gentlemen, girls and boys, I announce Larry and Joy husband and wife. Hip hooray.'

Everyone was on their feet, clapping and calling out congratulations. Kids began running around in circles, laughing loudly.

The waiters were bringing around trays with glasses of champagne.

Shaun waited until no one was talking to Joy and moved in to hug her. 'I am so happy for you, sis. I really am.'

She planted a big kiss on his chin. 'So am I.'

He waited for the dig about sorting his own life out, but it didn't come.

Instead she said, 'I hear you turned down Larry's offer of a job here.'

'I did.' When he'd gone into the ED where his mate worked, he hadn't felt the spark of anticipation at a new job that was normal and knew he was returning home.

Home. That was the thing. Christchurch was home. 'I didn't want to be there. I like the position I've got.'

'Sounds positive. Sorry, but I'd better keep moving around.'

'Go for it. This is your and Larry's day.'

'Thanks to you for introducing us.'

They were a perfect match. But what about him and Nikki?

Shaun had spent every free moment since that night they'd argued thinking about Nikki and asking himself if he was wasting an opportunity to tick that final requirement to be at home and completely happy. Opening up and talking about Liam's death would've been hard to do but also would've shown how hurt and vulnerable he was, something he didn't know how to do. It might've lightened his vulnerability. His family understood the pressure he'd put himself under by blaming himself for not being able to save Liam when in reality it had been impossible, but they never actually talked about it with him. If he wanted to become part of Nikki's life, then he had to toughen up, and take it on the chin if she didn't understand why he'd felt he'd let Liam down.

Though he doubted Nikki would think he had done anything wrong that day in the plane. She'd more likely fully understand why he'd been so hurt over losing Liam. She'd been hurt too and knew how hard it was to move on. Couples had to share their feelings, their fears and delights, their pain and joy, not avoid them.

'Looks like you're thinking too much.' Larry was handing him another glass of champagne.

He hadn't realised he'd drunk the first one. 'I'd better go easy.'

Larry smirked. 'It's our wedding. You will enjoy yourself.'

'You've only been married moments, and already you sound like my sister.'

Larry laughed, sounding happier than Shaun could remember him ever being. 'They say love is blind.'

Ping, it was like a bell had gone off in his head. He was blind. He'd fallen for Nikki fast when he knew little about her, and suddenly he made a decision. He didn't want to miss out on trying to make it work between them. Damn it, he'd get down on bended knee if that's what it took to make her give him a chance. 'You know what, you're right.'

'When aren't I?' Larry chuckled. 'Don't tell Joy I said that.'

'You owe me.'

'You won't change your mind about coming over here for that job?'

'Nope.' Not even if he didn't win over Nikki. He was going home to Christchurch. It was the right place for him, and everything had been slotting into place making him more comfortable by the week when he wasn't overthinking it. 'I'm sticking to the plan.' Larry knew what he was trying to do, and Shaun suspected the job offer was his way of toughening him up.

Larry clapped him on the shoulder. 'Good. Now looks like I've got to go get some photos taken. Beats me why we have to do this, but if Joy's happy, then so am I.'

'Yeah, right. I can already see a framed picture of the two of you on the lounge wall in your apartment.'

If he had a photo of Nikki on his phone, he'd be taking it out now and looking at her. He accepted he loved her. He missed her so much it hurt big-time. Would she give him a second chance when he'd hurt her? Face it, he'd kept her at arm's length too long and now might have lost her for good. They'd been too busy getting to know each other without giving anything away about themselves, which seemed unreal but in their case was true. Forget the list. This was about them and love and making a future together. He didn't care about anything else right now, only Nikki.

Monday night and the sun hadn't quite set, though darkness wasn't far away. Spring was inching closer. Her favourite season when the daffodils flowered in the park and the trees started to bud. Not that the air was much warmer, but it was a start. Nikki walked fast around the perimeter of Hagley Park. It was her second lap, and she felt good.

If she didn't think about Shaun.

Hard to do when he hung out in the back of her mind all the time, popping up to the front whenever she wasn't involved with patients. Annoying at the very least. She wasn't thinking how he affected her so much. It was too raw and too close to her heart. She had to stay in remote mode to get through this, and get through it she would. She'd done it before. She could do it again.

She had to, for her sanity. But this time she wasn't going into a funk and refusing to get out among other people when it came to dating. It was past time to move on and get a real life—the one she'd dreamed of and thought she'd had with Brett. Her strides lengthened. Decision made. She couldn't waste any more time wondering why everything had gone so wrong with Shaun. That was part of life.

When she reached her car, she checked her phone, but

no messages from Shaun. As if there would be. She was supposed to be getting over him. Yeah, right. At least she was thinking about doing it.

On the way home, she swung by the Thai takeaway shop and picked up an order of green curry, plus a chicken satay to reheat for tomorrow's dinner. Easy as. Cooking for one got to be a chore at times. Most of the time, she admitted with a wry smile. Brett used to say she should get a kitchen maid considering how much effort she put into cooking. Her argument was that being female didn't automatically make her a great cook. He never had an answer for that.

As she turned into her street, the car's headlights lit up a vehicle parked outside her house. A black SUV. Shaun. Wasn't he meant to come home tomorrow? What did he want? Come to tell her he was moving to South Australia? He might as well have waited until tomorrow at work when he could tell everyone. She didn't need a special visit.

Parking in front of her garage, she sucked in a deep breath and reminded herself she was not going to let him into her heart any longer. He was history before he'd been much else. Gathering up the takeaways and her handbag, she got out of the car and locked it, glad for the automatic lighting that came on when she drove in. Then, serious face on, she turned to look at the man walking up her driveway and waited. Her heart rate had lifted, and she had no idea to slow it down other than remain determined to get through whatever this was about without giving in to the love filling her at the sight of Shaun.

'Hello, Nikki.' He stopped and watched her as though waiting for a reaction of any sort.

She only had one. Wrong, she did have reactions that

wanted to burst free, only she was keeping those to herself. She couldn't rush up and wrap her arms around him, hold him like she never wanted to let him go, because she wouldn't. 'Hello, Shaun.'

Something was bothering him. He was watching her with an intensity she hadn't seen before. It was hard not to ask what was up, but he didn't like personal questions. This was how she protected herself. She waited.

'Have I come at an inopportune time?' he asked.

'No.'

'I need to talk to you, explain a few things. How we parted last week.' He paused. 'How we stopped getting along so easily—' Another pause. 'It's been hard not seeing you.'

She waited to see where this was going, ignoring the glimmer of hope tapping at her heart.

'I haven't been totally open with you.'

'Nor have I with you.' She shivered. The temperature was dropping now that the sun had disappeared, but her skin was tight. 'Come inside.'

'Thanks.' He followed her in quietly, not saying anything else.

Awkward. Nikki placed the takeaways on the bench and her bag on the table. The silence grew, and in the end she had to say something or lose her cool. 'How was Adelaide?'

He stood at the end of the counter, watching her. 'That's why I'm here.'

So he was leaving Christchurch. Plonking her backside on a stool at the kitchen island, she studied him. He looked tired, and worried, and sad all in one. She let go the hold she had on her emotions. He was too special for her to ignore his pain. 'What's going on, Shaun?'

'First, I'm not here for sympathy. I need to explain what makes me tick so you might understand me a little.'

Was he saying they might have a future together? Or was she getting ahead of herself? That was more likely. But her heart wasn't very good at doing as she told it. 'Go on.'

His wide chest rose as he drew a breath. 'I went across for my sister's wedding, and seeing her so happy brought me to tears.' He gave her a wobbly smile. 'Yes, I am capable of crying.'

'Who isn't?'

'Joy was in an abusive relationship until a couple of years ago when one day she got up, packed her bags and walked out of the house never to return. It took a lot of guts. She never once considered going back despite the threats the guy made.'

'Now she's moved on and is happy.' *Like I want to be.* With this man if he'd have her.

'Yes, with one of my friends. But that's not what I came to tell you. At least not entirely.' He was struggling, not used to being open about himself.

'Would you like a glass of wine?' It might help him relax a bit and get whatever was bothering him off his chest.

'I'd love one.'

When she placed two glasses on the counter, he sat down opposite her. 'Thanks.'

Taking a sip, she waited. There was nothing she could think of to say to help him overcome whatever was holding him back. If she apologised for her own mistakes now, he might stop what he was trying to say.

His glass was turning back and forwards in his fingers. 'Seeing Joy so happy woke me up to what I could have if I only let go what's been holding me back since Liam died. She made sure I knew I was wasting time worrying about being vulnerable again. She's right. I have been dodging around what's happened.' He paused and took a mouthful of wine.

'What would that be?' she asked quietly, still not sure where this was going but feeling more and more on edge. She wanted to help him, but she didn't know how and wouldn't until he told her everything.

'You know my friend, Liam, had a cardiac arrest while he was flying us back from Wellington in a small plane. I knew nothing about flying, but I'm a doctor. I know what to do when someone has a heart attack. Except there was no room to lie him out and do CPR, and if there had been, there'd have been no one at the controls to fly the plane.'

'You've blamed yourself ever since.' This was deeper than what she'd read, because it was Shaun telling her what happened.

'It probably sounds OTT, but yes I have. Not all the time, but often. At the time, I had to make a decision and figured getting Liam home to his family in one piece was more important than trying to manage compressions when I knew he was dead. I desperately wanted to do them. Instead I got on the radio and called for help. Liam had shown me how to keep a plane flying straight and level, even how to bring it lower, but in the circumstances, it all felt near impossible. Someone in the control tower who had a private pilot's licence talked me through keeping the plane level until an instructor came across from the nearby aero club and talked me down. It wasn't a great landing, but at least we made it without further problems.'

She couldn't help herself. She reached for his free hand. 'I don't know how you did that.'

'I don't either.' He took another gulp of wine. 'But it only got harder. I was married to Liam's sister, Amy. We were both devastated over what had happened to Liam and struggled to support each other while dealing with our own grief. Then there was her family. They never blamed me for what happened, and I know they were right, but I felt so guilty for not saving him. In the end, it got too much for Amy and me, and we agreed to go our separate ways.'

'So you've been married.' Somehow she wasn't surprised. It added to his reasons for holding back from telling her everything. 'You lost a lot that day.' After squeezing his hand, she let go to give him space.

'I did. Our marriage break-up coming on top of Liam's death made me vulnerable and therefore self-protective. I haven't let anyone in since. Until now. Meeting you has made me open my eyes and really see how I've withdrawn from living life to the full. I'm vulnerable and scared, and because of that, I've hurt you. I'm so sorry.'

Her heart slowed. *Here it comes.* He was going to say he couldn't trust himself with a new relationship.

'The thing is, Nikki—' Again that sexy chest lifted. 'I've fallen in love with you. I really, truly love you, and I want you to know that. I'm sorry I avoided talking about myself earlier, but—'

Nikki was off her stool and stepping between his knees. 'Stop right there, Shaun. We've both held back.' *He loves me.* 'I didn't tell you how I felt about Brett playing around behind my back, how vulnerable that made *me.* I haven't mentioned how hard it was growing up with an egotistical father making us constantly move homes and schools, having to make new friends all the time. I gave you the basics because the rest was too hard to talk about. I laid my heart on the line once, and after how Brett treated me, I've been afraid to repeat that mistake.' *He loves me.* 'Though since meeting you, I've decided being alone is more than lonely. It's ridiculous. I still dream about having a family with the man I give my heart to. You, Shaun. I love you. I think I started falling for you that day in ED when you had my back with the media.'

She couldn't say any more. Not only because of the tears blocking her throat but because Shaun had her head in his hands and was kissing her so gently she wanted to cry—if she wasn't already.

He drew back a fraction. 'Darling Nikki. You're everything I want. You're one amazing lady, and I love you so much it hurts at times.'

She had to kiss him better.

An hour later, they lay in each other's arms in bed, smiling non-stop. 'Wow,' Nikki whispered.

'Yes, wow. That's the way to start a serious relationship.' Shaun brushed a kiss on her forehead.

Pushing up onto her elbow, Nikki gazed at him. 'Serious relationship? You mean that, don't you?'

He sat up and took her hands in his. 'Yes, sweetheart, I do. To the point that I have to ask— Will you marry me, Nikki Marlow?'

Her heart was beating out of time. 'Y-yes. Absolutely yes, Shaun Elliott.' She'd be Mrs Nikki Elliott. Woo-hoo.

Their kiss was long and deep and filled with all the love they had in them to give.

I'm getting married, Nikki hummed to herself. *To the most amazing man I've ever known.* Life couldn't get better than that.

'I have something else to put to you,' Shaun said.

'What's that?'

'Would you be happy to move into my house with me and make it our home?'

She loved her cottage, but if Shaun was ready to move on from his past and settle down, the least she could do was be there at his side in all ways possible. She'd held back about herself, and this would help make up for that as she moved forward with the love of her life. 'Absolutely.'

'It doesn't mean you get to make all the decisions about the colour scheme and furniture,' he said with a grin.

'We'll see about that.' She laughed. She really couldn't have cared less about any of that right now. All that mattered was she loved Shaun and he loved her back. 'We're getting married. Woo-hoo.'

'That we are.' And he kissed her again. And again.

* * * * *

If you enjoyed this story, check out these other great reads from Sue MacKay

Parisian Surgeon's Secret Child
Wedding Date with the ER Doctor
Brooding Vet for the Wallflower
Healing the Single Dad Surgeon

All available now!

MILLS & BOON ®

Coming next month

EMERGENCY ROOM REUNION
Amy Blythe

He glanced at her mouth—again. And he wasn't the only one guilty of that look.

But she wasn't going to make the same mistake twice. 'We shouldn't have… That night you came in with a broken tibia, I didn't think you were staying.' Her words were running away from her, but she couldn't stop them. 'It felt like goodbye, like there was nothing to lose, but now you're *back* back, and there's something to lose. Oh god.' It hit her like a ton of bricks, the real answer to her question. 'You came back to give it another go?'

'No.'

'No?'

'I just wondered if there was still something.'

'How is that different?'

'Because there's no pressure,' he said, eyes pleading. 'Because you kissed me back and it was like nothing else.' His tone seemed to dare her to contradict him, to disagree, and she couldn't do it.

Without meaning to, without consciously making the choice to touch him, she reached out, grazed her fingertips to the back of his wrist. This was real. He was really here, really telling her he wanted her still, after all this time.

Continue reading

EMERGENCY ROOM REUNION
Amy Blythe

Available next month
millsandboon.co.uk

COMING SOON!

We really hope you enjoyed reading this book.
If you're looking for more romance
be sure to head to the shops when
new books are available on

Thursday 18th December

To see which titles are coming soon, please visit
millsandboon.co.uk/nextmonth

MILLS & BOON

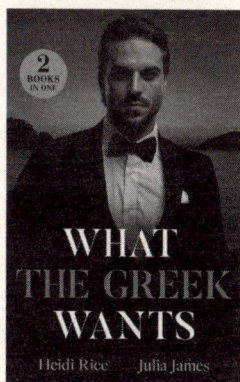

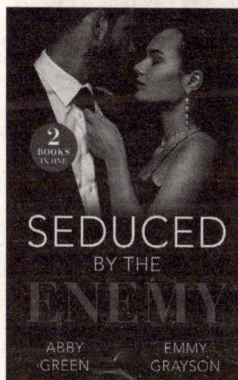

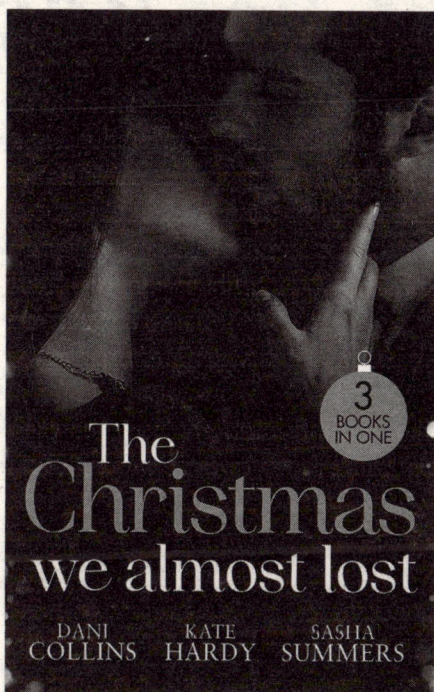

LET'S TALK

Romance

For exclusive extracts, competitions and special offers, find us online:

- **f** MillsandBoon
- **X** @MillsandBoon
- **◉** @MillsandBoonUK
- **♪** @MillsandBoonUK

Get in touch on 01413 063 232